Black Jacks

Works by Shaun Webb:

A Motion for Innocence

A Motion for Innocence, Second Edition

Black Jacks

Shaun's first novel, "A Motion for Innocence" has been featured in the Hometown life (Milford Times) newspaper, and on the Education Examiner, a weekly on-line publication. He has also been interviewed by the ARC radio network out of Oklahoma City.

The characters and events in this book are fictitious. Any similarity to real persons, living or dead, is coincidental and not intended by the author.

Manufactured in the United States of America.

A special thank you to my Editorial Contributor: Lynn Gillard

ISBN-13: 978-1-4538-7842-2
ISBN-10: 1-4538-7842-4

Published by Shaun Webb through *In Motion, LLC.*

Special acknowledgement to the Mayo Clinic for allowing the use of their material for inclusion in this story.

A very special thank you to Donna Gundle-Krieg for shining the light on my work.

Comments:

A Motion for Innocence

This book provides a disturbing and revealing look at our criminal justice system. You learn that the quest for the "almighty dollar" is alive and well in law enforcement and the so called "justice system". The author also lets you enter into his world to see how this was emotional wrenching for him and everyone who knows him. It will definitely give you another perspective on the sex offender list. ***-bcinok***

This is a book about an ordinary man named Sean whose life is unalterably changed when a schoolgirl accuses him of sexual misconduct. The book is a very personal and raw account of the events that unfold after young Blair reports Sean to the authorities. Sean's passion to prove his innocence translates superbly into text. We are right there with him, feeling and living this horrifying and surreal experience. Sean draws us in with his experiential understanding of the injustices of our legal and penal system. We are appalled and enraged. A Motion for Innocence exposes the unbelievable insanity and brutality of a system out of balance-a system that needs and must be changed. Men everywhere should be "up in arms". What might have been a crippling experience for others, Shaun Webb transforms into a work of art. He pours his heart and soul into this amazing account, which in turn, raises awareness and potentiates change. He gives a voice to all those who have been unjustly accused, shunned, and judged. Perhaps he gives a voice to those who are guilty as well. Our justice system is shockingly corrupt and inhumane.-***Vicki***

"A Motion for Innocence deals with the stigma of false accusations, which happen all the time. I had a lot of trouble putting the book down. I can't believe the hell that the main character, Sean West, went through, not to mention his family and friends. The book was written in first person, so you had a feel you were walking in West's shoes. That made it a bit scarier in the sense that you could almost feel the pain. I like how newspaper articles and court documents were interspersed, giving it a real-life feel. I recommend that at the very least, all men and teenagers give this book a glance. This book teaches a valuable lesson about our corrupt and flawed court systems. Any allegation by anybody could land you behind bars. 5 big stars!" – ***A. Reader***

An eye opening story into the injustice that can happen to anyone today. The message should scare the living daylights out of every person throughout America. Every elected official should have to read this book. The frenzy and hysteria have created a modern day Nazi hunt. Like the past atrocities during Hitler's rein many innocent people lost their lives, which is what the registry imposes. Law enforcement follows the legal traps under the justification of following the laws. The elected officials use the "lock 'em up throw away the key" to garner votes behind a false veil of safety. Soon everyone will be a felon & a sex offender. We are wasting precious resources to be administrators for law enforcement for those who have hurt no one. All the while the real sexual predators continue to harm the children they know. Stop this madness. Pass this book to every elected official. Stop the "one size fits all" Hitler mentality. *–**Google book result***

A Motion for Innocence deals with the backlash of false allegations levied against someone. It seems to be a pretty serious problem in the USA and this book deals with it in no uncertain terms. It is a work of fiction, but mirrors what it must be like to be falsely accused, convicted and sent through the criminal justice system. I liked reading it; it was a pretty good delivery with a little funny, a little sad, and a lot shocking. *–**Google book result***

I haven't been able to put the book down since I got it. Heart wrenching. Terrible how one man's life has been ruined.*-**Joanna***

This well-told story is a harrowing description of one man's journey through our justice system after a vengeful false accusation destroys his previously calm, happy life. It's a nightmare scenario that will make you think twice the next time you read a news story about an arrest or conviction. The trial scenes made me want to scream at the incompetent lawyer and the judge, and make me wonder how many people are currently behind bars because the jury didn't see the whole story. Some of the jail scenes are just as shocking. If even half of the things in this book actually occur in real life, we should all be out protesting our court and prison system right now. Despite all the negatives, the unwavering support of family and friends gets Sean (the lead character) through his ordeal, and provides some lightness to the book. I like how the author varied his narrative - mostly first person, but also court transcripts, newspaper articles, police reports, etc. Good read, page turner, I recommend this book.-***McB***

I just finished this book and had a hard time putting it down. It reinforced how corrupt the legal system can be and how a person is guilty until proven innocent. How frightening to know that one accusation without proof can dismantle someone's life. I look forward to reading more books from this first-time author.-*B & N reviewer*

Outstanding Read! Keeps u wondering and opens your eyes to many things! (Not all good) I plan on reading it a second time! AWESOME first book, I am waiting on the next one!! - *Lisa 1063*

Excellent! This book showed how easy it is to be railroaded into a corner with nary a lick of evidence. The only drawback was that it kept me so interested, I felt more tense than relaxed when reading. It was also a little sad and depressing. It does, however, put you directly into the main character's shoes. I cannot imagine going through what Sean West went through. I'm glad I only had to read about it. –***Rexreader***

This is a great read, by a first time author. The story is compelling and quite frightening to see what happens to a family when one of its members is unjustly accused. The story is told in a way that makes you feel like you are sitting with him talking over a cup of coffee. I recommend this highly!-**Jill**

A great read from start to finish. It is scary to see how easily someone's life can be destroyed by lies, incompetence, and people too busy to listen to the truth. I highly recommend this book.-**Best Read**

Black Jacks

Shaun Webb

In Motion, LLC
Michigan

To: Chris Kuzneski;

Thank you for the encouragement.

Schizophrenia demons live in my head.

Wesley Willis

Once upon a time...

INTRO

A Killer in Black

Black. This was the color of choice for the killer. Black shirt, black leather pants, black gloves and a black leather facemask. This color effectively deemed the killer invisible, especially at night when striking was best. A black leather strap hung from the killer's belt, with a Jack of Spades connected to it. He ventured out only in the deception of darkness. Lurking in the blind comfort of the alley made him that much harder to detect. He was awaiting the prey. The prey that lingered just a few feet away.

The five year-old boy only needed to venture away from his parents two more feet…the killer waited patiently, hoping for the new victim. Another foot and a half…his breathing became rapid. One more foot…the sweating was profuse and ran down his face, dripping out of the mouth hole of the mask.

The killer's hands reached out, grasping at the air just inches from the child. Open hand, grasp, open hand, grasp. Leather gloves stretching and crackling with each tightened grip. The anticipation swam throughout his body. He was feeling a surge of excitement as the prey neared. The killer's blood was pumping fast and hard. “Just another inch or two,” he thought to himself. Soon, very very soon.

*

Jimmy Joseph didn’t know any better. Why should he? He was always told not to go with strangers, and he wasn’t. Mom was right over there. Dad was in the hunting store, so he’d be out soon. His parents taught him not to so much as talk to anybody he didn’t know. Jimmy learned. He obeyed, staying away from oddballs. This tyke liked exploring though, and explore he did. The sidewalk made for a cool game of avoiding the crack, while the bricks of the tall building were fun to try to count all the way to the top. The youngster merely being a youngster. Mom wasn’t paying attention. She seemed more concerned with who was watching and noticing her. Kids sometimes wander without the adults seeing. They simply do whatever they do and meander away. Before you know it, you look around and....they’ve vanished.

*

Little Jimmy ventured those extra couple of inches. His mom was still watching the glitzy lights of the city. She was not heeding the little guy. As suddenly as a lightning blink, as rapidly as the wind, the black leather strap reached around his neck and…..little Jimmy was gone.

“Where is Jimmy?” Mrs. Joseph finally inquired. “Jim....JIM.....JIMMMMY!!!” The air was sucked out of her lungs. It was like a four hundred pound brick sat on her chest. Mrs. Joseph's husband ran from the store and to her side.

"Where's Jimmy?" she managed but a whimper.

"I th-thought y-you w-were watching him," he insisted with his trademark stutter.

Both parents' heads darted from side to side hoping to spot their son. Mom was finally able to release a blood-curdling scream, but it was much too late. Dad was also screaming his son's name to no avail. He was not answering.

They'd lost Jimmy before, only to find him by the toy stand in the store they were visiting, or by the nearest candy or ice cream display. Unfortunately, this time little Jimmy was gone. He would not be found by any displays or near any toys. Mrs. Joseph pounded on her husband's chest, "Why weren't you watching? Why? What were you thinking?" She then slumped down to Dad's knees, wailing and crying and whining. All the while grinding her long fake fingernails into his thighs.

"C-come b-b-back here, James, this instant", Dad stuttered.

No answer, no response, no hope. None of Mom or Dad's cries would change the fact that Jimmy was lost. Praying to their God in Heaven wouldn't change the brutal reality. These parents would now go through life without their precious child. They would feel the iron grip of guilt and regret. They would never recover from the day little Jimmy disappeared. Mom and Dad would suffer, but as it would turn out, so would others.

*

Jimmy was the second child to disappear from the Lincoln, Nebraska area in early 1995. The first, a six-year-old boy, went missing in February, presumably by the hands of the same killer. No leads, few clues, nearly nothing. Just two missing kids. The first child was recently found in a remote cornfield with a black strap wrapped around his neck. Connected to the black strap by a safety pin was the Jack of Spades playing card. Nebraska had a problem on its hands and the public would shout for "justice," cry for "closure", and clamor for "action". What are you supposed to do when the mobs want a head on a platter but you have nothing? You improvise. You try to calm the public's fear. The next question is how? How do you calm the masses without a suspect? You find one, that's how. Find a, *not necessarily the*, perpetrator and bring him or her to "justice".

*

Jack Beauregard, the Nebraska State Police Colonel, was running for Governor of Nebraska. Solving the crimes would go a long way towards the goal of winning the election. It would show the public that he's tough on crime and "on the case," thus ensuring votes and noteworthiness.

Mr. Beauregard thought he was God's gift to politics, women, and the world. He also thought of himself as "anointed" for whatever good karma came his way. He was "anointed" to be a cop. He was "anointed" to be a dad. He was "anointed" to become Nebraska's next Governor. The man was truly remarkable in his self-serving ways. He took the good credit when it wasn't due, and shoved off the bad when it was. "In some ways," Jack reflected, "you have to be cold like that."

He knew that the society wanted everything legislated. A job like that should go a responsible human, and Jack rationalized that he was, in fact, that person, although everything he did was motivated by greed and a lust for power.

It can be a very ruthless world, especially when it comes to the fear that is shared, especially since the 911 attacks. We as a society, want everything constituted and we pin our hopes on flawed humans to uphold the law. A vicious circle of fear results. Jack Beauregard *was* the law in Nebraska. He was counted on by hundreds of thousands to make the right decisions in the state, along with bagging and disposing of the criminals. The job should go to a responsible human, or humans in some cases, who legitimately try to do what's right for the good of the people. Jack would say he does this, but in reality it was for the good of Jack and his personal goals. He'd get what he wanted in whatever way was necessary. Jack was a true believer in the end justifying the means. Whatever had to be done.

*

We now take you to rural Hickman, Nebraska, about five miles south of Lincoln. This is where things will get really interesting.

Before

Fire: Summer, Youth, Energy, Blood

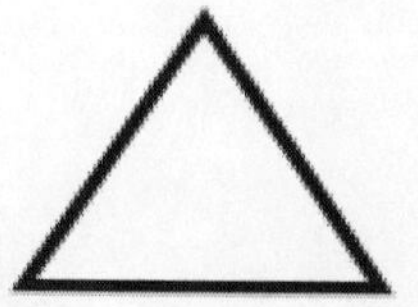

Sho 'nuff Dead

"Eyep! He's dead fer sure." Old man Garrison exclaimed. "Must'a been hit by a car."

The old man looked down at his feet and felt bad for the old mutt. It was a black dog. He guessed it could have even been one of those medium sized sled-pulling dogs. Chow-chow maybe. Garrison hadn't seen this animal hanging around before today and sure enough wouldn't see it again after the day ended.

"He must've been travelin' or somethin'," he thought. "Doesn't look like a car hit 'em, though. No blood and he ain't deformed."

The dog appeared to be about middle-aged. It didn't have any grey hair and his opened eyes weren't saggy. It also had nice manicured nails on all four paws, meaning it probably hadn't been gone long from wherever it came from. Rigor mortis had set in, causing the dog to take on a rigid form. Its legs were stuck straight out from the body, which was lying on its side. There had to be a crying child or upset doggie parent not too far away. John knew how disappointing it was to lose a beloved animal, as he had put down probably ten dogs in his lifetime. He was also forced to put down a horse two years ago due to a broken leg it suffered trying to jump out of the fenced pen.

"No matter," Garrison thought, "I still gotta get the mutt picked up and bagged." The old man threw the dog on his shoulder and headed for his garage. The walk was about the equivalent of two city blocks from where he found the mutt on his land. Garrison wasn't getting any younger, as his knees, shoulders, hips and arms told him each day. "It's frustratin' when ya have a mind that says yes, but a body that says absolutely not!"

The sweat beaded from his forehead and he made frequent stops along the way to wipe his brow. "Wow, you're heavy, feels like you've been eatin' lead", Garrison barked as he carried the carcass to his garage. John, like most people that lived through a Nebraska summer, always had a handkerchief at the ready. It was a rule of thumb in the sweltering heat. It was only April and the sun shone down with a persistent glare.

"Gotdamn, it's hot out here. It's gonna' be a hell of a summer," John moaned as he continued his trek.

*

John Garrison lived in Hickman, Nebraska, which is a stones throw from Lincoln. John moved to the area after the death of his wife. He liked living here because it was quiet and away from the bustle of city life. John wasn't crazy about hanging around with too many folks, except the guys at the local barbershop. He had just turned seventy-two and missed his lovely Mildred. He kept a shrine in the living room in honor of her. Nobody was ever allowed to touch it…hell, even look at it! He had no children, so that meant no grandchildren, which suited John fine.

"I sure don't need no snot-nosed kids runnin' around, for Christ sake. They just break everything and cause a real ruckus!"

Garrison was a spry man for his age, despite the thirty or forty year's worth of beer in his belly. He had a full head of snow-white hair and a crotchety, almost malevolent attitude. The old man just wanted peace and serenity so he could take care of his three-acre yard. Drama and such just didn't sit well with him, so he avoided it.

"A dramatic town is a lousy town to live in," John would preach. "I don't need the cursin' games."

John spent his days seeing to the chores of such a large property. His lawnmower, a brand-spanking-new fancy-riding rig he bought at the local John Deere was tuned to a cat like precision and never failed him when he has to cut this large area. He carried the blades as low as they'd go so he could give the grass a good scalping. This way, he only had to cut once every two or three weeks.

"A scalped, brown lawn is a good lawn", was another of the old guy's mantras. "I don't have to deal with a parched piece of land."

What with keeping the house tidy and neat, seeing to his three horses he owned (and had considered selling), and taking a two-hour nap each day, cutting grass was just a flat-out pain in his posterior. Garrison didn't feel much like working anyhow. He spent forty-two years at General Motors just outside of Detroit, and that was more than enough for him.

John liked going to the local barbershop, where he could spew his poison and hatred of the Government system. Basically it served as the town complaint department. Most of the old fogeys who could ambulate all gathered here, whether they needed a haircut or not. Hell, some of them had a grand total of fourteen hairs, but spent ten bucks getting them clipped. That's darn near a dollar a hair! The old men talked about everything. John always took over the conversations, harkening back to his days of youth and exuberance. It was kind of a "who has the best yarn" contest.

"These kids nowadays are nothin' like when we were young. Some of 'em need a good ass whippin'!"

The patrons almost always answered with an "amen to that," or a good grouchy looking nod of the head.

The quiet men just listened. It sure beat sitting on the front porch watching the grass grow.

"When I was young, I could whip anyone's rear end! Nobody messed with me. They knew better. I'll bet I could still whip some of these youngin's asses if I really needed to."

"Aw shut-up, Garrison." One of the coots would say. "You're always braggin' 'bout stuff you can't do. I'll bet you can't even get that soft noodle in yer pants to do anything anymore, ya old coot."

The entire barbershop would roar with laughter. John loved a good argument.

"Yeah? That's not what 'yer wife said last night."

Again, the roar of laughter. The boys in the shop having a grand old time. It was a rite of passage in Hickman, the most boring town in the state. The popular subject in the shop is what was wrong with the old geezers.

"My damn gout's acting up."

"I ain't crapped right in two weeks."

"If I don't get flu this year, it'll be a miracle."

On and on they went, exchanging war stories. Look at this scar, look at that scar. Medicine this, hip that. These guys were a hoot for about an hour, and then the subject always switched to the weather. It's the same thing every day with these guys. That's what made the small town life great.

*

Garrison called up his neighbor (the closest being three miles away) Robert Long, and asked him to come over and help bag up the dead dog.

"Long, getcha' ass over here and help me with this mess," John ordered.

The old man tended to be pushy and bossy to people, but he couldn't have cared less. If you didn't want to hear it, don't ask. If you didn't ask, you'd hear it anyway.

"What's goin' on over there, John? What kinda' mess ya talkin' about?" Long inquired.

Robert was trying not to sound stupid. It didn't matter, because to John, he sounded like an idiot. Garrison explained, "I got a dead dog over here and he's fixin' to rot on my property. He's heavy and I need help puttin' 'em in a bag so I can get rid of 'em."

"Oh, okay John, I guess I can give you a hand with it."

"Well that's a miracle," Garrison derisively spewed, "I thought I'd have to pry ya' out of 'yer lazy boy with a crowbar."

"I don't mind helpin' ya' John, it gives me somethin' to do for a while."

"Well, Robert, yer still on the phone, so ya' ain't helpin' me that way, are ya'?"

Long would always take one extra second for things to sink in.

"I'll be right over. Don't be such a grump."

Robert always took an annoyingly long time to do anything. It was a chore just to find his truck keys, even though he'd leave them on the table in the kitchen every single time he'd come home from wherever he'd been. This time would be no different. Find the keys, find his shoes, put them on, and finally go out to his truck.

The old Robert Long labored up into the truck seat, made all his adjustments, and then finally headed for John's house. The whole ritual would take an extra twenty minutes to complete.

*

Robert Long was tall and lanky, standing about six feet five inches, a skinny glass of water. He was retired, like John, and lazed about his life with a casual attitude. Robert had lost his wife of forty-five years two winters earlier, but he was more relaxed about it than grumpy old Garrison had been. Robert's wife browbeat him to the bitter end.

"Damn it Bob this, damn it Bob that, Bob where are you? Did you get the damn windows clean Bob? Is the trash out? What in hell are you doing now Bob? Bob, Bob, Bob."

It was a wonder Robert didn't kill her before the cancer did. Robert long didn't really miss her too much. At times, in fact, he didn't miss her at all. Being a laid-back type of guy was his saving grace; otherwise he would've been spending his life behind bars from shooting the old hen. In a strange sort of way, though, Robert must've missed his wife's constant berating, because he allowed Garrison to run him down every time they were together.

Robert, like John and most of the other old-timers, spent a lot of time at that barbershop in town. There simply wasn't a whole lot else to do. Long liked going to the theater to see a picture, but only on oldies night, which is one Saturday per month. The rest of the time it was the stab 'em up, teenage disaster movies where a female usually ended up topless, then was killed with a fire poker stuck in her eye. Long didn't care for that. He was a big fan of the John Wayne type of pictures. A good old-fashioned shoot-'em up western was more his speed.

John turned out to be Robert's best friend at the barbershop. John had learned that Long was a pushover, so it was easy to manipulate him. Robert allowed it, again harkening back to his browbeating wife of yesteryear. Every time John smarted off to him, he just chuckled and chalked it up as a joke. It usually wasn't though, because John would get big laughs at Long's expense. Mainly, Robert just wanted to be liked. He wasn't the brightest soul, but he was warm-hearted and kind. The man would do just about anything for you, including helping you pack up a dead, stinky mutt.

*

Upon arriving in his 1980 blue Chevy pickup with all of 350,000 miles on it, Robert eased out of the cab and noticed the mutt, giving it a little nudge with his foot.

"Dead fer sho'," Robert told the old man. "He ain't goin' nowhere."

"What was yer first clue, Sherlock?" Garrison deadpanned.

Sometimes the old man's sarcasm was a real turn-off. To Robert, it was a normal everyday thing.

"You don't have to be such a grumpy old coot about it John, I was just sayin'."

"Yea, well if yer gonna speak, say somethin' sensible. Obviously the gotdamn dog is dead. He's stiff as a board."

Garrison's patience left a lot to be desired. He was like this to everyone, so Robert shouldn't have felt singled out. He did, though, because Garrison sometimes made it feel personal.

"Now help me bag this critter and we'll call the animal control folks to come get 'em."

The old man rummaged through his garage and came up with some duct tape and a couple of black garbage sacks. After placing the dog in the sacks, head down and rear up, Robert taped up around the dog's front and hind legs, thus sealing him in.

"That should do er," Robert proudly stated. "He won't be goin' no place!"

"Ya think it'll hold 'em? Are you sure he won't run away?" Garrison sarcastically sneered. "Help me put this carcass at the end of the driveway."

Robert was beginning to get aggravated with Garrison, but helped him move the body.

"Dang, that mutt's heavy." Bob noticed.

Garrison rolled his eyes, but managed to keep his mouth shut this time. After placing the dog in the spot John wanted, Robert picked up his truck keys to head out.

"Ain't cha stayin' for a beer?" John asked with a pair of puppy-dog eyes.

Robert angrily interjected, "I helped ya move the dam dog, despite yer' smart mouthed attitude, now I'm goin' home." Robert then added, "By the way, go get bent!"

Garrison heartily laughed, "I love ya too, ya codger," and blew him a kiss.

Robert left Garrison to finish up. Long lurched back up into his pick-up and squealed the tires as he left the driveway, leaving a pair of black marks behind. John screamed at him as he turned out on to the gravel road, but only received a middle finger salute in return.

"That cursin' old so-and-so!" John whined. "I'll deal with 'em later."

*

"Animal Control, Lyla Helms speaking, what's your issue?

Garrison, though he'd never met Lyla, always liked the sound of her voice. It was soft and sexy with a hint of squeakiness for good measure. John was a flirt. He loved messing with the ladies, even if they became appalled by his perverted mind.

"I'll bet she's got herself a nice set-a-cans!" The old man thought. Old John Garrison was just that, old, but he sure enough wasn't dead. He thought if the situation called for it, he could "rise" to the occasion. If not, there was always Viagra.

"Hello, can I help you?" Lyla repeated with a slight sense of urgency. "Is anyone on the line?"

Garrison was snapped out of his nasty little fantasy just when it was getting good. “Lyla, I got a dead dog over here, 221 Chestnut Road. I don’t know what happened to ‘em, but he’s as stiff as a petrified two-by-four.”

“Is this John Garrison?” Lyla inquired.

She had her eyes rolled up in her head knowing full well it was another dead animal call. This was a regular occurrence with the old fart.

“You know it is, Lyla. Garrison, John Garrison. Now are we gonna small talk all damn day, or are ya gonna get an officer over here to pick this up before it starts stinkin’ up my yard?” Garrison continued, “He’s sittin’ at the end of my drive and I’m already startin’ to smell ‘em.”

Lyla waited a second, took a deep breath, and then retorted.

“We’ll get an Animal Control Officer over there shortly, but he’ll probably stink up your entire property beforehand.”

Old John grunted loudly and hung up, satisfied that by not giving her another second to speak, the process would move faster.

“Jerk,” Lyla quipped as she dispatched an officer. “I should make him wait until tomorrow.”

“Witch,” John said under his breath. “I should lodge a complaint with the civil authorities.”

Garrison retrieved a lawn chair from his garage and sat under the shade of the eave, where he drifted to sleep. Old John loved his naptime. It was his favorite part of the day.

*

Lyla Helms had worked in Animal Control for fifteen years, and dealing with the old cuss Garrison was a regular event. Every time a squirrel was run over within a five-mile radius of Garrison’s house, he called her. A deer hit? A call from the coot. A measly, stinking bird lying dead somewhere in Garrison's sight? Another call. It was ridiculous, but she grew to expect and deal with his silliness. In fact, Lyla had learned to deal with a ton of ridiculous requests since she'd been on the job. John wasn't the only old coot to call with dead animals needing to be picked up. There was the famous "birds in the eaves" calls, in which birds had the audacity to nest in the gutter. How dare they?

"That's what birds do." Lyla would explain. "If you don't want them there, remove the nest."

You have the road kill calls, which were everyday.

"Did you know a groundhog was run over on the freeway?"

"A bird just hit my windshield."

"My cat was run over, will you come get it."

Lyla was friendly and patient on the phone, but after hanging up she'd scream.

"I only have two guys on duty and road kill pick up is twice a week. If something's lying there, be patient. It'll either get picked up or eaten. If you can't wait, pick it up yourself."

She always yelled to herself in the comfort of her dispatch area. On the phone it was "yes ma'am," or "no sir."

*

The forty-eight-year-old woman stood about five feet without shoes, five-one-and-a-half with heels. She was a nice enough looking gal, but would not have reached the old goat's lofty expectations of her appearance. Her hair was a short dirty blonde, just below her ears or just above her neckline, whichever you prefer. She was small from the shoulders to the waist, thick, not fat, around her hips. Her body then tapered back down to small, short legs.

Lyla had never been married. She was too much of a "helper" type for that. She enjoyed cookouts at the church, garage sale shopping, and helping the less fortunate by handing out blankets and mittens to the homeless in the winter, while feeding them at the soup kitchen year round. It's the mother in her. Everybody who came across Lyla liked her. Her nice smile and happy-go-lucky attitude served her well and soothed others. She could also talk. My goodness could that woman talk. She always led the conversations and was very interesting. She talked about what was going on around town without sounding like a gossip. Basically, Lyla was your average, everyday looking woman who had a great dis-position. Although she'd never had kids, she certainly wished she would've. Caring for others came naturally for this woman. Garrison was one of those few personalities that brought out her snotty side. It wasn't very often you were given the "Lyla eye roll," but when you were, you'd pressed her nerves.

*

Lyla called out on the dispatch signal: "We have a dead dog at the Garrison house. You already know where that is. Over."

"10-4 Lyla, I'll take it, over," said the voice of Animal Control officer Dan Wheeler.

"Back at ya', Dan, watch out for the old geezer, over. He's being his ornery self again. Over."

"What's new Lyla? He's always a big jerk. Over."

"I'm just warning you, Dan, today he seems especially grumpy. Over"

"Okay, I'll take that under advisement. Over."

Dan let out a hearty laugh, fished out his Slipknot CD and began the twenty-five mile trip to Garrison's home. "I'll psych myself up with some good, hardcore metal!" Dan knew that dealing with the old goat was always a challenge, but he didn't care much, as nothing really bothered him. Mr. Wheeler tooled down the road with the music blaring, unaware of the horror that awaited him.

Beauregard's Dilemma

Nebraska State Police Colonel Jack Beauregard sat back in his reclining office chair scratching his head and trying to figure out who was abducting the kids in his town. A steel ball pendulum clicked and clacked on the other side of the room. The Colonel always gave it a push when he needed to think. More than a few thoughts filled his mind. He had a huge murder case to solve, while at the same time contemplating how to win the Governor's chair he so coveted. Other assorted items bounced around Beauregard's gray matter, but those two kept surfacing to the top.

One of the boy's bodies had been found, with no leads or clues, except for a black strap used to strangle him, along with a Jack of Spades playing card pinned to it. The crime scene was devoid of anything else remotely pointing to anybody who may have been involved. No prints, no DNA, nothing. The boy had been found two weeks prior just inside the city line. Jimmy Joseph was still missing and also feared dead. The pressure Beauregard felt was immense. So far, there was one boy dead, and one boy who had turned up missing, seemingly out of thin air. It would take all of Jack's skills and then some to get to the bottom of this.

Jack was very confident that he possessed the said skills and would, in fact, bring the criminal to justice. He leaned on his years of experience in law enforcement. You may pull the wool over Jack's eyes for a moment, but he'd get the best of you soon enough. This is what made Jack who he was. The ability to get to the bottom of a situation. No matter how he achieved it. A bit corrupt? Perhaps. A tad sinister? Maybe. In Jack Beauregard's mind, if it was a shade crooked, but nabbed the bad guy, then so be it. The public certainly didn't care how it was done. They just wanted it to stop. Whether it be murders, rapes, or simple burglary, it had to end by whatever means were necessary. Up to and including the prosecution of possibly innocent people.

*

Jack Beauregard had been a Nebraska state cop for twenty years, his last five as the colonel. He wore a full crown of brown hair with a slight hint of gray on his temples. He didn't appear to have suffered from too much stress in his line of work, but Grecian hair color for men went a long way towards hiding the wear and tear that encompassed his job. Beauregard spent a lot of time campaigning to become Governor, so he was usually dressed up. Jack looked far better in a suit and tie than he ever did wearing his police uniform. He didn't seem comfortable in his trooper gear. Perhaps the obsession with becoming governor affected his ability to "wear it well." When he put on a five hundred dollar Italian knit, he'd be upright with an air of confidence, smiling all the while. In his cop scrubs, his shoulders drooped slightly and he became a hardened version of himself. The smile disappeared, replaced by a frustrated scowl and a completely different attitude. He was a modern day version of Jekyll and Hyde. He didn't want to be a cop anymore. He was bored with it and wanted new challenges. The idea of being the state's leader, thus wearing a nice suit everyday, must've given him that extra boost. Beauregard stood six foot two and weighed about two bills. He wasn't muscular. He actually looked a bit soft. He usually wore the police jacket, though, even when it was ninety degrees outside. This hid any extra blubber that hung over his waistband. It also gave him what he thought to be a tougher look. It was very difficult for Jack to look threatening partly because he wasn't. He'd be the one sending patrolmen into the fight while he stayed safely behind a car door or better yet, in his office.

"I need to be the commander, so I stay out of the fray. Who'll lead if I'm dead?"

*

The public had been hammering Jack for a couple of weeks now since the Joseph boy went missing, and with the discovery of the first body, the cries doubled. If he didn't solve the case, his governorship would be all but lost. The election was in a few months and he had enjoyed a three-point lead in the latest polls over Democratic challenger Mel Critchett. This number could turn on him like an angry, stepped-on rattlesnake. He hoped something would break quickly, especially if he wanted that coveted seat. His mind kept drawing a blank, though, and frustration soon set in.

Jack's police scanner, which was always on, sounded.

"Daniel, could you go pick up a dead dog at Garrison's place? Over."

It was Lyla Helms, the Animal Control dispatcher, sending out yet another Animal Control officer to Garrison's roost. Jack had had a couple of traffic related encounters with John Garrison in his years on the force and thought he was one of the biggest assholes ever. Lately, it seemed, Garrison was making a lot of calls about dead animals. Beauregard contemplated this for a brief moment, then shrugged his shoulders and went back to thinking about the two things most important to him. Actually, there were four things that were important. The murders and the governorship, obviously, but also his girlfriend, Soo-Chin Xing, the State's licensed pathologist, and his son Kyle Beauregard.

Jack gave the steel pendulum another push….click, clack, click, clack.

*

Kyle was an eighteen year-old kid who toiled through high school and had been trying to get accepted to attend the University of Nebraska on a political science scholarship. Astronomy was Kyle's first career love, but, like it or not, politics are what he learned from his dad. Dealing with the stars and space along with delving into possible "nether" worlds intrigued the young man much more. He read his L. Ron Hubbard books on Scientology and paid close attention to Carl Sagan and his ideas about our universe. These subjects stimulated him. Jack was fine with that, but only as a hobby, or second career fallback. He would not allow it to be Kyle's career choice.

"We Beauregard's have political ties dating back to the eighteen hundreds, it's in our blood. You will continue our tradition, son."

Since Jack's ex-wife had divorced him and left five years earlier, it was his sole responsibility to raise this young man to excel and follow in his footsteps. So far he'd done an average job because he hadn't completely convinced Kyle that politics were the way to go career wise. The boy would be graduating in a couple of months with A's and B's on every report card since they started keeping records in the fourth grade. Kyle made his father proud. The only small problem Jack had was that Kyle didn't care much for politics or criminal law. With Jack's help, the boy would realize the dreams his dad had for him. Jack simply refused to believe that Kyle's interests rested elsewhere. No matter how much his son tried to talk to him, it always ended up a one-sided conversation.

"You don't know what you want yet. Listen to me. They'll be no more arguing!"

Kyle was a seemingly decent boy with a pleasant disposition. He didn't have many friends, though, because he thought that the kids who always wanted to fool around at the mall or chase girls were an immature bunch. They really didn't pay much attention to him anyway. He was a nerdy type and stood out from the crowd. A social butterfly he was not. Kyle had made the decision years ago that he would put all his energy into school and worry about the girlfriend, marriage and raising a family stuff later.

"A real sacrifice," Jack would think to himself. "The kid just fits for future governor of Nebraska."

Jack supported and looked after him as Kyle continued to do well and maybe, just maybe, would follow him as the leader of this great state. Beauregard pushed the issue more than he probably should, but Jack controlled the boat. He would skipper his son the correct way, or so he thought.

"Keeping it in the family," Jack would proudly say. "At any cost necessary!"

*

Jack met Soo-Chin on the job and the two hit it off pretty well from first glance. They'd been dating a few months and seemed ready to take it more seriously. Jack was falling in love with her, but at the same time, needed to have a wholesome family image to stand any chance of winning the election. The public wasn't all that keen on electing a bachelor to run a state.

Soo-Chin was exotically beautiful. She was from China and had come to the USA to study medicine when she was only fourteen years old. Obviously, her intelligence was also a turn on for Jack as he truly appreciated her views on the world and politics. She was as smart as she was sexy. Soo was all of five feet tall and weighed one hundred pounds soaking wet. She was a tiny thing. You could call her the opposite of Jack's tall and slightly soft physique. Together though, they were a good match, especially when they were intimate, which Jack surely appreciated along with her smarts and wit. Don't be mistaken, she wanted a piece of the power too. She was falling for Jack, but the money and attention he would garner as governor was at least a little intoxicating. By no means was Soo a gold digger, she just wanted to be comfortable. Drink fine wine, eat good food and shop whenever her heart desired. Soo didn't want to have it all; she just wanted to have enough, plus a little extra.

*

The killer, like Jack, also had a police scanner. He needed to keep up with any police information for the obvious reason of avoiding detection. He also heard the dispatching of an animal control officer to Garrison's place in Hickman and a brilliant thought occurred in his mind. Acting on impulse, he placed the body of Jimmy Joseph in his vehicle. It was off to Garrison's farm to hatch the perfect plan. A plan that would throw a wrench into everyone's future.

Upon arriving at the farm, the killer parked in the brush about twenty or so yards away from the driveway, leaving the vehicle undetectable. Carrying Jimmy's body was as difficult as anything he could have imagined. It was like a bag of solid bricks that didn't give an inch. The dead weight was more than a little heavy and the killer broke out in a profuse sweat.

When it was close enough to make sure that neither Garrison nor anyone else was watching, the plan would be materialized.

Garrison continued to slumber under the eaves of the garage. The temperature was rising, so the overalls he was wearing became damp and uncomfortable. The old man arose from his chair, stretched until he was suddenly dizzy from rising too quickly, bent over to reclaim his bearings, and then went inside to change. The killer hid in the brush only seventy-five feet away, watching and waiting for his opportunity. When Garrison went inside, the move was made. The killer struck quickly, moving the body of little Jimmy onto Garrison's drive. The bagged dog was snatched up and he fleetingly disappeared back into the brush. A start of an engine, then he was gone. Old John Garrison was none the wiser. As the killer drove back to his lair, a sardonic laugh escaped him. He was so pleased with the intelligence that he'd thought he had. This killer couldn't and wouldn't be stopped.

The Pickup

"A pair a shorts and a tee'll suffice."

The old coot grumbled under his breath while making the change. "I'm too blasted fat!" He acknowledged upon seeing his shirtless reflection in the mirror. Garrison continued his silent barking as he slid into his cooler duds. He was quite right about his weight, as his belly protruded out further than his penis did. He called it a dicky-do.

"My belly sticks out further than my dicky-do." He'd tell the boys at the barber shop. Lots of laughs.

The grumpy man stopped at the icebox on his way back outside and fetched a brew. After all, watching his figure took work, and what better way to work than chugging a cold one in the summer heat. One? Probably more like four or five. He might even polish off a whole six-pack.

"That'll burn a calorie or two," Garrison jokingly reasoned. "Bottoms up!"

It had been about an hour since he called Lyla, so Garrison thought the animal control folks better hurry their rear-ends up or they'll be another call, and Garrison won't be quite as polite.

"Blasted slowpokes. What in hell do they do all day anyhow?"

As the sun beat down, a wave of heat rose from the asphalt driveway, giving the black bag a dreamy air. Garrison reclaimed his seat in front of the garage and swilled his brew as he continued to wait for the officer and watch the dead dog at the same time. A dog that he figured was swelling in the high temperature.

"Better be hurryin' up! I ain't got all gotdamn day to sit around and wait." John took another swig of his beer.

*

Dan, after what seemed like forever, finally arrived at the Garrison home. He greeted John with an outstretched wave.

"About damn time," Garrison growled with the tenacity of a pit bull while ignoring Dan's greeting. He then added, "The dog's been layin' there fer almost two long hours. It's stinkin' up ma property."

Dan smiled and stuck his hand out in a greeting manner. "How are you Mr. Garrison? Is life treating you well? How's that beer?"

The old man wrinkled his face into the meanest expression he could muster, and then spewed forth at Dan with a venomous tone.

"Just get that dog outta here; I'm tired of babysettin' it. Christ Almighty." The old timer waved his hands about in a dramatic fashion.

Garrison walked to the end of the driveway with the officer and together hoisted the carcass into the air conditioned compartment built for such pick-ups.

"That dog's a heavy one." Dan announced as a bead of sweat dripped off his eyebrow and onto his cheek.

"What do ya expect? He's been layin' here in that hot bag fer hours." Garrison countered, then added, "it ain't losin' no weight doin' nothin'! Probably all bloated up."

The young man just gazed at the old fogey and nodded. He thought to himself how miserable it must be to live in the codger's shoes. He was glad to be young and vibrant without the grumpiness.

"Well, I guess that's it. I'll be on my way," Dan hurriedly said. "I have a lot of work to do."

The old timer mulled over whether or not to throw out another smart-aleck comment, then decided against it. He figured this officer wasn't a big thinker anyway.

"He must be some kinda dimwit," was all Garrison could think up in his mind.

Dan drove off, carcass in tow, no wave or even a thanks from the old codger.

"That's one grumpy, miserable dude," Dan thought. "I'm sure I'll be back again when he (hopefully) finds a dead rat in his kitchen."

With a shake of his head, Dan turned up the Slipknot CD as loud as it could go and still sound good, and then headed to the incinerator at the pound. After dealing with that old crab, the heavy beat seemed to mellow him. At least Dan thought it did.

*

Dan Wheeler was a simple enough guy. Twenty-five years in the world and nothing but good times ahead, he hoped. Dan liked his music hard and loud, his women soft and quiet. He was a good-looking guy who lived in a loft above the hardware store in Bennet, just a stone's throw from Hickman. At 250 bucks a month, Dan had a modest living room, small kitchen, bathroom and TV (with cable access.) He had no trouble picking out his evening conquests from the batch of single late-teen and early twenty-something ladies living in and around town. After all, he was the best looking, athletically built, and most relaxed of all the men in the area. He was also one of the few young bachelors available. The women fought over him, wanting to be the future Mrs. Wheeler, but he wanted no part of marriage. Dan was having way too much fun for that. He kept that secret under his belt, though, for fear of running any of the girls off. He loved the "no strings attached" sex. Companionship was no big issue.

"What they don't know won't hurt them," was Dan's logic. "If they want to just hook-up for a night, who am I to say no?" Not a bad deal for a guy with no cares in the world and women swooning over him.

This guy also loved his job. Picking up or trying to catch animals was as easy for him as it was fun. Live trap a coon? Great! Use the rabies stick on a nasty dog? Wonderful! Pick up dead animal carcasses? That was his least favorite thing, especially when there was road kill duty, which was twice a week in this area. It was okay, though, because the other three or four days (depending on if he had to work Saturday) allowed him to meet almost all the folks living in the area, as well as the cute females! Many of which he would bed down.

*

"You can't see California without Marlon Brando's eyes, you can't see California without Marlon Brando's eyes, you can't see Cal-i-for-nia with-out Mar-lon Bran-do's eyes!"

The Slipknot song jammed loudly in Dan's truck. Even though he had no idea what the lyrics were, he sang along thinking he had it right. That's a wonderful part of youth. It doesn't have to be right to be good. It only needs to be cranked to ten.

Dan finally pulled up to the incineration building of the Animal Control Center and backed his truck up in line with the open-mouthed pit of the char broiler. This was another cool part of the job; throwing the carcasses in and watching them burn. It seemed kind of sick, but it was what it was, so you might just as well enjoy it. The smell was bad, but he'd gotten used to it.

"Dan, you out there? Over." Lyla inquired on his radio. "Where are you at Dan? Over?

"Yea Lyla, I'm at the incinerator about to throw this dog carcass from Garrison's place in, over."

"When you're done with that, come see me. We have another run. Over."

"10-4 you good lookin' hunk of woman you, over!"

When she heard that, Lyla rolled her eyes. Dan was so proud of himself for being the ladies' man. He had just impressed Lyla, he was sure.

"I told you not to talk like that on the radio, Dan. Next time you're getting written up. Out."

Dan ducked his head down in embarrassment, and then went on with his duty. He opened the truck's back door, unlocked the air conditioned compartment that held the black bag, and dragged it out to the edge of the bumper. When he ripped open the bag with what he thought to be the dead dog, horror and anxiety gripped him with a stranglehold he'd never felt before. Ice water filled his veins and his lungs felt heavy and burdened. A lump formed in the center of his throat, seemingly cutting off the air and the ability to swallow. He fumbled for his radio and dropped it on the ground. Dan was frozen in an icy grip of fear. His heartbeat raced to a scary speed, his breathing felt as though it had stopped cold, and his stomach churned with a combination of nausea and cramping. Dan finally corralled his radio and called out.

"L-ly-l-la, g-get out h-here n-now!" Was all he could whimper with his rapidly closing windpipe. He again dropped the radio.

"What's-a-matter? Over!" Lyla casually asked.

Dan was as frozen as an ice sculpture in the arctic.

"Dan, what's going on out there? Come in! Over."

No answer. Lyla shook her head again; more forcefully this time. She arose from her desk, and headed out to the incinerator. Dan's boss was beginning to get quite aggravated with him. Lyla loved Dan to death, but sometimes he could be a real pain in her backside.

"I'll write his ass up," she thought. "Goddang kid."

Lyla walked up from Dan's left side, ready to humble him once and for all. "This better be good," Lyla warned with a pointed finger.

She noticed that Dan was looking a little gray in his cheeks. His back was against the edge of the incinerator, about ten feet from the truck. He looked like he might be having an episode of some kind. Heart Attack? Seizure? She suddenly became very concerned and worried. "Are you all right, Dan?" She stepped closer, looking at Dan's ashen face. Her concern mounted.

"Dan, what the hell's wrong with you?"

As Lyla turned away from Dan and into the back of the truck, her inquisitiveness turned into a look of shock and outrage.

"Oh my dear God in heaven," she said as her open hand went up to cover her mouth, muffling what would normally be a scream. Her eyes darted to and fro and the terror caused goose bumps to break out.

"We have to call Jack Beauregard now!" She had seen the young boy's body with a black strap tightly wrapped around his neck and the Jack of Spades pinned to it. His bloodshot eyes stared back at her blankly with no emotion. He was a pale blue and most assuredly dead. No doubt about it. Lyla called out on her radio,

"Jack, Jack Beauregard, are you out there somewhere?"

Let Sleeping Dogs Lie

The lights were flashing and the radio static was hissing in the thick, dusky air. The Nebraska State Police, along with Colonel Jack Beauregard, were on the scene. A scene that Jack himself couldn't actually believe existed. What a boon for his election chances. This would be the break he was looking for.

Dan Wheeler sat off on a bench near the incinerator, head between his knees and a puddle of vomit at his feet. His skin was in a cold sweat and his face was pale. He had beads of perspiration running down his temples while having a tough time lifting his head up. Dan felt very much like he would drop over dead right there on the spot. He half-wished he would, but no such fate would find him. Anxiety doesn't kill, it tortures.

Lyla stood next to Beauregard. They were studying the dead boy's body in the back of the Animal Control truck. The Jack of Spades playing card was attached to the choking device tightly wrapped around his neck.

"I think that's the Joseph boy, I saw his picture in the paper the other day," Lyla told the Colonel. "Dan picked up the bag at the Garrison house. What's with that Jack of Spades on the strap?"

Beauregard couldn't comment on the playing card, but remembered hearing something about the "dead dog" situation on the police scanner earlier in the day that he had chalked up as more nonsense from the old man. Little did he know at that time that such a break in the case would occur just a few hours later.

"I'm heading over to the Garrison house now," the Chief told his second in command, Lt. Colonel Ed Michaels. The Lieutenant nodded an affirmative Jack's way.

"I want an APB out on John Garrison, and I want the press at his house. I'll be there in a half hour and I expect cameras and reporters."

Lt. Michaels again bobbed his head in agreement.

Beauregard thanked Lyla, told her to keep quiet about everything she'd seen and heard, and help Dan, who was obviously in some major discomfort. He then jumped in his car and headed to the Garrison house with the sirens blaring. Beauregard was flanked by two additional trooper vehicles as he tore down the highway at a dangerously high rate of speed. The adrenaline Beauregard was feeling coursed through him like a finely tuned pump.

*

The Colonel's mind was whirling around faster than a spinning top. This collar would most certainly be his ticket to the governor's mansion, because the public would eat it up. The entire state would hear about this and cheer the lawman's tenacity and grit. "What a wonderful payoff for unwittingly solving this case." Many other questions bounced around Jack's head, though. He was already thinking about the "whys" and "what if's."

"Did the old man really think they'd just toss that sack into the fire, bag and all, and not notice that it was a child's body? Why do it that way? What was he thinking?" None of it mattered, because in Jack's mind, the old timer had tried and failed to conceal the murdered boy. John Garrison was a cold-blooded murderer. A child murderer at that. He was no better than a serial rapist or a mass murderer. No better than Bundy, Manson, or that goofball Berkowitz in New York City in the 1970's. Garrison, in fact, was worse because he killed children. He was the creepiest of the creepy.

This seemed open and shut to him and he continued down the road with even more motivation. Jack figured Garrison to be responsible for the other boy found with a strap around his neck and a Jack of Spades pinned to it.

"That's his MO." Jack thought aloud. "This is how he likes to do it, for whatever reason."

Jack had studied up on how the criminal mind works, and while there is no distinct psychological reason why people do these things, it struck Jack as some kind of twisted fantasy gone awry.

"Something in their head just snaps and it's an all out killing spree. Maybe it's the attention they get. Perhaps it's just for sexual kicks," were Beauregard's theories. Lt. Michaels listened, nodded, and kept his concentration on the road ahead.

Although Jack would never really know for sure what makes these people tick, he would take great joy in removing their poison from the public sector.

*

Upon arriving at the Garrison home, Jack was met by a throng of salivating reporters and other media hard-hitters. The barrage of questions hit him fast and furiously.

"What's the story, Colonel? Did you find the Lincoln child-killer? What is old man Garrison's role?"

"I will answer all your questions momentarily. Please stay back, we are cordoning the area off."

Beauregard waved his arms in a "get back" fashion and ordered his troopers to herd the newsmen and women to the edge of the lawn by the dirt road.

That's when old man Garrison came storming out of his front door donning his boxer shorts and tee-shirt. He was as angry and obnoxious as ever, and, he thought, with good reason. It's not everyday you see a throng of lights, TV vans, police cars and other activity on your own front lawn.

"Freeze!" one trooper shouted from behind his car door. "Don't move!" His pistol was zeroed in on John's chest.

Garrison, never fazed, spoke up loudly and with vigor. The old man was steaming. "What in the fires of hell y'all doin' here? Get off my gotdamn lawn!"

"Put your hands up, turn around and walk backwards toward my voice," a trooper ordered.

Jack was watching from the safety of his car door and clearly saw that Garrison was unarmed.

"Rush 'em, rush 'em now!" Beauregard ordered. "He's unarmed, get him!"

At that instant, three troopers hurried toward Garrison. The old man, his eyes as big as saucers, felt as if he had the football and the defenders were closing in on him to make a bone-crunching tackle.

"You get the hell away from me ya damn lunatics." Garrison said. "I ain't done nothin' wrong here."

That's when another trooper barked out a new order, "Taser him! Taser him!"

A trooper crouched into a shooting position and gladly fired his electric weapon. The lightening that entered John Garrison's chest felt like a bolt from a transformer. All went black and Garrison fell flat on his face. John's body twitched and jumped while lying on the ground. The old man looked like a fish out of water, gasping for much needed oxygen. Soon the effects of the Taser started to lighten up and Garrison opened his eyes to the face of Beauregard standing over him.

"You're under arrest for suspicion of murder of the two boys." Jack dramatically stated. "You have the right to remain silent......"

Garrison tried to shout at Beauregard, but "Kizzz ma azz ya ficken ah, uhhh," was all he could muster.

Two troopers roughly cuffed Garrison and began carrying him to the paddy wagon waiting at the end of the driveway. They had the old coot by the arms as his feet dragged behind. Television cameras and microphones followed John as he was being hauled to the vehicle. John couldn't talk and didn't try. He was in a foggy daze and would not remember all that went on here tonight.

Beauregard ordered Michaels to get the lectern out of the trunk, and then shouted his plans to the media throng. "I'm calling a press conference starting in five minutes on Garrison's lawn!"

The reporters, camera operators and news teams crushed to the front of the faux podium in Garrison's yard. It was a free-for-all to get in rows closest to Jack. He soaked in the attention and loved every second of it. A satisfied look adorned his face as he looked left and right, happy in the devotion that couldn't be matched by the proudest of humanity.

*

Robert Long, watching the mini-standoff on his TV, was confounded as to what was happening. He was also a bit surprised, but that was par for the Robert Long course.

"Why, they're carryin' the old fart to the paddy wagon?" Long wondered, "What the sam-hill!?"

Robert thought it better to sit in his living room and wait for Beauregard's news conference to hear exactly what was up rather than go over there. He figured that staying away from the action was his best bet. Robert did not like to get involved in things that weren't his problem, even if it was a friend in trouble.

"I sure ain't riding down there into that mess," Long wisely concluded. "I don't belong there."

At that moment, he started laughing in an uproarious way. At what, who knew? Then he spoke. "That old goat's wearin' his damn underpants, ha, what a dumb son-bitch."

Long laughed heartily for about two minutes until he couldn't breathe and tears rolled down his cheeks, before again being gripped by the seriousness of the situation. Robert was a flighty, aloof man who perplexed everyone who knew him, especially when it came to situations that called for a more serious attitude. He'd cry at a wedding and laugh at a funeral.

"I gotta stop laughin', Christ that's funny though. I wonder what the old codger's in trouble for?"

Robert cracked open another beer and sat down on his recliner to watch the news conference. He was interested as well as baffled by the happenings just down the road.

*

The Colonel started the news conference by mentioning that they'd found Jimmy Joseph's body within the last hour. "While we will not be answering any questions that would jeopardize our investigation, I will say we have apprehended someone of major interest in the child's death." Beauregard continued, "His name is John Garrison, and he lives in the house behind me." Jack turned and pointed at Garrison's dwelling through the heat and humidity of the evening. "At this time, we are treating this case as an open investigation and we'll give you more details as they become available."

Jack was staying with the serious look, but inside was beaming like a child on Christmas morning. *"This could very well be the path straight to that coveted governor's chair,"* was all he could think. He looked over his admirers with a matter-of-fact stone jaw. He wanted to look as serious as possible for the photographers.

"I will be personally questioning the suspect and I will find out if he is, in fact, our man. After which I will again supply the media with the needed and relevant information. Any questions?"

The reporters all spoke at once, and then settled on the first inquiry from the channel 15 news. "Is Garrison your only suspect? What brought you to him? "

The Colonel answered. "I do not know at this time if he is the only culprit, and as for why we think he's involved; no comment."

Another question, this time from a young Journalist. "Will you be seeking the death penalty? Will this enhance your run for governor? Did you know Garrison's a seventy-two-year-old man?"

Not having listened to a word he'd said in his opening statement about not supplying exact details, Beauregard's patience wore thin, "That's all for now folks. We'll get back with you as soon as we know more. Thank you for being here. I'll be available for a couple of photos."

Jack mingled with the throng as he stepped away from the makeshift podium. Flashbulbs clicked and reporters asked questions in a garbled manner. Too many voices made it impossible to hear any single one inquiry. He had some questions of his own, only he had to talk to Garrison himself for answers.

Lt. Michaels picked up the podium and put it in the trunk. Jack followed him and the two left the scene, making their way to the station to get down to some serious business. A huge opportunity had presented itself and there was no way Jack was letting it slip through his fingers.

Raising Suspicion

Jimmy Joseph lay on the gurney looking very little like a dead boy. Besides the strangulation marks on his neck, which formed a thin red-purple ring, and the pale color of his skin, which bordered on blue, it seemed as if the boy was simply sleeping. Unfortunately, he wasn't and Jimmy's parents were summoned to come in to the station and identify their child. It was a tough call for a trooper to make, so Lt. Michaels did the dirty work. He was a surprised, though, at what seemed like a twinge of disinterest. The child's mother answered the phone nonchalantly.

"Hello, this is Kathy Joseph, may I help you?"

"Mrs. Joseph, this is Lt. Michaels from the Nebraska State Police, do you have a moment?"

After a short delay, Mrs. Joseph spoke, deep down knowing what the call encompassed. "Yes. What is it? I'm a very busy woman and I have a lot to do, so let's get to the point shall we?"

Taken aback, Michaels informed her of the possible discovery of her son and asked her to come down to the morgue and make a positive ID. Mrs. Joseph only then showed some emotion, "Are you sure it's little Jimmy? Oh my God. He's dead, isn't he?"

Her voice was choking and her disposition changed, but only slightly. Trooper Michaels reluctantly informed her that yes, the boy was deceased, but an ID had to be made. It wasn't his job or general practice to tell a family member that their loved one was deceased, but in some rare cases, dealing with a mother who appeared to have a slight attitude; he thought it to be the preferred method. It was a judgment call all the way. "All right then, my husband and I will be down to ID him."

Michaels spoke again, "I know it's tough, but we have to get this identification before we can continue our thorough investigation. We'll see you in a few minutes then."

"Did I say we'd be right down?" Kathy coldly asked.

Perhaps the shock of knowing that this could be her son was hitting her and she was reacting the only way she knew how. After all, it had been awhile since Jimmy went missing, and the healing and recovery had begun. Still, Michaels had to think this would at least give some closure to the couple.

"I know, and I'm really sorry...," Michaels tried to say with a sympathetic voice.

Jimmy's mother was now becoming more aggravated. The woman interrupted, "**FINE!** Fine, we will be right there." CLICK! Michaels put the phone back down on the cradle, much gentler than Mrs. Joseph did, he assumed.

"It sure doesn't seem like she cares."

This perked up the trooper's suspicion. "Maybe this is just how some people take pain." His raised eyebrow lowered back down to an even hairline across his forehead.

Michaels shrugged his shoulders, went back to his paperwork, and waited for the Josephs' arrival.

*

Colonel Beauregard arrived at the police post and instantly wanted to know where Garrison was being held. He was on a mission, as anyone could tell.

"Interview room # 3," the dispatch trooper informed him.

Jack headed straight to that room with a head of steam. He was beyond angry, with a touch of excitement mixed in.

"I don't want any disturbances," he told the trooper guarding the door, "I want this guy alone for thirty minutes. **I mean it!** No disturbances."

"Don't hit him, Colonel, you know that would ruin everything we're trying to build."

Jack leered at the young trooper for a solid ten seconds, but couldn't decide whether to fire him or kick his ass. Beauregard took the high road and headed for Garrison. Jack slammed the door open, slammed it shut behind him and thus began the mental chess match.

"Why'd you kill those kids, you dirty old man? What's with the Jack of Spades? I want answers and I want them this instant."

Garrison looked up at the Colonel Trooper, still feeling a bit woozy from the stunner he took earlier.

"Go fuck yerself punk cop! By the way, what gotdamn Jack of Spades are you talking about? Have you lost your head? Maybe this police thing isn't for you. Ever thought about politics?"

John gave a wide grin when he came up with that gem. Jack reached across the table and grabbed Garrison by the collar, pulling him so close the old man could smell the tobacco wafting from the deepest recesses of Beauregard's lungs.

"You better talk now, or I'll beat you within an inch of your existence," Jack threatened.

The old man looked down at Beauregard's fists full of shirt when another coy smile crossed his lips. He gazed up at the Colonel, and replied, "I want two things, Colonel. I want my phone call, and I want a cup of hot fuckin' coffee! Maybe after that, I'll spill. No guarantees, though."

Jack pondered Garrison's requests, and then reluctantly complied. "Here's the phone. I'll be back in two minutes with your coffee, *cold* and black, just like what's inside that brain of yours!"

Lt. Michaels and a couple other troopers watched the proceedings on the monitor. The Lieutenant wanted to make sure Jack didn't hit Garrison, *even though he thought he deserved it,* so it wouldn't impede the investigation.

*

As Beauregard left the room to get coffee, he passed by Mr. and Mrs. Joseph, who had just arrived to identify their son. She of her over colored and upswept, split-end ridden blonde hair, caked on makeup, and dressed in too tight blue jeans and a tee-shirt that accentuated her artificial curves. Beauregard had to take a double glance behind him. She had a great body along with a trashy, easy look that drove men to lose themselves while walking, talking or otherwise standing around watching her. She took a bit of pride from seeing other women smack their boyfriends and husbands upside the head for ogling a second too long. You could definitely tell this woman was tasteless, along with being a difficult type of person to deal with. Jack squinted, then turned back to re-focus on his tasks as the Joseph's arrived at Lt. Michael's office.

Michaels again explained that he needed them to go in the back room with him to ID their son. Mrs. Joseph, with a look of contempt, asked her husband to go with Lt. Michaels to ID the body. The mister straightened to attention.

"Y-yes dear," he delicately and pusillanimously agreed.

"I just can't push myself to go back there. It would be entirely too tough for me." Mrs. Joseph whimpered. "I'm not suited for such a grisly task. My husband, on the other hand, should handle it fine. Please go Kurt."

"Y-yes d-d-dear," Mr. Joseph whimpered. He looked to Michaels and whispered. "M-Mrs. Joseph always g-gives m-me the short end of the st-stick," he told the Lieutenant. "I w-wish she'd ju-just admit that wo-once in a w-while. I d-do all her b-bidding."

Michaels tried to ignore the annoying stutter. He shook his head and pointed the way down the hall. Mr. Joseph took one more look back at his wife, and then concentrated his eyes forward behind the trooper.

Lt. Michaels led him to the back for the grim task. This was the toughest part of his job, leading someone back to see a dead body, especially that of a young boy.

*

John dialed up Robert Long, who finally answered after fifteen rings.

"Hey Robert, I need your help."

Long, on the other end of the wire, started his laughing jag again, "Hot damn, John, you shoulda' seen yerself on that TV. You looked like a floppin' trout just brought up in the boat."

Garrison scowled, "Dammit Long, can you shut your pie hole for a minute? My time's limited."

The old man was aggravated; this was no time for any funny stuff. "I need you to come down here and give these idiots a statement that we packed up a dead dog, not a dead kid. Can you do that for me, Bob?"

Long mulled for thirty seconds or more, then spoke up, "I don't wanna be involved, John, I'm scared ah them cops. You go on ahead and just tell 'em about it. They'll understand."

Garrison shut his eyes, painfully squeezed the bridge of his nose and snapped back, "I ain't tellin' 'em nothin' without a lawyer, but you can and you WILL! Now get down here, ya old fool."

Old John figured his little shout at the end of his sentence would spark Long into action.

"Nah, I ain't gonna do it John. I ain't gettin' involved."

This was a lousy time for Robert to finally get defensive and stand up to the old coot, but he was doing it anyway. John's face was turning a beet red color. "Fine then," Garrison said, "Call me that lawyer down on Hickory Street. Amy Fraser's her name, I think. We always see her on that commercial she does."

Long agreed to do that, "Okay, I will, but that's as tangled as I'm gettin'."

"You're already in it, you moron," Garrison warned. "Don't think yer just walkin' away from this nonsense. Now stop actin' like a pussy and get yer act together."

Garrison slammed the phone down on its cradle, looked at Beauregard, who had returned with the coffee and told him, "I ain't talkin' till I see my lawyer."

Jack wanted to beat the living life right out of the old man, but couldn't, as being a lawman *seemed* to keep him in line, not to mention that he was on camera. He did, however, tell the geezer he was under arrest on suspicion of murder.

One count so far, and probably two, the way he figured it. He'd work it out with the D.A. later.

"You're staying here in my jail until this is straightened out," Jack told him in a threatening manner.

The old man took one final stab at the chief before being led to the booking area and then his cell.

"If you think I did this, you're nuts. I know you're runnin' for Governor, but you can't just pin this shit on anybody you see fit. I have rights, and I intend on usin' 'em!" The old man crossed his arms across his chest defiantly.

Beauregard glared at the coot, stifled his anger, and then ordered him taken away. "Take this scum bucket out of my face." The trooper assisting Jack did as he was told.

"Wait a second," Beauregard snapped, "Give me that damn coffee." He ripped it from Garrison's hand. It spilled everywhere. Garrison chuckled.

*

"Y-yeah, th-that's J-Jimmy alright." Mr. Joseph stated with nervousness, "I n-never thought-y-you'd f-find him."

"Why would you say that, Mr. Joseph?" Michaels inquired, "Did you know where he was? Do you have information you're withholding?"

Lt. Michaels covered the boy's face back up and waited for an answer as he led the father back to his office where Mrs. Joseph had been waiting.

"Y-yeah, th-that's him honey," Mr. Joseph told her, then looked at Michaels, "and n-no, Lieutenant, I d-don't kn-know where he w-was and I do n-not have anything t-to add."

That exchange caused the missus to raise an already suspicious eyebrow, "What'd he ask you, dear?"

"N-nothin'," Mr. Joseph annoyingly said, "N-n-nothin' at all." Lt. Michaels smartly left it at that.

Once again, Mrs. Joseph did not appear to be terribly broken up about her child's death. Then again, how are you supposed to appear?

"Okay, if that's it, we'll be on our way." Mrs. Joseph stated.

"Wait just a minute," the Lieutenant insisted. The couple stopped and turned to face the trooper. "Aren't you even going to ask if there's a suspect or where he was found. Aren't you a little curious about the particulars?"

Mrs. Joseph rolled her eyes and impatiently answered, "Yes, okay, where did you find him? Is there a suspect? What do I need to know?"

She asked these questions with an exasperation that suggested she was bored, her head cocked to one side, her hands on her hips. Mr. Joseph kept looking at his feet the whole time, too shy or ashamed to speak.

"He was found at the John Garrison place over in Hickman. He's our lead suspect," Michaels told them, *told her*. "That's where we're at now."

"Great," Mrs. Joseph quickly uttered while widening her overly made up eyes. "You guys get that creep and see that he fries in the chair for this. Okay?"

Michaels carefully responded. "We have him already; he's jailed right down the hall." The Lieutenant continued, "The autopsy will be done tomorrow, we'll get back with you when we have the findings." Mrs. Joseph was still fidgeting to leave. She tired of continually being held up.

"Anything else trooper?" she asked with a tart and sarcastic tone. Mrs. Joseph wasn't exactly known for her sensitivity. This time was no different.

"No. That'll be it for now. Oh, one more thing." Michaels nodded his head as he raised his index finger. "Do me a favor and hang around town, will you?"

"Are you insinuating that...?" The missus asked with a hint of shock.

"No," the Lieutenant interrupted, "just procedure, I guess." It wasn't, but Michaels wanted them to stay close in case he had more questions. With that, the couple quickly left the station.

The next morning's Lincoln Times looked like this:

Lincoln Times

**Jimmy Joseph's body found.
Beauregard nabs suspect in child killing case.
Colonel now frontrunner for Governor Seat.**

AP-In a stunning development, the Nebraska State Troopers have found and apprehended the man believed to be responsible for the two child murders in Lincoln. John Garrison, 72, of Hickman may be arraigned in District Court on charges of murder. Although he only remains a suspect, there is evidence to believe he may be the man responsible. Currently, Garrison is being held in the Lincoln State Police jail until the investigation is concluded. Jack Beauregard, the Lincoln Trooper Colonel, would not comment on the extent or progress of the investigation. We will report further as details become available.

-Angela Page

The paper also included two photos; one of Garrison being hauled into the paddy wagon, the other was Beauregard beaming and mugging up for the camera. It couldn't have been better had he scripted it himself. Jack drank his coffee and ate his toast while smiling over the article.

"Boy this sure makes breakfast taste better!"

"Good job, Dad," Kyle grinned from the other side of the table.

"If there was any doubt before, it's gone now." Jack interjected, be it ever so slightly. "Let's not get too far ahead of ourselves. I need to cross every "t" and dot every "i" before this goes any further."

"No problem, Dad, you've never had any trouble solving stuff before and this will be no different."

Jack gave his son a giant smile, rose from his chair and walked over to give him a hug. He believed this had convinced Kyle that a career in law enforcement and politics was, in fact, the right choice.

Amy and the Old Coot

Garrison sat in his cell wondering why he was a suspect in a murder case he knew very little about. A dead boy was found in the bag he laid out for Animal Control, yet he knew that #1, he killed no one and #2, it *was* a dead dog in that sack. Robert Long could, and with any luck, would testify to that. John was a bit concerned about Robert. He had, for some odd reason, decided he wasn't going to take the ribbing any longer. John insisted to himself that he simply joked with Long and really didn't mean any of it in a literal sense. He liked Robert and thought him to be a friend. They had met each other at the barbershop and he was closer to Long than any of the other old coots that hung around up there. He felt he had a connection with the tall drink of water that he did not have with anyone else. He also felt that camaraderie slipping a bit. He hoped his neighbor would come around before it was too late.

John was understandably very angry about being accused of something he truly didn't do. "I don't know what the hell's goin' on here," Garrison thought, "but I ain't takin' the fall for some murders I ain't got nothin' to do with."

The more John thought about it, the angrier he became. Lots of folks sitting in jails say they didn't do it, but in John's case, it couldn't ring more true. He was telling the truth and no one in law enforcement cared for it. They had their man and nothing was going to change that fact with them. John's only hope of escaping this rap appeared more and more likely to be in a court of law. "It's the way of the system." Garrison argued to himself, "If in doubt, go to trial. The truth will surely come out there." John then thought about the scarier part of the mess. "It doesn't matter to the police, state prosecutors or even a judge if a jury comes back with a guilty verdict. As far as they're concerned, once a jury of your peers has spoken, its gold."

John knew his chances would probably be less than fifty-fifty, because he himself had been reading about the murders in the newspaper and wanted the law to catch the bad guy(s). Now it was different because *he* was the center of the investigation. He wasn't even sure that a boy had really ever been found in any bag since he himself had not seen the body. He was harassed by his fellow inmates, the police, and almost everyone else involved, save for Robert. "You know you stashed a dead kid in the sack." They all said. He knew what was in the bag he placed in his driveway, and it was not that of a dead child.

*

The guard brought John his dinner tray, slid it under the cell gate, and had it suddenly returned to him courtesy of John's right foot.

"Get that shit outta here!" John grumped, "I wouldn't eat that trash with your mouth."

"You're cleaning this up, you old shithead!" The guard ordered. "Why'd you do that anyway?"

The clumped mashed potatoes and gravy covered Salisbury steak were strewn about the corridor, dripping from the wall and cell bars. A mess had been made and John was proud to own it.

"Clean it yourself, ya fuckin' good for nothin' badge wearin' pencil neck."

The guard gave Garrison a cold stare then told him he'd be thrown in the solitary lock-up of the small office jail. John did not care one bit! "I don't give a rat's fat ass what cha do. I ain't scared of your threats."

The guard retrieved a mop and bucket, and then began the cleanup himself. John returned to his cot, grumbling and cursing under his breath. He hoped Long had done what he'd said and called that lawyer. The old man wouldn't be surprised if he didn't though. He was worried about Robert. "He's probably sittin' in his stupid lazy-boy tryin' to figure out whether he wants to help or not. I'll kick his ass when I see him."

Garrison was right. Robert was sitting in his lazy-boy looking at the news and contemplating whether or not he wanted to be involved. Robert really had no idea that he was a part of this, like it or not.

"That old codger Garrison's ruinin' my peace and quiet. Why does he have to do that? I didn't do nothin' 'cept help out a little. That old fart's been bossin' me around since day one. I ain't callin' nobody for him! He can do it his damn self."

As Robert continued to hem and haw over what to do next, he fell asleep in his chair. Nothing was happening tonight, that much was definitely determined. The call would have to wait.

*

Morning arrived early for Robert. He threw on bacon and eggs as he thought about his friend sitting in jail. He had a huge decision he was pondering and wasn't making any progress simply obsessing over it. Just then, Amy Fraser's commercial ran on the TV. She was standing in front of her desk with a nice blouse, along with glasses to make her look a bit more mature. Robert goggled at her because this woman was "fine as wine," in his eyes. Amy used her hands a lot as she emphasized each and every point. She was also holding a pen in her right hand. Here was the pitch:

"Are you in a bind? Do you need expert help at a reasonable price? Is winning in court no matter what a must for you? Well look no further, because I'm right here. I'm Amy Fraser and I win cases. My costs are low but my aim is high. Call me at 800-AFRASER and consult with me today! Don't wait that extra minute. Do it now!"

The tall, lanky, Mr. Long went with his gut instincts and finally gave Amy a call. He had to help John, mainly due to the fact that yes, a dog was what they wrapped up in the garbage bags. He also considered John a friend, even when he was a harassing old goat. Deep down, Robert thought that there was a very slim chance that Garrison had a dead boy stashed somewhere and was just using the dog as a ruse. Yes, he helped him pack the dog up. No, he did not stay to see the pickup. The switch could easily have been made after he left John's house. As painful as it was to consider such a possibility, it had to be addressed in his mind. Still, he did not believe John killed a child. It just didn't make sense. "That old man ain't never hurt nobody that I know of."

Robert picked up the phone and made the call. Amy answered.

"Hello, Amy Fraser please." Long requested.

"This is she. What can I help you with?

It wasn't a big surprise Amy herself answered because she owned the business and worked alone. She called it Fraser law. Why not? She operated the practice herself. Secretary and lawyer. She was a savage workaholic. A damn good attorney, too.

*

Amy Fraser was a motivated self-starter, relatively new to the world of live courtroom action. This included dealing with real people and real problems. She attained her law degree from Lincoln School of Criminal Justice. She went straight into the law school after high school graduation and put in a tough four years grooming for the chance to become a defense lawyer, her lifelong dream. She passed her classes perfectly and scored a 100% on her State Bar Exam. The woman was tenaciously dedicated to her craft. It was Amy's first year as an attorney and she had already handled three cases, all resulting in victory for her clients. One of the cases was a hit-and-run, resulting in injuries, not death. The other two were for unarmed robbery and an alleged breaking and entering. Amy was outstanding in the courtroom, thus convincing three juries of her clients' innocence. She was not prepared for the news of what would turn out to be the biggest case in her young career, but that's what she trained for.

Ms. Fraser was beautiful. She of her long jet-black hair and green eyes. Her skin had a hint of olive coloring, which gave her an exotic look. "Just right," men would say behind her back. "Easy on the eyes." Her lips were full, not puffy. Very kissable, if you dared to try. Amy only stood five feet one and a half inches and weighed one hundred and ten pounds, but a sharp edge and firm assertiveness more than made up for her small stature.

Along with her good looks came a competitive, fiery attitude. You wouldn't cross this woman or else! If anyone mentioned how she appeared physically, they would get more than an earful; they would receive a full-scale lecture on sexual harassment and the punishments that came with it. Only one time would an individual venture into that territory with her. They learned quickly that she was neither intimidated nor shy. Amy was not interested in dating and she was less interested in men, sex or any relationships. She wanted all her energy to go toward her career. All the other stuff would fall into place if it was meant to. She was a driven woman. She was also as tough as she was pretty. More than one man had been socked in the eye by Amy at a nightclub or bar. The reasons for her tough and tenacious determination ran deep. It is a dark and abusive upbringing that had given Amy her edge.

*

"What can I do for you sir?" Amy said when answering Robert's call.

"Uh, yes ma'am, my name is Robert Long and I'm callin' for John Garrison. He's in the county lockup right now; they're blamin' him for the child murder. You know, the Joseph boy."

"Oh yes," Amy retorted. "I saw what happened on television last night."

Long stalled for a second, searching for the proper words to say to this woman. "Um, I guess John has seen you on the TV and he's interested in hiring you to represent him in this case. He asked me to call. So I did."

Long paused another second before speaking one last time. He was again trying to choose the right words. "I don't want to be involved in this shit, so I made the call for 'em and you can take it from here."

Right words indeed. Robert quickly cradled the phone. He was scared to death.

"Mr. Long….hello? Mr. Long… are you still there?"

Robert had hung up the phone smack in Amy's ear. Little did he know that he was involved even deeper for making the call. Out of sheer curiosity, she decided to make a trip down to the lockup and speak with Mr. Garrison one on one. It wasn't her everyday method of operation, but the phone call from Long was anything but normal. She'd simply check the Garrison guy out at the jail and decide then if it was something she was really interested in pursuing. If not, it was no skin off her nose except for an extra trip. Amy would not only find out she was interested, but she would find out a whole lot more than she ever bargained for.

*

After going through the obligatory search and frisk upon entering the jailhouse, a trooper led Amy down a long corridor, the end of which was Garrison's cell. The whistling, catcalling and harassment started almost the second she stepped into the cell block. She tried to pay no heed to this nonsense as much more important issues existed. They finally arrived at John's cell. The trooper warned Amy not to make physical contact with the prisoner. He gave her a chair to sit outside the cell and talk. After Amy saw the guard was out of sight, she put her hand right through the bars to greet Mr. Garrison. It was the Amy way. "I'm pleased to meet you Mr. Garrison. I'm Amy Fraser and I was called by your friend, Robert Long, but he hung up so abruptly I didn't get any details about your situation except what I've heard on the news. By the way, are you alright from that nasty Taser strike?

John looked Amy over with squinted eyes and shook hands with her, happy that she was there. John told her right off the bat, "I ain't no gotdamn child killer, ma'am, and this is a frame-up. These are some double-dealin' pigs!"

"May I call you John?" Amy asked.

The old coot nodded his head affirmatively.

"You're in a world of unadulterated trouble, John. I'm here to try and help you out of it. I saw the news stories on TV and the internet. None of it was good.

You are also a YouTube sensation from the stun gun incident. Nevertheless, I have to ask you, why do you want me? I'm not really experienced with this type of casework."

Amy cracked a small smile John's way and the old grump ate it up.

"You're a woman after my own heart, and perty too! My you're a good-lookin' lass."

Amy wiped the smile off her face and shot back, "I may be a woman after you're own heart, but me being pretty is not going to win your case. Please refer to me in a business-like fashion, if you don't mind Mr. Garrison; *John*."

The entire cell block went silent fast. All that could be heard was the tick-tock of the hallway clock. John broke the silence, as he leaned forward, hands on his knees, so he could explain some things to the young lawyer. "I didn't say I was aimin' to jump yer bones Ms. Fraser. I'm about to pay you upwards of fifty grand, and I believe that gives me the right to call you pretty if I see fit." John then leaned back in his seat and crossed his arms. "Anyway, I picked ya' because I liked what I saw on your TV commercial. You seemed very confident and you even said, "If you can't afford to lose, hire me." Well, I can't afford to lose."

Amy couldn't really do much but agree. She figured John to be fairly harmless, not to mention what fifty grand could do for her and the business, even though that was obviously too much money.

"All right, John, start from the beginning and do not hold back. I want the complete truth A-Z. Tell me everything you know. Don't lie!"

The young lawyer took out her notepad and listened intently as John told her the whole story, warts and all. Her mouth fell open while trying to soak in what she was hearing.

*

The old man started from the moment he found the dead dog all the way through to being tased, cuffed and jailed. He left nothing to chance. The truth and nothing but, so help him God.

"So you found a dead dog, and picked it up. With the help of your neighbor, Robert Long, you bagged it and called the pound. Beauregard said you're the murderer and asked you about a Jack of Spades playing card. It sounds like a railroad job if I've ever heard one."

Amy was trying to make sense of it. Why would someone claim such a story if it weren't real? A dead dog? She also believed him when he talked about the playing card. He truly seemed unknowing. Either that or he was a very good liar. So far everything he said seemed legitimate.

"That's right," Garrison told her, "I'm gettin' railroaded for the good of that gotdamn Beauregard."

"Why do you say that?" Amy asked. "What makes him so special?"

"He's goin' for the governorship. Everyone knows that. Where the hell ya been? Under a rock?"

Amy served up a nasty sneer and again scolded Garrison, "Don't talk to me like I'm a child. I hate being patronized, and I don't appreciate your sarcasm"

The old grump was getting grumpier and he was tired. He ended the interview. "I gotta get me some sleep. Let's finish this later."

Garrison limped over to his cot and lay down hard. Within five minutes he was snoring. Amy sat outside the cell finishing up some notes. At the same time, she was trying to get a better feel for Garrison's story. She stared in at a sleeping Garrison and tapped her index finger against her lips. After a few more minutes of this, she packed up her stuff, walked the catcall-ridden corridor and went home.

*

Amy Fraser lay in her bed wide awake. It was very early in this case. The autopsy wasn't until the next day, so there were plenty of new facts and figures that would be coming in. Her stomach started to churn. A wave here and a wave there. This was not indicative of Amy's disposition. She didn't take kindly to feeling out of the ordinary.

"Maybe my period's coming," she thought to herself, "or it could be I ate something bad."

Still, stomachaches did not happen to Amy and it concerned her. This woman was known for taking stress and fear, strangling it to death, and then throwing it in the trash can. After an hour or so of tossing and turning, the ache diminished. She fell asleep knowing deep down inside there was lots of work to do. When morning came, Amy dragged herself out of bed, still feeling a tad drawn.

"Flu? Possibly. No time for that though. Way too much to do today."

She started her day by calling Beauregard and leaving a message that she had been hired as Garrison's attorney and all inquiries would go through her. That done, Amy took a shower and got dressed. Her next trip was to her office to check her messages, then to the morgue to wait for the autopsy results.

Despite the upmost fight from Amy, the stomachache worsened. It wouldn't stop her though. The woman was determined to help Mr. Garrison, and no pain in her gut was getting in the way of her goal. Rolaids, Tums, Maalox, or whatever else was needed to quell the nausea, she'd use it. It would take a whole lot more than this to slow down the bullheaded attorney.

Little Jimmy's Autopsy

Col. Beauregard, Lt. Michaels and the Forensic Pathologist, Soo-Chin, gathered at the county morgue for the autopsy of Jimmy Joseph. In the waiting room, Amy Fraser sat with a magazine and patiently read as she waited for the team's arrival. She met, shook hands, and exchanged words with Jack before he and Soo-Chin abruptly disappeared into one of the inner offices adjoining the autopsy room. His mood was downcast and arrogant.

"I'm Amy Fraser. I called you earlier to let you know I'm handling Garrison's defense."

"Yes, I got your message, Ms. Fraser," Beauregard said, "My question is why you would want to represent a scum-bucket like him? You must be a desperate lawyer."

Amy was taken aback, although only slightly. She fired back at the trooper.

"You let me worry about that, Mr. Beauregard," Amy insisted. "I thought people were innocent until *proven* guilty. It sounds to me like you have a completely different idea about that cardinal rule. By the way, I'd like access to the autopsy, please."

"No chance, Ms. Fraser, this is strictly police business. You'll be notified of the results."

Beauregard turned to his partner and barked his order, "Lt. Michaels, stay out here and guard the door, and no one is allowed access. There will be no disturbances, understood?"

The Lieutenant gave Jack a salute as Amy protested loudly, "I have a right to see what's going on in there, and make sure there's no tampering of evidence. I know you and Pathologist Soo-Chin have been dating. I've seen you two around town hand in hand. I want to see the Jack of Spades playing card that's in question, and I want to make sure everything's on the up and up."

Jack countered, "This is strictly a professional deal here, so take it up with the Judge." Jack looked at his watch and cracked a grin. "You have about five minutes to garner a warrant for entry. Good luck to you." Jack's smiled unapologetically widened.

That was the extent of the conversation, very short and not so sweet. Amy stood frustrated and particularly angry. She could at first see and now heard how these people were not going to give an inch to help her defense. When you're hiding evidence, or a lack thereof, this is usually how it worked. Her stomach started acting up again. Amy fumed as she sat back down on the chair. She was waiting right here until the autopsy was complete, then she'd ask more questions. Amy also made a phone call to the Lincoln Times and let them know the autopsy was underway. They said they knew and were en route. She flipped through a magazine, but didn't take in any of the contents.

*

"Two dead boys, two black straps around their necks and two Jacks of Spades. What was the connection? Is the killer trying to get *Jack* Beauregard's attention exclusively?" Soo smartly asked.

"I think the killer is simply a big fan of black," Jack reasoned. "This has nothing to do with me *per se*. It's a calling card."

Soo-Chin didn't have much to add, "Maybe so, Jack. People who kill children really don't have much rhyme or reason for doing it except in their own minds. It's too early to know for sure. Let's perform the autopsy and see what we find. I need you to be quiet and let me work, okay?" Jack nodded.

Armed with a menthol mixture smeared under their noses and a mask over their faces, they began the task of trying to decipher whatever clues may be hidden with Jimmy's corpse. Soo-Chin started by describing into a tape recorder the body as it looked on the table.

"Body appears normal except for black belt strap tightened around the neck. No hair missing, no obstructions inside the ears, nose or mouth. Eyes are fixed and dilated. Front side of body shows no bruising or broken bones. Reproductive organs appear normal with no sign of sexual abuse. Fingernails are present, with no sign of struggle."

Soo-Chin then rolled the body over on its face, backside up. She did this quickly and methodically.

"No bruising is visible on back of torso. No damage to the head or skull. Black belt strap is visible on nape of neck just under the cortex. There does not appear to be any sign of sexual abuse in the anal area. Legs and feet normal. Toenails are present with no sign of struggle. Okay, Jack, help me roll him back over and I'll begin the internal exam. Hope you have a strong stomach. It can get pretty graphic."

Jack accommodated Soo-Chin and the boy was ready for the next step. Soo marked the torso with a sharpie pen in the exact spots she wanted to cut. She then placed the scalpel at the base of Jimmy's left collarbone and cut down to the middle of his chest and then back up to the opposite collarbone. She followed that with a slice straight down from his mid chest to the bottom of his abdomen. A classic Y-shaped incision. After sawing the ribcage apart, Soo-Chin separated the cut openings, thus revealing Jimmy's inner system. The examiner began poking around the internal organs while talking into her tape recorder. She used her fingers and a probe stick.

"Normal, normal, lungs look good. Liver intact and functional. No disease visible." She continued with her examination when Jack finally spoke, "Do you see..."

"SHHH!" Soo-Chin turned toward Jack and scolded him while clicking off her tape recorder. "You cannot say one word while I'm doing this, Jack. You know that. I have to rewind and start again every time you speak."

Jack was mildly embarrassed, "I'm sorry; I just need to know..."

Again Soo-Chin interrupted, "When we are finished, I will tell you what I think. Until then, let me do my job. I shouldn't have let you in, but I'm trying to help you solve this case."

Soo's face was pinched into an aggravated scowl.

"OK, OK," Jack agreed and went quiet again. He checked the watch on his wrist and looked at the wall clock. Both kept the same time. He remained hushed.

After examining the rest of the torso, which included inspecting and weighing Jimmy's heart and lungs, it was time to cut Jimmy's scalp and inspect the brain. It revealed nothing to her, although it unsettled Jack a bit. He turned away during that part of the exam. Soo-Chin peeled off the latex gloves and concluded the autopsy.

"Well," Jack asked impatiently while motioning in a circular pattern with his hand.

"I see no sexual abuse of any kind," she answered, No brain injuries, no bruising, and no heart issues.

Jimmy seemed to be well fed and pretty healthy. He simply died of strangulation from that black strap around his neck. It crushed his larynx. It's the same as the Wilder boy."

Jack looked at Soo-Chin with a gaping mouth, "That's it? Nothing more?"

She explained that DNA testing on the garbage bag and Jimmy's blood work may tell more, the bag being most important. "I know you long to solve this and stamp your ticket to the mansion, but you must be patient and let the system work. I can't make a magical discovery that's not there."

Jack reluctantly agreed and washed up before stepping back into the hallway and right into the teeth of the media. A throng that was foaming at the mouth for answers.

*

Beauregard ordered Lt. Michaels to go to the car and get his podium from the trunk. This podium went everywhere the could-be-next governor went. The front of the lectern had two circles; one was a State Flag encircled with a Nebraska State Police printing while the other was the same State Flag, only this one with the words Nebraska Gubernatorial Candidate around it. Jack thought there was nothing like being ready for any public appearance that may come along. Beauregard intended to use the media to enhance his chances for election by explaining how *he'd* caught up with the alleged child killer and it was *he himself* who'd put the collar on him. This probably wouldn't thrill the other troopers, but he figured they could watch and learn from a pro. He would not mention the Jack of Spades, though, in fear of potential copycat killers. That would be saved for a trial.

As Jack surveyed the media before him, he felt a surge of pride flowing into his temperament. He was in the world he loved. The world of attention and concern brought onto him by the *little* people. Mr. Beauregard loved every ounce of focus he received. When at home or away from the throng, he wasn't as happy. It just was not the same thrill going on vacation or out of state and not being recognized. If he were to land the governor gig, it would help him spread his name, but he'd still need to do more or go further, say the Senate or Congress, to stretch his image. Perhaps one day it would be Jack Beauregard, President of the United States? Well, he wasn't prepared to go that far yet, but in the future? Who knew?

*

Flash bulbs cracked and questions filled the room. There was no way one could decipher them. It was an all-out frenzy, with Beauregard taking great pleasure in it. As he stepped up to his podium, the first thing he requested was that all questions wait until after his statement. The room went relatively silent and Jack spoke. Hand and face gestures were prevalent during his address.

"As the defender of the law in Lincoln, it is my duty to bring to justice any individual accused of or found to be breaking the law. We think it's safe to say that we have found a lawbreaker in John Garrison of Hickman, Nebraska. A young boy's body was found at his home and we have ample reason to believe that Mr. Garrison is the man responsible. I will be seeking a warrant from the prosecutor's office to charge Garrison with first degree murder. I think it's safe to say we have the culprit."

Soo-Chin looked at Jack like he was crazy. She had just told him it was too early to determine anything. Without toxicology exams to link Garrison, there was still nothing. She was visibly aggravated.

Jack continued his news conference. "While we still have plenty of information to go through, and while there's still a few people to interview as far as possible witnesses go, I remain confident that the killing will stop right here, right now. If you have any questions, I will take them one at a time."

"JACK, Jack, how do you link the murders to Garrison?"

"Simple," Jack cleverly stated, "We believe that he was trying to dispose of the body through animal control. It didn't work."

"JACK! Will you be suggesting or pursuing the death penalty?"

Jack smiled brazenly, "I will suggest death, but the prosecutor has final say on charges and possible sentences. Nothing's imminent. Ma'am, your question please." Jack was pointing into the crowd. "Yes, you in the blue shirt."

"Mr. Beauregard, will this collar enhance your chances of becoming Governor of Nebraska?"

While all this was going on, Amy was frantically jotting down notes. She could not believe her ears. Amy thought that she should be privy to any evidence gathered before the media was. Apparently that was not the case, but if Beauregard was linking her client based only on a bag in his driveway, this could bode well for her defense. The stomach ache that had earlier inconvenienced Amy was now threatening to bend her over. She hoped the conference would end soon. She kept up her intent listening, hoping for more cracks in Beauregard's statements. It was tough with her stomach throbbing. Amy was concerned.

"God, my stomach is killing me!" Amy thought to herself. "I think I'm going to puke."

The news conference continued, despite her ills.

"If this doesn't enhance my run for governor, I don't know what will," was Jack's reply to the last question. "My job is to get killers off the street. That's what I'm doing. No one slips away from me or my troopers. We are the best at what we do."

The excitement gripping at Jack was electrifying. He wanted that office worse than anything he could ever think of, and this was doing nothing less than helping it along. He did, however, feel that he'd said enough and it was time to move forward and let the people clamor for more.

"That'll be all for today folks. We will keep you informed."

"JACK…. JACK, Jack....."

"No more questions, that's it."

Jack rifled through the reporters and almost ran smack into Amy on his way out the door. Lt. Michaels followed closely, podium in hand.

"Give us room. Let us through please." Lt. Michaels ordered.

Amy left the building with the other reporters, hid behind a wall and puked her brains out.

"What the hell?" She thought, "I've never felt this rotten before." Amy reassured herself yet again that it had to be a touch of flu. She dusted herself off and headed towards her vehicle when two media members recognized her from the courthouse. She did not feel like talking, as the nausea still pursued her.

"Is that you, Amy Fraser?" One of them asked, "Are you defending Garrison? Is that why you're here? AMY, AMY, Amy Fraser, would you answer some questions please?" The news people begged as they stuck microphones and tape recorders inches from her face.

Amy struggled to hold back the vomit that was knocking on the back of her throat. "I have to go guys; I have a lot to do. I'll answer your questions later."

With that, Amy fled into her car, turning her head and spewing onto her passenger seat. She would have to clean up the mess in the morning. The two reporters who had followed her to the car saw the accident she had and turned away, no longer interested in her at the moment.

Jack, meanwhile, flew down the road in the cruiser with all the confidence he could muster.

"Michaels, I think this will all but cement my run for governor."

Lt. Michaels, ever agreeable, nodded in agreement. He knew that Jack's election would open the door for him to take over the Colonel's chair in the State Police Headquarters. Lt. Michaels also knew that the evidence thus far was weak at best, but someone really did need to go down for this. The public was already outraged and this would soften them considerably. Michaels wanted to do it right, although it wasn't his call.

The media ran with it in the next day's newspaper:

Lincoln Times

Beauregard has collar on killer; Amy Fraser to defend Garrison. Charges in case expected soon; Autopsy results pending

AP-Charges in the homicide of two local youths will be announced soon, according to Trooper Jack Beauregard. The autopsy results of Jimmy Joseph, the second murdered boy in the area, are pending. The suspect, John Garrison of Hickman, allegedly was found to have possession of the dead Joseph boy at his home. It was also discovered that the suspect has hired Amy Fraser to be his defense council for all future proceedings. Garrison is suspected of murdering both boys in the Lincoln area. When the charges, if any, are announced, we will inform the public.

-Angela Page

Dreams (Amy's Torment)

It took all of her power to concentrate on the road ahead to make it home. Her stomach churned like razor blades in a blender, while her head ached right down to the core of her brain. Luckily, the case was just starting, so that would give Amy plenty of time to ward off whatever was troubling her at the moment.

She thought deep down that there may be more going on in her mind than the Garrison situation alone. The glimmers of her forgettable past could be trying to rear up and give her a jolt. It seemed to her that for some strange reason, this case was a trigger of sorts.

"Why now?" She asked herself. Amy was intense and serious all the time. It could very well be that some kind of disquiet had decided to pay a long, overdue visit. A rapidly beating heart for no distinguishable reason, cold sweats, numbness and tingling in her arms and a warm rush from her feet to her head caused Amy to think she may be dying. Panic attacks have a way of doing that to the strongest of personalities. You may wish you'd die, but the Grim Reaper always fails to show up. Amy pushed these thoughts away and doubled her resolve.

"I need to get myself together. I have a huge case that will most certainly go to trial and I'm representing a man who could DIE if I am not the very best lawyer the State of Nebraska has ever seen. There is simply no time for feeling sick or tired."

Amy had the tendency to place enormous amounts of pressure on herself. She simply refused to accept anything even slightly out of the ordinary. She could see a doctor and possibly find a reason for the discomfort, and then medicate it. Amy was too stubborn, but she would reconsider, especially with the intensity in which these "spells" occurred. Bullheaded Amy. She was the type to stare down discomfort and overcome it. This is no different then when she was a kid being raised in Lincoln.

*

Growing up with an alcoholic mother and an abusive father drove Amy to excel where most teenagers would fold up like a house of straw in a hurricane. She was determined to rise above the din of her troubled home life and make something happen that would be exciting, enriching and most of all, would help others in need. This woman loved helping people in trouble. It seemed to draw her in. Amy decided that being a lawyer, a defense lawyer at that, was what life called her to do. She could have been a model, but wouldn't hear of it. Amy was adamant about not being exploited because of her looks. She knew she was pretty, but ignored it. Amy knew men wanted her so bad it hurt, but she chalked it up to pure lustfulness. They would not, could not, have her.

"Anybody can have sex," Amy reasoned, "But few can make love." She had not found the special man that could love her unconditionally. Not that she would allow someone to get so close to her, mentally or physically.

Without that worry, she put her concentration fully toward her goal of becoming a lawyer. This girl loved arguing and she really valued proving someone else wrong. Being an only child in a dysfunctional home was seen by her as a challenge, not a weakness.

"So you don't think I can do it? Watch me!" was her stubborn refrain.

Amy decided to shower and try to sleep. She really needed the rest and she was frankly, pretty tired of feeling like death warmed over. As Amy wrapped her hair into a towel, put on her bathrobe and laid on the edge of the bed, the thoughts crept back into her mind. The thoughts of childhood…the thoughts of her now deceased parents…all the thoughts that haunt Amy. Her eyes grew heavy and tired. Her bodily functions started to settle down. Amy's breathing mellowed and her heartbeat, racing earlier, ebbed into a comfortable, unnoticed rhythm. The sandman had arrived, and just in time. She finally fell asleep, and then the dreams came.

*

"You'll nefer amount to anything," her overweight and couch ridden mother slurred in a drunken stupor. "You're a looser and a bish."

Sixteen year-old Amy stood with her arms crossed over her chest and her head cocked to the left. Her hair was pulled back in a tight, yellow ribboned pony-tail. She had been listening to this tirade since she was seven or eight. That's when her mom started thinking alcohol was her personal savior.

"Jus because you're cute, it does not gif you a free pass through life."

Amy was a stunningly pretty teenager who wanted nothing more than to become a lawyer. Mom and Dad thought she would become a model, due to her good looks, but Amy would not be exploited. Besides, the chance for success in that world is minimal due to the extreme competitive nature of the business. More importantly, it was not her passion. Lawyering was. She wanted to defend people against the harshness of a cruel society. She wanted to save people from a system that encouraged punishment first and fairness never.

"Mom, I'm going to be in law and I'm going to help humanity." she would reason.

Drunk off her rocker, Mom said nothing that would support her daughter's dream, "You are one stufid bish, you will nefer make it. Not a looser like you."

As Mom slumbered in and out of consciousness, Dad walked by and gave Amy a small smack to the back of the head, knocking off her hair ribbon.

"Listen to yer ma, Amy, and don't be stupid. You need to take your looks and run with 'em."

Amy was undeterred and her smart-aleck mouth sometimes got in the way. "I'm going to be a lawyer, and as for my "good looks," I'm lucky to have them considering the mess you and Mom are."

Her dad lunged forward at a lightning- fast rate and clocked Amy with his fist just below her nose and just above her upper lip. It was a powerful punch. "You shut yer damn mouth ya little bitch. I'm the leader around here and you'll do as I say!"

The blood ran out of Amy's nostril and into her mouth, causing her to experience a bitter, copper-like taste. She rose from the floor, retrieved a tissue from the bathroom and fled into her bed face first, crying into her pillow as hard as she could. Amy remained undeterred. These instances only made her more resolute.

*

Amy awoke, sweating, and lay in her bed, staring at the ceiling while reviewing her life up to now. Despite her Parents' discouragement, Amy spent all her spare time pursuing her dream. She had a 4.3 GPA in school and was continuously perusing law books, journals and watching each and every case she could on LAW TV. Learn, learn, learn was her mantra. She would study her backside off and ignore her surroundings. Amy was stubborn and driven-the right combination if she were to be in law. No boyfriends, no parties and no goofing off. There was no time for games if she were to attain her dream.

Nearing the end of her senior year in high school, Dad joined Mom in the out-to-lunch drinking sessions. Dad stopped hitting her so much because he was usually too drunk to even stand up, let alone swing a fist. They were a pathetic pair who she thought would probably be dead before she completed college. Amy graduated high school in the third week of June without Mom and Dad's presence. She had no brothers or sisters to watch her, as she was an only child. These factors caused her to be even more determined. Where others would fall by the wayside and probably become blithering drunks themselves, Amy would have no part of it.

The University of Nebraska called her with an offer of a full ride scholarship to study law. The excitement ran deep inside, but alas, there was really no one to share it with. Amy kept her poise and started her education. "One step closer," she thought, "One step closer."

The study habits Amy forged were that of legend. She had two roommates in her dorm that were both astonished and worried about the girl. She could spend eight hours in class, ten hours studying, four hours working, two hours sleeping and wake up with that same bright, rosy smile and dogged determination. This was not just once in a while; this was six and sometimes seven days a week for *five* years! She seemed healthy and strong. She never looked tired. She wasn't. She was excited and thanked her Lord everyday for the opportunity given to her. Proving any doubters wrong was part of her motivation. Reaching her goal and becoming a lawyer was much more important to her than anything else this world had to offer.

Amy studied hard and graduated from U of N with honors. Near perfect scores to go with her near perfect smile. Mom and Dad were not there for her college graduation, just as they had not been there for her high school honors and just as they had not been there for her acceptance into a major university. They were too inebriated to even remember what had happened five minutes ago, let alone pay attention to their daughter's accomplishments. This girl was as alone as she could've been. Amy learned how to deal with it and kept her nose to the grindstone.

*

Mom and Dad died not two months after her graduation. The car accident was bad. It was a good thing it was just those two and no one else. Dad hit a curb, became airborne, and sheered the car in two on a metal electrical tower. Both were D.O.I. (dead on impact). Amy shed a tear or two at the funeral, and then moved on with purpose. At least she had made it to *their* celebration. If anybody thought it didn't bother her some, they would've been wrong. These were her parents after all, not just a couple of strangers she never knew. Amy was not heartless, simply focused. Having to ID the bodies was painful, not only because they were mutilated, but because on some level she cared. She cared in a very cautious way, though. She was abused mentally, sexually and physically, which she buried as deep in her psyche as she possibly could. It was the only way she could cope. Unfortunately, those types of traumas have a tendency to reappear when they are the least welcomed. Your spirit does not have a schedule.

*

Amy tossed and turned throughout the night, dreams coming and going. It was never quite this vivid before. She was seeing into the depths of her tormented soul. Could she have had a better relationship with her parents? Absolutely, but not without effort from both sides. All the feelings had to be stowed away for the sake of her career. It seemed now that they wanted to surface. There was no time for that, because the biggest case of her young life was upon her. Amy tossed a bit more and fell back into her slumber. She hoped she would sleep restfully the remainder of the night. She would not.

*

"No Daddy, please, no!"

A young Amy cried as she took yet another pummeling from her father. ***"How many black eyes and bloody noses will there be?"*** *she screamed.*

"NO, No, Daddy, NO!"

Dad ripped Amy's clothes off and stood before her, soaking in the beauty with which Amy had been blessed. Amy tried to cover herself, but her entire body was impossible to hide with two hands. Dad ordered her to put her arms to her side so he could see her, lust over her, and then violently shove her on the bed. Amy's tears couldn't hide the pain. Her father attacked her with an evil intent in his eyes. The rape was savage as he punched, bit and sweat on her while performing his vile act. The rancid language coming out of his mouth gave Amy the most fetid feeling imaginable. She thought about biting or scratching him, but it would only make the experience worse. Amy would cry for help. ***"Help me Mom, please. Please help, HELP,"*** *until Dad hit her in the mouth. It was to no avail as Mom was a miserable shell of her former self. She had no idea what was happening. The blame would be placed on Amy's head regardless.*

When her father finished, Amy re- clothed herself and went into the bathroom to vomit up the wretched stink of the deed. Amy was no longer a virgin. Her purity had been bled from her loins. Her dad stole that gift from her and it could never be returned. Amy would never tell anyone, as she did not want this kind of attention following her through life. She finished her puking, put herself together and lifted her chin high, trying to look the part of a strong girl. These rapes continued through high school. Amy expected them and was somehow able to shift her mind into a different place when it happened. Her father had violated her sacred trust and watched her develop into a young woman the wrong way.

"Why has he done this to me? Why has he tormented me in this way?"

There is no answer for these questions, only excuses. Alcohol, drugs, perversion, lust, greed, sickness. Amy felt that she had to move forward and block it out. School would help to do that; school, along with counseling, would give her the tools to cope. Although she would never admit to the disgusting rapes, she would see a therapist and talk about life. She thought it helped, but how could she suppress those awful feelings?

The dreaming became even more pronounced. Suddenly it took a darker, more sinister turn, sending a jolt of terror through Amy's mind. She saw and heard things that were never thought of in a conscious state.

John Garrison bent up on a gurney in the morgue with his hands outstretched and stared straight into Amy's eyes. He was pale and drawn with electric burn marks clearly visible. "Help me, help me." He said with a voice as dry and raspy as the rustling wind. The old man cried out to Amy but she could do nothing except stand there with her feet weighed down by lead shoes. Beauregard was there, her awful perverted father was there, and her mom was also there. Little

Jimmy, the murdered boy, stood next to Amy. She looked down to her right and suddenly saw him staring back up at her. His skin was a pale-blue and his eyes had no whites to them. "Why did you let that old man die, Amy?" He asked her this in a gravel voice, a direct result of his strangulation. She turned away from the ghoulish boy and saw, curled up in the corner on her left, a nude, bloodied sixteen year-old Amy Fraser, moaning for relief while reaching out for her. "Help me Amy, help me," the spine-chilling group chanted together as they drew nearer and nearer to the adult Amy. "Don't let him die in vain, don't turn your back on him." Amy tried to scream, but nothing short of a small murmur came out. Her heart raced and her anxiety peaked. She wanted to run, she wanted to get away. Closer they stepped, inches away. They reached for her, they wanted her. Cold fingers, cold skin. Dad lusted for her. Garrison despised her. Sixteen year-old Amy needed her. Beauregard laughed at her. Little Jimmy grabbed her arm.

"STOP! STOP! LEAVE ME ALONE!" I'M A GOOD PERSON, I WILL DO MY BEST, STOP!!!

*

Amy reared up with the speed of a striking cobra. The dream was suddenly over. She raced to the bathroom as fast as possible and heaved. It helped her feel better.

"I really need to see a doctor," Amy reasoned to herself.

She did need to see the doctor. Not being sure about symptoms that were new was a definite concern for her. On top of that, the images of her dreams reverberated in her head for the next few minutes until she was finally able to shake them and move on with her day. Shower, brush teeth, comb and style hair. The usual.

"What's going on in my mind?" she kept asking herself. "I feel *off* somehow. Whatever it is, I have to get over it."

Amy managed a piece of dry toast and a cup of mild coffee. She chewed up a couple of Rolaids and slid the rest of the roll into her briefcase. Amy wasn't sure how much the antacid would help, but it certainly couldn't hurt. Getting on with her day may help her to feel more normal again. Whatever normal was.

*

She was off to check on the autopsy report, try to talk with Soo-Chin, see Garrison in jail and then begin the tedious job of working up a defense. On her way out the door, she caught a glimpse of herself in the mirror where her keys hung. Amy thought she may be a bit pale. Tiny black bags hung under her eyes. "Is that a slight wrinkle creasing out from my mouth? I'm far too young for that." It wasn't noticeable except to Amy herself. "I've a touch of flu, that's all. I'll call the doctor and get an appointment today." With that, Amy crashed out the door and back into her world of work, work, and work.

You can be a Governor, too!

"Gawd Dad! Why does it always have to be the same dang argument every single day?" Kyle was sassing up a storm and having a hissy fit.

"I don't want to be a governor or a politician or even a cop for that matter. Geez!"

Jack was smiling slightly out of one side of his mouth as he listened to Kyle's patter. Then he spoke.

"Listen son, you are acting the same way I did when I was heading for college. It's in the family; from my Grandfather to his Grandfather, all the way back to the late 1800's. We Beauregard's are meant to be in the political arena. We are destined to keep the name alive."

It didn't seem to matter much that a non-Beauregard was currently serving as Nebraska's Governor, because Jack knew it would all be back to normal with his win in the upcoming election. He figured a win because he was not only solving the child killer case, but he also considered himself a political master. The public would clamor for him and victory would be all but assured. It was his marketing strategy.

"Hello! Dad! hello!" Kyle was snapping his fingers to lure Dad back from his star gazing trip.

Jack shook his head and picked up where he'd left off a minute or two ago. "Like I said, Kyle, you don't think this is your destiny now, but you'll see the light soon enough."

Kyle shrugged his shoulders and responded in a very condescending way. "I'll tell you what, Dad, you keep it in your silly brain that it's my destiny but I can tell you right now I'm not going to do it. I'm studying astronomy and that's that! Stop pressuring me about it."

Jack took a sudden move toward Kyle, causing his son to duck. Jack pointed a finger inches from Kyle's nose.

"Listen to me, kid, I'm paying for your damn school, so you'll study political science and that's final. In the meantime, I'll buy you a telescope so you can stargaze anytime you want."

Kyle shook his head while looking at the floor. "You just don't get it, Dad. You don't understand."

Kyle's grades in high school were a mid-to-high B, which kind of shot down his free scholarship possibilities, but kept his dreams alive. It was frustrating for him, though.

"I hate you sometimes Dad, you don't care about anything except your stupid governorship and sitting in your rotten leather recliner in the oval office."

This time when Jack lunged at Kyle, he didn't bluff and he didn't miss. WHAP! Kyle grabbed the side of his head and quickly ran into the bathroom, locking the door behind him.

"Kyle…Kyle, I'm sorry," Jack pleaded through the closed door. "I lost my head, I'm sorry kid."

Kyle was trying to regain the hearing in his right ear while his dad was apologizing. He twirled his finger in the auricle over and over while checking in the mirror to make sure the numb appendage was still connected. The ringing was terrible. Kyle placed his hands on the sink and stared into the mirror, wondering how he could change his dad's mind.

*

Amy took the last bite of her dry toast and washed it down with a swig of coffee. Her stomach felt better after her on-the-go breakfast. In a few minutes, she would arrive to see Soo-Chin. The fiery attorney was still trying to figure out, or convince herself, as to why her stomach had been in such knots. She continued to think it was the stress of the case or the flu, or perhaps a combination. She really wanted to push it to the side. It would become evident to her later exactly what the problem was. For the time being, it was back to the grind as she arrived at the county morgue.

Soo-Chin was trying to finish the last of her paper work from the autopsy the night before. Jimmy Joseph still lay on the slab in her laboratory, engulfed from head to toe in a white, sheet-like body bag. Some people have no idea that after the autopsy, you must sew the body back up. It's just another of the behind-the-scenes tasks, along with the note taking, that some people took for granted. Amy knocked hard on the office door and Soo-Chin was stricken with momentary paralysis from having the bejesus effectively scared out of her. "Come in," she invited. "This better be good. I hate being interrupted." Soo-Chin took in a deep breath.

Amy entered with a smile and an outstretched hand so she wouldn't appear to be coming off in an unfriendly, business only manner. She was not met with a handshake. "Hello, Soo-Chin, can I please ask you a few questions about the autopsy?"

The Chinese-born, naturalized American who was dating Jack Beauregard and served as the head pathologist in Lincoln, sharply chastised Amy: "You know that I'm not giving you any information that hasn't already been released and I do not appreciate your uninvited drop-in."

Amy was unfazed, "Soo-Chin, I only need to ask you a couple of quick questions and I'll be on my way. Please. It's very important."

Soo's eyes rolled up and she blew out an aggravated sigh, but allowed Amy to ask her question.

"I just want to know what you found that links Garrison to the murder."

Soo-Chin replied, "The body was found in his driveway at his house, what else do you need?"

Amy was stunned at that response.

"So what you're saying is that you have nothing else whatsoever that links the old-timer, just a location and a trash bag? You do know that hindering or hiding evidence constitutes a felony criminal charge, right? A charge that brings hefty jail time."

Amy was standing with her arms crossed as she tapped her toe on the floor

"Enough of your stupid questions and threats," the Pathologist spewed with a wave of her hand. "Talk to Jack if you want more answers. I stand behind him fully and will continue to do so."

Amy sensed a slight weakness in Soo's response, but knew there would be no answers. She thanked Soo for her time and left the facility, heading now to see John at jail. Soo-Chin picked up the phone the second the door shut, obviously calling Jack to give him a heads up on her surprise visitor.

*

Jack tried to continue his discussion with a provoked Kyle when the phone rang.

"After I take this call, we're going to figure this thing out Kyle."

"Fuck you," is what Jack could've sworn he heard Kyle say from behind the door while searching for his cell.

"Hello. Jack Beauregard, next Governor of Nebraska speaking. Can I help you?"

Soo gave a tired "spare me" look, and then spoke. "Hello, Jack, its Soo. Do you have a second to talk?"

Jack chuckled, "Yeah, Soo, Kyle's just having one of his shit-fits, but he'll get over it. What's going on in your world?"

Soo-Chin gave Jack some unwanted advice, "Not to pry too deeply, Jack, but Kyle seems a bit tense lately. You may want to lighten up on him a bit?"

"Don't you worry, doll, he's just fine. All he needs is a little guidance and heavy hand now and then. I'll take good care of the boy, trust me on that."

Soo-Chin pondered Jack for a moment, and then guided herself back on task. "Amy Fraser came up to the morgue today, Jack. She was asking questions and poking around a bit. It was very uncomfortable."

Jack instantly gave Soo his full and undivided attention. A seriousness gripped him.

"I told her she needs to talk with you if she wants her questions answered. She was kind of a smart-ass. She wants to know how you're pinning the murder on her client."

"What did you tell her?" Jack inquired with much more than a passing interest. His voice was deep and tone rich. It sounded like a low growl.

"Nothing except the official word of Garrison being named as the lead suspect."

Jack reassured Soo-Chin, "Good, I'll take care of that nosy lawyer; you just stick by your guns and pass any questions off on me."

This comment made Soo feel a lot better, as she didn't want to anger Jack. She was falling for him and tried very hard to keep peace between them.

"Okay, Jack, I have to go. I have a ton of work. I love you."

"Ditto!" Was his clever response.

After Jack hung up, he reminisced about the fun times he and Soo-Chin were having. Making love in her office, his office, anywhere they could find. The sessions used to be incredible and particularly orgasmic, but were losing some of their intensity lately. Jack figured it was all the business going on at the moment. It'll pick up again, he figured, after the election. He knew she wanted a taste of the power Jack was gaining, and Jack, for that matter, didn't care to be alone any longer. He wanted a mate to decorate his arm. A sudden flash of light brought Jack out of his daydream. He looked around, wondered what it was, and then dismissed it as an electrical surge. Now with his call from Soo finished, Jack made a mental note on what he'd been told, then re-focused on the task of bringing Kyle to his senses. He knocked lightly on the bathroom door.

"Look Kyle, I'm just trying to see that you don't make a horrible mistake in life, that's all."

The door slowly squeaked open and Kyle reached out to give his dad a hug.

"I'm sorry, pops, I just get a little stressed from time to time. I hear you loud and clear. It's just that I want to do something in life I enjoy, like astrology. Why would anyone want to have a livelihood they can't wrap their arms around and love?"

Jack rubbed his chin again, something that Kyle didn't care for. Whenever his dad rubbed that chin, a lousy answer followed.

"Kiddo, you'll wrap your arms around politics fine. I do have to get going now, so we'll pick this up later. I'm not going to change my mind about it, however. Please don't make me force the issue."

The young man just sighed and gave his dad another hug, a very lazy hug at that.

"Okay, pops go do your thing. I know you have a huge crime to work on."

*

The next stop for Amy brought her back to old man Garrison's jail cell at the county building. She had visited the Pathologist earlier and wanted to let John know where everything stood. Amy did the jailhouse routine again. Frisked, searched, screened and questioned. She was then allowed down the corridor to Garrison's cell. The catcalls began anew, "Hey babe, I got somethin' for ya!" as a man reached out for her. "Woo-Hoo, you a foxy mama," another said while gripping his crotch, "Why don't you come over here with those sexy lips and kiss this." Revolted, Amy recoiled. It was nauseating. Her stomach started tightening again. The same painful and sickening feeling was washing over her. She kept walking while the disgusting, vulgar remarks continued. Amy couldn't hear all of it because it was starting to run together. One huge, perverted mass of nastiness. The air started getting thin and her head began to swim around with dizziness, while her heart rate accelerated noticeably. She began getting small doses of blackout-like symptoms accompanied by hot flashes. Finally, after what seemed like hours, she reached Garrison's cell. The trooper pulled up what looked to be the same chair from the last visit and gave Amy the mandatory instructions about lawyer-prisoner protocol. Taking a seat was wonderful. The swimming head and tightened gut started to relieve itself as she tucked her head toward her knees. She felt steadier. Her ticker settled down. Garrison approached the gate and started on her right away. It was his standard operating procedure.

"Boy, you sure look like shit, girl. You're paler than a bleached bed sheet. You gonna' be all right?"

Amy lifted her head towards Garrison and opened her notebook. "John, are they treating you well here? Are you doing okay?"

The old man roared with laughter. "If you think eating maggots, cockroaches and whatever else is crawlin' around my food is "well," then yea, I'm doing great. I sleep on a rock-like cot, I crap in a filthy, out-in-the-open toilet and I don't have any dirty magazines to at least have a little fun with, know what I mean, wink, wink."

Amy curled her face in absolute disgust. "Spare me the gory details, John. Simply put, 'I'm functioning despite my surroundings' will suffice."

"Yeah?" the old man shouted. "Then don't ask me stupid gotdamn questions!"

Amy sighed, then explained to John the visit with the Pathologist and updated him on her work thus far. She was trying to enlighten the old codger. "It's only been a couple of days, John, but based on my meeting with the State Pathologist and from what I've heard through the grapevine, I'd say you're the fall guy for Beauregard's case."

Garrison grunted, and then spoke, "I already knew that, Ms. Fraser. Anybody with half-a-brain knows that!"

"Please, Mr. Garrison, call me Amy, and don't speak to me in that tone. I'm just updating you on the progress." Amy continued, "I think today or tomorrow they're going to charge you with two counts of capital murder, not to mention whatever other charges they can tie in. So your arraignment will probably be next week sometime."

"What the hell does *capital* murder mean? Lincoln? Because the boys were from Lincoln?"

Amy looked deeply into John's eyes and searched for the right way to tell him. This was the first time she ever had to explain to anybody what the penalty encompassed. "Well John, it means that if you're found guilty of even one of the two murder counts, then they'll uhhh…" The words escaped her.

"Then they'll what Ms. Fraser? Just spit it out."

"Then it's the electric chair…you know…execution."

John eyeballed Amy from the side of his face, head turned slightly to the left.

"Did Robert Long pay you yet?" He inquired.

Amy was snapped out of her trance-like state that developed while trying to think of a good way to tell John he faced death.

"Uh, no, not yet, but don't worry, I'll tabulate everything together when this is finished up."

Garrison growled at her, "Well ain't fifty grand gonna' cover it?"

"John that will more than cover it, by about twenty-five grand."

"Good," Garrison said, "then fifty it is. I'll let Long know to get that to ya."

Amy shook her head, "Don't you even care about what I said the penalty would be if you're found guilty of even one count?"

John rubbed his face with the palm of his hand in an inquisitive gesture. Amy could hear the roughness of his stubble against his hand. He spoke.

"Yep! I know what it means now. I also know that you'll not let that happen. It's all up to you Amy. If ya screw up, I go down. 'Member what you said? 'If you have to win, call me.' You 'member?"

The knotting and the sweating, along with the dizziness, returned in droves. "Yeah, John, I remember."

"Then ya better keep yer promise, Ms. Fraser."

"Great, John, thanks for your uhh…*confidence* in me."

John sheepishly smiled. "Don't mention it."

Amy looked back down the corridor. She knew the "walk" awaited her. Sweat dripped and her palms were clammy. She made the trek through the hideous perversion and managed to hold her cookies.

A Meeting of the Minds

It was time for Amy's trip to the doctor to see what was going on with her. Her nerves were a little on edge. She did not want to be told she was deathly ill, or any kind of ill for that matter.

"That's highly unlikely," she reasoned. "Geez; can't I even get a stomach flu without thinking the worst?"

Dr. Connie Abraham was one of the finest doctors in the state, or so everyone said. She had a wonderful, soft bedside manner and acted as if she truly cared about your problems. Amy trusted her thoroughly and had had nothing but good experiences with this woman.

"Come on in, Amy," Dr. Abraham said with a huge smile and a welcoming wave. "What's going on, girl? You look a bit peaked today."

"I'm not sure, Connie. I was feeling okay until just a couple of days ago. Now I can't seem to keep anything down and I'm horribly thirsty. I'm not diabetic, am I?"

The Doctor smiled again, and had Amy lay back on the office bed so she could look her over.

"I'm going to push in your stomach region and you let me know if it hurts, okay?"

Amy nodded her head and the exam began.

"Hurt here?"

"No."

"How about here?"

"Nope, but it tickles."

The Doctor continued pushing and poking from Amy's lower abdomen up to just below her breasts.

"Here, Amy, how about right here?"

"Nope," Amy answered again.

Dr. Abraham checked Amy's stomach in a few more spots, concentrating mainly on the vital organs such as liver, spleen and digestive tract, and then moved on to her chest, neck and finally, her head.

"Amy, are you pregnant?" Dr. Abraham asked with a deadly serious look.

The young lawyer laughed out loud. "Unless I'm the second coming of Mary, there's no chance whatsoever."

The Doctor chuckled and asked Amy if her periods were regular and if she had bouts of diarrhea.

"My periods are good, even though I haven't had one yet this month and no, no diarrhea, just some vomiting."

Abraham scratched her head and tapped the side of her face with her finger. She decided to send Amy down the hall for a couple of quick tests. "I just want to rule out ulcers or any blockage in your stomach. It'll only take about thirty minutes or so, and then I'll meet you back here.

Amy nodded in agreement and headed into x-ray.

*

Dr. Abraham met Amy back in the room about forty-five minutes later with, thankfully, no bad news to report. "I don't see anything on your x-rays, Amy. No ulcers, no blockages and nothing else abnormal. If you don't mind me asking, are you stressed about anything lately?"

Amy mulled for a moment or two, and then spilled to the Doctor. "I'm working my first high profile case. The *alleged* Nebraska child killer. I'm defending him."

Abraham couldn't help but to ask the following question. "Why? They found the body in his driveway, I read."

The lawyer responded, "I don't want to get too deep, but that situation does not make this man a killer. There's way more to it than meets the eye."

Doctor Abraham then brought forth the possible solution to Amy's problem. "Counseling, Amy. You need some counseling. It's tough to be in your line of work and not take at least some of it to heart."

The next inquiry surprised the Doctor a bit.

"Am I healthy? Because if so, I have a hell of a lot of work to get done."

"Yeah, you're healthy physically, but mentally I'm not so sure. Take my advice and talk to someone."

Amy thanked the doctor. "I'll think about it. I'm not nuts, you know."

"I didn't say you were. Just think about it okay?"

Amy hopped up off the table, straightened herself out and headed back to her office to get some work done. On the drive, Amy tried reasoning to herself. "As long as I'm not physically ill, I'm moving forward. I can handle a little stress."

She hoped she could. The question still lingered in the back of her mind. "Would it get worse?"

*

Jack Beauregard was waiting on the sidewalk outside Amy's office when she pulled up. The building was just a simple, small-bricked facility with an outer waiting area lobby and two inner offices. Amy didn't use a secretary or greeter up to this point because it wasn't necessary. This case could change that. The press that she'd receive could very well be extensive. Amy figured there would be a number of messages on the phone when she arrived, but dealing with Mr. Beauregard would take center stage. She welcomed the challenge that was sure to come up when she spoke with him. The young lawyer parked in front of the building, just off the curb, exited her vehicle and approached Jack with an outstretched arm, ready for a handshake. Jack did not oblige her welcome.

"Does anyone shake hands in this town anymore?" Amy.

"We need to talk NOW!" Jack barked. **"I have a bone to pick with you."**

Amy made a puckering motion with her lips as she mulled over Jack's request.

"Yes, absolutely we can talk. Follow me into my office, Mr. Beauregard. Oh, one thing sir." Amy turned to face Jack. "Do not talk down to me, do not patronize me, and do not disrespect me. Are we clear?"

Jack nodded very slowly, squinted his eyes in an angry manner, and followed Amy into her office.

*

Jack and Amy entered her main working area where Amy had all her awards and accolades on display. This not only included her many awards for scholastic excellence, but also for the athletic achievements she had received. Amy was a rowing champion in high school and a hell of a 3200 meter runner. She wasn't the state champ, but she dominated her school. It was obvious to Beauregard that he was dealing with a very talented woman.

Ms. Fraser brought Jack a cup of black coffee, placed a cream and sugar tray on her desk, then asked him to have a seat. **SMASH!** The coffee, cup and all, flew across the room in a burst of liquid heat. The mug hit the wall and smashed into a thousand tiny pieces, the coffee dripped down and onto one of the many plaques.

"You listen to me, Fraser," Jack was pointing a finger inches from her face. **"I couldn't care less how much you think you know. Do not fuck with me and my investigation. It's bad enough that you're representing that lousy scumbag in trial, but I will not let you sabotage this case."**

Amy's eyes widened to the size of silver dollars and she shot back with as much, if not more, venom than Jack thought she could squeeze into her tiny frame.

"You dirty S.O.B.! How dare you come into *my* office and disrespect my profession." Amy was jamming her index finger into the desktop as she vented. **"I am going to defend that man with a vengeance. I do not believe he committed these murders, and damn it I'll prove it!"** The last poke of her finger was the most audible of all.

Jack scoffed at her with a sarcastic smile. **"You won't do a thing, Fraser. There's no jury within five thousand miles of here that would acquit this guy. If you think you have any kind of shot, you're in the wrong business."**

Amy decided that having a shouting match would not solve this problem, so she shifted gear.

"Mr. Beauregard," she said in a softer tone with her hands lowered in front of her, "I know you're running for governor and I know you think this case is a slam dunk for the election, but remember, you haven't faced a lawyer like me in court. You have ZERO forensic evidence linking Garrison and you have ZERO proof that Garrison was even involved. How do we know it wasn't Dan Wheeler, the Animal Control officer? Why is Garrison your only suspect?"

Jack responded with more anger resonating in his voice. He kept it to a low groan. "Because the damn body was lying in Garrison's driveway. Dan Wheeler is no murderer. He's young and stupid, a little like someone else I know!" Jack squinted Amy's way.

Amy continued to keep her cool. It was tough, but she managed.

"Okay, Mr. Beauregard, if you're not going to at least be reasonable, then we may be wasting our time here. Why don't we try talking when we have cooler heads?"

Jack let out a rich, deep laugh, and his tone suddenly went back to loud. **"Please do not talk to *my* witnesses anymore. I will tell you right now that will get you nowhere. I will get you a list of discovery soon."**

Amy couldn't believe her ears. This was ludicrous.

"Garrison hasn't been charged and you're coming up with discovery? That's just great Jack."

"Don't you worry your sexy little head about that, Amy. He'll be charged." Jack told her this with a wink and a sexy smile. It wasn't a good idea on his part.

The knotting started in Amy's stomach, and she responded to Jack with nastiness. **"Do not talk to me about anything "sexy" Mr. Beauregard or I will cry harassment so fast your head will spin off its swivel. If you don't believe it, try me. I dare you. And I'm *Ms. Fraser* to you, not Amy!"**

Jack rose from his seat and headed for the door, paused, then turned around for one more swipe.

"My prosecutor will soundly rout you in court. We all lose a time or two, but I will not be on the short end of this one. By the way, send me a bill for the coffee stains.....*Amy*."

Jack slammed the door behind him as he let himself out. Amy stood proud until he was out of sight, and then ripped through her purse looking for the Rolaids she stashed earlier. It struck her that perhaps the stomach trouble was coming when men talked to her in a sexually suggestive way, or when she felt harassed. Jack himself was making Amy sick, but that was no surprise because his threatening attitude and the way he talks off the end of his nose could make anyone nauseated. It was time to get some work done, so Amy made herself useful and started a long grind.

*

"Let's see, we have John Garrison, Robert Long, Dan Wheeler, and Lyla Helms as *possible* witnesses for the state, while we have Beauregard, Trooper Michaels, Soo-Chin and the Joseph parents also involved on their side. I'm going to have to go one by one and see if I can't figure out who belongs where. If they'll talk, that is."

The work habits that Amy made famous were again kicking in. She had forgotten, for the moment, Beauregard's rather rude visit. Simply put, Amy needed to make sense of all the involved parties. She already figured Lyla and Dan to be simple witnesses to the dead child, while Robert helped John pack the dog up. "Where did the body come in?" Amy asked herself. "At what point did a possible "switch" occur?"

She knew she needed to speak to Robert, because he appeared to be the number one witness that could help exonerate Mr. Garrison. She didn't care that Jack had ordered her away from the involved persons, due to the fact that she had every right to question them before they were named on either the Prosecutor's or her own list of people to testify in court. Amy continued to work, sort, figure and go over everything a number of times when the sandman paid her a visit. Eyes heavy, body relaxed, big yawn. "I can't sleep now, I need to work, lots of work to do…lots…of…wo…." Amy's head bobbed down softly on her desk and the dreams came.

*

"Amy, Amy wake up. Amy?"

The lawyer slowly lifted her head from the desk and noticed that the room was very dark and eerie. The next thing she saw was her desk completely devoid of any paper work.

"I had a whole desk full of notes," she disconcertingly thought.

Amy was trying to get her bearings when she heard the voice again, "Are you awake now Amy?"

She looked around again, this time with more alertness. She looked behind her to see if anyone was there. When she turned back, she was shocked at the sight of sixteen year-old Amy sitting in one of her guest chairs, looking directly into her eyes.

"Who are you, and why are you here?" the adult Amy asked.

"You have to help me Amy; you have to look deep into your soul. I cannot live without you, and you cannot live without me." The young Amy's voice quivered with a ghoulish, unnerving tone.

Adult Amy knew she was looking at herself as a sixteen year-old, but didn't know why.

"What do you want me to do? What would you have me do?" She asked.

The teenage Amy rose from her chair, her face bloodied from her battles with her father.

"Make this go away," she said as she rubbed the wounds on her cheeks. "Make the scars disappear before the time runs short."

Now adult Amy found herself trying to reason with a dream. "You're just an imaginary vision of my dream. You don't exist. I have moved forward since I was a teen. Why don't you?"

The ghostly Amy raised her voice slightly, sounding worried. The words left her mouth with a shaken, vibrating tone. ***"If you don't help me, you don't help yourself. Don't make that mistake, Amy."***

After she made this statement, she was gone. Amy wiped her eyes and shook her head, sure that this was about to pass and she would wake up to her work. From a far corner of the room she saw a figure standing in the shadow. It walked toward her slowly and without much movement, almost as if floating, or levitating. The figure came into the dim light. It was Garrison, electrocuted almost beyond recognition.

"Don't let this be my fate, Amy. Don't let me die for a crime I didn't commit."

Amy was becoming unexpectedly angry. ***"You cannot come into my dream, my head, and make such statements. I am only responsible for giving you the best defense I can, nothing more and nothing less."***

"Don't let me die, don't let me die."

Amy again shut her eyes tightly and rubbed her thick black hair as hard as she could.

"Just go away," she repeated over and over. "Just go away and leave me alone."

When she opened her eyes again, Jimmy Joseph was reaching across the desk to grab a handful of Amy's hair. His eyes were dead and his teeth were bared in a yellowing, rotting smile. Amy was frantically trying to pull away from the boy's grip, but couldn't.

"I'll kill you Amy, I'll kill you. Why did you let Garrison die?" *were the words Jimmy kept repeating. Pulling Amy's hair, harder and harder. She could feel the follicles being ripped from the scalp. Now she was screaming.*

"Leave me alone! I'm trying to help! Leave me alone."

*

Amy awoke suddenly and found handfuls of her black hair in her gripped fists. She released the hair onto her untidy desk and began to weep. Her midsection pained and her head ached. Amy was struggling with her demons.

"I'm doing what I can; I cannot take this case personally."

After a few deep breaths in and out, in and out, Amy began to calm. She ventured to the bathroom and splashed cold water on her face and turned on the office light. She mulled over the piles of paperwork sitting on the desk before her. It was now mixed with strands of black hair. Amy swept the pulled tresses into the trash can and decided in her mind of minds, "I have a lot of work to do. I better get busy."

Amy went back to the grind and thought little about the dream she had just experienced. With so much to do, she was somehow able to immerse herself so deeply, it allowed very little else to distract her.

Garrison takes the Fall

Jack was to meet with the top state prosecutor, Richard Headly, give him a copy of the police report, and go over the Garrison case to determine what charges would be brought. Headly had led the prosecutor's office in convictions in each of the twenty years he'd been doing the job. His dream was to become Nebraska's attorney general, and working with Beauregard to see a conviction in the child killer case would be a huge step in that direction.

"I, as governor, can make damn sure that you would be looked on very favorably to reach your goal," Jack told him. "It's right there in the palm of your hands, Richard. This is the time to step up and be heard."

Headly was as power hungry as anybody else in politics and figured he and Beauregard scratching each other's back would be nothing short of good politics between two powerful men.

"Listen Jack, I received the coroner's report on the body and the bag samples. Nothing except the boy being discovered in Garrison's driveway implicates that man. There was zero DNA found on the garbage sacks and no proof that Garrison's lying."

Jack mulled over Headly's logic and came up with a feasible political solution. "Look Richard, we have two dead boys, two Jack of Spades pinned to the bodies, and five decks of cards from the Garrison house we searched. Even though the decks are full, it seems pretty funny to me that there would be five decks in his house. Besides, the public is crying out for a killer. No other killings have taken place since the Joseph boy was found, and you already know a jury will convict on circumstantial evidence, especially since the thirst for a perpetrator is so intense right now. Who really cares about that old codger? I think he did it, but if not, well; his life is almost over anyway. No harm, no foul." Jack continued his sale, trying to convince the DA. "Besides, this is your ticket to the job you've coveted for so long now. It's pure win-win. I get my seat in the mansion and I see to it that you get your seat as attorney general."

Richard mulled deep and hard about the Colonel's idea. It was a tough decision, but he's made them before. "You really think this is my ticket in, Jack?"

Beauregard patted Headly on the knee, reassuring him. "I know it is. No doubt whatsoever. You'll be the prosecutor of the century. The man who took the killer down in court."

Jack decided to offer up the prime scenario as to facilitating charges against Garrison. "Listen to me Richard. The old man stashed the dead boy in his garage. He called his neighbor, Robert Long, to come and help him clean up a dog. *Clean up a dog, indeed.* It's the perfect cover-up. Garrison thinks Long will go along with the dog story, but there's a gap when Long left and animal control arrived. That's when Garrison made the switch. A jury will buy it. Hook, line and sinker."

Headly looked deep into Jack's eyes. They were unnervingly serious and he knew they meant business. After taking a deep breath, the deepest of his life, Headly finally shook hands with Jack and agreed. "This better work Jack or our dreams will be crushed like cinderblock under a sledgehammer."

Jack once again told him not to worry. "You just come into court with your game face on. You've always been a slick talker and I have no doubt that you will shine in front of the media and in front of a jury that wants justice."

*

Richard prepared the charge list and sent it to Amy's office for her perusal. He felt a twinge of guilt because he wasn't so sure Garrison had committed the crimes, but that quickly disappeared when he thought about the position he so coveted as attorney general.

"I would have the final say over anyone in the courts except for a judge. I'm sure I could even put them in my back pocket if it were truly necessary. Jack as governor and myself as attorney general sounds like a team that couldn't be stopped."

After his final fit of pondering, Headly went forward and this time did not look back.

*

The rain was pouring hard against the front glass façade of the building Amy occupied. She was still going over the case files and reports late that afternoon when a delivery truck pulled up in front of the office. The UPS man walked in, drenched to the gills, and handed Amy a manila envelope, which contained Garrison's proposed fate.

"Thank you sir. Would you like a hot coffee to go?"

"Nah," said the soaking wet man. "I have a lot to deliver and very little time to deliver it."

Amy fished a ten spot out of her purse and handed it to the young man. "This is just a little something to keep you motivated. Go get a hot drink or something."

The UPS driver beamed, "I'm not supposed to take tips, but I'll keep quiet if you do."

Amy smiled and nodded as the man exited back into the deluge.

Amy was almost afraid to open the envelope. She knew in her heart Garrison should not take the fall. She also knew he would. The young lawyer opened the mailing and laid it out on her desk. The following is how it read:

State of Nebraska Prosecuting Office
Lincoln Branch

In the case of The State of Nebraska vs. John Garrison, the charges and sub-charges are as follows:

Count 1. Capital Murder. For the murder of Jimmy Joseph. Punishable by death in the electric chair.

Count 2. Kidnapping (1st degree). For the kidnapping of Jimmy Joseph. Punishable by 25-50 years in a maximum security prison.

Count 3. Capital Murder. For the murder of Anthony Wilder. Punishable by death in the electric chair.

Count 4. Kidnapping (1st degree). For the kidnapping of Anthony Wilder. Punishable by 25-50 years in a maximum security prison.

Richard Headly,
Nebraska State Prosecutor

There it was in black and white. Four charges brought against Mr. Garrison. Amy had her work cut out and knew it would be an uphill battle. She also knew she had to make a trip to the jail to let Garrison know what he faced and to prepare him for the formal charge proceeding before the State Magistrate that would take place two days later. Garrison was being charged with the other boy's murder because both kids had been found with a black leather strap and a Jack of Spades-The M.O. that Beauregard had thought of earlier.

*

Amy stopped up at the jail to advise Garrison of the situation. After forty-five minutes of his smart mouth along with the perverted jeering of the prisoners, Amy was going for a ride to Robert Long's house. She hoped she could get him as a defense witness and enhance Garrison's chances for survival. Acquittal was the ultimate goal. Less that, it was life in prison. The stomach pain and headache followed Amy all the way to Robert's home. The sexual catcalling from the prisoners was getting to her. She so loathed these perverts and their disgusting actions. She was also concerned about Garrison. Amy knew he could handle himself in jail, but she worried about his health. He was looking wishy-washy today and his energy wasn't at the usual level. She concentrated on the road and thought about the case when straight out of the blue she swore she heard: **"AMY, AMY!"** In a female voice. It sounded exactly like the girl in her dreams. She looked around frantically, but saw nothing. Amy directed her concentration back to the road. The voice she heard was very much like the voice everyone hears when they're on the edge of sleep. Lying quietly in bed, all of the sudden you hear your own name loud and clear. It's alarming for a moment, causing your eyes to blink open, but then you settle back down and sleep comes.

The young lawyer knew that counseling and psychotherapy would help her with the visions she had during sleep. Amy knew they were just dreams, but they were disturbing ones. They felt so real and seemed so vivid. After the trial, Amy would give herself a break and find the assistance she needed.

"Could it be that I'm going crazy?" she worriedly thought to herself before reasoning it out. "Nah, I'm just going through some post-traumatic something or other. My subconscious is just playing a few tricks on me. It'll pass."

She refused to be hindered by such nonsense. It wasn't a ghost and it wasn't some evil spirit. It was just her earlier experiences in life trying to wreak havoc on her bright future. Amy tried convincing herself that she wouldn't have it, but it was getting tougher with each episode.

*

Robert Long was cutting wood out by his shed when Amy arrived at his home. He swung the axe with determination, but needed two swings to split each log. Back when he was a young man, his output was tripled by comparison. The sweat was dripping off his face like a running faucet. He was in his late sixties, so he needed to be careful and give himself a break now and then. Being a couch potato wasn't helping him because he lacked the athletic ability needed for this type of work. Long's face was a deep crimson, so Amy figured this to be a good time to talk to him. The break he needed was long overdue.

"Hello, Robert, I'm Amy Fraser, John Garrison's attorney. You called me a few days ago."

"I know who you are, and I ain't interested in gettin' involved." Long went back to swinging his axe. He had turned his back to Amy, but she circled around to force him into looking at her.

"I'm sorry to share the news with you," Amy stated, "but you're involved, like it or not."

This statement was effective enough to get Robert to stop and toss the tool down. He grabbed a handkerchief out of his pocket and had a much required seat.

"Okay, ask your questions. But I'm not gonna' be much help to ya'."

The lawyer was pleased that she had stopped Long from his chopping and started getting down to business. "Robert, please answer this for me: John said you guys packed up a dead dog. Is that right?"

Robert looked closely at the young, beautiful lawyer and replied even though he was still panting. "Yep. It was a dog alright. Ain't no doubt about it."

"So then you'd testify in court to that exact statement?"

Robert gave half a smile and let Amy know that he'd answer what he had to, but the truth would be told. "If they ask me if I was watchin' the old coot all the way 'till they picked up the bag, I'll tell 'em no. That'd be the truth."

Amy asked more difficult questions. Inquiries that were more to the point. "Do you think Garrison killed a boy and packed him up while you were gone? Do you really, truly believe that?"

"I don't know what the hell to believe." Robert's hands rose up, and then slapped down on his thighs. "I know he's a grumpy old cuss who loses his temper. Killin' youngins' though? I don't think so, but I can't know for sure."

Robert was getting agitated and wanted to go back to his work, but Amy wasn't done quite yet. "I'm going to put you down as a witness for our defense. When you're on that stand, I'll make sure to help you get through the Q and A without much trouble."

"You can put me down on whatever list you want, Ms. Fraser, but I'll warn ya' that Beauregard already stopped by and spoke with me. It seems I'm a value to both sides, which kinda' goofs things up, doesn't it now?"

The wind gathering in Amy's sails began to deflate slightly with that statement, but she thought she could get him a summons before Beauregard could. At least she hoped so. There were not many people involved here and she needed at least one witness to defend Garrison.

"Well, Mr. Long. Thanks for the time. You should be hearing from me soon."

Long shook her hand lazily, picked up his axe and started chopping once again. As Amy was pulling out of the driveway, she noticed that Robert was now splitting the logs with just one swing instead of two.

Lincoln Times

Garrison charged with capital murder
Murder, Kidnapping among charges filed
Prosecutor Headly promises justice

AP- John Garrison of Hickman, Nebraska has been charged with the murders of two boys found dead in the Lincoln area. He was charged with capital murder and kidnapping in both cases. Capital murder means if Garrison is found guilty, the jury can impose the death sentence. All charges are packaged in a way that allows the suspect to be found guilty of the lower count if convicted of murder. If he is acquitted, then he is acquitted of all charges. He cannot be found guilty of the lower count if he is found not guilty of murder. Richard Headly has been assigned the case by the State of Nebraska and will represent the prosecution. Amy Fraser has been hired by Garrison to defend him. Neither party was available for questions and did not return our calls. The trial date has yet to be set. More information will be brought to you when it becomes available.

-Angela Page

*

Amy had one last stop to make. This time it was at the Lincoln Animal Control office to see Lyla Helms and Dan Wheeler. These two would be tough for her because they had seen the dead boy in the bag near the incinerator. Allegedly, Dan picked up the bag from Garrison and drove it over to be destroyed. Amy had to think that Wheeler would have had just as much opportunity as Garrison did to make a switch. It certainly seemed like the old man was taking the hit on this one due to some underlying reason. A governorship on the line? Perhaps. It's tough to prove, but Amy figured it was so.

"AMY!" That damned voice again. It rang off Amy's brain with a more solid punch this time. She shook her head violently and kept her wits about her. Massaging the bridge of her nose helped relieve some of the stress the voice was causing. When she finished her rubbing and looked out to the road, she screeched on her brakes as hard as she could. There was a young girl standing in the middle of the lane wearing a white nightgown, and she looked exactly like the girl in Amy's dream. Knowing her brakes weren't enough to avoid hitting her, she swerved hard to the right to get out of the way. She nearly crashed into a tree and drove halfway into a ditch. Amy manipulated her vehicle back onto the shoulder, stopped, and then composed herself on the side of the road. Upset, frightened and pissed off, Amy exited her vehicle to give this young girl a good scolding. She wasn't there.

"Hey, where are you?" No answer. **"Come out and show yourself. You were nearly run over."** Again, nothing. Only the sounds of buzzing cicadas and birds happily chirping. Amy stood on the pavement and looked around at the wooded area for a few more seconds, then decided to chalk it up to a stupid kid playing chicken, not some silly apparition. The young girl and her friends were probably watching from an undetectable spot in the woods and giggling at their effective game playing. The lawyer went back to her vehicle, took a huge breathe, and continued her journey to the animal control building.

*

Upon arriving, Amy parked out near the incinerator in question, grabbed a quick peek at the burner itself, and then walked around to the front of the building. She entered and asked the secretary if Lyla Helms was working.

"May I tell her who's calling, please?"

"Tell her I'm Amy Fraser, John Garrison's attorney, here to ask a few questions."

The secretary offered Amy to have a seat and went into the back of the facility. Amy sat down and opened a wayward magazine that was lying on the table and she waited. She waited and waited and waited. Fifteen minutes, thirty minutes, an hour. Finally the secretary returned with Lyla. Amy rose from her seat and offered a handshake.

"Save it," Lyla spit, "I'm not talking."

"Why? I only have a couple quick questions."

Lyla seemed aggravated. Her impatience spoke for itself. "Dan Wheeler is still off work from the shock of seeing that dead child and personally, I hope the old piece of shit Garrison fries for it."

Standing with her mouth agape, Amy tried one more time, with understanding in her voice. "Miss Helms, I know it's tough, but can't…."

Lyla loudly interrupted, inches from Amy's face. **"I said save it! We're done here. Can't you take a hint?" Don't try talking to Dan either. He won't help you.**

"Thanks for nothing, Mrs. Helms." Amy sarcastically chastised.

Lyla Helms stalked back through the door and disappeared while her secretary simply shrugged her shoulders. Amy knew it was an uphill battle, just not quite this steep.

"At least I have Long, *I think*." She gathered her things and headed back to the office to write up and send out a summons for Long to appear on behalf of the defense.

A Killer Waits

The killer's lair was situated in a secluded and thickly limbed area near a swamp. It was a small shack that he had pieced together using old wood stolen from the local lumberyard. The lean-to was drafty and damp, much like the killer's personality. The makeshift hideout was completely hidden by brush and it was far enough back in the wooded area that nobody would ever find it. Even if, say, law enforcement did a manhunt, they would be hard-pressed to locate this hidden burrow. The killer was strong and dug a small tunnel from the outskirts of the thickest part of the woods, until it reached an opening he fashioned near the bottom of the wooded side. It was about seventy-five feet total in length. This is where all his rituals were hidden. This is where the killer of children came to worship his Satan, set up his shrines, and cut himself. It also brought the two young victims here to terrorize them before strangling the life out of their bodies. A psychopath needed the hideaway to unleash the hate and madness. This gruesomely haunted abode served the purpose.

*

The killer was waiting. Waiting and watching. The Jack of Spades playing card adorned the lair. Two dead children yet no heat whatsoever on this, the real perpetrator. He knew he was smart and knew he was safe here. The killer had pictures of the two recently killed boys, plus other pictures and varied images of dead people, adults and children, scattered about the room. The killer kept his mask on at all times. Breathing and sweating into it until the foulness would offend even a skunk. It was the stink of body odor, unbrushed teeth and vinegar. This was not your everyday normal human being; he was a troubled soul patiently waiting for the time he could kill again. The killer was counting the hours, the minutes, even the seconds until he could lash out at another unfortunate child and strangle them to death. The killer loved watching people die. Nothing could match the intense rush that draining someone's life force supplied. The lights in the room shone low so the glow cast shadows on the floor, walls, and ceiling. It was a scary place, most certainly. A place of death, destruction and insanity. The killer knew who Amy was. Anyone involved in the case had their picture on the evil shrine surrounded by the Jack of Spades. John Garrison's photo lay directly in the middle of the killer's homage. He wanted to maim, hurt and tear apart seemingly normal families and friends. His purpose in life was to spread evil around and pit men and women against each other. He learned from reading the satanic scriptures that man was doomed. The killer thought it could both sacrifice the children it chose and terrorize the adults it despised through murder. There was, however, a small glimmer of heart and feeling in his tormented soul. The killer thought to some degree that he was actually helping humanity toughen up to the agony that was to come.

Watching the news delighted him. He loved hearing about the murders and rapes especially, because he thought of those transgressions as the highest evil people could perpetrate against themselves and each other. It was also the most painful way to die: Slow and without remorse. Politics was also amusing. The governorship right here in Nebraska was interesting, as was the U.S. presidential race and affairs overseas that involved the hurting of human beings and the human soul. People shot to death; blown up, and with severed limbs made him tickle with excitement. At the same, he would shake his head with the knowledge that man was its own worst enemy. He didn't consider himself only a killer, but Satan's underling.

Collecting newspaper articles connected to his killings was another hobby. Pinning them on the walls with the rest of the hideous shrines was important to him. The more hideous and disgusting the pictures, the better. Watching society destroy itself gave him some satisfaction, pleasing the soul within. He formed a pentagram on the floor using some of the items belonging to his victims, along with dead animals and other scraps such as sticks and twigs. The killer would pray to this design using candles, and outlining the Satanist star with chalk. It needed work, but it would be perfected later. He wanted to satisfy the master he worshipped.

Fits of rage took up more time as he hungered to kill again. Bloodlust coursed through his veins. It was getting tougher and tougher to hold back, but he knew that he had to wait for the trial to conclude before restarting the bloody rampage. This killer was confident that Garrison would take the hit, thus freeing the way to continue his murderous spree, along with the game he was playing, which was already in motion. Throwing and breaking glass, strangling mice, rats and whatever other rodents that could be found helped a bit, but not enough. He would squeeze the life out of these critters with bare hands, the still warm blood oozing onto his skin. He stapled a Jack of Spades to everything he killed, so there were rows of dead creatures along the wooden walls with cards hanging from their lifeless bodies. The killer giggled through his leather mask and would occasionally touch, even caress the stinking bodies. This would give him energy, causing him to remember why he wanted to kill in the first place. Slaughtering rodents calmed the rage within, but not like killing a human being did. The murdering was a drug he could not get enough of. It was an addiction that would never calm itself. This killer would nearly spin out of control when taking life, but never lose focus of the deed. Talking to the victim after death was also a huge turn on for him. Bending low and within inches of their faces, he wanted to know what death was like. "Where do you go? What do you do? Can you fly? Can you see God, or is it Satan?"

Alas, there were no words coming forth. He touched their faces, their eyes, their lips and their hair. The strangest thing about the killer was that he would not harm the child before killing them. No rape, no abuse, just a strangled child. Death was the only answer. There would be no other way. The killer reveled in his confidence.

"They'll never find me. They'll never see me. I come in the night and leave undetected. I'm invisible and invincible. I cannot be destroyed. I am the Black Jack of Spades."

Politics Aside

The debate was set to begin. Jack was in the back room with Soo-Chin rehearsing his points and counterpoints. He was facing the Democratic nominee, Mel Critchett. Mel was a well-known philanthropist made popular for helping the middle and lower classes who struggle to make ends meet. Mr. Critchett opened several businesses throughout the State of Nebraska and had a reputation for hiring people who were felons, sex-offenders, or simply down on their luck. A large population of people respected and supported Mel, but with Jack Beauregard's mere insistence that he had a collar on the Lincoln child killer, the flock started migrating toward his camp. The case wasn't solved; Garrison had not even been tried yet, much less convicted, but a huge number of people trusted that the Colonel had it in the bag. Assumptions seem to go a long way in politics and this situation was no different. In the week after Jack made his announcement of catching the perpetrator, his poll numbers went from a three-point lead to double digits. A successful debate and subsequent conviction of Garrison would sew up his victory in the election. Critchett knew this and had to have a dominant showing. The Lincoln Plaza Hotel would serve as the debate stage, while Ed Brenner of the Lincoln ABC news would serve as moderator.

*

There were two major differences between Beauregard and Critchett as they entered the debate area and were introduced. Number one: Jack looked fantastic with his nifty polyester three-piece suit and tie. Mel looked ill. He appeared pale and overweight, with dark circles under his eyes. Number two: Jack Beauregard had an aura around him. It was a kind of electricity in the air. Mel Critchett looked overwhelmed and had no stage presence. He was seemingly going through the motions. It probably would not have mattered if they had traded spots. Jack had the killer by the throat (at least in his mind), while Critchett did not. Mel knew it was an uphill battle. He was glad the killer had been caught (even though he hadn't been tried or convicted, the *alleged* killer was caught), but wished someone else had caught him. He figured Jack caught a lucky break in that regard. Mel had to fight, though. He wasn't one to simply concede and quit. Mr. Brenner asked the following questions as related to the issues:

Beauregard	Gubernatorial issue	Critchett
No	Free Choice (Abortion)	Yes
No	Embryonic stem cell research	Yes
No	Equal rights for gays or lesbians	Yes
Yes	Small business credits	Yes
Yes	Job creation incentives	Yes
No	Green energy research	Yes
No	Green manufacturing zones	Yes
No	Overhaul big business tax	Yes

It was pretty obvious that Jack was looking out for big business while Critchett wanted better for the middle class. You would think that the people of Nebraska, mainly farming land, would favor Critchett. They did for the most part, but these issues were not *all* of the issues.

*

The typical nerf toss questions were presented for the first three quarters of the meeting, with the best of the debate saved for last. The questions about crime in the state and how each candidate would deal with the subject were now in the forefront.

"Mr. Beauregard, this question is to you. What will you do, and continue to do, about the increased crime rate statistics in the state?"

Jack smiled wide when asked this question. He made a quick glance towards Mel, and then fired away.

"Since I've been on the job as Colonel Trooper in this state, the crime rate has actually fallen by six percent. We lock them up and throw away the key."

The crowd cheered when this point was made, and Jack beamed. He continued the momentum, feeling the crowd's enthusiasm pump in his veins. "I have seen a significant improvement in the crime fighting ranks and I can promise you one thing, no one *but* no one will pull any wool over my eyes. I can also tell you that we will prosecute to the full extent of the law any person or persons who breach our peace here in Nebraska."

Another cheer rose from the audience. Jack was careful not to mention anything about the Garrison case in fear of jeopardizing it. Beauregard's time was up and it was Mel's turn to try and top what seemed unstoppable. The crowd hushed in anticipation of Critchett's counterpoints.

"While I will agree with Mr. Beauregard that crime is down and the police forces across the state have been tightened, we still had children being murdered under this man's watch."

Critchett pointed at Jack while making the point. "Mr. Beauregard failed to tell you that a killer had been running free for months and kids were dying.

Why hadn't he stopped it sooner? How many kids had to die before it ended?"

This time the crowd remained tentative and a little subdued as they waited for Beauregard's rebuttal. Jack stepped back up to the podium and with fire in his tongue, lashed Mr. Critchett.

"Mel, Mel, Mel," Jack repeated as he shook his head and smiled at the same time, "I wasn't going to mention this because I wanted to give you at least a fighting chance, but you've left me no choice. As many of you have read in the Lincoln Times the last few days, we have a prime suspect in custody that will be tried in a court of law by an impartial jury."

The cheers reached a crescendo as Jack tried to quiet them with hand gestures. "I defy you, Mr. Critchett, to try and dispute the fact that our determined and tenacious police force has more than done their job in bringing this case to a close and saving many, many *more* children than we've lost. I'm not saying that this man in custody is guilty because we all know he's innocent until proven otherwise. However, we have a damn solid case working against him. What have you done, Mel, to fight crime? What have you done to solve this case? Nothing, that's what. Shame on you Mr. Critchett for using such cheap and pathetic tactics to try to win a governorship that obviously belongs to me."

This time there was no silencing the throng. They stood and gave Beauregard a solid five minute standing ovation. Jack savored each and every second of it. His ratings were rising at that very moment, while Mel's approval slipped away.

Mel stepped up to the lectern for his final point, but this time he tried to deflect the subject some.

"I will be tough on crime and I promise an improvement over what we have seen in Mr. Beauregard's tenure as chief."

It was far too little and way too late. The crowd turned on Critchett with boos and hisses. Jack was winning the biggest debate before the election and there was no changing it.

The crowd began a chant, **"We want Jack. We want Jack."**

Beauregard sauntered across the stage with his hands held high over his head. It was much like a boxer KO'ing his opponent with a huge right cross and watching his lights go out. Critchett was pirouetting to the floor. Ed Brenner called for time to be up and the debate was history, with the clear winner being Jack Beauregard.

*

Jack and Mel exited the stage and walked side by side in the hallway leading to their respective cooling down areas. Jack couldn't resist throwing one more barb out there before separating with Critchett. "You're underhanded and cheap, Mel. I'm really surprised with you. How dare you try to throw a challenge as weak as that my way. I will not be beaten by the likes of you."

Mel said nothing. He just kept walking until their paths parted under the bleachers of the plaza hall. Jack simply nodded and found Soo-Chin and Kyle, who greeted him with huge hugs. The stage was set for the final election, which was three months away. By that time, Garrison would be history and the voters would love Jack like no other.

"You were awesome, Dad!" Kyle happily stated.

"Way to go my big handsome man," was Soo-Chin's loving remark.

People all around were shaking hands with Jack and congratulating him on a job well done. Pats on the back, high fives and cheers. Jack kept moving and disappeared into his personal dressing area with his two favorite people.

As the door shut behind them and silence filled the room, Jack looked at Kyle and winked.

"So Kyle, you still not interested in following in the old man's footsteps?"

Kyle was still very skeptical, but didn't want to ruin his dad's night. "That was pretty exciting, Pops. That's a tough gig to turn down. All the cheers and ovations were spine-tingling."

The boy gave himself a mental "Atta boy" and let his dad rejoice. Soo-Chin looked at Jack with those wonderful, beautiful Asian eyes and he knew exactly how this night would end. It was all good in Beauregard's world.

Lincoln Times

Beauregard nabs huge win in debate

Challenger Critchett on the ropes

AP- The race for governor just became a lopsided affair as Jack Beauregard routed Mel Critchett in the final gubernatorial debate last night in Lincoln. Beauregard's nabbing of murder suspect John Garrison went a long way toward clinching the huge victory. The crowd that gathered was one-sided from the beginning of the evening, giving Critchett virtually no chance of victory. Beauregard strutted around the stage with an aura of invincibility as he rode the crowd's momentum. The election is scheduled for November and without something astounding happening for Critchett, we will have a

Beauregard back in office. More details upcoming as they become available.

-Angela Page

*

The next morning's polls showed Beauregard's lead had gone from 6 percent all the way to 60-40. The advantage he gained from last night's stellar performance was astronomical.

"It had to be some kind of record," Jack thought to himself.

He would be right. The only thing that could possibly stop him were the words "not guilty" in Garrison's trial. Jack knew that was unlikely and he also knew that the end justified the means, even if an innocent man took the fall. Jack refused to believe that Garrison was not responsible, though. Although the evidence was flimsy, it still pointed to the old man. Jack Beauregard would not take "no" for an answer. Anything to win, baby. *Anything*.

The Trials Begin?

The time had come for Garrison's hearing before the Magistrate. Beauregard walked down the corridor of cells to let John know he had thirty minutes to button it up before they left.

"Go fuck yerself, ya' railroadin' piece of trooper shit."

Jack was going to scold Garrison, but that probably wouldn't work. He tried a fear tactic often used by bullying officers. Garrison re-buffed it.

"You do know I could charge you with disturbing the peace, among other things?"

Garrison gave Jack a broad smile and fired away once again. "Let's see pig, your gonna' try and put me in the electric chair, yet you wanna' slap a little pussy charge of disturbin' the peace on me? Where do I sign, jerk-off?"

"Nope," Beauregard thought, "that didn't do a thing to chill him down. I guess I'll just block it out."

Jack then blurted out, **"Thirty minutes, Garrison. I'll be back for you."**

John mumbled another expletive under his breath and continued shaving. He was not going to let the Colonel get the best of him. It was bad enough he was on his way to an unwarranted court date.

A few minutes later, Jack returned. He ordered John to the front of the cell and had him turn around and place his hands outside the bars. John did so and Jack slapped the cuffs on him.

"Open gate C," Jack yelled down the corridor, and the gate slowly opened with a rusty squeak and a loud moan.

Garrison exited the cell and faced the wall to be frisked. As Jack searched him, he gave John some riding orders. "Don't try anything stupid, John, and do not give me a hard time. I'm simply taking you to the Magistrate then straight back here. Can you give me a little respect?"

John gave Beauregard a little puppy dog-eyed look and said, "What, me give you a hard time? Not in a million years." Garrison then let out a low toned snicker with his mouth pushed to one side.

"Let's go, John. The sooner we get this over with, the better."

"Eat it, cop!"

Beauregard led Garrison out to the police garage and placed him in the back seat for the twenty minute drive to the District Courthouse.

*

Amy woke up bright and early, ate a piece of dry toast, and then jumped in the shower. As Amy was lathering her hair up with shampoo, she heard it again, **"AMMMY!"** It was as loud and as clear as the other time in the car. She swore it came from in the bathroom, just outside the shower. Amy quickly threw open the curtain and saw nothing. Before her eyes, as always, was a steamed up, yet empty bathroom.

"What the hell? Why do I keep hearing that voice in my head?"

Amy panned left, then right. Nothing. She continued her shower. As Amy rinsed the soap out of her hair, a faint shadow crossed outside the shower curtain. It was ghost-like and quick, gliding from one side of the room to the other.

A whisper floated through the steamy air. "*Don't let him die in vain.*"

Amy again ripped open the curtain, tearing two hooks clean off the rod. **"What? Answer me! What do you want?"**

Again, no answer and no movement. As was the case before, it was only Amy and a bathroom.

"I'm not killing anyone!" Amy shouted to the empty room. **"It's not my fault he's been charged! I have no control over that! Stop holding me responsible!"**

Amy quickly came back to her senses. "Who am I talking to? This is nuts, there is nothing here. It's all in my head."

Tears welled up in Amy's eyes, but she wiped them clean and toughened up, as she has always been prone to do. The tension gripped her insides, whether she liked it or not. "I have way too many things to worry about, let alone that stupid voice *in my head.* It is and always will be nothing but my imagination playing games."

Ms. Fraser wiped herself off, dressed, dried her hair and gathered her briefcase together, ready for her first defense of Mr. Garrison. She grabbed her keys from the hanger next to the door and again caught a glimpse of herself in the mirror. Amy saw the reflection staring back at her. It appeared to be sixteen-year-old Amy, bloodied and bruised. Amy quickly turned away, wiped her eyes and looked in the mirror again. It was nothing except her normal reflection. She looked the same as always, less those damn dark bags under her eyes. They appeared to have grown slightly, but they were not out of hand. "A little skin cream and some good sleep will take care of that."

Amy ignored what she had seen just fifteen seconds earlier and continued out the door and to her car, heading for the courthouse. Amy felt frightened.

*

"Shut up, Garrison! Geez-Louise can't you just stop whining for one second?" Jack was getting impatient with John's constant griping from the back seat of the car.

"If you're going to put me on trial for some kid's murder, even though ya' damn well know I didn't do it, then you have to endure the unpleasantness." Garrison told him.

Beauregard shot back with what had to be the worst possible excuse in the book. "I'm not putting you on trial, the Prosecutor is. I simply forward my findings to him, and they make the final decision."

John was not the least bit fooled by that statement. He wasn't born yesterday. "How dare ya' pass the buck like that, *Pontius*. You really do think I'm stupid, don't ya'? Everyone and their brother knows yer doin' this for the press ta get ya' that Governorship."

Jack pulled the car over to the curb so he could turn around and tell Garrison in no uncertain terms what he felt. "You old creep. You murdered one child and left him in your driveway for us to dispose of, and I personally think you're responsible for the other dead kid, too. Your M.O. is that damn Jack of Spades, which was found on both bodies. I think you did it, murderer."

John laughed out loud and snubbed Beauregard. "You go right ahead with yer stupid thinkin', cop. Ya' know it was a dog, not a kid, and I think *you* made the switch. You're a dirty double-dealin' piece of shit that'll do anything to get what ya' want. I'm not fooled by the likes of you."

Jack made one more threat before moving on to the courthouse. "One more word and I'll crack you one. Shut-up."

John gave him a final pretentious laugh, and then just looked out the window the rest of the trip. He knew he'd inched under his skin and would continue his verbal assault later. John didn't feel his best physically, but that only succeeded in making him even crankier.

*

The image of sixteen-year-old Amy showed itself in the rear view mirror of Amy's car and she, like Beauregard, pulled off to the side of the road to have a face-off. Amy started ranting at the vision.

"I've had enough of your….."

As Amy turned around to the backseat, it was gone. She looked in the rear view, and that too was a reflection of the *empty* back seat. Now Amy was becoming angry. It was more a case of heated than scared at the moment.

"This… is… getting… annoying!" she slowly announced, "I've had enough of your nonsense! Leave me alone!"

Passengers from other vehicles drove by as Amy was parked on the curb, and shook their heads as they saw a young woman talking to herself in an unoccupied car.

"She's crazy, Dad!" One child said to his father as they drove along.

Amy began pounding on the steering wheel and made her ultimate announcement to whatever was messing with her head. A warning of sorts. **"I'M TRYING THIS CASE AND I'M WINNING, SO BACK OFF AND GO AWAY!"**

This was her way of not only trying to ward off the visions, but attempting to take back full control of her situation, which she appeared to be losing. The young lawyer pulled the car back onto the highway and continued her drive to the courthouse. She was even more determined now and drove on with a head of steam. Amy still felt frightened.

*

Jack and Amy arrived at the courthouse about the same time, both exhausted from the morning's trials and tribulations. It was 9:00, so the plea before the magistrate wouldn't start for another hour or so. Jack walked John into the court's holding cell, while Amy checked her briefcase in through the scanner and found a seat to wait for Garrison. The building was packed. There were two Magistrates for all of the cases, so it could get a little edgy as people waited. Amy continued to be nervous and frightened, although she felt a bit safer in a room filled with people. She sat quietly and kept to herself.

*

John was stuffed into a cell with at least another fifty men, so it was a bit cramped. He was immediately recognized by a couple other inmates who had seen him on TV.

"Hey, you're that child killer, ain't cha?" one said.

Another piped in, sounding undereducated. "Yea, dat's 'im, dat's da old pervert 'ew likes ta kill kids!"

Garrison stood his ground, fearful of a beating. "Back off ya little punks, I'm here for a drunk drivin' charge. I don't have any idea what yer talkin' about with this killer thing."

The brutes in the cell didn't buy the story. Four men rose from their seats and headed toward the old man. They had angry looks on their faces and it seemed they meant to pummel him. Not a moment too soon, the cell door creaked open and Garrison was summoned out to the hallway. John hightailed it and the door slammed behind him. He looked back and saw those angry faces staring at him through the glass. He flipped them the bird.

"We'll see ya' in the hoosegow, old man." They announced, "Watch yer back."

Garrison felt a sense of relief as he walked with the man that had just pulled him out of the cell.

"I'm sure glad ya' came when ya' did," John exclaimed, "I was fixin' to take an ass-kickin'."

"Shut your mouth, killer. I'm only here to decide what your bond will be." The bondsman was not very friendly and continued ripping John. "I'd put you back if I could; let them tear you to shreds."

As always, Garrison didn't take the comments sitting down. "Whatever happened to innocent until proven guilty? All you lawmen are as crooked as busted pencils. You should be ashamed of yerselves."

The bondsman mulled over John and came right out with it. "No bail will be granted. I'm not taking the chance of you killing any more kids."

John countered with a matter-of-fact attitude. "I didn't expect ya' to grant bail. Especially with the crookedness that exists in this whole damn run around. Ya'll can kiss my ass!"

At this very moment, Jack came around the corner to claim his suspect. "I'll take him. He's my guy."

The bondsman concurred, making a repulsed face when he looked at John. "Good, I'm getting sick standing here with this killer."

Jack led Garrison to a large lobby centered in the middle of the fancy courthouse and sat him next to Amy, who was waiting.

*

"You okay, John?" Amy asked.

"Almost had my ass handed to me in that cell, but yeah, I'm alright."

Amy looked up and noticed Beauregard hovering over them, eyes squarely fixed on Amy's cleavage, which was visible because of her button down shirt.

"Excuse me, Mr. Beauregard, but my eyes are up here. Mr. Beauregard?"

Jack shook his head slightly, trying to ward off the image of Amy's allure. "Oh, sorry, Ms. Fraser, I was daydreaming."

Amy grunted and spoke again, not very happy with Jack's ogling. "Could you excuse us please, I only have a moment with my client before were called."

Jack again snapped back to the focus at hand. "Yes, yes of course. I'll be watching from over there."

"Yeah, I'll bet you will."

Jack took a seat about ten feet away and Amy continued her conversation with John. "You look much better than you did the other day, John. You're not so pale and tired looking."

Garrison wasn't interested in Amy's small talk and urged her to the point. "What in hell are they gonna' do Ms. Fraser? I'm getting' mighty sick of this madness."

Amy soothed John the best she could, and placed a caring hand on his knee. "Hang in there John; it won't be a whole lot longer until your trial. A month or two, maybe."

John spoke up again, as sarcastic as ever. "I asked ya' what's gonna' happen in the meantime. Damn, don't ya' listen?"

Amy took a deep breath and leveled with the old coot. "You're staying in jail until trial. There's not one thing I can do about that. I'll fight for bond, but I'll probably lose. In the meantime, I need you to stay positive and keep your mouth shut before the Magistrate."

John sneered and gave Amy a disgusted look. "I can't guarantee nothin'; I just wanna get this shit over with."

Amy had time to tell him one more thing. "I'll fight for you, John, but you have to listen to me. I'm not telling you anything to hurt you."

The moment came for Amy and John to enter the Magistrate's area. Amy prayed that John would keep quiet.

*

Amy stepped up to the lectern situated in front of the Magistrate.

"We know the charges your Honor; we simply wish to enter a plea."

John stood at this podium with his hands cuffed to his waist at the side of his body and shackles on his feet. Amy turned and noticed Mr. and Mrs. Joseph and Lyla Helms seated behind the prosecutor's table. They all had looks of anger and revenge on their faces. Only Mr. Joseph seemed distant and uninterested. He was looking everywhere except to the front, and mostly at his own feet. Suddenly Amy thought she saw the young Amy near the back of court. She stood in stunned silence as the sweat beads began forming on her forehead and a trembling gripped her body.

"How does the defendant plead?" The Magistrate asked.

Amy said nothing. She kept looking at the young Amy smiling back at her.

"I ain't guilty, yer Honor. I didn't do nuthin'."

Amy snapped out of her trance and took over, angry at John for speaking. "My client does in fact plead 'not guilty' and we'd like to apologize for his outburst."

Amy gave Garrison a little kick on the shin as she said this. She turned around again and young Amy was gone, replaced by a typical teenage girl. Amy thought she simply mistook the teen for her bothersome little friend. She was relieved.

Richard Headly stood to their right and piped in, flaunting his importance. "We request no bond be given for the defendant. He poses a danger to society as well as being a definite flight risk."

Amy was going to speak, but the Magistrate beat her to the punch. "Bond is denied and the prisoner will be remanded until trial."

Headly requested a preliminary hearing in two weeks. Amy requested waiving the hearing because she already knew what the outcome would be and she did not want to give away one piece of information.

"The preliminary hearing is waived and pre-trial is scheduled for three months from today in the Honorable Donald Wiley's courtroom at the Lincoln circuit. Anything else?"

"Yeah," Garrison blurted, "ya'll can go straight to the fiery pits of hell!"

Now the Magistrate was really infuriated. "Get this vermin out of my sight before I throw up!"

Garrison was hastily escorted from the court. As they were leaving, Amy briskly walked next to John, who was being escorted away by Beauregard. "I told you to keep your mouth shut. What is your problem?"

Garrison smiled and gave her a simple explanation. "What were they gonna' do? Put me in the chair?"

Amy stopped walking at that instant and watched Garrison continue out with Beauregard.

"He'll be the death of me," she stated while slowly shaking her head, "The death." Amy needed help. She still felt frightened.

Amy's Descent Continues

Amy knew she needed to see a doctor about the little "visions" she was having, but she was a stubborn woman with a scorching defiance. She thought most of it was nonsense brought on by her tumultuous past…*At least she hoped so*. She was to meet with Doctor Doris Baxter today. Dr. Baxter was a leading psychiatrist in the Lincoln area and was also a woman,-something Amy insisted on when dealing with anyone in the medical field. She felt as though women better understood her emotional situation and were more in tune with the workings of female intricacies. This was not to say that men didn't do a good job in the medical profession; she just preferred a woman. Amy was tortured by a man while growing up and this also fed into her choice of Dr. Baxter.

*

Amy arrived at the Doctor's office, checked in, and had a seat on the comfy sofa that was placed in the waiting area. She opened her files and began working on the Garrison case.

"What can I do to dispel the nonsense of John trying to get rid of a body?" Amy asked herself this question over and over, trying to make sense of it. "If I were trying to dispose of a body, I wouldn't do it like Garrison did. I'd just burn it myself."

Amy thought John to be innocent, but that would mean a killer still lurked. There had been no further killing since John was jailed. That did not bode well for her defense. The one good thing is that she would have Robert Long testifying for Garrison in court. She had managed to get a summons to him before Headly did. She still had the other players on the Prosecutor's side, so her cross-examinations would have to be effective and show the jury that they couldn't be trusted. That would be especially tough, seeing as these witnesses had no real reason to lie. No reason, that is, unless Beauregard paid them off.

"No," Amy thought, "This was a very doubtful probability, as Jack did not want to hurt his run at governor by having one or more of these folks running to the press with such allegations." A good solid defense by making the jury believe that the Prosecutor's witnesses were mistaken was about the only way she could win. It would be very difficult, and depended much on Headly's strategy.

*

"The Doctor will see you now, Ms. Fraser."

Amy stood up and made her way across the lobby and through the glass door to meet her possible savior. Dr. Baxter welcomed her. "Well hello, Amy. Won't you come in and have a seat?"

Amy smiled and sat in a soft chair directly across from Dr. Baxter. The Doctor hit a button on a small desk clock, which Amy figured to be a timer. "Sixty minutes and out," Amy thought to herself. "Who can time feeling better?"

Dr. Baxter thumbed through some notes her assistant had taken when Amy first called, then started the task of helping her get back to a more normal life. Baxter already knew that she was a lawyer. She knew from television reports saying that Amy was handling John Garrison's defense.

"What bothers you, Amy? What is it that concerns you the most?"

Amy pondered for a moment while acquainting with her surroundings, and then replied. "The visions and the voices. The teenage Amy, which for some odd reason wants me to see and hear her. She's been in my dreams and just lately, my waking hours."

Baxter thought about this for a moment and asked more questions, all the while jotting down notes on a pad of paper. "Tell me about your teen-age years, Amy. I want to know all about it."

"Well Doctor," Amy answered, "it was rough. I studied to be a lawyer like it was nobody's business. My parents were drunks who never once supported my dream and my Dad…well…"

"Well what, dear? You know you're safe in here, right? You can tell me anything."

Amy paused for about thirty seconds, just enough time for one tear to run down her cheek and nestle in the corner of her mouth. "My dad….he….raped me. Okay, he raped me. He ripped my clothes off. He made me stand with my arms at my side so he could see me naked, then shoved me down on the bed and hurt me. He would bite me, slap me and he spit at me.

If I bit or hit him, he would kill me. I had no choice. My mom was too drunk to do anything. It was a nightmare. A miserable nightmare. That's what happened… a lot… okay?"

Doctor Baxter walked around her desk and rubbed Amy's shoulders very lightly in an effort to soothe her. "I'm so sorry, dear. I'm sorry he did those awful, disgusting and vile things to you. You do know it was not your fault. You shouldn't blame yourself."

"Then who do I blame? Whose fault is it? Why didn't I kill him when he slept?" At that point, the tears were streaming out of both eyes and the emotions were swelling inside her. It felt better, though. It gave her a small sense of release.

Doctor Baxter spoke again, in a most understanding tone. "It's not your fault that your dad was so despicable, but I don't think blaming the teenage Amy helps you. You really need to stop blaming that girl."

The toughened up Amy now made her appearance. The strong and able Amy who was a lawyer and a winner. "I do not have time for this, Doctor. I have a huge case to defend and I will not waver in my obsession with winning it." Amy wiped her eyes dry. "If I lose, an innocent man could go to the chair. Plain and simply put, he dies if I fail."

"I think you may have bit off more than you can chew right now Amy," Baxter advised. "Perhaps you need to stick with smaller cases that don't have life or death consequences."

"No," Amy shouted, then calmed, "I'm capable and strong. I just maybe need a prescription help to get me through. For some odd reason, I'm letting this get under my skin more than it should. I have to harden up and go to it."

Amy nodded her head in a very confident manner when she said this and the Doctor looked concerned.

"Okay, Amy, I'm not going to get in the way of your obsession, but I warn you, young Amy might. I can't promise you anything. I will give you some meds to help calm your nerves, but that's all they'll do."

"Is she real?" Amy asked. "Is young Amy real?"

Baxter gave her another look of concern and leveled with her. "To you, yes. To everyone else, no. She's not really there, but she seems to be calling for you. Until you come to terms with what happened in your teenage life, I'm very afraid young Amy will continue her visits."

Amy thought it made sense, but it just seemed so real to her. She asked the doctor one more question. "Can young Amy hurt me?"

Doctor Baxter sat back down in her desk chair, leaned forward on her desk, and propped her chin up with two fists underneath for support. She answered Amy as honestly as she knew how to. "I don't think she can hurt you physically, but mentally I suspect she can do major damage. I sense Post Traumatic Stress Disorder, *PTSD,* going on here, but so far it's not so severe it would disrupt you too much. That's today, Amy. I can't possibly tell you what tomorrow brings. You'll have to find out for yourself. I am going to ask you one more time to consider passing this case to another lawyer. I don't think you're ready."

Amy's eyes formed into that determined look she develops. "Nope, I'm saving this man's life. Nothing can talk me out of it." Amy stood self-assertive.

"Very well, Amy. I want to see you next week. In the meantime, I'm prescribing you a low-dose medication to deal with the visions and voices plus anxiety. It should help, but no guarantee."

Amy took the script and headed for the reception desk to make an appointment for the following week. Doctor Baxter followed her, handed her a business card, and told Amy one more thing. "Call me if you need anything."

Amy nodded and went for the door.

*

As she headed home, Amy made a pit stop at the local drugstore to get her script filled so she could get started on the medicine right away. There was much work to do and she needed all her wits to do the job right. Yes, Amy was a little scared and yes, she was skeptical. The biggest thing about her, though, was that torrid determination that hounded her like a stubborn swarm of gnats. It was both a blessing and a curse. The personality that Amy possessed was a definite high B, low A type. She didn't think she was OCD, ADHD, or depressed. She may have a touch of PTSD, like Dr. Baxter said, but it could be managed with meds and therapy. In this case, it really wouldn't matter because she thought the hauntings would undoubtedly continue to pester her. It was just an issue of dealing with them in the right way. Amy would try to look at them as a pure mirage, "but were they?" she asked herself. Deep inside, she thought that maybe they were more than that. Perhaps they were as real as the day is long. She would soon find out. Amy would be tested in two arenas: The arena of court and the arena of *(in)*sanity. Amy was confused.

She filled her prescription and continued on her journey home. She was hungry, so she stopped by the local burger joint and picked up some food. She wolfed it down, took her first pill and washed it down with the soda she purchased with her sandwich. Amy finally arrived home at ten that evening and was wiped out. She quickly changed into her PJ's and hit the hay for some much needed rest and relaxation.

*

Inevitably, the dreams came. She would drift off into a world that both frightened her to death and aroused her curiosity. It started slowly, like a howling wind, "*AMY, AMMY, AMMMMMY,*" increasing as she neared the point between waking and slumber. Soon she fell into a full tilt REM sleep……*Amy found herself in a very empty space. Not a field or a city, just a kind of chasm. There was nothing around her. No light, no dark, no color, nothing. It was, simply put, pure emptiness. This caused Amy more fear than she had experienced up to that point. It was far stranger and more unpredictable to be in nothingness rather than a space that was at least somewhat relevant. Suddenly and without warning, young Amy appeared before her. She was angrier looking and seemed to have a fight to pick. "You cannot hide from me. You cannot escape me. You will never erase me from your memory."*

Amy tried at first to reason with the ghost. She closed her eyes and concentrated as hard as she could. "You are a dream, a mirage formed from my deepest darkest realm. You cannot hurt me and you cannot beat me..."

"SILENCE, WOMAN! I AM THE RAPED, I AM THE TORMENTED, AND I AM THE INNERMOST WOUNDED SOUL! YOU FEED ME AND GIVE ME STRENGTH! I AM YOUR WORST NIGHTMARE!" *Young Amy's voice rang with a heavy, frightening tone. It put Amy into a sort of paralysis. She kept her eyes on the young girl and what she saw next sickened and repulsed her. It was bad enough that the young Amy had the bloodied face and bruising on her cheeks, but she now was forced to witness why it was that way. As suddenly as she found herself in this abyss, the scene changed to Amy's childhood home. Mom was drunk on the couch and Dad was raping the young girl. Amy tried to look away and even shut her eyes, but the images would not be blocked. She was going to see this whether she liked it or not. Amy was forced to watch as her neck, shoulders and head became paralyzed.*

It sickened her to the core. She became nauseated and attempted to vomit, but could not. She again tried to shield her eyes from the attack, but could not move. Young Amy pleaded with her older twin, begging for mercy. "Help me. Save me and spare me from the torture I'm under."

Amy screamed at the top of her lungs. ***"STOP, STOP*** *hurting her…me…us. For the love of Jesus,* ***STOP!"***

It would not stop until Dad completed the act that Amy couldn't control. Her Father then slowly turned his head toward Amy and told her, "You cannot let him die….you cannot let her die….you must save them all Amy, all of them."

Her Dad's face melted before her and he yelled a hideous, distorted scream, causing Amy herself to scream. She suddenly found herself back in the chasm with her teenage twin, who had one final message. "You must save us, Amy. You must save Garrison; you must save yourself before it's too late."

Young Amy disappeared. The older Amy folded herself down on the ground, knees tucked inward, and wept.

Amy woke up in the corner of her room. Her knees were tucked into her chest and she was naked. Her nightgown lay strewn in pieces on the floor next to the bed. It appeared as if it had been ripped off her. Amy looked in horror as she felt, and then spotted bite marks on her arms and thighs. She stood up and dashed to the bathroom to look in the mirror and yes, her face was bruised and swollen, blood trickling down from her lip. **"Oh my God, oh my God. What's happening here? What's my problem? Why is this happening?"**

Amy fell to the floor and cried herself back to sleep. This is where she spent the rest of the night.

*

Morning came and Amy opened her eyes to a spot of sun filtering in from a crack in the shades. She rose from the floor and to her utter surprise, had her nightgown on and intact. She looked in the mirror and there were no bruises or injuries on her face. She tore the nightgown over her head and saw no bite marks or any other flaws on her skin. Amy blew out a deep relieving breath, rubbed her forehead, and smiled slightly, aware that the dream was just that, a horrible dream. Amy drew the shower on and jumped in, taking it as hot as she could stand. She finished, dried her hair, ate a slice of toast with coffee, then dressed for the day. On her way out the door, she again saw herself in the mirror. It was not good. The bags were darkening and her skin looked older, like she was over tanning. She knew *it* was gnawing at her, eating away at her youth.

"I'm taking meds and going to therapy. In the meantime, I *will* defend Mr. Garrison."

Amy headed out the door and shut it tightly behind her. A ghostly shadow crossed the room just a second after she left it. Amy sensed it, almost saw it, but steadfastly moved forward into the future.

Old Coot in the Hoosegow

There Garrison sat, all alone in a single man cell in the beautiful town of Lincoln. It really was good that it was a single; otherwise the old man would probably be dead by now. The men occupying the adjoining cells to the left and right of him were frothing at the bit to kill the old codger. They assumed he'd killed the kids and wanted him to pay dearly.

"It'll be the chair for you, pervert," from one side and "You'll fry you old fuck," from the other. Somehow, Garrison was able to block out their nonsense, but other times he was looking for a good argument. It kept his edge and helped him stay his ornery old self. "You guys wanna kick my ass, eh? Come on over here and do it. I'll even tie one hand behind my back and still whip yer asses."

That kind of lip enraged the men, causing them to reach through the bars in an attempt to grab John. It was to no avail, as the old coot scooted his cot to the center of the cell and slept somewhat peacefully. After a few days of harassing him, the other inmates grew tired and bored. They would occasionally spit at him, but John figured out that using a bed sheet on each side of his bunk created a nice blocker in which to catch the nastiness. When it came time to clean the laundry on switch-out day, the troopers chewed out the spitters for making such a mess. After threats of solitary, the spitting, for the most part, stopped. This was another delight for the old man. He would continually rub the solitary card in their faces. "What's a matter, boys? You all dried out?"

On one occasion, a dumb inmate stuck his hand through the bars to try and catch Garrison with his back turned. It turned out to be a rather stupid move, as the old timer showed he still had some of the quickness of youth in him. He grabbed the man's arm, which was stuck through to the elbow, and dropped to the ground while holding his wrist under his armpit. When the arm hit the divider bar situated in the middle of the cell gate, there was a loud crack and instant pain. Garrison landed on his butt with his back to the man, and the arm was still under his grasp. The man's screaming brought two troopers instantly.

"What the hell happened here, Garrison?"

The old man calmly explained. "He's the bonehead who put his arm through the gate. I accidently fell on it. He should 'a kept his hands to himself."

The geezer roared with laughter. The guards did not.

"We should put you in solitary; you're a real piece of work Garrison."

John welcomed that threat too. "Go ahead; I don't give a rat's rear end what ya do. I ain't got nuthin' to lose."

Frustrated, the troopers scratched their collective heads and warned the other inmates to keep their hands to themselves. The broken-armed inmate was put in a cast up to his elbow and placed in a different cell.

*

Food flying, expletives flowing, urine on the floor outside the cell. Whatever John could do to aggravate, he did. Finally, Trooper Michaels had enough and sent John to the solitary cell at the end of the block. John really didn't care. He preferred the quiet of the single, out-of-the-way cell. It had a sink, toilet and cot. The only drawback was that there was no TV he could watch. He had become quite interested in Beauregard's run for governor and was following it pretty closely. The election was coming and his trial, it appeared now, would be right around the same time. John found it comical that Beauregard had taken a commanding lead since he was arrested for the murder of the boy, mostly due to the fact that he had nothing to do with it. How ironic that this man would use him as his stepping stone. Anytime Jack came down the hallway to check on the prisoners, John would stand up in his cell and salute the would-be governor.

"Hail to the Chief!" John would yell, after which he would grab his balls and give Beauregard the credit he thought was more deserved.

"Shut up, Garrison! You aren't getting under my skin. You can say and do anything your heart desires, and I still won't give a shit."

Just putting a charge into Jack tickled John silly. If Beauregard was reacting, it meant it bothered him. John came up with a slew of salutes for Jack. The one-finger salute, the hands-to-balls salute, and his personal favorite, the throwing-food-at-Jack-and-then-saluting salute. The last one pissed Jack off more than any.

"Stop throwing your food at me Garrison or I'll…"

"Or you'll what, big shot? Throw me in the solitary cage? How about the sewer? You don't scare me, copper."

"I'm putting you in the chair, John; I'm really tired of your crap."

Garrison, as smart-assed as ever, welcomed the challenge. "I'll sit down in it ma self, asshole. I don't even need yer help. I ain't scared of yer intimidation tactics."

Jack ordered Michaels to get the chair, and he was more than excited about the prospect of shutting the old man up, at least for a day or two. This chair is awful. It is made exclusively for back, leg and butt discomfort. The muscles in your body are not made to stretch to such unnatural position. After four hours or so, your legs become numb. After eight hours, your back screams in pain and after about twenty-four hours, you're begging for mercy as your body shouts for relief. It really comes down to a form of torture. For some strange reason, the powers that were at the top of the criminal law food chain seemed to think it was okay to use such a device. I guess, that is, if it wasn't them sitting in it.

*

The pain came much quicker to the man in his seventies. The legs went numb after but one hour and the back pain came after three. John kept quiet and took the pain, but deep down inside he screamed for mercy. *"Okay, okay, you win, I will be good, I won't do anymore bad stuff, please let me out, please."*

Nope! Not for John Garrison, doggone it! He was as tough as rusted metal, and as stubborn as a sick mule. There was no way in the world he would ever admit that they were getting to him. His face paled a bit and his mind struggled, but John sat quietly while appearing as if it did not bother him. After twelve hours, John felt sick to his stomach and vomited violently onto the floor in his cell. Trooper Michaels came to check on him.

"You had enough old man? If you behave, I'll let you out."

Garrison mustered enough strength to lift his head and answer the cop. "Go fuck yerself, boy. If I were thirty years younger, me and you'd go at it. Just the two of us, you pussy."

"Well," the trooper said, "you're not thirty years younger and I'd kick the living shit out of you anyways. Besides, you were probably soft as a young guy. No gumption."

John cussed under his breath and tilted his head forward until his chin rested on his chest. Drool ran from his mouth to his stomach. He stayed quiet the rest of the night. Not a peep out of him.

Twenty-four hours after being placed in the torture device, John was released and placed in his cot. He didn't make a sound except for a minor groan while being carried. The troopers put John back in his regular cell with the other inmates surrounding him on both sides, and they promptly spit on his listless body until they became bored. The old coot lay on his cot for sixteen hours after being unstrapped from the chair. He wet himself and didn't care. Finally he was able to rise. It would take another three days before he felt somewhat like himself again. Amy had visited recently and thought John to be sick, but he was too proud a man to admit any weakness and chose not to tell Amy of the torturous experience.

John began feeling a bit better. He still hated the grub ridden food and only once in a while did he throw it out of the cell. The threat of that chair calmed him, though, so he wouldn't take things as far as before. Messing with the inmates on either side of him became his favorite hobby. It was the same as before, only this time they were smart enough to keep their arms inside the cell. The inmate with the broken arm was down the wing a bit and John would, from time-to-time, call out to him to see how that arm was. It was in a surly and sarcastic way in which he did it. The old man was getting a little frustrated and jaded waiting for the pre-trial hearings, and especially the trial itself. John was not afraid of dying; he just wanted to do it for the right reason. He paid Amy a handsome amount of cash to defend him, but he knew in his mind he was probably a sitting duck.

*

The TV talked more about the governor's race and it was all but assured that Beauregard would easily win it. That was also a craw in John's side, because he knew he was being railroaded just for that reason. Jack was not going to change his mind and let Garrison off the hook, and although John could never prove it, he thought the prosecutor, Richard Headly, probably had some incentive from Jack to continue pursuing the case. One TV set was shared by every three cells, and news was not a popular item among the inmates. John had to fight each and every day at 6:00 to see it. "One gotdamn half-hour a day, ya morons. That's all I ask."

The inmates countered. "You don't deserve anything you old shit, except for that electric chair. You're a filthy warped old man."

"You don't know the facts, ya idiots, I was framed up to take the fall," is how Garrison attempted to reason with them. "I bagged up a dead dog, not a dead kid."

The prisoners usually pondered John for a split second, and then ignorance would rear back. "Shut up old man, we know you did it and you're taking the fall."

There was no reasoning or talking it over. John didn't necessarily care what they thought; it just worried him because he was sure a jury would see it the same way as these bozos did. What else could he do besides shrug and blow off the negative comments. It reached a point where John became tired of talking at all, so he just clammed up. On occasion the old firecracker personality would appear, but it was rare, and appearances started getting less and less each day. John was very worried and concerned about his trial. The old man was tiring and he knew it. This was very much like caging a wild animal that deserved freedom. Too bad other incentives took precedence over the truth.

*

"TROOPER, TROOPER!" The inmate next to Garrison's cell screamed out with a bloodcurdling holler.

"Shut yer damn mouth," John ordered, "I don't want no attention comin' to me."

The inmate looked at a pale, weak and obviously in distress old man.

"I ain't letting you die in here, killer. You have a date with the chair. **TROOPER, TROOPER! HURRY THE HELL UP!"**

John Garrison sat next to his cot having what appeared to be a heart attack. His face was an ashen color, he had trouble breathing and his left arm felt like it was being yanked from his body by a grizzly bear. Finally after what seemed like forever, Lt. Michaels walked up to the cell. "What the hell do you want? I'm tired of hearing your damn infernal mouth screaming."

The prisoner pointed at Garrison and Michaels instantly took action.

"Dispatch, Trooper Michaels here. We have a prisoner down. Repeat, prisoner down. I want an ambulance NOW. Over."

"10-4 trooper, EMS ETA is about five minutes. Out."

"OPEN CELL C RIGHT NOW!" The trooper ordered.

The gate slid open and Michaels quickly went to Garrison's side.

"Get away from me, ya frickin' pig. I don't want yer help. I'll die right here. This is as good a place as any."

Michaels chuckled a bit. "No chance, old timer. You're seeing this murder rap through. I refuse to let you die."

John sneered at the cop and tried even harder to die, but so far it wasn't good enough.

"I hope I die right in yer pathetic arms, pig. I never murdered anyone and I fix to expire right here before you can railroad me any further." Michael's sensed a hint of truth in the old man's voice. It bothered him.

EMS arrived seconds later. The other prisoners were hooting and hollering like wild hyenas. After stabilizing the ornery old man, they transported him to emergency, where more treatment followed.

*

John lie in the hospital bed with one hand cuffed to the bedrail and one leg shackled to the bed leg. There was no way he was going anywhere in his condition, but you know the police have to do their jobs.

"Where the hell they think I'm goin'?" He asked his nurse.

"Mr. Garrison, it's not my choice to cuff you up like that, and I wouldn't, but it's out of my hands."

John grunted and mumbled something about letting him die.

"Oh, we can't just let you die, Mr. Garrison. *It wouldn't be morally correct."*

A firm smiled formed around the old guy's face as he listened to that bit of nonsense. "But frying me in an electric chair is sooo responsible, right? Yer just as bad as the rest of the finger pointing pieces of shit in this godforsaken town. I suppose you'll be the one checkin' my stats to make sure I'm good and crispy-critterеd."

The nurse scolded John. "You just had a catheter put in your main aortic artery, either remain calm or we WILL strap you down to stay still."

John laughed again, finding it funny they would cath his heart when they wanted him dead anyway.

"How can ya' pin me any more than you already have?"

"Try me!" the nurse warned.

John wouldn't. He knew she meant business and he wasn't going to stick his toe in that pool of cold water.

"Fine then, ya' two-bit excuse for a medical professional. You're a gotdamn railroader, just like the rest of 'em."

The nurse left the room and looked unpleasantly at the trooper stationed at the door.

"I told you he was an ornery cuss," the trooper said. "You can't say I didn't warn you."

The nurse scoffed aloud and went about her business. The guard trooper cracked the door open and gave John a word of advice. "Stop messing with these folks John. They're just trying to help you." The old grump shouted back. "You leave me alone too; you're a poor excuse for a lawman."

The trooper shut the door just before the lunch tray hit it, sighed, and went back to his copy of *US* magazine.

*

Amy received a call from Colonel Beauregard letting her know that Garrison had suffered a mild heart attack at the jail. She gathered up her things and left immediately to see to her client at the hospital. Amy drove fast and focused, wanting to make sure John was alright.

"They probably caused it, those jerks; they just can't stop messing with people."

The "they" she was referring to was obviously the troopers at the jail. They had always been known as a cruel and inhumane bunch, but no one had the guts to approach them about it in fear of retribution. It was just another of many forms of intimidation practiced at that facility.

Amy reached Lincoln Memorial and quickly cut in front of two people at the reception desk, grabbed the rolodex, found where Garrison was, and then thanked the secretary for nothing.

"Room 221, room 221," is what she kept repeating for fear of forgetting and having to start her search over. She took the stairs in lieu of the slow elevator and arrived at Garrison's ICU unit when the trooper at the door stopped her cold.

"Who are you and what are you doing here?" she was asked.

"I'm Garrison's attorney. Now let me in please."

"No dice, "the trooper insisted. "I was told to keep everyone out, and that includes some bimbo broad who says she's this guy's attorney."

Amy stood with her mouth agape, and then spoke sharply and without manners. "Did you just call me a 'bimbo broad?' Was 'bimbo broad' what you really said, trooper?" A fight was developing.

When the trooper was about to answer, up walked Jack Beauregard, as cocky and overconfident as ever.

Lt. Michaels flanked him. “She’s okay, Ron, you can let her in.”

Amy nodded slightly to the Colonel, lipped an expletive to the trooper and let herself in.

*

“Hey, you old whipper,” Amy enthusiastically said to John, “how’s that ticker doing?”

Garrison choked out a semi-sincere smile. “I’ve been better, but I wished I’d just died. Leave it to the stupid law to save my life so they can take it later.”

Responding in her usual confident way, Amy tried to cheer the old codger up.

“You are NOT going to die in that god-awful chair, John. I’ll see to that personally. I’ve never lost a case and I won’t now. Have faith in your lawyer, huh?”

“Whatever you say,” he said. “I don’t have any trust in the system or the fools runnin’ it. I’m probably a goner. You know it and I know it.”

Beauregard, after chatting with the trooper in the hall, let himself in to check on his “prize” for himself. He walked past Amy with nary a glance and started talking to John. “So killer, you wanted to die before your time? What’s that all about?”

Amy swiftly rushed to his aide. “Do not talk to my client in that way, Colonel Beauregard. I’ll warn you that it is illegal and immoral to assume guilt before it’s been decided.”

“Easy does it,” Jack gently pushed his hands against the air in front of him, “Easy, I’m just kidding, right John?”

Garrison was not amused. "Kiddin' my left nut, cop. Yer just hopin' for a big win come election day, and I'm the chess piece you're playin' to get that victory. You ain't nuthin' but a fake, Beauregard, a plain fake."

Amy stood toe to toe with the Colonel, trying her best to inflict some guilty intimidation on him. You could see a confrontation developing which would became testy and loud when the nurse barged through the door and began a scolding, her ire directed at the three that were not lying down with heart trouble.

"Both of you get out of my ICU. I have a patient to look after and you're crowding us both out. Now leave this second!" The Nurses eyes glowed with anger.

Astonished, Amy and Jack stood in utter silence before the determined nurse.

"Do you know who I am, ma'am?" Jack rudely implied.

"Yes, I know who you are and you're in my domain, my ICU, my jurisdiction. Now leave before I call security."

Jack mumbled something about owning the security and reluctantly left the room. Before he could get out the door, John asked him for a second more and gave him the one fingered salute he so adored. Beauregard grumbled and left. Amy asked the nurse one last question before leaving. "When do you suppose he'll be back to his cell?"

The nurse gave her a deceptively caring look and answered. "When he gets better. Now OUT!"

Amy gave her a quick fake grin and told John she'd see him later. John waved at her and shut his eyes, exhausted from the whole rigmarole.

*

Jack and Amy walked side by side at a breakneck pace, Michaels trailing them, as they headed for the exit. A conflict awaited in the parking garage. When exiting the garage elevator, Amy started in on Beauregard. She was circling him much like the little dog circling the bulldog in the old Bugs Bunny cartoons; only in this case she wasn't happy and bouncy. Amy was screaming at him as she desperately vied for Jack's attention. She wasn't having a whole lot of success as he continued his march towards his vehicle with tunnel vision.

"How dare you label my client, how dare you speak to him in such a way, how dare your stupid guard called me a 'bimbo broad?' Are you listening, Jack?"

A quick flash of light illuminated the area. All three looked around and saw nothing. Amy attributed it to be a bad light bulb in the parking facility. Beauregard, along with Lt. Michaels remained focused on the task at hand; getting in their vehicle and getting away from what Jack perceived to be a lunatic. At the very moment Jack reached for the car door handle, Amy grabbed him by his wrist. Beauregard stopped in his tracks, turned, and lashed out at the young attorney. **"You mean zero to me; nada, nothing, zilch. You are the wad of old bubblegum stuck to my shoe. You, Ms. Fraser, of all people, will NOT hinder my goal, which is the state governorship. You will lose in a court of law and the court of public opinion. Good day, Ms. Fraser."**

Jack whispered something to Michaels who then walked over and gently shoved and held Amy against a support post as Jack entered his vehicle, revved the engine and peeled out of the scene. Michaels then released Amy, who was struggling to free herself, gave her a little wink and headed to his own vehicle, leaving her to fend for herself in a largely empty lot.

This was just about as infuriated as Amy had ever been. She realigned her suit jacket, which Michaels had wrinkled at the left shoulder, and gave her silky jet-black hair a push toward her temple. "Well," Amy said in a quivering tone, "I guess I showed them."

Amy fished for her keys and set out trying to find her own vehicle. Then it started again. It was just a whisper at first. "Ammmyyy." It then proceeded to get a little more volume, "Amy, Amy, **AMMY!**"

The last cry caused Amy to break out in goose bumps as she trawled through her purse for her car keys while simultaneously walking. She walked forward with purpose and determination, passing the pillars and listening to the haunting cries of her name. This time it wasn't only the young Amy's voice, but that of her mom and dad, along with a tiny male, presumably Jimmy Joseph. The lawyer picked up her pace and continued toward where she thought her car may be, looking over her shoulder every twenty feet or so. "Was it level two? Or was it three?"

Amy's heartbeat started to race and her breathing swelled as her gait picked up to a slow jog. It was getting darker and emptier, it seemed, as she struggled with the voices calling her. Suddenly, from around a concrete post, it was the young ghostly Amy. She was standing in a white nightgown stained with blood. Her body tilted to the right, as if she had a stroke, and her arms lay at her side. Her face was pale and drawn, her eyes a frighteningly deep black. Amy circled around her and took off in a dead run. The young Amy turned and followed, but not nearly at the speed at which Amy was pacing. She felt like a zombie was pursuing her, but at a tad quicker gait. When Amy looked over her shoulder, she saw that she was putting some distance between her and the ghostly figure. This gave her a little more confidence until she turned back to see where she was going and was abruptly confronted with her dead parents.

Mom and Dad were hideous. The injuries from the car accident, which claimed their lives, were now on full display. Dad's midsection was badly gashed and bleeding, his entrails visible and spilling out near his alcohol damaged liver. His head was smashed in on one side and he appeared to have only half a mouth. Mom was much worse. Her face was barely a shape as her skull cap fell over it, presumably from the cut she received when going through the windshield. They both reached their mangled arms out to hold their daughter. Amy released the most bloodcurdling scream she could muster. It was loud and unmistakable. This episode was disturbing and unlike any of the visions up to now. Amy regained some composure and continued her mad dash. When she looked behind, she saw them coming. When she turned back to her path, she saw them waiting. Amy zigged and zagged through the garage, desperately trying to find her car, as if that was a safe haven. The panic and anxiety were crushing her as she fled. She again heard the voices, now shouting her name.

"AMMYYY! DON'T LET HIM DIE AMMMYYY!"

Fear gripped her mind. The need to stop and vomit was overwhelming. She wanted to escape, but seemingly could not. **"HELP,"** she shouted, **"HELP ME!"**

It was to no avail, as the ghostly figures pursued her with a vengeance. Finally and thankfully, she saw her car. It was parked exactly where she left it. She fumbled for her keys and reached the door. As luck would have it, she was too shaky and nervous to insert the sharp piece of metal into her lock. She dropped the keys and bent over to pick them up. She turned…and they were all there, just two feet from her. It was young Amy, along with her mom and dad. Amy sat with her back against the car door as she wept. She felt like giving up. Her stomach churned a warning of impending sickness and her heart fluttered with fear. The three ghostly figures before her separated, two to the left and one to the right. This is when little Jimmy walked up between the ghouls and faced Amy from six inches away.

He spoke, "Don't let him die, Amy. You cannot let Garrison die. You let Amy die, you let your mom and dad die, and you let me die. Don't make the same mistake again."

Amy cried and wailed. **"I'm sorry. I'm sorry. I won't let him die. Just leave me alone. Let me be."**

Amy covered her face with her hands and continued crying when a warm feeling touched her fingers.

"OH GOD NO! DON'T HURT ME!"

When Amy opened her eyes, she was shocked. It was a family; a seemingly normal family. Mom and Dad, Daughter and Son.

"You alright lady?" The ten-year-old son asked, head cocked to the right. Dad chimed in. "Do you need an ambulance? I can call on my cell."

Amy looked around. The light in the garage was bright. There were people milling about, whispering about the crazy lady who was rushing through the garage. Amy arose from the ground, straightened herself up, and thanked the family for their concern. "Uh, no... no, I'm okay, just a little freaked out. I'm fine. I'll be going now."

She was still quaking on the inside, but it was calmer now.

"Are you sure, ma'am? It's really no…"

"No, I'm sure. Thank you all the same. Goodbye now."

Amy jumped in her car, gave herself one more once-over in the mirror, and then, with a screech of her tires, left the parking garage. She looked in the rear view and saw the family standing there. She was embarrassed and spooked. She managed to make it all the way home before upchucking. She took her meds and went to bed-with the lights on. Amy was horrified.

Deadly Headly

Time passed and preparations intensified. Garrison was back at the jail, his health almost as good as new. Amy fought her demons, which were lessoning a bit with the medication, while at the same time preparing for John's trial and seeing Dr. Baxter weekly. Beauregard toured the state seeking his victory and trip to the mansion in Lincoln. Sitting out of the limelight and almost forgotten was Richard Headly. He was the prosecutor trying the Garrison murder case. He knew winning probably meant he would have the attorney general post he so badly coveted. He continued to deal with Jack and the two had seemingly become quite good buddies. Dinners at each other's houses. Trips together to state mandated events all over the USA. The girls even blended well. Soo-Chin and Sonya Headly, Richard's wife, were getting along splendidly. Even Kyle took to the Headlys and he was not easy to impress.

*

Richard Headly grew up in Omaha. He was interested in politics since his teen years, but had never seen law as a way to govern or make big decisions for the state. He had no idea that the two tend to go hand in hand. He wanted to be in a position of power-not the corrupt kind, he always thought to himself, but the kind that serves his own purposes. If someone gets in the way and needs to be bulldozed? So be it. He would just turn his head and walk away; acting like it wasn't his doing, even if it was. So yes, like it or lump it, Headly had some shrewd and hurtful tactics in his arsenal. If something nasty needed to be done, he'd do the dis-honorable thing and have someone else do it. An employee needs firing? His secretary passed the life changing information on. Somebody getting a little big for their britches? "My assistant will deal with that." Richard wasn't all that well liked at the office because he was considered, plainly put, a sissy with no backbone. Never there for the bad, but always present to collect the accolades. His face was featured on the Lincoln Times front page more than a few times and Richard loved it, as long as it was a positive. If you thought about it enough, it was really no surprise that he and Jack got along the way they did. Two men out for the same type of prize, running over anyone and anything in their way, while at the same time keeping their hands relatively clean. It seemed volatile and poisonous, but to them it was necessary. If it came down to these two needing to crush each other, they would without regret.

Mr. Headly wore two thousand dollar spectacles. Only the best for the best. He stood a thin six-foot-two, and combed his hair with a part on the left side. He had a receding hair line, but waved it off as a minor annoyance. Richard met Sonya in '82 while going to school in Omaha. She was now a touch past her prime, but carried herself very well for a woman in her early 50's. What helped most is that she could afford all the latest face-lift and tuck techniques available. She was overly-tanned, but thought it looked perfect on her. If medium well is perfect for the skin, then she hit the nail on the head. When Richard and Sonya were out on the town or visiting friends, they were blinging it up. The finest rings on her fingers, the finest wine in the restaurant, the finest clothes. Over-the-top and excessive is how it appeared to most, but for them it was marvelous. Richard was involved in a shady scheme or two, but nothing ever came of it. He was alleged to have ripped off over a hundred grand from an old business associate just after college. The two worked on a computer software service together and it was quite successful in the mid '80's when computers were beginning their ascent into mainstream living. The venture lasted about a year and a half before a lack of funds did it in. Richard's then partner tried to implicate him, accusing Headly of cooking the books. It made it to Civil Court, where it was dismissed and dropped due to a lack of evidence. The newspapers reported it as a case of sour grapes. Headly continued on, living a luxurious lifestyle while his ex-partner, broke, took a .357 caliber handgun and tried to swallow it. Unfortunately, the gun discharged and that was that. Following another failed venture or two, Headly opened a law firm, defended accused criminals, and became famous in the Omaha area for rarely losing cases. He defended would-be felons over 250 times, remarkably losing only 3 cases. Richard and Sonya hoarded up as much cash as they could and just five years later, Headly was hired by the Lincoln

Prosecution Office to try cases for the State. Since then, every case he's had, he's won. A flawless record that the big guns loved. He became known as "Deadly Headly" due to his sterling conviction rate. He was moved up to lead state prosecutor and has his eyes on the attorney general gig, which is part of the reason he's so close to soon-to-be Governor Beauregard. A smart and shrewd man, this Richard Headly-If not at a small part crooked.

*

Headly was working very hard on the Garrison case. He knew the evidence was flimsy. Hell, he knew Garrison probably didn't commit the crime. No matter, because a seventy-some year-old man going down for the good of his future was more than worth it. Richard would call Beauregard regularly and complain about the lack of evidence present. "Jack, dammit, how do you expect me to do anything when I have nothing. I've received the coroners report, nothing. I've received the forensic report, nothing. All we have is a dead kid in a bag in Garrison's driveway."

Jack always managed to calm Richard down. "You're the best, Richard. There is no attorney in the state, hell, in the country with your record. Nobody can come close to beating you, especially this little Fraser rookie. It's in the bag, along with your AG position."

This always made Richard feel better. He was the best and he knew it. He was cocky and arrogant, which goes a long way in the world of criminal law.

He knew he could impress these jurors beyond belief. He would charm the pants off them. As for Fraser, she was a lightweight with an attitude. She was overmatched against the best lawyer in the country. Headly needed to be at least a little careful about being over confident, so he'd often tone it down a bit and ask him what it would be like to be beaten. "Can this Amy Fraser beat me? Will I choke under pressure? Do I have what it takes?"

He knew he did and he didn't feel the challenge as he used to. Not only beating Fraser, but humiliating her would be a great joy. They didn't call him deadly for nothing.

*

More trips with Jack, more dinners at the fanciest restaurants, and more money. That's all Headly wanted in life. The upmost in comfort and security. He vied to keep his wife happy and he worked to keep his record perfect. If he wasn't careful, he would start believing his own headlines. He could easily fall prey to indifference or malaise. Not in this case he wouldn't; not for a second. He'd find a way, even if it meant stretching the truth just a hair or two. He would figure it out. He'd stay perfect and be the state's new attorney general. If he lost to the "rookie," he'd be better to just quietly retire and lick his wounds from far, far away. In his mind, he wouldn't lose. He could not accept defeat.

*

Richard loved his wife Sonya. She could be a real pain in his ass though, as she was a pure spendaholic. Richard had been forced to hide credit cards, cash, and anything else that could be pawned to keep the woman in check. The prosecutor made $100,000 a year, but Sonya went through it like melted butter. Lately though, with his new strategy of hiding everything, the spending fell dramatically. This would make Sonya as grumpy as a mama bear protecting her cubs, but it was the only way. Richard wanted to have it good for both of them, but he needed her cooperation to succeed. The man would be challenged by his wasteful wife, and it would be up to the future Attorney General to keep things under control.

Lyla's Love

Lyla Helms was trying to help Dan Wheeler through a tumultuous time in his life. He had seen a dead child up close and it was very difficult for him to process the terror. He was visiting a therapist and taking nerve medicine that helped offset the anxiety that had gripped him like an eagle's talons on a helpless mouse. Dan had been on disability since the grisly discovery and wasn't sure he could ever do his job again. He was losing his mojo, as the women in town that were regulars at his apartment found other things to do. It would only take a visit or two to Dan's place to turn them off, and then turn them the other way.

"I can't take it. I don't know how to handle it. Can you understand what I'm going through?" Were the questions and comments Dan would use, weighing down the female's interest in him.

It was okay once or twice, but fifty, sixty, seventy times? The women disappeared and Dan was left alone. Left alone except for Lyla, that is. Lyla took Dan under her wing like a mother swan and did everything she could to help him through the trauma. Dan could ask the same question as many times as he liked with her and she treated each one as if it was the first time she heard it. She answered with enthusiasm and openness, helping the young man feel a tiny bit better each time she expressed interest.

Dan was getting more depressed each day, it seemed. Having to testify at the upcoming trial also left Dan blue and dejected. Lyla had talked him down off of a chair twice. He had a rope slung over the rafter and knotted around his throat. Just one step and it would be curtains for the handsome guy, but Lyla twice walked in just in time to save him.

"Its God's will that you don't do it, Dan, because I keep showing up to stop you. Don't do that to yourself, hun. It's going to get better with time."

Dan Wheeler cried and wept on Lyla's shoulder. She would do whatever it took to get him feeling like his old self again. Yes, she would even do *that* if necessary. Lyla was a very nurturing woman and really liked the guy even though they sassed back and forth at work. He was still her animal pickup man, and hoped it would be back to the same old, same old soon. She didn't think she could actually date Dan on a regular basis, and if this recent event hadn't happened, wouldn't even consider sleeping with him. This was a special circumstance. "Sometimes," Lyla figured, "you have to give of yourself to help someone else."

Dan never really thought about that kind of relationship with his boss. It never crossed his mind to have sex with her. If the situation were right, though, who knew? Dan was not beyond it by any means. Right now, he simply appreciated his boss's encouragement. It was good old-fashioned fostering by Lyla because the situation called for it. Lyla needed to be careful, though, because she tended to get clingy after getting too close. Dan had no idea how clingy.

*

Richard Headly had to meet with Dan and Lyla, and after a little inveigling by Lyla, was talked into having these meetings at Dan's apartment. Richard was a much bigger fan of meeting any and everybody at his office. It was his "home field advantage" so to speak. In this case, he really didn't have a choice because Lyla would have it no other way.

"You meet us at Dan's place or don't meet us at all. It's your choice, counselor."

With a deep breath and a moan, Richard agreed. "If I knew it'd be this much of a damn headache, I never would have taken the stupid case." He really didn't mean that, but it sure felt better to say it to himself occasionally.

Mr. Headly met the pair at about four in the afternoon, purposely that late because after the meeting, Headly would want to go straight home. He figured to be exhausted having to meet his witnesses in a strange dwelling. Richard arrived and was shocked at the sight when he walked in. He was taken aback immediately by the odor of the apartment and the mess lying around on the floor and couch. He also could not believe how someone could live in such a tiny space. He could see the kitchen, bathroom and bedroom ALL from the same spot in which he sat. It seemed that Mr. Headly had forgotten where he came from. He grew up in modest surroundings…"but this?" he thought, "Never in a million years." Lyla sensed Mr. Headly's slight discomfort and tried to make him more comfortable.

"Cup of tea, sir, or perhaps a cold soda?"

"HMMPH!" Was the reaction from Richard. "No, let's just do this."

"That's no *thank you*, Mr. Headly. Where are your manners?" Lyla looked him over, head tilted slightly to one side, mouth in a circle shape, and eyes wide open.

"We are in a situation, sir, where a young man has been traumatized and is having some difficulty getting his senses back. Could you be a bit more-what's the word? Gentle? Alternatively, is it caring? Possibly even patient?"

Ms. Helm's matter of fact outburst had little to no effect on a man who listens to people's complaining everyday. He had a very thick skin. Nonetheless, Headly tried as hard as he knew how to conform and overcome his uncomfortable surroundings. "Okay, Mrs. Helms. I understand and I apologize. Can we now get on with the unfortunate task of getting our stories down for court?"

Richard still looked perplexed. He wanted to leave at that moment, but held his tongue and tried to cast the right body language for the occasion. "Whom shall I talk to first? You Ms. Helms, or Dan?"

"May I be in the room when you speak with Dan?" was Lyla's request.

"Not at first. I want to get his statement separate from yours, and then we'll fix what needs fixing."

Lyla looked a bit startled at Headly's answer. "If we are being honest, what difference does it make? We both saw what we saw, right?"

The patience Richard was struggling to exhibit began growing thin very quickly. "I'll start with Dan, and then I'll speak with you. Afterwards, we will speak as three. Do you understand, Ms. Helms that this is the way in which I desire to work?"

This time Lyla grumbled and went to fetch Dan, who had been lying down for most of the afternoon. Dan walked out to the living area and God almighty, Richard thought he looked and smelled like death!

"Hey, Mr. Headly, Lyla told me you wanted to see me?"

"Yes Dan, have a seat, will you? We need to get your story down exactly as you saw it."

Dan plopped on the chair across from Richard and let a long fart escape.

"Oh, sorry, my stomach's been a little upset lately."

Headly wanted to pull out his handkerchief and stuff his face into it, but resisted.

"Let's do this as quickly as we can, Mr. Wheeler," Richard stated with a disgusted glance, "It looks like you could use some rest."

Dan yawned widely and Headly started his interview.

"Okay, Dan tell me what you remember."

The young man rubbed his scruffy unshaven neck as if he were choking himself and did his best to recall the horror without losing his composure. "I picked up a bag at Garrison's place. He was the same old smart-ass that I've always dealt with, nothing different there. He helped me throw the sack in the control truck, it was heavy, I told him, but he said it was heavy when he and Robert Long, his neighbor, set it on the end of the drive."

Richard interrupted, wanting more information. "Could you tell what shape it was? Did you have any reason to think it was anything other than a dog?"

"Nope," Dan answered, "no reason. It seemed pretty normal to me."

"Go on please," Headly requested.

"I don't know what else to say, really. It was heavy. I loaded it up with Garrison's help and took it to the incinerator."

"Did you stop anywhere on the way?" Richard asked.

"Nope, went straight to the burner."

"What happened next?"

"I'm not sure," Dan replied, "I remember ripping the bag open and the next thing I know, I'm puking all over the place. How much longer do we have to do this?"

"Just one more question, Dan. Do you remember seeing the dead Joseph boy in the bag?"

Dan put a hand quickly to his mouth and ran for the toilet. He threw up loud and violently, further nauseating the already queasy Prosecutor.

"That's all, Dan," Headly gently whispered from across the room as he jotted down notes.

Lyla came dashing out of the bedroom to check on Dan, whom she'd heard vomiting. She suspected the entire street heard him.

"What did you say to him, Richard? Can't you see he's not well?"

It was more than obvious to Richard that Dan was not well, but he was a key witness for the state. "Well or not, he's testifying," Headly told her, "That is of course, if he doesn't string himself up first." Lyla smoldered at that comment, but kept her mouth shut this time, with much difficulty. "When you finish attending to him, Lyla, I'd like to speak with you."

"Yeah-Yeah, I'll be back in a minute."

Richard sat back against the support of the couch and blew out a perplexed sigh. "Half way home," he thought to himself. When Lyla returned, he reiterated his point with a softer manner. "Lyla, you must have Dan ready for that trial, like it or not. He has to be there to support the damn case. It all hinges on him."

"I'll do what I can, Mr. Headly, but as you can plainly see, he's worse than not well, he's flat out miserable."

Richard leaned forward in his seat and put it rather bluntly. "I don't care if you have to pour Pepto-Bismol right down his throat or if he needs a puke bucket on the stand. If he's not there, we get no conviction. Period, end of story." Richard was glancing around repulsively at the surroundings in the apartment, which continued to disgust him. Lyla became unglued and gave the discourteous prosecutor a piece of her mind.

"You, Mr. Headly, are the rudest, most insincere man I've ever met. You're cold and callous. You're horrible."

Richard rubbed his rapidly aching temples and wondered at that point how high his blood pressure must've been. Lyla was now standing across from him, hands on hips and head bobbing to the left and right like a swivel on her shoulders. She was angry and it was showing.

"Look, Mrs. Helms, I'm not in this business to be popular. I'm also not Mr. Congeniality when it comes to putting together tough cases, but I know that you, as well as me, want this murderer put away. Any slip-ups and a jury could easily acquit. I don't want that and I know you don't want that, especially with what Dan has been through. He deserves justice as much as the dead boy. Am I making myself clear to you ma'am?"

Lyla calmed significantly and sat down on the sofa next to Headly. Dan's upchucking had settled, so she could give the Prosecutor more of her attention.

"Mr. Headly, isn't my testimony good enough? I saw the kid in the bag as well as Dan did. It was both of us, you know."

"Dan made the pickup, Lyla, so he has a broader picture. He was helping Garrison put the body in the truck. That would sway a jury much further than you simply seeing the corpse. Besides, how will they know it wasn't Dan?"

Lyla's face reddened and she felt this meeting went far enough.

"How dare you even suggest such a thing! Dan's no killer. He has trouble with a smashed cat or dog in the road let alone murdering a child. I believe you should go and we'll pick this up later when cooler heads prevail."

Richard shook his head. She wasn't getting what he was trying to say. He thought that her asking him to leave was the best idea that came from this meeting.

"You're right, Lyla, let's do this another time and definitely at another place. I'll call you." Headly gathered his notes, placed them safely in his briefcase and headed for the door, and not a moment too soon.

"Good day, Ms. Helms."

Lyla gave him a dagger-in-the-eye look and Richard let himself out.

*

"You did not tell me I was dealing with complete idiots, Jack," Richard said into his speaker phone while driving home. "These people are as strange as they come. They had better come around if we're to have any chance with this case. Incidentally, I still think the case is weak, but hey, I'm aiming for a higher calling, so I'll deal with it."

"Calm down, Rich, it's going to be just fine. Don't get your ire up. I'll see that they cooperate without you having to endure anymore trouble. It's really no problem at all. Let me make some calls and everything will be under full control. Go home and have a drink, kick your feet back, relax."

Headly was now a sucker for Beauregard's soothing tone, so he agreed and went home, but had one more small comment before hanging up. "You'll take care of it, right?"

"It's really no problem at all," Jack said with a cunning edge.

Headly unwisely countered. "You know if this backfires, I'll take you with me Jack."

Jack was keeping his patience, even though Richard was severely testing it. "Number one, Richard, don't ever threaten me. I'll snap your career like a twig. Number two, trust me. If you don't, then you're no good to me and again, I will destroy you on the spot. If you'd like to take the chance, try me."

This time Richard backed down in earnest. "No problem, Jack, I trust you. We'll move forward."

"Good, now see how nice that feels? By the way, you'll be meeting with Jimmy Joseph's parents in a few days; I'll arrange it and let you know."

Richard finally hung up and this time went home without a worry.

Beauregard dialed up Lyla's cell and when she answered, he made it short and sweet. "Lyla, It's Jack. Do not fuck with Headly again or your job as dispatcher is ancient history, got it? Good."

Jack hung up before Lyla could comment and he knew he'd made his point. Lyla was still holding the phone to her ear on the other end, mouth hanging wide open and in complete shock. Jack was beginning to show signs of being unyielding, yet knew he had to be as tough as nails for the new job that soon awaited him. Nothing but *nothing* would stop him.

*

Jack was getting meaner and more impatient in other facets of life as well. Soo-Chin bore the brunt of Jack's tirades each morning while reading the newspaper together. "Stop paying attention to all the negative stuff people comment about. It's always going to be there, no matter how popular you are. As a matter of fact, stop reading that garbage altogether. It does you no good." Jack always clenched his teeth and threw the newspaper in the air. It would slowly float to the floor as he stormed out of the room. He would yell from a distance. "You don't know the difference; you're just a stupid pathologist."

Soo learned to let Jack blow off steam, figuring the stress of the upcoming election was getting under his skin. It hurt her when he would say such nasty things, but she always forgave him. She would eventually decide to sleep at her apartment until the election was over, giving Jack the space she thought he needed. She did spend much of her free time at Jack's place, though. Soo needed to keep the peace between him and Kyle, as Jack would ride his son hard about following in his footsteps. Kyle did the smart thing and retreated to his room when his dad would have his fits. It was his only true refuge, as Jack rarely crossed the boundary of Kyle's door. Jack always apologized and soothed his son's tattered ego, but these explosions were happening in closer proximity as the vote drew closer. Soo tried her best to keep Jack calm. "C'mon honey; let's go to your bedroom. I'll give you a rubdown and maybe even a really good *something special*." Soo licked her lips seductively.

Jack was usually open to that, but keeping focused long enough for her to finish her performance was getting tougher and tougher. It progressed from Jack chasing Soo around the house to her begging him to follow her into the bedroom. "Don't stop," became "hurry up." Snuggling in the afterglow of lovemaking turned into Jack instantly falling asleep, or jumping out of bed to "get back to work," even if it was four in the morning. Still, Soo-Chin stayed patient and understanding, knowing that his election would calm him significantly, *she hoped.*

Along with everything that was happening, Jack would see that strange flash of light from time-to-time. At first, it had him concerned that he may be having a problem such as stroke symptoms, or worse. After a few instances of seeing this light, and with no apparent physical problems spotted by his doctor, Jack chalked it up as a flash of power given to him as the "anointed one."

Going Through the Motions (Election Day)

It was finally time for the big election day in Nebraska. Tuesday, November 7th was here, and Jack was going over all his acceptance speech notes. He did not have concession notes, because he knew he wouldn't need them. Victory would be his, and the coveted leather recliner in that beautiful mansion is where he'd be sitting on January 21st. He knew he'd win despite the Garrison trial not being scheduled for another month or so, because as far as the public knew, the murderer was caught. There had been no other deaths since they put Garrison in jail, so it *must* be him. "The public can be so fickle." Jack would think, "It doesn't matter that the killer hadn't struck lately. It doesn't even matter whether the man being held was guilty or innocent. What mattered was that we caught someone." It was just as Jack had predicted it to be. Couple it with the fact that the victims were children, and you have a rabid community who'd love to try Garrison themselves. Dragging people through the streets or drawing and quartering had long since vanished, so the courts were a good enough option.

They'll put him in the electric chair, which is much more....*Humane*? As long as it's done through the system, that makes it okay, as far as the people were concerned. In a "what have you done for me lately world," Beauregard had done plenty to satisfy their thirst for justice.

*

It seemed hard to believe that Jack could possibly lose. There was just too much support for his challenger Mel Critchett to overcome. Mel had put together a victory and concession speech, so he was prepared for both possibilities. He knew deep inside he was an overwhelming underdog. The only way he figured to pull the upset was to kidnap 75 percent of Nebraska and hold them hostage until 8:00 p.m., when the polls closed. Even then, the remaining twenty-five percent would probably vote Beauregard in. Despite the odds, Critchett was a good sport and waited with everyone else to see the final results, which would be around midnight. In the meantime, he would spend the entire day touring the state with one final election push. His crowds were relatively small and he was resigning himself to going through the motions before conceding defeat. Jack, on the other hand, was also touring the state with his last ditch effort to garner more votes. Jack knew he would win, though, and that made a world of difference when it came to enthusiasm and confidence. Beauregard's main selling point was having captured the killer and having brought him to justice. He said it over and over throughout the day. "We know a man is innocent until proven guilty, but I believe we have our man. There has been no further killing since John Garrison was apprehended. That tells me we are doing our job and remaining tough on the criminals who think they will take over our beloved state."

The crowds cheered wildly with this point alone. Oh, he would talk a little about jobs, government, D.C. and even the future, but the citizens of Nebraska had a very short attention span. Jack Beauregard had done a lot for them, most of all protecting their children.

Mel's speeches were repetitive and boring. There was no real juicy gossip to share with the voters, so he ad-libbed and did what he could. Government, jobs, pro-choice and so on. It wasn't enough though. He needed to capture the murderer himself to have any chance, and everybody knew that it was way too late for that.

Jack finished his last runs around 6 p.m. and settled into the Lincoln Towers Hotel for what would probably be a victory speech later this evening. Mel went back to his campaign headquarters just outside Lincoln to watch what would probably be a sound thrashing by his opponent.

*

The news crews arrived at around 7:00 p.m. to both candidates' locations. News anchor Ed Brenner, who moderated the last debate between the challengers, would be stationed at Jack's headquarters while Vicki Ford, Ed's co-anchor, would provide coverage from the Critchett camp. At about 8:20, the polls started to trickle in with their results. Brenner took to the mike and made his first announcement.

"As of 8:25 p.m., Jack Beauregard had a 20-point lead over Mel Critchett. This with 4 percent of the precincts reported."

A wild cheer erupted within the banquet room they were stationed in.

"Vicki, do you have reaction from the Critchett camp?"

"Yes Ed, the mood here is somewhat somber after the 20-point lead was announced, but hope is still being held out that Mel Critchett can come back and win this thing."

At that very moment, Vicki walked up to Mel and asked questions. "We have Mel Critchett right here, Ed. How are you feeling about the lection thus far, Mel?"

"Well, Vicki, we have a long ways to go, and we aren't giving up. This election can still be ours. There are a lot of precincts yet to report."

Deep down, Mel still knew he was toast.

"There you have it from the Critchett camp. Back to you Ed."

The screen switched from a somber camp to a joyous one as you could literally feel the electricity in the room. Ed Brenner had one more blurb to throw out before signing off for the moment.

"We will be interrupting your regular schedule television programs from time to time to bring you more reports from here at Lincoln Towers. Ed Brenner reporting."

Jack was mingling with his constituents on the floor of the banquet room, shaking hands and thanking the contributors for their support. He was still tense, but he felt better knowing he had a sizable lead in the voting thus far. Kyle and Soo also worked the room, thanking people, shaking hands, toasting, and putting Jack on a pedestal. Critchett was doing the same thing at his camp, only there were fewer hands to shake and fewer pockets jingling.

*

The night wore on and now it was just after 11:00. Jack had been maintaining his 20-point lead all night and was all but a shoo-in for the nomination. At around 11:30, Ed Brenner made another appearance, this time on the stage at the front of the large hall. A microphone was set up and a television cameraman took his place in the front of the stage. Ed Brenner walked out with an envelope and a smile. “Ladies, gentlemen, could I please have your attention? Thank you. I have just been informed that Mel Critchett is ready to give a concession speech at his headquarters!”

Beauregard’s crowd again threw their collective hands up and shouted with glee. Jack was about to win.

“The latest polls,” Brenner announced, “show that Jack Beauregard has garnered a record 70 percent of the vote. Let’s hear it!” Big cheers again.

“There are now 90 percent of the precincts counted, so it appears we can unofficially crown Mr. Beauregard our new Governor of the State of Nebraska.” Big, wild, loud cheers this time.

“Let’s now go to Vicki Ford at the Critchett headquarters. Vicki?”

"Yes, hello Ed, hello everyone. As we speak, Mel Critchett is giving his concession speech. As everyone probably knows, this is a new Election Day record for the most votes received by a single candidate. I will be leaving here shortly to join you Ed, at the Beauregard camp. Until then, this is Vicki Ford reporting."

Behind Vicki, the workers were cleaning up posters, flyers, buttons and debris strewn across the floor. Mel's concession speech was all of five minutes and he disappeared. It was a quiet, drab room. Vicki, in the meantime, gathered her cameraman, equipment and whatever else belonged to her and bolted over to the Lincoln Towers.

*

Jack was still walking around shaking hands with Lt. Michaels at his side. It was then that a small-time reporter stopped Jack mid stride to ask questions. "So Jack, how's the trial preparation coming? Do you really think Garrison's guilty?"

Jack tried changing the subject. "If you have questions regarding tonight's election, I'd be happy to answer them for you."

"No, I have questions about the trial, Mr. Beauregard. I want to know how that's going."

Jack stared at the young reporter for a moment, and then whispered in Michael's ear; "quietly get rid of him." In an instant, Lt. Michaels commandeered the young man toward the exit door at the corner of the hall.

"Wait…hold on…I'm not through asking questions, I want an answer!"

"You're through tonight, son, have fun." Lt. Michael's insisted.

Michaels pushed the reporter out the door and into the chilly Nebraska air. His car was parked at least three city blocks away and he didn't have his coat. He walked around the front to get it, but was met at the door by none other than Michaels.

"I need my coat, sir." He said sarcastically.

"Too bad, kid, your coat is long gone. If you don't leave now, I'll take you into the alley and beat your scrawny ass. Would you like that?"

"Fine, I'll leave, but you guys are a crooked bunch." The reporter turned his tail and headed away, satisfied that his zinger had landed. The power of the governorship was already going to Beauregard's head, and Michaels knew it. The lieutenant had a job to do, though, and did it.

*

Jack met Kyle and Soo-Chin in a private room just behind the stage to celebrate with them a bit before giving his victory speech.

"Hey Kyle, I'll bet this gives you even more incentive to be my follower in the mansion, huh?"

"I'm really happy for you Dad," Kyle proudly said, "but this is just not my cup of tea, you know?"

"Nonsense, you will one day follow me in giving a victory speech."

The next comment out of Kyle's mouth was sharp and to the point. He stood up fast. "Don't you get it Dad? I don't want politics in my life. Just because you like it does not mean I do, now chill out, geez!"

Jack walked over and gave his son a sharp slap across his cheek. The look on Jack's face was that of anger. He gave an "I told you so" expression to the boy. Soo stepped between them and tried to calm Jack. "Jack, you have an acceptance speech to give, so go give it. We'll be out in a minute."

Beauregard left the room and headed for the stage.

Soo walked over and attempted soothing Kyle. "Are you alright? You know it's a tense night for your dad. Try to bear with him, okay?"

Kyle, shoving Soo's friendly hand away, responded. "I know it's his night, but he's so fucking nasty lately. I've never seen him like this."

"Neither have I Kyle, I'm in the same boat with you. Do me a favor and come out with me to listen to the speech."

"No," Kyle blurted, "I'll watch it from the bar and grill down the road." Kyle walked out and left Soo to take the stage with her boyfriend.

Jack noticed Kyle was missing during his speech, but had a large group of people to cater to. He did not have time at this moment to deal with whether his son was with, or against him. He'd deal with it tomorrow. Soo politely clapped and smiled. It was the most see through smile ever.

*

Here were the headlines from Wednesday morning's paper:

Lincoln Times

Beauregard crushes opponent Critchett 70-30 is widest advantage ever in state

AP- In a record rout, Jack Beauregard destroyed his opponent, Mel Critchett by 40 points in the gubernatorial election. The voting booths stayed open until 9:30 p.m. due to record amounts of people turning out. Upon exit polling, the consensus seemed to be that Beauregard was elected mainly for his handling of the two child murder cases in Lincoln. Mr. Beauregard stayed at the Lincoln Hotel late into the evening as he celebrated with family and friends. Beauregard will take the oath of office in January, thus ensuring a Beauregard will be in office again. Jack Beauregard is the fifth of his family to be Governor of Nebraska.

-Angela Page

Jack had his campaign managers fetch two-hundred papers from the Lincoln Times and bring them to his house. He wanted a copy for all his family and friends, plus a framed copy for his trophy room. That's the area where all of his life accomplishments were kept. Soo-Chin and Jack sat down for breakfast, but Kyle was missing. "Where's my boy?" Jack inquired to Soo.

"I think he was pretty upset last night. He may have stayed with a friend. You know Jack, I'm not completely in my rights saying so, but you need to calm down on that kid. Let him decide what to do with his life without all the pressure. He might surprise you."

"The only surprise I want is for him to follow me to that leather recliner at the mansion. Nothing less will do."

"You're so controlling Jack," Soo's eyes were glowing, "just like a cop."

Jack grabbed Soo by the arm just over her elbow and squeezed tight. "You too, huh? I'm really getting tired of you backing him up on every damn thing."

Soo ripped her elbow free and grabbed her coat as she headed for the door. "When you want to act like the old Jack, give me a call. Until then, stay away from me. You hurt my elbow, you jerk."

Soo left and Jack sat alone eating his breakfast. He gave the matter at hand one final thought, and then picked up the paper so he could gloat all over his pictures and praise. "I have been anointed by God to run this state. I am the king of the roost now."

Jack was the king. Jack was anointed. Jack was only getting started.

A Killer Watches

He was watching and patiently waiting. There was a slight sadness in the killer's world. He wanted so badly to kill again that he was actually shedding a tear. The killer was impatient. Who or what would ever want to have these kinds of tortured thoughts? It had to be a something very deep and very dark that was causing him to think this way. The killer had turned to Satan as a way to lash out at those who belittled him, tried to control and dominate him. Murder was the way of retribution; when the killer killed he was in control, he was dominant. The only creature who ruled him was Satan; his dark Lord.

The killer ventured out from time to time, even in broad daylight. He had been to one of Jack Beauregard's speeches and even shook his hand afterward. He was watching everything that was happening in the City of Lincoln and its outskirts. The killer knew what was going on. The chess pieces that came together to create the trial of John Garrison were very interesting. All the people involved were because this killer wanted them to be a part of it. He kidnapped and killed the boy, set-up Garrison, and was watching Beauregard win the election because of it. The killer was thrilled with Mr. Beauregard for pushing the old man's trial, even though he did not, could not, know if the geezer was guilty or not. The killer was very proud of the way he meticulously planned the chaos. Another Jack of Spades would be blessed and placed on the circle of death, which the killer used to curse the "bad ones." Why did he feel emotional pain followed by rage, then pain again… rage, then pain? He had no idea how to control the emotional aspects of that which attacked his brain. This killer *simply* murdered and felt right about it, but lately that had changed into more of a challenge, and that was dangerous. It was hazardous for the future of all children that lived within his range. He was watching and waiting for the next opportunity. Not until after the trial, though. He did not want to interrupt the plan that he had unleashed and would spring forth after.

*

The steel bowl was filled with the blood of the dead children, along with urine, tears, and saliva. It was placed on a wire-like cooking utensil and a fire was placed underneath it. The killer used fifty-two black Jacks of Spades to stoke the flame. The cards were treated with the same mixture as the bowl, along with a bit of kerosene to allow it the ability to light and burn. The stink that rose from this hideous mixture was gruesome and nauseating. That was what he wanted; disgust, torment, and evil. The killer called upon his master Satan to accept the sacrifice being offered. He raised his hands and prayed; hoping the leader of the dark world would hear it and come.

"OH HAIL SATAN, MY DEMON OF WORSHIP, MY RIGHTER OF WRONGS, ACCEPT THIS SACRIFICE! I COME BEFORE YOU WITH THE BLOOD OF CHILDREN, THE BLOOD OF ANIMALS, AND THE WASTE OF HUMANITY."

The killer repeated this invocation five times, and then the fire that burned below it flamed out. He waited for a minute, then picked up the awful mixture and chanted once more while holding the bowl toward the middle of the pentagram.

"MY SATAN, MY EVIL DARK FRIEND, I ACCEPT THIS SACRIFICE UNTO YOU. I DRINK THE STINK OF HUMANITY IN YOUR NAME. MAY THE POWER OF YOUR DARKNESS ENTER MY HUMAN SOUL."

With that, he drank the vile mixture and felt what he believed to be a surge in power, an increase in energy and a refreshing outlook. Despite all his efforts, was Satan even present for this horrible ritual? The killer didn't even know how to worship the dark prince. The mortal was ad-libbing as he went, but thought to be getting the Devil's attention. No matter because he continued with the rituals and customs.

*

The last of the killer's deeds was to stand before a mirror and cut. He cut himself along the inner thigh, from just under the crotch all the way down to his knee. It had to be done on both sides in the exact same direction. When the knife penetrated the skin, the killer felt the warm blood run down his leg and the pain exit the body. The blood was collected in a small plastic rectangular plastic holder. This blood would be mixed with other various fluids for the next ritual. Already cut, he took off his mask and used it to rub himself in the injured areas. The blood collected would add to the horrifying concoction. The mask was placed back on his head and face after this vile ritual. The stink and smell of nasty leather, body odor and blood was a comfort.

*

He planned and surveyed. He thought and figured. What is the best way to destroy more people's lives? The killer paced back and forth in the lair, a rat hanging from the leather strap connected to his hip. The strap tightened around the rodent's neck, causing its eyes to bulge out unnaturally. The killer was smart and calculating. His plans were hatched. The time of reckoning couldn't come soon enough. In the meantime, he waited and watched. He dreamed about the next child that he would strangle the life out of. The deed would be done soon. The killer continued pacing until he dissolved the nervous energy built up inside. He would go into town and stake out the next target. This killer felt the need to stay sharp and ready for future kills.

One Final Push

Amy was feeling better than she had in quite a while. The medication was helping to suppress the visions that had been haunting her, although they were still faintly present. The voices also remained, but were more distant. The meetings with Dr. Baxter seemed to be doing the trick in helping her deal with her past. She knew it would still be a tough road ahead.

The young attorney was studying the case, and couldn't come up with a whole lot of additional information because it didn't exist. The cross-examinations would be the key, as she had to convince the jury of reasonable doubt. To Amy, reasonable doubt included a lack of evidence, but as she's learned through the years of studying and practicing, juries can be very odd and sometimes ignorant of what the correct verdict should be. If they bought the story the state would give them, it would be curtains for Garrison. Amy definitely *thought* she could win outright. Less than that, she would hope for life in a prison rather than death in a chair. She figured the case to move rather quickly, being that only a few people would be testifying. The questioning techniques would surely tell the tale. She had seen

Headly in action and always liked his style. He has a gift of putting the words into your mouth. Yes, he's that good. Amy thought she was good too, and that would come in very handy for the upcoming showdown, although she still had some doubts.

*

"I don't know, Jack. This case scares the bejesus out of me. I don't want to lose, but I so want the AG job." Richard and Jack were talking at Jack's apartment he kept in downtown Lincoln. They were going over any last minute details that needed to be addressed.

"Stop your constant worrying, Rich; it's going to be fine. I'm getting real sick of telling you that."

"Look here Jack. If I lose this case it's no skin off your hide. You just keep your little seat in the mansion while I have a blemish in my record. I may drop out Jack."

These were words Richard should have kept to himself. He inadvertently angered the Governor-elect. Jack grabbed Richard by the shirt just under his neck and whirled him around, slamming him into the wall. It looked and sounded very painful.

"Stop that infernal nonsense talk, Richard. I'm losing my patience with you real fast."

"Unhand me! You hurt my back! Unhand me or I'll spill everything about your offer to me!"

Beauregard pulled out his .357 from the hip holster he was wearing and stuck the barrel of the gun on Richard's right cheek. A dark circle appeared at the crotch of Headly's trousers. Richard saw and felt the flash of Jack's power.

"Did I hear you say you'll quit? Did I also hear you say you'd spill all the beans about our little deal? You had better answer the question right, Richard, because there are no repeats. This gun's locked and loaded."

"Did I say quit? I didn't mean *quit-quit*. I just mean for the night, that's all." Headly felt the urine release from his bladder and begin collecting in his underwear. He bore down to stop the flow.

"N-no worries Jack. I'll keep m-my mouth shut. I'm just a little n-nervous before the trial. It's just my w-way, that's all. Y-you understand? R-right Jack?"

Jack re-holstered his gun and released his hand from Richard's collar. The answers had been correct.

"Don't disappoint me again, Richard. I hate being disappointed." Jack then moved within inches of Richard's face. "Don't you ever fuck with me, Headly. By the way, the bathroom is right around that corner. Go clean yourself up. You're pathetic."

*

Lyla had been taking good care of Dan. He was starting to come around and seemed to be doing well with a combination of therapy and Lyla's help. She usually stopped by his place after work and stayed with him until about 10:00 or so, when she would have to get home and take care of her business, and then get some sleep before the following day of work. On the weekends she stayed a few hours longer, which suited Dan fine. Lately, they had been taking car rides to the courthouse to practice for the day they really had to go.

Dan was so shocked by what he saw, he was afraid to do anything or go anywhere that brought back the memory. When the drives first started, it was usually a couple of blocks, then back home with Dan suffering a major panic attack. It advanced to more miles away from the house and closer to the courthouse. Before he knew it, Dan Wheeler could drive far enough with Lyla to actually see the court. These were baby steps, but he was on schedule to make it to the trial. They finally reached the pinnacle together, which was a drive through the parking lot, staying longer and longer each time.

Dan truly appreciated Lyla, and she him. About a month before the trial, Lyla was at Dan's place and was dirt tired. She decided to just sleep at his house that night. She didn't have work the next day and didn't feel like driving home.

"I'll sleep on the couch Dan, if that's okay."

"Absolutely not Lyla," he said, causing her to have a minor letdown from fear of being sent home. "You sleep in my bed and I'll sleep on the couch."

Lyla was happy. She did not want to drive and she liked being with Dan. He was as polite as he could be plus he was coming back to the real world. Maybe he could even work soon. That was her hope.

Lyla told Dan she was jumping in the shower to freshen up. Dan was watching TV and nodded to her. As the water in the shower ran, Dan started thinking impure thoughts. "Gosh, she's in my shower. I wonder what she looks like naked."

Dan looked down and saw that something was happening which hadn't happened in some time. He was getting excited, and it was over Lyla. Dan rose from his chair, made a minor adjustment for comfort sake and headed to the bathroom door, which was slightly ajar.

"Should I go in? Nah, stop this silliness."

Dan was confused, his first two fingers tapping his lower lip. He thought about it and came up with a great plan. He would just barely nudge the door open and see if he would get a reaction. If she flipped out, he'd simply apologize and go back to his chair. You know, "Sorry Lyla, I forgot you were in here." That type of pathetic excuse.

He very slowly and carefully nudged the door open; he felt the guilt coarse through his veins. He peeked in and saw Lyla standing in the shower, facing him, with her hands rubbing shampoo into her scalp. Her eyes were closed because of the soap, and Dan was able to stand and watch her for a moment. He couldn't believe how good she looked for a woman in her forties. Her curves were smallish, round and smooth, and she appeared calm and relaxed. A tiny puff of brown hair sat nicely between Lyla's thighs. No longer being able to resist temptation, Dan entered the bathroom, dropped his robe on the floor and stepped in behind Lyla. He was shocked when she turned around and gave him a perusal from top to bottom, and then smiled. He kind of thought he would be thrown out on his ear, but wasn't. Their mouths met softly and sensually. Both tongues doing a soft, sensitive dance between each other's lips. Lyla picked up the soap, rubbed some suds into a washcloth and began washing Dan's body. She started at his neck and worked her way down. Dan felt as if he would explode at any moment. She paid especially close attention to his manhood, which Lyla found surprisingly, yet pleasantly large. After finishing her little wash-up routine, she again kissed Dan's mouth. She warmed his neck, his chest, and his mid-section with soft pecks, and slowly moved back up until she could caress his mouth and lips again. Her eyes met his. His eyes rolled back in his head as she continued to kiss him and message his lower region. He returned her touches with those of his own, sending Lyla into a moaning ecstasy.

The night was long and sensual. They made love and passionately satisfied each other. It went on for six hours until she fell asleep in Dan's strong and reassuring arms. Dan lay next to her awake for a short time, smiling while at the same time wondering what the hell he was doing. He thought this woman to be so much better sexually than any of the younger girls he'd been with. She was a bit more mature, thus able to better satisfy a man. Dan finally fell asleep next to her, temporarily pleased with his wonderful night.

*

It was time for Amy to go see Dr. Baxter again. She started thinking that this would be her last visit because she was improving so rapidly. The visions were waning, the voices were fading and Amy's stomach aches were improving. The wrinkles forming under her eyes had tightened back up and looking at herself in the mirror was like it used to be, beautiful olive colored skin that was taught, firm and young. The fiery attorney was still working hard on the case, but had taken a day here and there to relax and try to enjoy life. Amy had turned down all other possible clients while this case took her attention. She headed for the Doctor's office, confident and happier. Dr. Baxter would still encourage her to drop off the case, though. Amy wouldn't hear of it.

Amy had gone to the local bookstore and bought CD's that dealt with relaxation, self-hypnosis, and breathing techniques to help her better deal with stress. Coupled with the therapy and medication, Amy figured herself to be cured and ready to start dealing with the rigors of life on her own. A tough woman, but oh so stubborn.

The self-help CD was playing when she arrived at Baxter's office. Amy felt relaxed and had a sense of well-being. She walked in with a slight arrogance about her. She wanted to show the Doctor how nicely she was coming along.

"Hello, Amy, please stretch out on the couch."

The Doctor gave her a wave towards the couch, much like the models on a game show do when they introduce the fancy new prizes revealed as the curtain opens.

"Are you doing okay, dear? How's this week been for you?"

"I'm doing great, Doctor, and I think I'm ready to be on my own from here on out."

Doctor Baxter squinted Amy's way and placed her index fingers across her lips, supporting her chin with her thumbs as she listened to Amy.

"You have given me all the help I can soak in. Standing on my own two feet is the next hurdle, which I can and will handle. I've gone full circle."

"I'm going to agree to disagree, Amy. I really think you've made strides, yes, but I don't think you're ready to go on without my help."

"C'mon, Doctor, I've been doing better than good. No more visions, very little in the way of voices and my anxiety level has dropped dramatically." Amy was pleading.

"Look, Amy, coming here to speak with me and release that stress that had built up in you is why you feel better. You still need to practice your techniques and I'm the one who can coach you. If you keep coming for a while longer, say three or four more months, I'll teach you how to avoid these visions and voices forever."

The attorney remained stubborn and undaunted. She was getting ahead of herself. That's what Amy did, though. She tried to control every single situation. Sometimes, help was needed.

"I'm putting the rest of my energy into the trial Doctor. If afterwards I need to see you, I'll let you know."

Dr. Baxter tried scolding and threatening Amy to help her see the point she was trying to make.

"If you don't come to see me, no more meds. If you think you have this beat, you're very wrong. You may well find yourself back to square one, Amy, and that can be dangerous. As for the trial, I know you're going through with it even though I think you need to stand down."

Now Amy's ire was lit. She does not like being told what to do or how to do it. She also thought that Doctor Baxter may be in it for the money.

"I can't believe you'd actually have the gall to pull me off those meds, Doctor. You know it's more the meds and less your blabbering bullshit that helps me feel better. I'm tired of talking about my screwed up, perverted dad and my drunken, useless mom. I'm sick of going over the past and rehashing the bad memories that mess me up in the first place."

"Amy, please calm yourself. You're not seeing the point clearly."

Amy leapt up off the couch and grabbed her purse and coat, ready to head out the door.

"Can't you get it through your thick skull that I'm tired of talking about it? Don't you know when enough is enough? Good Lord in Heaven, can you just shut the hell up? If you didn't hear me the first time, I said I don't want to talk about incest anymore. I don't want to think of my perverted, sick father or my hopeless and stupidly drunk mom! GOD!"

Amy reared around and headed out the door with a fury and determination. She didn't need those damn pills anymore. The bottle went flying across the room, bashed into the wall and broke open. Oodles of little white tablets rolled under the desk, around the Doctor's feet, and toward the center of the room. Amy was talked out. It was time for her to move on and do this herself.

"Foolish woman." Doctor Baxter thought to herself. The door slammed behind Amy.

Doctor Baxter leaned back in her seat, the office chair creaking with her movements. She shook her head and hoped Amy would see the light, and soon… before it was too late.

*

Dan Wheeler woke up and found Lyla Helms in his arms. He didn't know quite what to do. He had slept with his boss last night. He made love to her, or did he? Perhaps he only banged or screwed her. He wasn't sure. He slowly freed his completely numb right arm from under her, and then quietly snuck out of the bed. Dan stood before her, taking a long look and thinking about the night before. She lay in the bed with one leg hanging out from under the sheet and the covers only concealing up to her belly button, thus exposing her "not as ample and firm as he first thought" breasts. Dan was a tad sickened, not by the fact that he'd had sex with Lyla, but because she *was* Lyla. He thought he should not be having this type of relationship with her. What was done was done, though, so he had to face it and accept it. Dan slipped into the shower to wash her perfumed scent off him.

Lyla arose from the dreamy world she had been a part of just minutes earlier. A smile graced her face as she stretched and yawned. The night before was wonderful, and she felt rested and ready to face the world. It was, by far, the best night of sleep she'd had in what seemed like ages. Hearing the shower already running, Lyla marched into the bathroom as naked as the day she was born. She had felt no shame nor had second thoughts about the night before, as Dan did. She stepped into the shower behind Dan and touched his slight love handles.

"Oh my!" Dan jumped. "Ah, er…good morning, Lyla. What are you doing in here?"

"Good mornin' silly. I just wanted to see you first thing today. It was wonderful, Dan. That was the best night I've had in years!"

Dan was visibly shaking as Lyla attempted to soap his back for him.

"That's okay, Lyla, I can get that. Um, er, uhh." The words escaped him. "Can I kinda' ask you to wait until I'm done here? You can have the next shower."

At that precise moment, Lyla got the point. Her smile turned into a frown and her hands fell to her side. It was a tough pill to swallow.

"Sure Dan, I'll just go. I see how it is now. Fuck 'em and forget 'em."

"Lyla, please," Dan said as he turned to face her. "I didn't mean to sound rude. I just don't know if what we did is, what's a good word? The right thing. Do you get my drift?"

"Yeah, I get your drift alright." Her voice was cracking. "I served as your latest whore last night." Dan lowered his head.

She quickly removed herself from the shower and toweled up, now embarrassed by her nakedness. She stepped into the living room and started to cry a bit, then composed herself. She dressed, gathered her things and left for her house. Dan finished his shower and stepped out, knowing he had severely hurt her feelings. He knew she'd be gone when he finished. Dan would be on his own from now on.

*

Richard was very careful not to tick off Jack again. A gun up your snout tended to make you more aware of your wording. Headly saw Jack a few days later and offered his apology for being a troublesome prosecutor. Beauregard would not shake; he only gave Richard another warning.

"Like I said, Rich, you don't fuck with me, and I won't fuck with you. It's that simple."

Richard nodded yes and said no more, in fear of getting punched in the eye. It's amazing how you get the point when you "get the point."

Jack had one more thing to say before leaving Richard. It was yet another warning. "Don't lose this case, Headly, or there will be trouble."

Now the pressure doubled on the Prosecutor. He not only had to try the case, he had to guarantee a victory. A jury can be a peculiar group that blows all your best laid plans right up in your face.

"I gotcha' Jack. I won't lose," Richard said. Jack was already down the hall and heading out.

"Pompous idiot." Headly quietly whispered. "I wish he'd drop over dead." Being the nervous type, Headly worried about his mental well-being. He felt angrier than usual. He wrote it off as a reaction to the pressure Jack was putting on him.

*

Jack had some patching up to do. He had his son angry again and Soo was not a happy woman. He knew he really needed to fix up the situation before he could move forward. Beauregard hadn't realized it yet, but he was becoming a real jerk. He was bossy, arrogant, cocky and manipulative to everybody he came across. He felt that he needed to be tough to be governor, but he seemed to be missing the point. Soo had said it herself; He needed to pick and choose his arguments, not look for them. In this case, power was corrupting, not being used in a positive manner. To be honest, a lot of people felt that Jack really didn't have the first clue on leadership. He would balk if anyone would dare say that to him, so nobody would. Jack felt that he was king of the world. It would backfire on him if he wasn't careful.

*

Jack arrived back at his place around noon, and called Soo-Chin to ask her over for a talk. She agreed and arrived about thirty minutes later. Kyle was at school, so Jack would catch up with him later.

"Hi, doll. I've missed you a lot."

"It's only been a day, Jack, so spare me the theatrics."

Beauregard had to calm himself from the inside out. His temper was already flaring and if he wanted an adult conversation, he would need to suppress the anger.

"A day without you Soo is like a day in hell. I'm so very sorry I lashed out at you. I feel like a real schmuck."

"You should," Soo said with presence, "and I'm still listening."

Soo-Chin stood before Jack with her hands on her hips and her body cocked to the left, thus putting all her weight on her left leg. She had a spoiled baby look on her face with her thin black hair hanging slightly in her eyes.

"I love you, Soo. I want so badly to be your husband. I can't stand life without you."

"Are you *really* sorry, Jack, or just feeding me another line of bullshit?"

"No, I truly mean it. I want to marry you. I want you to be my wife." Jack pulled a small box out of his pocket and bent down to one knee.

"Will you marry me?" Jack asked with a smile.

Soo opened the box and saw one hell of a stone reflecting back at her. This was probably the first of many gifts that would come her way in the next few years. She picked material over substance.

"Yes, YES Jack, I will! I will be your wife."

They clutched each other as tightly as they could and headed for the bedroom, clothes flying off as they went. Jack was very proud of himself. That day, they had the best sex ever.

"One crisis averted," he thought with a sly, tongue-in-cheek grin.

*

It wasn't one hour since Amy left the Doctor and already the voices seemed louder.

"Amy, Amy, **A-m-m-m-y**," they chanted.

Amy chalked it up as her mind playing tricks after her heated meeting with Baxter. At this point, she was far too determined to turn back. Once this girl made up her mind, there was no stopping her. She was stubborn and simply willed herself forward. After a few minutes, the voices settled down.

"See? I have the ability to shut it off. I will NOT be consumed by these figments of my imagination."

There was a lot to do on the eve of the trial and Amy boor down to work. She brought everything she'd need to the office with her. Clothes, female essentials, plus food and drink. She locked herself into her "home away from home" and studied as hard as she could. This was a big deal in Amy's life. It was the trial that could make her a household name in Nebraska and perhaps beyond. The notoriety was secondary to Amy, but would certainly help business.

"Preparedness is the key," she preached. "Especially since I'm facing one of the best in Headly."

As the night wore on, Amy became aware of the voice again. This time it was just the young Amy and no one else. She attempted to will it away, but it wouldn't stop. She had saved a couple pills just in case of emergency and in her mind, this constituted one. She popped the meds, washed them down with water and tried to get back on task. Young Amy wouldn't allow it. As the clock struck 11:30 p.m., Amy looked up from her desk and was again confronted with her past.

"I'm here to take you home, Amy. I'm here to save you." The teenage version said with an outstretched hand. Amy balked.

"Well, I'm not going home, dear. I have a trial to conduct, so don't mess with me."

The young Amy roared her disapproval. **"YOU WILL COME HOME. I WILL SEE THAT YOU DO. I NEED YOU. I WANT YOU. YOU ARE A PART OF ME, AMY!"**

Amy shut her eyes tight and screamed at the top of her lungs. **"GO AWAY! LEAVE ME ALONE!!"**

As she opened her eyes back up, the vision had disappeared. This relieved Amy in a significant way. It was like a large two ton weight had lifted off her. Amy was pleased with her resolve.

"I'm going through with the trial, and nobody, human or otherwise, will stop me."

*

Amy Fraser rehearsed and prepared. Richard Headly rehearsed and prepared. Dan Wheeler rehearsed and prepared. Lyla, Mr. and Mrs. Joseph, Soo-Chin, Robert Long, and Lt. Michaels all rehearsed and prepared. Jack Beauregard watched Headly rehearse and prepare. The trial was starting the next morning and everyone needed to be ready. The Honorable Judge Donald Wiley was to preside over the biggest case in Nebraska's long and rich history. It had to be right. It had to be accurate. Potential jurors were on the edge of their seats. Summons had been mailed and received, so each and every person who held one knew they may be a part of the grand stage. The news at 11, featuring Ed Brenner and Vicki Ford, talked extensively about the action that would take place in court. John Garrison sat in his cell, wishing the heart attack had spared him the seat at the defense table. He was worried, but not like you'd think. John was more obnoxious and annoyed than he was overly concerned. The trial of the century was set to begin. How it would go was anybody's guess. One thing was sure, though. It would be a circus.

A killer also prepared.

During

Earth: Winter, Old Age, Night, Feminine Energy

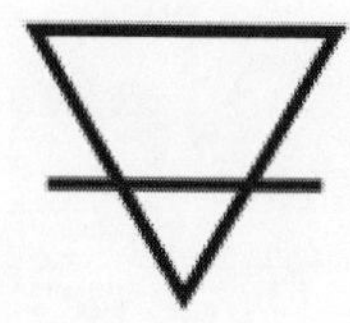

The Trial of John Garrison

Day 1

Jack Beauregard milled about the court building. He was patiently waiting for Richard, while at the same time mugging for cameras and conversing with a few VIP's. Jack had spoken with Lt. Michaels earlier and ordered him to transport Garrison to the courthouse for the jury selection. He had not spoken with Amy in the last couple of weeks and did not know if any motions would come up from the defense side. He really didn't care much either way, because Richard would handle it.

The Governor-elect was a bit nervous. Not so tense that it would ruin his day, but enough to keep him on edge and in his sharpest state of mind. That's what he thrived on: tense, emotional, troubling subjects that would send an ordinary person scurrying for cover from the onslaught of anxiety. As Jack finally took a seat and sipped on his coffee, a local newspaper reporter walked up and asked for an impromptu interview. Beauregard granted it.

"Mr. Beauregard, have you and the prosecutor built a strong defense in the Garrison case, set to begin today?"

"Yes. We have this man dead to rights" and I feel with the superior council we have working for the state, there's really nowhere for Mr. Garrison to run. He can't outsmart us, because we have the best police force in the country."

"How about the defense lawyer, Amy Fraser? Tell me what you've heard about her and what you may expect from her side."

"Honestly, she's a rookie. She has never covered anything this intense in her young career, and I do not expect her to hold up against Richard Headly." Jack took a long slow sip out of his cup. "I also think she's in way over her head. She really has no idea what kind of tricks we have up our sleeves. She'll learn a hard lesson in this case."

"What kind of tricks, sir? Please elaborate."

"You'll have to watch and see, young man. I'm certainly not going to simply give away our strategy."

The reporter frantically jotted down shorthand in his fold up notepad while breathing hard through his somewhat congested nostrils. It was an annoying whistling sound.

"One more question Jack, please. Is it possible that Ms. Fraser could pull it off and win, thus severely hurting your public approval rating before it even gets comfortable?"

"Impossible! Let me tell you two things, sir. Number one, we will win, and number two, the state elected me for more reasons than this case. The trial is but a drop in the bucket in the big picture."

"I spoke with a lot of folks, Mr. Beauregard, and the consensus was that since you had the killer at your fingertips, they voted for you."

"How many people did you include in your 'poll?' The consensus of this state, sir, is that they wanted a leader and a winner. With me they get both. Polls mean very little now, since I *was* elected."

The reporter looked up and saw Amy Fraser walk through the front doors. Jack also caught a glimpse of the stunning attorney. Jack gave a short thought in his head to what it might be like to bed her down. He tried to push the thought away, but his loins had other ideas. The reporter broke Jack's perverted chain of thought.

"Excuse me sir and thank you for the time. I'd like to talk to you again sometime."

"Yes, sure young man, anytime. Just call my office."

With a quick handshake, the reporter dashed over to talk to Ms. Fraser, who was rapidly being surrounded by other media members. Jack appeared a tad miffed as the attention shifted to the "rookie" lawyer. He arose, uttered a small throat clearing "ahem" and made his way towards Wiley's courtroom.

*

"Ms. Fraser, Ms. Fraser, please! May we ask you some questions?"

Amy greeted the throng with a wary smile as she weaved her way between the tape recorders, pens, flashbulbs and the mass of humanity.

"Give me a few minutes' people, please. I have some items I need to attend to, and then I'll speak."

"But Ms. Fraser, please just one question. Can you win this case, Ms. Fraser? Do you have a chance?"

"I promise I'll talk with you later. I have to move. Excuse me please."

Amy finally reached the light at the end of the human tunnel and dashed toward the courtroom. She moved very quickly on her feet while still maintaining a calm appearance. Only certain people could run and look like they were still walking. Amy was one of them. She finally reached the courtroom and unloaded her armful of folders on the table. Along with this she had a rolling briefcase that followed her every move. It never left her side and always showed up wherever she did. It was as if it had its own personality, but alas, it was simply leather and wheels. No emotion or caring. It carried Amy's thoughts and ideas. She never let it out of her sight.

The courtroom was already filling up for the Judge's 8:30 arrival and no one wanted to be left on the outside looking in. It was 8 a.m. in Lincoln and was to be the biggest day for this town in some time. Amy peered to her right and saw a trooper directing court traffic.

"Have a seat, have a seat; you, you there, have a seat."

"Have a seat" appeared to be the day's language of the law.

Amy heard a small "psst" behind her. She turned and there was Robert Long, dressed to the nines in a slick, three-piece suit. She shook Bob's hand and asked if he was ready for action.

"Are you nervous Bob? I know I am. I do hope you've studied up for the trial."

"Naw. Ain't nothin' to be nervous about. Just answer the questions and get on outta here, that's all."

"Do me a favor Bob and try to remember what I told you when we went through our training sessions. Speak clearly and concisely and try to use proper grammar. Don't slur and please use the whole word. Instead of 'ain't', use 'aren't'. Don't say 'nothin'', say 'nothing'. Can you remember this Bob?"

"Oh! Fer sure, Amy. Don't cha worry none about me."

Robert was smiling as he said this. Amy simply sighed and put her fingers on her temples. Was it a headache already? She hoped not. This was going to be a long haul. "Good grief!" she uttered.

As Amy was surveying the courtroom, she caught a glimpse of the Joseph parents entering. Mrs. Joseph stood tall and with good posture. Her shoulders were placed high and firm, while the rest of her appeared so-so. Her blond hair was unbrushed and her aura was dull. The blouse she wore was way too tight, and her ample cleavage spilled out of the top of it. Mr. Joseph appeared to be his same meek, pussycat self. She barked and he obeyed. He even wiped the seat in which she would sit, and then covered it with a small handkerchief. Amy thought him whipped and trained. "What a pussy!" She thought silently.

Lyla Helms and Dan Wheeler sat behind the prosecution's table, but were about four rows apart. Lyla sat quietly near the rear while Dan looked very uncomfortable ahead of her. She stared daggers straight into the back of his skull. Amy thought there may have been a falling out of some sort, but didn't know for sure. In fact, she really didn't want to know.

As Amy was turning back toward the front of the court, she saw the young Amy. She was sitting dead-center; last row, with her arms crossed and a pale, rigid look on her face. She said nothing while glaring at Amy. The young Attorney was transfixed on the teen-age version of herself.

"Is it going to start now?" Amy wondered. "This would be one hell of a time for that."

"Ammy-AMMY-**AAAMMMYYY!**"

Startled, Amy took a quick deep breath and turned back to her right. Standing before her was Richard Headly.

"Amy? Amy? **MS. FRASER?**"

Headly was trying to get her attention. Ms. Fraser shook her head and returned to the real world.

"What? Huh? Oh. Mr. Headly, oh I'm sorry, I was deep in thought. Sorry, how are you?"

Richard looked at her with a confused look, one eyebrow up.

"You alright, Ms. Fraser? Do you need some water or something?"

"No, no. I'm good. Are we about ready to begin?"

"You better snap to it Ms. Fraser, or this will be much easier than I originally thought."

Amy gave him a half sneer and looked back over her shoulder to the spot where her young trouble-maker sat. It was empty. No one there. Amy breathed a slight sigh and fumbled with her notes.

The side door near the jury box opened and in walked John Garrison. He was shackled and cuffed at his wrists and ankles. Boy, Amy was glad to see him. Now it felt real.

*

"What in gotdamn hell ya lookin' at lady?" These were Garrison's very first words upon entering the court. They were directed to Mrs. Joseph. John had his neck craned in her direction.

"Well speak up, blondie. You got a problem with me?"

Mrs. Joseph ran a finger slowly across her neck, then flipped the old coot a quick bird. Amy saw the exchange and immediately stepped between them. She spoke to Garrison in a quiet, calmed tone.

"Mr. Garrison. I need you to settle down this instant. They'll turn your ass around and take you out of here so fast your head will spin off its swivel."

"Well you tell that fake-tittied bimbo ta keep to herself. I don't need her drama along with everyone else's."

"That's the victim's mother, John. She's a little upset right now. This is an emotional time for her."

"Well, if they'd catch the gotdamn killer, she'd feel better now wouldn't she?" Garrison dead-panned.

Amy felt the sarcasm that dripped from John's lips. She knew she would be exhausted after this whole thing was over, no matter what the outcome. Amy Fraser, lawyer and baby-sitter.

It was time for Amy to explain to John for a second time about courtroom etiquette and what to expect on this first day. "John, I really need you to behave yourself in here. If you want me to win this case for you, you must cooperate with me wholeheartedly. The jury, after it's been chosen and finalized, will frown on your antics. Do you understand me sir? Any questions?"

"Yeah, I got a question. When are they gonna serve lunch? I haven't had nothin' good to eat in forever."

Amy took a deep, cleansing breath and continued her tutorial with the grump. "I'm going to tell you the same thing I told Robert. You must speak in a clear, concise manner. Nothing else is going to cut the mustard. Do you get that? I need you to get that, John."

"Yes, Ms. Fraser, I get it. What do you think? I was born yesterday?" John was curling his lips and attempting to legitimately speak with manners and correct grammar. He was used to speaking in an inflection of his choosing and did not want to conform. Call it set in his ways. If he wanted any opportunity to escape this mess, though, he was going to have to follow orders to a fault. Amy kept the pressure on John so he'd at last try.

"Amy, what is it I do if I disagree with somethin' that's said and I don't like it?"

"You allow me to do my job. That's what you've paid me for John. Don't try to slip in any words at all. I want you to sit stone-face and quiet. Please John, I beg you."

"Okay. I'll write down what I disagree with and you can look at it. Don't expect me to be different, though, just because I'm up against somethin' I never did. I should be home sleepin' in today."

"Well, you're not. It's reality in its worst form. Now promise me you'll behave. Don't make it tougher on me than it needs to be. I'm nervous enough already with everything that's going on."

"So what exactly is it that's goin' on, Ms. Fraser? You ain't felt nerves till ya sit in my seat. Whatever it is, it can't be that bad. Don't go gettin' all jittery on me now."

"Don't worry about me, John. Just keep your wits about you."

Amy started shuffling through her paperwork and heard her name again from the back of the courtroom. It was eerie and made Amy very cautious. She could not show weakness though, as she had a man's life in her hands and he was sitting right next to her.

"*Ammyy*!" was said in a quick, short whisper.

"***AMY!*** *Don't let the old man die Amy*."

Amy turned to peruse the courtroom and saw young Amy again sitting in the rear with Jimmy Joseph sitting next to her. They both wore sly, intimidating smiles on their pale, blue faces. Young Amy had her arm around the little boy as if she were comforting him. Were these actual ghosts Amy was seeing? Were they just figments of her imagination? Whatever they were, they seemed as real as they did when she saw them over the last few months. Her heartbeat began to race and she felt a hot flash come over her. She turned back to the front of the court, poured a glass of water and swigged it down. Amy wanted to splash her face with it, but that would obviously draw negative attention. She turned back around and they were gone…..for now.

"Why now?" Amy asked herself. "At least wait until after the trial. I don't need this now!"

There was no sense of time, as far as the young Amy and others were concerned. Could it be that the pressure Amy was feeling perpetuated the voices and visions? Time would certainly tell.

*

"Order! ORDER IN THE COURT! THE HONORABLE DONALD C. WILEY WILL NOW ENTER. PLEASE RISE AND REMOVE YOUR CAP IF WEARING ONE."

Following the announcement from the bailiff, the Honorable Don Wiley entered his court and made his way up to the bench. In his courtroom, the pledge of allegiance was to be spoken every morning, so without delay, the bailiff started the chant.

"I pledge allegiance, to the flag, of the United States of America……."

Once finished, Wiley gave permission for everyone to sit and then began his lecture on courtroom rules and behavior that he expected in his domain.

Don Wiley was a little man. He was no more than 5'2" and couldn't be 130 lbs. on his heaviest day. He wore his hair around his head, but not on top. He was as bald as a bowling ball except for the tuft that circled ear to ear and had grayed through his thirty years on the bench.

Mr. Wiley had started as a state prosecutor thirty-five years ago, and was known as a very gentle man who took issue with other prosecutors who brought up charges based on circumstantial evidence. This point alone would bode well for Garrison, seeing as the state had no physical proof of his contribution to the murder. What did not pose an advantage for John was Wiley's faith in the jury system, which he absolutely swore by. Even if he thought they were wrong, which was rare, he kept his faith because he thought juries of your peers were the best decision makers one could hope to have. Mr. Wiley had a reputation for being fair and unbiased, along with patient, and could be tested for a very long time before reacting. Lawyers liked this aspect of his rule, because they could "push the envelope" so to speak. All in all, Garrison and Fraser lucked out to get this Judge assigned to the trial. It could have been much worse.

*

"I expect a quiet courtroom. I expect a clean fight and I expect above all else, respect. No outbursts will be directed at the defendant or the state. If I hear outbursts, I will have you removed. Mr. Headly, Ms. Fraser, while I consider this a war in my court. I do not allow unfair fighting. You will conform to my rules or this trial will be a long one for the both of you. As for the people sitting in the gallery, I have the same rules. You will not badger or bother either team. You will stay quiet, even if you don't think you should. Do not force me to have you removed, because my bailiff will take great joy in tossing you out on your ear. Troopers, this is for you: You will show respect to the defendant, the state, and the people sitting in my court. You will not conduct yourself with an attitude. You are not guarding the jail right now and you are not on your beat. You will act accordingly."

Wiley asked everyone if he made himself clear and they all nodded yes. A few said "yes" in a very light voice, not really wanting to be heard, but agreeing all the same. Don Wiley had one more thing to say to the Court TV cameramen who were present for the live coverage of "IN SESSION."

"I expect you to keep your cameras focused toward this part of the court." He pointed to the prosecution and defense tables. "I have reviewed the angles and find them to my liking. You will not point at the gallery and if you, even one time, expose a juror, I will have your entire operation removed on the spot. Clear?"

They also nodded their heads yes and Wiley was satisfied.

"Bailiff, please run downstairs and bring a potential jury up."

Wiley's bailiff enthusiastically bobbed to his superior and headed out to gather a group of peers.

Selection Day

The men and women of the potential jury filed in and took their seats in the middle of the gallery. The people present to watch the trial were asked to move as far to the left and right as they could so that all the potentials could have a seat. There were forty people in the pool. Twelve, with one alternate, would be selected.

"I want a jury selected today, if at all possible council." Wiley said. "Don't rush your decisions; just try to hurry it along. We have an important trial ahead and I want to stay on task. If a jury is not selected today, I expect that tomorrow morning, at the latest, you will accomplish this task."

Amy and Richard tipped there heads in agreement and it was time for Voir Dire.

The bailiff instructed the potentials with the numbers 1-12 to take a seat in the jury box with the corresponding number. He asked for number 13 to have a seat in the chair next to the box. Judge Wiley, as was his tradition, made his way down to the edge of the box and had a seat there. He liked to help with the selection process by being close to the jurors. He felt it made them feel more comfortable. When ready, Richard and Amy would begin questioning each juror and decide who stayed and who didn't. Each council could eliminate five jurors during this Voir Dire selection process. Richard was first to question juror number 1, a white middle-aged man.

"Sir, thank you for being here. My first question is simple: Do you have a prejudice in this case?"

"No sir, I do not."

"Have you read in the newspaper about this case?"

"Yes, I have."

"Thank you. No further questions."

"Ms. Fraser, it's your juror," said Wiley.

"No questions, Judge."

Judge Wiley took over. He had a question. "Sir, do you have an opinion one way or the other in Mr. Garrison's case?"

"No, Judge, I feel I can be fair and un-biased."

"Thank you."

Wiley looked over to the council tables and asked if they had objections.

"No prejudice, Judge, he's fine," Headly stated.

"Yes, your Honor, I would like to excuse this juror," Amy said.

Wiley excused the potential juror. "Thank you and you may be excused."

It was going to be a tedious task in selecting this jury. Who hadn't heard about the case? Who wasn't biased? These were the puzzles each council had to work out.

"Voir Dire." "Voir Dire." Each council took turns saying this.

The bailiff called out; "Potential juror number 14, please take seat 1." A young, white female took the seat. It was now time to move to juror number 2. The questions would continue. This is how the first half of day one played out. It was surprising that they had so many jurors seated by lunchtime. Wiley was especially happy with the results.

At the end of one round of questioning, Headly had expelled three potential jurors while Amy had also expelled three. They would have six new potentials to interview in the next round. Seat numbers 2,3,5,6,7,11 and the alternate at number 13 would remain. The weeding out continued, but Judge Wiley called for a two-hour lunch break to give everyone a chance to recharge their batteries.

Garrison was cuffed and placed under watch in the holding room. Amy promised to pick him up a burger and some fries so he could enjoy a meal that wasn't crawling with bugs. The clock had just struck noon and Wiley wanted everyone back at 2:00. So far it had gone well. Seven seats filled and six to go. It should be handled on day one, but only time would tell for sure.

Amy stopped at the local Burger joint and picked up some food for her client. She opted for a small salad and water for herself. Amy did not want to upset her already fragile digestive system. Headly went to lunch with Beauregard, who had sat at a bench behind the prosecution table and would remain there through the jury selection. He did not have much to say during the break and in Headly's case, that couldn't be all bad. If Jack wanted to say something or worse yet, complain, he would. Amy returned and fed John, who gobbled down the food with the gusto of a lion standing over a kill. It was pretty disgusting, to say the least. Food dribbling onto the table and Garrison's full red cheeks staring at Fraser. She ordered him to put a napkin in his shirt and try to eat like a civilized human.

"Mmphh! I eapht how I font!" Was Garrison's muffled full-mouth response. "Phesusph frist!"

Amy got the picture and let him be. She had much more important matters to consider as she planned for her after lunch questioning of the remaining jurors.

*

Back inside the courtroom, the jurors took their seats in the box, while the prospects sat in the gallery as before. A young, white female sat in seat number 1 and this time, Amy was allowed to lead off. After all the questions from Amy and Richard, all the jurors remained the same except for two spots. Potentials in seats number 4 and 12 remained up in the air. Both attorneys would have one more round of questions to decide their court fates. Amy had used up her allotment of five dismissals.

Amy started off with number 4, a middle-aged black female.

"Do you have a prejudice against older white men?"

"I ain't got no prejudice, ma'am, 'cept I think he did it. Keep me on the jury and watch me find 'em guilty as hell."

"Your Honor, I would like to excuse number 4. I believe she would be a hindrance to fair and impartial decision making during deliberations. I call for excusing her."

Richard spoke, "I think she should stay, Judge. Perhaps she can challenge the other jurors or vice versa and the decision they make would be more carefully founded."

"I'm keeping her for now," Wiley said, greatly disappointing Amy. "But let's see what else happens."

Both attorneys requestioned number 12 and decided to stay with him, a young black male.

Amy continued the argument with Judge Wiley as to why the potential in seat 4, the last seat, should be expelled. "She will disrupt the jury system, your Honor. That woman will not be fair and impartial because she is obviously biased against my client. It would be a plain tragedy if she's allowed to remain."

Wiley spoke to the potential, a middle-age black woman named Cylinda. The judge paid careful attention during this exchange.

"Ma'am, do you believe John Garrison committed the murders he's here to stand trial for?"

Cylinda smartly replied, easing her stance a bit, "I don't know whether he really did it or not, all I'm sayin' is that I think he did. I can be swayed with a good argument. He ain't gonna' get no breaks from me, though."

The judge looked over at the councils and asked again, "Any objections?"

Headly said "no" and "Voir Dire," while Amy balked, this time with more emotion.

"Your Honor, please. For the good of your honorable court, don't let her sit on the jury." Amy looked and felt very concerned. The woman in question stared at John with a look of hate, but was still managing to hold her seat.

"She will sway the jury in a misguided direction. Sir, I implore you."

Wiley looked over Amy, then Richard, and finally the juror. He thought very hard about the decision he was about to make. He did not take it lightly.

"I have listened to the potential juror and I have listened to both arguments from council and I've decided that she will sit on my jury. Mr. Headly made a good point by saying she would challenge the other jurors. I like that idea and I agree." A smack of the gavel drove the point home.

Amy sat back hard in her chair, very disappointed, while Beauregard gave Richard a small clap on the back. They had won the first battle. There were many more to come.

It was running about 4:00 when the final juror was decided, and Wiley had one more order of business before the day ended.

"Do both councils agree we should sequester the jury for the duration of the trial?" Amy rose and spoke up quickly. "Yes, that's very important, considering the press coverage, your Honor."

She fully expected Headly to agree, but alas, he balked. "The jurors should be trusted that they will not talk about the case. They will be more relaxed and come to a better, more thought out verdict that way. I move they be allowed to go home."

Amy stood back up, looked at Headly like he was nuts, and decided she would win this little fracas right now.

"As you can see, Judge, the TV cameras are already here. I trust that these folks are good upstanding citizens," Amy looked straight at number 4 when she said that, "but I think they'd be better served to come to a decision based on facts in the courtroom, not on court TV."

"Good point, council. I find that the jury shall indeed be sequestered for the duration of this trial. They will be kept in separate rooms away from each other until such time as deliberations begin."

A muffled moan came from the jury box, but it wouldn't change a thing. They would be sequestered at an undisclosed downtown Lincoln hotel through the trial. It was good because this way no one could get to them or influence them in any way.

"That will be it for today. We will reconvene at 8:30 a.m. sharp tomorrow."

The judge instructed the jurors on their expected conduct and he understood, with sympathy, their obvious displeasure with his decision. He then called for his bailiff to take them to another location within the courthouse until a bus arrived to move them to the unspecified location.

"Court's adjourned. See you bright and early."

The jury consisted of: Liz, a 21-year-old white female; Frank, a 45-year-old white male; Felicia, a 25-year-old black female; Cylinda, a 54-year-old black female; Desmond, a 22-year-old black male; Alberto, a 53-year-old Hispanic male; James, a 73-year-old white male; Melody, a 27-year-old white female; Sam, a 31-year-old white male; Wilma, a 47-year-old black female; Oscar, a 67-year-old white male; and D'Andre, a 30-year-old black male. The alternate was Alyssa, a 19-year-old white female. Together, this group held John Garrison's fate in their hands. It was a capital murder case, so it was even more important that they worked well together and did not make the wrong decision. A life depended on it.

*

Amy gave John a couple more words of encouragement before heading out. Jack and Richard left together. John was led away by a trooper, and Amy left for home. The first day had given Amy and Richard a sense of accomplishment, with both councils winning one argument each. Headly was pleased to have a juror who seemingly hated Garrison, while Fraser was very happy that a sequestering had been ordered. There was simply too much TV coverage, led by Ed Brenner and Vicki Ford, to take any chances. Headly really did not care much whether they were put up in a hotel or not. He felt he had his first major victory, and he also felt he had the edge on day one.

Richard was driving back to the State Police Post with Jack and a mild conversation turned heated with just one sentence uttered by Headly. "So Jack, how am I doing so far?"

The right-hand punch lit Richard up like a Christmas tree. The pain jettisoned from his jaw down into his neck. It was a square and very effective blow by Jack, especially due to the fact that he was driving when he delivered it. The target was squarely bulls-eyed.

"Does that answer your fuckin' question counselor? Does that tell you how the hell you're doing?"

Jack pulled to the side of the road, shut the engine off, circled around the front of the car, and yanked Headly from his seat and out onto the curb. The rage in Beauregard's face was frightening to behold. Something had snapped in Jack's mind and Richard had no idea what it was. Cars drove by slowly and Jack noticed this. He was easily recognizable in Lincoln. He eased up, then let go of Richard's arm. A political smile replaced his nasty glare.

"What is your problem, Jack? Why'd you slug me? You're acting like a damn bully."

"I told you before Richard, stop stressing about the trial. When you start asking stupid questions, I tend to get a bit tense."

Jack continued smiling at the passers-by.

"A bit tense? You slugged me in the jaw, Jack. I'm going to have a mark on my face in court tomorrow."

Richard frantically rubbed his sore jawline as Jack's reddened face began to mellow some. Headly was right, it would definitely leave a mark. The left jawline between the ear and mouth was a deepened red. It would probably leave a bruise in its wake.

"Are you losing your mind Jack? Are you going crazy, or what? We're grown men here."

Headly cowered his hands toward his face when he asked this question, fearing another thrashing. Jack smiled as he straightened out Richard's wrinkled suit coat.

"Don't push my buttons, Richard. No, I'm not crazy and no, I haven't lost my mind. If you keep up your whining though, I just might. Don't test those waters."

"What the hell did I say that made you so mad? What deserved a fist to the jaw?"

"You asked 'am I doing okay.' That shows me you're worried, and worry means mistakes. Mistakes lead to losses in court. Do you get my drift, counselor? This is one case you will not lose under any circumstances. An acquittal for Garrison could hurt you in ways you just don't understand."

Richard thought to himself that Jack was becoming arrogant, bullish, and maybe even a dash nuts. He wasn't the first to think this way and this also made him worry more than anything else. What if a jury didn't see it his way? Would that mean the next step is death? Could Jack actually kill him if he lost? This put Richard in a very tough spot that he wanted nothing at all to do with, but there was no turning back. He would have to hide in the deepest jungle if he backed out now.

"Richard, listen, I'm sorry I slugged you, but I need you to see that I will not tolerate any negatives from you. I cannot and will not put up with it."

Jack gave Richard a pat on the lower back, causing Headly to flinch severely. It felt like he was in the mob and was being warned in a violent way. Apparently, Jack was losing his cool way too often and way too easily. This would have Richard thinking about far too many other things that didn't involve a trial. Richard had to try and keep his focus throughout, or God forbid, he could lose this case.

"C'mon Rich. Let's go get a bite to eat and let bygones be bygones. I won't clobber you again, I promise."

Headly reluctantly agreed and they headed off together to the local diner.

*

Amy drove home without hearing so much as a peep in her head. There also weren't any vision encounters during the commute. It was a welcome relief. No ghouls and no voices meant less stress. She hoped in her heart that it would continue this way, but deep inside, she expected more. She was still terrified by the anomalies but was getting more used to them. She didn't think for a second that she could get to a point where she could simply shut it out and forage onward. Not without some anxiety and fear. Amy wasn't your ordinary person, though. This girl would duke it out with Godzilla if she had to. It would be a no-win situation, but hey, David slayed Goliath, so she figured that one never knows for sure.

Amy had been fairly satisfied with the day's proceedings and thought she had done an adequate and professional job for John. She lost the juror argument, which was a bit damaging for her defense, but won the right to have the peers hidden for the duration. As far as the juror went, Amy figured that with at least one angry juror, she would, at the very least, get a mistrial. This would be much better than life, *or death* for Garrison. The sequestering would effectively cut off all the peers from the outside world. She knew that thoughts tended to fade as time went on, so the jury could have a nice fresh outlook on a trial that would last at least a few days.

Amy did not think that Headly was all that impressed with her, but it really wasn't her problem. Psychological warfare is waged in a court of law the same way motions and evidence are fought over. She would not let that Prosecutor get under her skin. Amy knew from long ago to keep her wits about her and stay tough and thick-skinned through the harshest of roads.

Sleep came easy for the young woman. She took a couple of Xanax pills, changed into her cozy PJ's, and lie quietly in the bed for a few minutes so the medicine could take affect. She read one of her People magazines and flipped on the TV to anything other than news. She found a wonderful program about love and relationships that made her smile. After her meds took hold of her, Amy felt relaxed and calm. The movie she was watching had numerous love scenes, which made Amy feel good about herself and the world in general.

"There are wonderful things in this life." She thought. "Perhaps I'll someday find love."

She rubbed her arms, legs and shoulders slowly, allowing a stress releasing feeling. She also gave herself a tummy message because it was a rare time when it didn't hurt. After thinking about all of it for a few more seconds, Amy took to sleep. No dreams, no problem.

A Killer Prays

The pentagram lay before the killer. He had taken a step forward and actually painted the design on the floor of the lair. It looked like this;

Satanists use a pentagram with two points up, often inscribed in a double circle, with the head of a goat inside the pentagram. They use it much the same way as the "Pit" or "Void" in Christian terminology (the word is used as such in the Bible, referring to the place where the fallen angels are fettered). The Satanists use it as a sign of rebellion or religious identification, the three downward points symbolizing rejection of the holy Trinity and the horns pointing up in defiance of conventional religious (spiritual) dogma. [1]

This is what the killer was spending his time learning about. Books and literature littered the floor, tables, and countertops inside the smelly den. The killer was following a very dangerous and potentially lethal plan-Lethal not only to the children that he planned on sacrificing, but lethal to the himself. This killer was starting to think he was invincible. He thought he could not die.

On the pentagram itself, the killer laid out each picture of the court participants. On the two upper tips of the Satanist graph laid pictures of Amy Fraser and John Garrison. The two outer, middle points had photos of Richard Headly and Jack Beauregard, while on the lower point rested a Jack of Spades with blood stained blades, a design the killer himself created. In the middle, where the goat's eyes met, were photos of all the other courtroom participants. He was planning on putting an evil, deadly curse on each and every person involved. The killer felt the power of Satan entering his body as he prayed to the prince of darkness.

He started chanting strange incantations in a completely different language. It must have been a Latin or middle-eastern dialect, although it was very difficult to decipher. The voice of the killer changed, he now spoke in a deep, growling tone, which chilled the heart and even scared the small bugs and other critters right out of the swampy cabin. The killer was surprised with his newfound ability to speak in

---

[1] Grünbaum, B. and G. C. Shephard; Tilings and Patterns, York W.H. Freeman & Co., (1987)

tongues. This made him feel like he had Satan's ear, and that was the whole point. As the killer continued the chant, he dropped a Black Jack of Spades for each participant on the pentagram. One Jack for each photo. Now the diagram held photos on each point accompanied by a Jack of Spades with the scary blood stained blades. He had one more task to finish before the evil curses could come to life, as the killer hoped they would. He needed a sacrifice. The killer heard it in his head. Satan was telling him to find a suitable sacrifice to complete the circle of dread and evil. After thinking about it for some time, the killer went outside and fetched a black garbage bag from the side of the lean-to. He brought the bag in and placed it next to the pentagram, and then continued the evil chants. This would continue for another couple of hours. The killer was now hearing in his ear what to say and do. Someone or something was communicating through his mind. Was it Satan, Lucifer, the Devil? The killer thought it to be exactly that. The dark one was personally telling him what to do. He truly believed that to be the case.

Two-and-a-half hours went by. The killer then stood up, cut his finger, and bled onto each card and photo encircling the diagram. It was time for Satan's sacrifice. The killer prayed hard that the contents of the bag would be an acceptable gift. He took the black garbage bag and opened the end of it, which had been tied tightly shut with Lyme added to avoid any decomposition stink. He then turned the bag upside down and dumped out….the dog! The black dog, which he had traded in Garrison's driveway, was serving as the sacrifice to his new found god. The dog had decomposed somewhat and the odor was still unbearable despite the Lyme. The rotting teeth of the animal were totally exposed and the eyes had decayed from its head in a jelly-like ooze. The fur that was remaining was matted and damp. The dog's tongue hung out of its mouth with a sickened green hue. It was the vilest and most disgusting sight imaginable. That was exactly what the killer wanted: a nasty, dark, and evil entity in which to offer his master The killer fell to his knees and continued the prayer. The dog represented the evil and death that the killer had inflicted in the name of his Satan.

Apparently, Satan was accepting of this sacrifice, as the floor began to glow with a fire red shade. The room seemed to move under the killer's knees and he was ordered to place his face on the floor while Satan took the gift. An awful roar was heard by the killer and he kept his head down. The footsteps walking through the lair were heavy and sloppy, much like someone who was walking through mud or boggy ground. The roar was deafening as the entire room shook with wind and energy. The killer was frightened, but trusted his god to do what was right. He felt a real and true presence in the room but did not dare to look up, in fear of death. The next sounds heard were bones crunching along with a splashing, gut-wrenching noise from within the pentagram. Satan was accepting the sacrifice and was dining on the half rotted carcass. The killer continued to keep his head down as the blowing and shaking continued. A few seconds later, the lair began to calm. The winds died down and the shaking stopped. The roar of the Devil silenced as the sacrifice was considered suitable. A voice in the killer's head told him to look up and he did. What he witnessed was a dog still present, but twisted into a hideous and incomprehensible shape. The cards and photos were gone, and left behind surrounding the dog was a painted note on the floor….

IT WILL BE DONE

The killer now knew that the plan would move forward. The plan he had hatched with the help of his god would come to pass. The killer knew what the plan was. It was swimming in his head and became crystal clear during the séance. He would unveil the evil intent after the Garrison trial was concluded. A smile followed by a long, hard laugh escaped from the killer and all was well in the world. They would pay. They would all pay for their transgressions. They would pay for the corruption they bequeathed upon humanity. It would be a sweet and succulent justice that the killer would, by his hand along with Lucifer's, inflict upon the unjust. The waiting would continue, but not for much longer. The hour was coming when the real terror would begin.

The killer was tired and drawn out. His energy level was low and the power of sleep was calling. This was a human being, not a spiritual entity. He was flesh, blood and bones that had emotion along with normal bodily needs. After placing the dog's carcass back in the bag, he added more Lyme, and then tossed it out the door. The killer stretched out on the wooden floor of the cabin and drifted off into a satisfying and restful slumber. Spreading curses and calling on Satan proved to be very hard work. The killer would wake later, refreshed and ready to implement the next part of the cycle when the time came, or when Satan himself gave the order.

The Trial of John Garrison
Day 2

The morning brought hope and fear. Hope for Amy and fear for Richard. Jack had given Headly a good thump the day before. He was swollen and bruised on his jawline. He knew he had to make up a good excuse as to why, so Jack wouldn't thrash him again. He decided to go with the "I slipped in my kitchen last night, and smacked my face on the counter," card. Yes, that would work for the salivating media, the Judge and others. Most of all, it would satisfy Jack. Headly knew he had to be very careful with that man. "Jack is becoming nasty," Richard thought, "now that he's been voted in." Keeping the Governor-elect happy would be a big job for Headly, but not impossible. If he can fight the case the way he did normally, he would easily win and have the man off his back. After, that is, he makes him the state's attorney general. Yes, Richard held that in his back pocket. He wasn't as sure now as he had been before, but he thought Jack would keep his word. Richard's wife Sonya had asked about the bruise, and he explained what happened.

"Why, that no good creep!" was Sonya's response. She wasn't finished. "You should tell him to get bent and that you quit. Don't be pushed around by that cad!"

"It's not quite as easy as you may think, dear," Richard told her, "that man is more dangerous than you may imagine. He pointed a gun at my face. Sonya, you better keep that big mouth shut, you hear me?"

"Why do you let people push you like that? Why didn't you slug him back?"

"I'll tell you what, Sonya, *you* slug him back. He'll turn that pistol on you just as quickly. Now promise me you'll keep that trap door on your face shut!"

Sonya looked at Richard with a very angry, squinted left eye. She wanted to shout at what she considered to be a big sissy of a husband, but kept her cool and kissed his forehead instead.

"Okay, darling, I won't say a word. I'll do as you tell me. Just be careful. Get through this case, win, and we'll be on our way."

"Sonya, I need to tell you one more small thing." Richard backed to the other side of the room when he said this.

"What is it Richard? What kind of surprise do you have this time?" Standing in her bathrobe, she was tapping her toe on the wooden floor as her arms lay crossed on her chest. Her right index finger was tapping her left arm in unison.

"If I win this case, Jack will appoint me attorney general. That's why I took the chance."

Rich expected another outburst, but was pleasantly surprised by the response.

"Attorney General? Does that pay well?" Sonya quizzically inquired.

Headly nodded, "About $400,000 a year-$300,000 per year raise from where we are now."

Sonya ran over to Richard and gave him a huge hug and a deep, wet kiss. She started carrying on about how they could drastically improve their lives.

"Oh Richard! You are the best. Imagine how wonderful our lives will be. We'll have so much money, which will mean so much shopping."

After making her statement, Richard warned her about getting too anxious. "You need to relax until I have that job, Sonya. Nothing is guaranteed yet."

"Oh Richard. I'm so proud of you. Our lives will be so much better."

Richard suddenly wished he hadn't mentioned this to her. His immediate fear was that she would be unwise and start a shopping spree they could not yet afford. He felt a slight muscle twitch in his eye, rubbed it away, and gave Sonya one more bit of advice. "Don't spend it before we have it dear. Please. I implore you."

He saw the twinkle in her eyes and it deeply concerned him. Now he had pressure coming down on him from two fronts.

*

Amy was getting dressed for the morning ritual. She had a sense of relaxation from her restful, dream free sleep the night before. She was humming a little tune and listening to the birds sing through her open window. It was Amy's way of attempting to ignore the voices that tried to take up space in her head. It was also a good day. She was chomping at the bit to have a crack at the state witnesses who would be taking the stand today.

Ms. Fraser looked terrific. Her black hair shone in the sunlight while her skin gave a radiant glow. She did a touch of eyebrow plucking due to the fact that they grew in very thick and very dark. Eyeliner, mascara, lipstick and hair. Amy always did her make-up at home. She hated seeing women do that stuff while driving and would honk at them if she saw it. That and texting while operating a motor vehicle drove her nuts. She wasn't crazy about legislation being passed to make it a misdemeanor offense for doing incredibly dangerous stuff while driving, but she also thought people should be smart enough to know how easy it was to have an accident when you weren't paying attention. These and other thoughts crossed through the attorneys mind while she continued getting ready for her day.

The toast was toasting and the coffee brewing when Amy smelled a strange odor that seemed to be emanating from the kitchen. It was a burnt smell, but not like overdone toast, it was more like the scorched scent of burnt hair. She made her way toward the dining area to see if she could track down the smell. When she entered the kitchen, she saw the popped toaster with normal looking golden brown bread and a full, very fresh pot of coffee.

"What the heck?" she asked herself.

"I know I smelled burnt *something*."

"Ammyy!" the voice said very softly.

Amy whirled around quickly and violently, knocking off and smashing ceramic cups from the counter as she did. Sitting at her dining room table were young Amy, Jimmy Joseph, her mom and dad, and Garrison. The smell had come from the charred John Garrison. He was burnt to a crisp and smoke was still rising off him as he slowly turned his gaze from the table to her. Fraser gasped and moved a hand to her throat, contorting at the shocking scene that lay before her. Young Amy, her parents and Jimmy also moved their eyes from the table to Amy, causing a creepy tingle to shoot through the lawyer's body. Amy looked in the center of the table and saw a grisly scene. The black dog was lying on a tray before the five ghouls. It had been cut open and the spirits were serving themselves from the carcass. Amy bent forward and fiercely spewed out dinner from the night before. The morbid, graphic scene was just too much for the woman to bear. After expelling her cookies, Amy bent back up and the young Amy stood before her with a plate of rotted, stinking dog inches from Fraser's face. She screamed a loud, had-to-be-heard-around-the-neighborhood scream and suddenly, as fast as a lightening strike, found herself looking into her bathroom mirror.

"OUCH!" Amy screamed as she threw the hot curling iron into the sink. Amy's hair was smoldering under her ear and around the back. She had left the iron on her locks too long and it was causing the burning, nasty smell of hair to proliferate around the bathroom. She quickly jumped in the shower, fully clothed, and turned the water on. The cold burst put out the hair fire and Amy was left with a mess that was singed beyond repair.

"YOU FUCKING BASTARDS!" Amy screamed at the top of her lungs, fists clenched. She slid down the back of the shower wall until she was almost lying on the floor with the water saturating her. She cried. She cried hard and she cried long. The hair was irretrievable. It was ruined. She saw some of it whirl pooling down the shower drain. She would have to think hard and fix herself up before court. She climbed out of the shower, removed all of her soaked clothes, and pulled a pair of scissors out of the drawer. Amy gave herself a haircut. She continued to cry.

*

It had been another dream, or so Amy thought. The kitchen table was clean and devoid of anything that resembled a *dog* dinner. The kitchen itself was in perfect harmony, toast perfectly toasted and coffee wonderfully brewed. Amy sighed and buttered her bread. She pulled the coffee pot out of the holder and turned to get a cup, but they weren't there. She always kept them on the edge of the counter so to be easily accessed and in plain view. She replaced the pot and walked around to the other side and found them. The three cups that had sat on the edge were now smashed on the floor. Little bits and pieces everywhere. One had an image of Amy and one of her U of N classmates on it. That was her special cup, made with one of her only friends in the world, but it was gone. The other two were basically insignificant, but they too were in smithereens. Amy felt that fear creep into her stomach and a headache instantly manifested itself. This was entirely too weird for her to comprehend. After standing in place for minutes, she opened her mini-closet, which sidled up with the kitchen, and pulled out the broom and dustpan she had stashed inside. Amy, despite her uneasy feeling, swept the mess up off her (thankfully wooden) floor. She put away the equipment and finished getting herself ready for court. The toast went down rough and the coffee tasted flat and uninspiring. She choked it down and gathered her rolling briefcase and folders, then made her way towards the door. Amy lifted her keys and caught another glimpse of herself in the mirror. Everything looked fine except her hair, which had gone from beyond shoulder length to now just below her ears.

"It'll grow back," Amy reasoned. "It could've been a lot worse, I suppose. It was Amy's new look. A short bob that did not come close to doing her beauty justice. "When they ask, and they will, I'll just tell them I'm doing something a bit different....for luck. Better yet, they would be wise to not ask at all."

The lawyer blew out yet another long sigh and headed out the door. She was frustrated and angry. Knowing her though, she would keep up the fight. Tough as nails, you know?

Opening a Can of Worms

Richard entered the courthouse and before any reporters even had a chance to ask him questions, he was confronted and quizzed by the two policemen manning the metal detectors.

"Richard, what in the hell happened to your face?"

"Yeah, Richard, what gives?"

"Oh, no big deal. I had a little slip and fall at home, that's all." Richard kept his eyes on his briefcase as it wheeled through the scanner.

"C'mon Richard. You can level with us. That looks like a punch to the jaw."

"Well it isn't, okay? Listen guys, I have to run, would you mind?"

The officer standing next to Richard waved him through. The policeman sitting at the scanner muffled a small chuckle.

"Okay, counselor, I get it. That's your story and you're sticking to it."

The laughter from both cops finally burst forth.

"Yeah! Okay Richard, whatever you say! See you later."

Embarrassed and feeling slighted, Richard moved forward. He saw Beauregard sitting on a bench reading a newspaper. Headly sucked in deep, then blew out a large breathe and forged toward him. Jack moved his newspaper and saw the handiwork he'd left on the lawyer's face.

"Good grief, Rich. What the hell? Did you have a bar fight?" Jack was playing dumb and Rich knew it. He explained his miserable excuse. "Fell in the kitchen, smacked my face, okay?"

Jack winced, and then smiled. You could tell he was holding back. Something the cops at the scanner couldn't do. Jack could burst at the seams with laughter, but didn't. "Wow, Richard, you'd better be more careful. You could get hurt real bad slipping in the…where did you say…..oh yeah, the kitchen. Boy oh boy."

"Can we just go to the courtroom please? I've heard more than enough already."

"Sure bud, let's head that way. I don't think you've fielded your last question about it, though."

Headly looked up and saw the throng of media headed straight toward him. He blew out another tired sigh. "Richard, Richard, what happened sir? What happened to your face?"

"If you have questions about the case, I'll take them. As far as my face goes, things happen, okay?"

"Whatever you say, Richard, but it looks like you were punched."

"That is not a question about the case," Richard angrily responded, "I said the case, not the face."

Big laughter shot out from the throng of reporters. Richard Headly unknowingly made a poem and it completely amused all the people around him, including Jack.

"What are you laughing at, Jack? You think it's funny, huh?"

"Come on Richard, let's get to the court," Jack blurted, holding in the residual giggles.

Both men headed down the hall and away from the throng.

*

"Amy? Amy Fraser?" the screener's asked. "Is that you?"

The two scanner cops saw Amy and were in awe over her short bob haircut. They obviously did not like it in the least. They said so, too. "Why'd you go and do that, ma'am? You had such pretty hair."

Amy's face was turning into a growl. She scolded both men on the spot. "What does my hair have to do with *your* lives? Better yet, are you judging me based on my new haircut? Are both of you harassing me? Huh? Are you? Speak up!"

Ms. Fraser had a razor sharp look on her face, bordering on out-and-out fury. Both cops backed down on the spot. They knew better than to mess with this one.

"No Ms. Fraser, we just wanted to let you know how nice it looked. That's all."

"Good, now would you both please step aside so I can get through?"

The scanner cops moved quicker than they had in years. The counselor let herself through, took her items off the roller and headed for court. Here came the media, right on time and right in Amy's face.

"If you ask about the hair, you're finished," she warned with a pointed finger and an angry looking scowl. "I'll never answer another of your inquiries again! Any questions?" Amy's fists were of tightened balls, squeezing hard enough to dig her nails into the palms of her hands.

The seas parted and Amy walked through. She had effectively shut all their mouths in one fell swoop. They did not follow, but she turned around and added one more thing with a demeanor that had drastically changed. Now she was pleasant. She had brightened a bit. "I will be available for questions after court today. Thank you."

The reporters looked at her with their mouths gaping. One cleared his throat and many others just looked at the floor or the ceiling. Amy had actually scared the mass silent. It was a rare sight indeed. As Amy turned back around and headed for court, a small smile budded on her face.

*

"ORDER! Order in the court. All rise and remove your caps, please." The bailiff shouted the same statement as the day before and out came Judge Wiley. All the ladies and gentlemen in his court went through the pledge, and then it was time to get the trial officially underway.

"Could we please have the jury enter, bailiff?" Wiley asked and ordered at the same time.

The jurors filed in through the side door and took their respective seats in the box. John Garrison looked at his peers with a squished-nose frown. It was as if something smelled funny. Amy gave him a good kick under the table.

"Behave yourself, John," Amy whispered.

John grumbled silently and straightened his crooked face.

It was with grimaces and half-mast eyes that the jurors entered. Apparently, sleep was not a success the night before, especially in strange beds. Wiley noticed it and hoped they would get used to it. He felt a bit sorry for his crew of peers.

"I know it's a new experience, but please bear with it. It won't last too terribly long. I do understand your discomfort, so please don't think I'm uncaring."

The jurors nodded to the judge and then he turned his attention front and center. He was shocked at what he saw with the two counselors. "What in Sam Hill's name happened to you, Mr. Headly?"

"Unfortunate accident, Your Honor, a fall in the kitchen."

From his seat behind the DA, Jack smiled oh so cleverly. He had the prosecutor wrapped right around his finger. No way would Richard ever put him out. Jack felt the power.

Donald Wiley then turned his attention to Amy, who was sitting at the defense table with John.

"I'm not even going to ask, Ms. Fraser. I know better."

"Thank you Judge. I'm even confused about it."

The gallery laughed very politely as Wiley shook his head. It was time for the trial to begin and enough time had been wasted up to now.

"Is the State ready to proceed?" asked the Judge.

Richard gave an affirmative nod.

"Defense, are you all set?"

Amy gave a quick yes nod in return and added a comment. "Yes Your Honor, the defense is ready."

"Fine, let's proceed. Witnesses to the hallway please. Mr. Headly, opening remarks."

Richard Headly stood up tall and walked to the lectern situated near the jury box. He spread his notes out, cleared his throat, and then began.

The official opening statement by Richard Headly, State Prosecutor:

"Good morning ladies and gentlemen. My name is Richard Headly and I'm here to prove to you that the man sitting at the defense table, one John Garrison, is guilty of a pair of murders involving young boys here in Lincoln, Nebraska. You will hear many different facets of testimony. You will hear many different emotions. You will hear *and* see for yourself how cruel life can be. You will ultimately find yourself sitting in a room with a cold-blooded child murderer. Can you imagine how that will feel? Sitting in the same room with a killer? A killer of children, nonetheless. Boys. Young boys whom he murdered. They were strangled to death. A leather strap wrapped around their tiny necks and squeezed until they could not breathe. They slowly and methodically and, might I add, painfully died at the hands of the man sitting right there: One John Garrison."

"I object, gotdamnit!" The perplexed Garrison stood up and butted in.

Wiley's gavel slammed down on the bench with a loud thud.

"Your Honor, objection! He's interfering with my opening statement!" Headly protested.

"Ms. Fraser," Judge Wiley scolded, "your client will not interrupt again or he will be dismissed from my court for the duration. I'm not going to play these childish games."

Amy grabbed John by his arm hard enough to leave a mark and pulled him back into his seat. She hissed through clenched teeth.

"Leave it to me to object, if needed."

She then stood up to address the Judge. "I am so sorry, Your Honor, I will make sure it doesn't happen again. My client is obviously emotional and he doesn't know his court etiquette very well."

"I suggest you teach him, Ms. Fraser. That's part of your job, you know."

"Yes, Judge, I am sorry," an embarrassed Fraser said.

Amy gave John a look like she might kill him with her own two hands. She thought the electric chair would be child's play compared to her punishment. John took the point and silenced himself.

"Mr. Headly, please carry on." Wiley permitted.

"Thank you, Your Honor. As I was saying, ladies and gentlemen, before being so rudely interrupted, this man sitting before you is a murdering madman and, apparently, a hothead. It appears that the defendant cannot keep his wits about him, which to me is very telling of his inability to maintain control. The specifics I will give you will prove beyond a reasonable doubt that Mr. Garrison committed these crimes. As a matter of fact, there will be no doubt at all left in your minds when I'm finished. I have never lost a case in my career and do not intend to now."

"Objection," yelled Amy. "His record in court means nothing to this jury. He is simply trying to insert a subconscious thought in their minds that he never loses."

"Sustained." Wiley pointed his gavel at Headly. "Counselor, don't make me warn you twice. You know better. The jury will disregard Mr. Headly's statement and it will be stricken. Carry on, Mr. Headly."

Richard had said what he wanted the jury to hear regarding his perfect record, so in his mind, the seed had been planted. Strategy at its creepiest.

"Thank you Judge. I would just like to remind you as a jury, that letting a guilty man walk free, especially a man that's guilty of these heinous crimes, is much more damaging than ever sending an innocent man to prison. That being said, this man sitting to my right is flat out and 100 percent guilty. When my case is finished, you will understand why I say that. Please listen closely when I speak to the witnesses you will be introduced to and hear for yourselves exactly what I mean. They will supply you with details and facts that will be disturbing, yet necessary in the prosecution of a killer. Thank you."

Richard stepped away from the jurors and took his seat at the prosecution table. Judge Wiley reminded the jurors to disregard his statement regarding his record in court and asked if they had any questions. They did not and his Honor proceeded.

"Defense, are you prepared with your opening statement?"

"Defense is prepared and ready, Your Honor." Amy confidently said.

"It's all yours council."

The official opening statement by Amy Fraser, Defense Attorney:

Hello ladies and gentlemen. I would like to start by saying thank you. Thank you for sacrificing your own time to be with us here in court. It is truly a very tough situation to deal with. I'm talking about the death of two young children. It is tragic and it is sad. It tears you apart on the inside. I myself cannot begin to imagine how tough and soul-ripping the loss of a child must be. I can only think that if it were my children, I would rather be dead than have to deal with the aftermath. That being said, my client, John Garrison, who sits before you, a jury of his peers, would not, could not, and did not kill anyone. Especially children. My client appears gruff and hardened to you. That's because, ladies and gentlemen, he is. John Garrison has worked hard all of his life and is as tough as a petrified two-by-four, to put it bluntly. He is hard-edged to a cruel and ruthless world of violence and degradation. He moved to Nebraska to get away from the harmful nature of this world. He worked all his life in Detroit. Detroit is rough, tough and callused. It is a blue-collar town full of hard-hitting blue-collar workers. John did his work, retired, and then moved here. To rural Nebraska. Lincoln, Nebraska. A much slower paced, non-violent town. That's not to say it isn't violent like other cities, but it's a lot less so. The question that keeps ringing in my head is this: Why move here to be violent? Why move here to murder children? John could do that in Detroit and stand a much better chance of getting away with it. He would have had all the access to young people he wanted there. John is no murderer, people. John Garrison simply did the right thing, which you will hear about during testimony. Mr. Garrison was, in actuality, looking after the best interest of the city in which he lived. That city is Hickman. It is one of the nicest cities in the USA. A nice city filled with nice people. They know each other, trust each other and love each other. Nobody in that small, quaint town is out to hurt, much less kill, anyone. All the information being put before you fairly, and without prejudice, will allow you to see that the state will have no physical evidence linking Mr. Garrison with the murders. You will see that the state has nothing….NOTHING, linking John Garrison to anything, much less murder." Amy glared at Richard during this key portion of her statement. "I will prove to you, rather easily I might add, that Mr. Garrison was, has been, and will continue to be a law-abiding citizen in our great state of Nebraska. Thank you and I wish you the best, not only to make a good decision, but that we have a nice speedy trial."

After Amy finished, the Judge spoke. "Ladies and gentlemen, we will take a thirty-minute recess and meet back here after. Please, jurors, do not talk to each other or anyone else about this case. We are in recess." BANG, with the gavel.

All in all, it turned out to be a very good morning for both councils. The jurors listened intently to both parties and appeared to be in tune with the happenings so far. Opening statements are just that, and everyone needed to step out and take a quick breather while everything soaked in. The day had only just begun, though. Much more awaited on the other side of the break. It would be time for the witnesses, and that meant more than anything else up to now.

Witness the Madness

The recess would be a short one, and Amy needed to make some major points with John, so she accompanied him to his holding room and asked the bailiff to shut them in for a few minutes.

"I don't know Ms. Fraser, I'm not supposed to…" the bailiff tried to tell her.

"Lock us in for twenty minutes, damn it! I'll take responsibility."

The bailiff just shrugged and did what she asked. He even knew better than to mess with the fireball on this day.

Amy looked at John long and hard. She paced left to right, right to left. She was looking for the right way to scold her client, then blurted forth with a combination of anger and frustration. **"ARE YOU A MORON JOHN?"**

John responded, "I'm just lookin' after my….." Amy did not allow him to finish. She knew what he was about to say. She repeated her inquisition.

"I SAID ARE YOU A MO-RON? Her eyes were on fire and her olive-colored skin transitioned into a red tint. Amy was as angry as she could ever remember being. Again, she did not allow John to answer and she continued her loud scolding. **"I'm**

here to defend you John. If you would like to defend yourself just say so. I'll refund what money I haven't used and you can do whatever you like." On she went, "I have enough shit on my plate to deal with less having you blurt out dumb statements in court. You will ruin this defense before it starts. You have started the jury off on the wrong foot. You messed up bad, John." Amy tried to calm herself by stepping up the pacing in the room. Her blood pressure was at an elevated level. John attempted to calm her a bit.

"Okay, okay Ms. Fraser. I'm just tired of bein' the fall guy for this nonsense. I tend to get a little emotional and I pipe in more than I should."

"Don't pipe in again, John. If you do, I'm out. On the spot, sir." Her hands were placed on the table across from John as she leaned toward him.

Even grumpy old John Garrison knew he had completely cheesed his lawyer off. Now he was feeling bad. "I won't do it again, Amy, but cha better win."

"I better win, huh? Well then you'd better help by following my orders. I'm going back to the table; see you in a few minutes."

Amy knocked on the door with attitude. After the guard let her out, she slammed it shut behind her. She left John to wallow in her tongue-lashing. John was regretful for the first time in a long while. He didn't want to lose Amy as his attorney, so he agreed in his mind to behave. He would now let her do her job. John just hoped he wasn't too late. A tear ran down the side of the old codger's cheek. He was in this thing for real and felt the strain. As much as he knew he had never hurt anyone, he also had to leash up his frustration and attitude to have any chance of winning. He had put his trust and cash into this woman and it was time to straighten up. He convinced himself that he would.

*

The recess ended and all parties were back in court. Amy sat at the table and fumed. She knew she needed to keep her head together so she could adequately defend her loud-mouthed client. The young Amy sat in court, watching her older twin work. Amy sensed it, but would not look back to meet her eyes. She knew it would throw her off her game. She had seen young Amy out of the corner of her eye during the opening, but successfully ignored her. Not to be outdone, the spirit moved closer. The young Amy was now sitting just two rows behind Fraser and Garrison. Amy knew it. She hoped someone would come and take that seat, thus forcing the "ghost" to find another spot. At least Amy hoped that's how it would work. It didn't matter much, because the vision would move around wherever it wanted. This went for the other visions that sometimes accompanied the young Amy. It was a challenge for the lawyer to try and look past all this and give Garrison her full mental capability as his council. Fraser was a very tough girl, but the stress was beginning to rattle her. She was dangling by a proverbial thread. It felt to her like she was on the edge of sanity. She hoped she could just hang on to her wits until the trial was over.

At that point, Judge Wiley dismissed the witnesses to the hallway, and then called for the state to present its case. Richard stood up and asked for Soo-Chin Xing to come forward as the first witness.

"Soo-Chin Xing, please come forward," the bailiff ordered.

Soo entered the main courtroom doors and made her way down the aisle toward the stand. She smiled politely to Jack in the hallway as she passed him and he gave her a half smile, half sneer in return. It was tough to gauge what he was thinking. Jack sat in the hallway with Robert Long, the Josephs, Dan Wheeler and a visibly miffed Lyla Helms. No one spoke.

"Do you swear to tell the truth, the whole truth and nothing but the truth, so help you God?"

"I do," Soo said in a nice loud and clear voice. She sat down for the questioning.

Direct Exam by Richard Headly, State Prosecutor:

"Hello, could you please state your name and spell it for the court?" Richard asked. He would ask the same question for each witness that he would call. Amy would do the same thing when beginning her defense.

"Soo-Chin Xing. S-O-O C-H-I-N X-I-N-G."

"Thank you Ms. Xing. Are you ready?"

"I'm as ready as I'll ever be, I suppose."

"Good. Can you tell the court what you do for a living, Ms. Xing?"

"I am the Forensic Pathologist here in Lincoln."

"Would you please tell the court what exactly it is you do?"

"I perform all the autopsies that involve suspicious death within the Lincoln City Limit."

"Did you perform autopsies on Anthony Wilder and Jimmy Joseph?"

"Yes, I did."

"What were the results?"

Soo had all the paperwork in front of her and shuffled through it as she prepared to answer the questions. She was very articulate about all her record keeping. She had her "ducks in a row," so to speak.

"Both children were strangled with a black leather belt strap and a Jack of Spades playing card was left pinned to those straps."

Richard picked up a bag lying on the table and opened it. He pulled out two black straps and two playing cards. "Are these the items you found during the autopsies, Ms. Xing?"

"Yes, they are."

"Your Honor, I move to enter these items as evidence numbers 1 through 4."

"Any objections?" the Judge asked.

"No, Your Honor." Amy responded.

"The evidence shall be entered. Publish exhibits 1 through 4. Please continue council."

Richard went back to his table, catching a glimpse of Amy as he did so. He quickly moved his eyes away from the attorney and thumbed through his paperwork.

"Ms. Xing, is it your opinion as a certified expert that these two boys were murdered?"

"Yes."

"Nothing further."

Headly sat down at his table and Amy took the floor. She appeared cool and confident, despite the watchful eyes that followed her every move.

Cross Exam by Amy Fraser, Defense Attorney:

"Ms. Xing, are you dating Jack Beauregard, the soon-to-be Governor of Nebraska?"

"Objection!" Richard shouted. "Relevance."

"Sustained." Wiley said. "Ms. Fraser, her love life means nothing here. Move on."

"But Judge, I want to show that there is a conflict of interest here."

"MOVE ON COUNCIL!"

Amy gathered herself and did as she was told. She was feeling tired and run down, more so at that moment then ever. John sat at the table quietly, as he had been ordered to do. He sat with his fisted hand on his lower lip, listening intently. Amy paused for a moment to study her fatigue, then continued.

"Ms. Xing, do you have forensic evidence of Mr. Garrison's involvement in the murdered kids?"

"All I know is the bag containing Jimmy Joseph was found on Mr. Garrison's driveway."

"Was Mr. Garrison's DNA present on the bag, tools or body, Ms. Xing?"

"No. We could not lift any DNA off of anything. All the items and the body were well cleaned."

"Do you know for a fact that the bag in Garrison's driveway contained the body of Jimmy Joseph? Or did you find out later?"

"I can't say for sure, ma'am. The body in my lab is all I saw. But I read about it in the paper."

"Ask to strike, Judge. The newspaper is completely irrelevant."

"Strike the last statement by the witness. Jury, please ignore the last answer."

"Thank you and no more questions, Judge."

Amy knew that she severely hurt the prosecution's case. No evidence of Garrison's presence is vital. It was very early, but Amy thought she had already gained a valuable edge.

"Re-cross, council?" Wiley asked Richard.

Re-cross by Richard Headly:

"Ms. Xing, did you do your job to the best of your God-given ability?"

"Absolutely! I always do."

"That's all, Your Honor."

"Ms. Xing, you may step down. Thank you and please stay on standby if you are needed later. State, call your next witness please."

*

"The state calls Kathy Joseph."

Kathy Joseph strolled up to the stand with a self-assured stride and a very straight face. She looked trashy. Dyed blond hair, tall, and her cleavage wobbling with every step. Her skirt curved around her hips and legs snuggly while her blouse was unbuttoned just one too many, revealing the obvious. She thought she was a knock-out, but that sentiment wasn't shared by the rest of the gallery.

Kathy took her place on the stand and Richard began his questioning.

Direct exam by Richard Headly, State Prosecutor;

He started with simple inquiries pertaining to the night of Jimmy's disappearance. "Where were you Mrs. Joseph, when you noticed your son was missing?"

She told the prosecutor she was standing on the sidewalk in downtown Lincoln enjoying the sights and sounds of the cityscape. One minute little Jimmy had been by her side and the next minute he was gone. "He seemingly vanished into thin air. Poof. Gone."

Richard extended his deepest sympathies on her loss and asked her how she felt.

"How would you feel if you lost your child, sir? He was my only son."

Kathy wiped the tears from her eyes and struggled to compose herself. Amy sat at the defense table wondering if those were crocodile tears running down her cheeks.

"Did you and Mr. Joseph identify the body, ma'am?" Richard inquired.

"Mr. Joseph did, sir. I could not possibly go into that room and have to look at my son again. I wanted to remember him while he was alive. I have no interest in seeing him like that."

Richard thanked Kathy Joseph for coming up and it was Amy's turn with the blond mother of Jimmy.

Amy's strategy was to sound sympathetic to her plight and not raise her voice, while at the same time, try to get Kathy to shed some light on Mr. Joseph.

Cross-exam by Amy Fraser, Defense Attorney;

"Mrs. Joseph, I noticed that Mr. Joseph has accompanied you to court, but he keeps his head turned downward and doesn't say much."

Mrs. Joseph explained that her husband, Kurt, does not speak well in groups and is very shy. He keeps his eyes toward the floor to avoid contact and conversation that he doesn't want to be involved in.

"Where was Mr. Joseph when your son disappeared?"

"He was in the store at the corner. So what?"

"Did you keep your eyes on him while he was, in fact, in that store?" Amy put her hands up and signaled a quotation mark with her fingers when she stated "that store" thus trying to lead the suspicion in Kurt Joseph's direction. Kathy began squirming a bit on the stand and answered with a dose of sarcasm.

"I don't watch my husband's every move, Ms. Fraser, I am not his keeper."

Amy's line of questioning was forcing Richard's hand and she knew it. He would have to call Mr. Joseph to the stand to testify. This is something that may be better avoided. If Richard didn't call him, it would look like they were hiding something. By calling him, Amy would have an opportunity to cross. A win-win for the young lawyer. Amy had her back turned away from Mrs. Joseph as she responded. She was confident and airy. She turned back and saw *young Amy* instead of Mrs. Joseph sitting on the stand, staring back at her. Fraser gasped at the vision and rushed to her table for water. This threw Amy off. It was enough of a challenge without those ghoulish eyes zeroing in on her. Wiley furled his brows and asked her if she was okay.

"Ms. Fraser, is there a problem? Are you well?"

Amy needed to respond to the Judge, but had to wait for the rush of adrenaline to cool down. Her breathing had become tightened with the vision. Finally, after what seemed like an eternity, she was able to again speak. She kept her back turned as she did so.

"I'm okay, Judge. I just choked a bit."

Turn and face me Ms. Fraser. Speak to me, not the gallery."

Of all things for Wiley to request, it would be that. Amy slowly turned back toward the front of the court and sitting on the stand with a puzzled look was Mrs. Joseph. She looked at Amy, and then the Judge.

"Ms. Fraser, I asked if you were okay. Are you able to continue?"

The jurors were also witnessing this little "spell" Amy was having and quietly mumbled among themselves in an inquisitive manner.

"Yes, your Honor, I'm fine now," Amy said. "I'm prepared to continue." Amy was being sapped of more energy by the episodes.

"Please do so, Ms. Fraser."

Amy composed herself and straightened out her suit jacket. She pushed the tiny lock of black hair away from her eyes and appeared to be back on track.

"So, Mrs. Joseph, what you're telling me is that you lost sight of your husband for a period of time. The same period of time that Jimmy disappeared in?"

"Objection!" Richard roared. "Speculative and leading."

"Sustained." Wiley responded. "Strike the question."

Amy was perplexed and out of focus at the moment. "No more questions, Your Honor."

Amy sat back down next to Garrison as Mrs. Joseph was dismissed and noticed he had scrawled something on his pad. It said, "What the hell happened? Are you losing it?" She slid the pad to her side of the desk and wrote, "I'm fine, just choked, "and slid it back to John. He seemed satisfied and nothing more was written.

*

Just as Amy had assumed, Richard was forced to bring Mr. Joseph to the stand and clear up this little miscommunication that had occurred seconds earlier. Kurt Joseph was called but didn't like it. Kathy gave him a sour look and a push. You could read her lips as she told him to get up on that stand. Kurt slowly made his way up, head turned toward the floor and took his seat. He was sworn and Richard took over.

Direct exam by Richard Headly, State Prosecutor;

"Hello, Mr. Joseph. Please don't be nervous, you'll be just fine. I only have a few questions and we'll be all done."

Kurt murmured something into the microphone and was told by Judge Wiley he'd have to speak up while testifying. Kurt nodded at the Judge and sat up straighter.

"Mr. Joseph, where were you when your son disappeared?"

"I w-w-w-was i-in the s-s-store." Kurt was a stutterer. Richard would have to be patient with him.

Amy heard this and knew she'd have to exercise kid gloves as well. Headly continued. "Okay, Mr. Joseph, do you know what happened to your son?

"N-no. I w-w-was j-j-just as su-su-surprised as K-k-Kathy."

"So you don't know what happened to your son, then?"

"No."

Kathy was staggered at the extent of Kurt's stuttering. She knew he was quiet and stuttered, but he had never exhibited this level of shakiness. She hoped he'd make it through without blowing his top or possibly even accidently incriminating himself. She kept all her fingers crossed.

"No further questions Judge."

"Defense, your witness." Wiley nodded to Ms. Fraser and she took over, still somewhat shaken by the latest vision. *Shaken, not stirred.*

Cross-exam by Amy Fraser, Defense Attorney;

"I'll keep this brief, Mr. Joseph. I will also ask my questions slowly and calmly, okay?"

That sat well with Mr. Joseph. It also sat well with the jury. Ms. Fraser was being polite and kind so not to upset the man. When people are handicapped, it's good to be humane. People like that a lot better than the cold, hard, calloused approach.

"Did you testify, Mr. Joseph, that you were in the store when your child was abducted?"

"Y-Y-yes, I was i-i-in the s-s-store."

"Then how did you know Jimmy was abducted?"

"K-Kathy s-s-screamed! I c-came running out. Sh-sh-she was u-u-upset. I c-c-came to he-help."

"Did you abduct that child, sir, and hide him? After which time you came running to help your distraught wife?"

"**OBJECTION**, Judge! Leading; and to be frank, pretty tasteless."

"Overruled. Answer the question, Mr. Joseph."

"I d-d-didn't do a-a-anything, M-M-Ms. Fraser. I w-was ju-ju-just helping m-m-my w-w-wife."

Mr. Joseph was getting vexed. He was making a nasty face at Amy and tightening his fists into balls. He was not of a low I.Q., he was simply nervous and upset. "Was the line of questioning effective for John's defense?" Amy asked herself. She wasn't so sure now and looked over at the jurors. They had a sort of "easy does it" look on their faces. Amy ended there.

"No more questions, Judge."

Wiley asked Richard if he had anything to add. Headly said no and Mr. Joseph was thankfully excused. Even Judge Wiley thought that was painful.

Kurt slinked his way back to his wife's side and sat emotionless the rest of the day.

*

Ms. Wilder, Anthony's mother would have testified next, but she had hanged herself by the neck in her son's tree house just weeks earlier. She couldn't handle the loss and did what she thought she could to possibly reunite with her murdered youngster. Overall, it was an eventful day that brought out a few tidbits for the jurors to chew on. They would be sequestered for the night and listen to more, hopefully enlightening testimony again tomorrow. The State had three more witnesses: Dan, Lyla and Jack. Headly hoped to get an edge with his main subjects. Amy had two people on her defense: Robert and John. Other than that it would be closing statements and deliberation. The trial was moving quickly, thanks to Judge Wiley, who had a propensity for politely speeding things along.

Amy stopped after court and answered a few questions for the media. They did not ask about her hair, though. The rough, tough posse knew better than that. After routine questions about the case, Mr. Garrison, and her small "choking" spell were answered, Amy headed home. She wondered why the visions were trying to sabotage her efforts. They didn't want John to die, but they also try to terrorize her every step. Amy was still hanging tough, but the images were wearing her down.

Headly headed out by himself, not with Jack. One walloping was enough, he thought. Jack also left.

Everyone went home to rejuvenate and try to get an edge for the next session.

John Garrison went back to his cell, as ornery as ever, and Robert Long headed home, frustrated that he had to be put in the back room for many hours. He complained and whined the whole trip, but no one was listening….he was by himself.

*

In the background, the killer had been watching the trial from *inside* the courtroom. Nobody was the least bit suspicious or knowing. He walked out with everyone else, even tipping the hat he was wearing to other people as they walked by. Richard Headly was right; everybody in the courtroom had been sitting with a cold-blooded child murderer.

A Bone of Contention

Lyla was fuming. She was so angry with Dan she could've spit. She had given him the love he needed, the love he desired, and instead of being at least a tiny bit appreciative, he shooed her out the door like old trash. It wasn't that Lyla wanted a lasting relationship with Dan, but she felt blown off, used and betrayed. Lyla did everything for this guy. From pampering him, traipsing him around town, cooking, cleaning and doing his laundry, Lyla was right there for the man. She agreed in her mind that yes, she would give him sex if he needed it, but a piece of her thought he actually cared. Deep down she hoped he did. It appeared that she was wrong. Dan was a twenty-something guy with a teen-age attitude. Lyla being older did not matter as much to her as it apparently did to him. She had thought on more than one occasion since that night that she should go check on him, but it would prove to be too painful for her. It may even be tough for him. He hadn't even given her a phone call to see how she was doing. No letters or e-mails. Nothing. To Lyla it was another enormous slap in the face.

"How dare he just use me and toss me in the rubbish," she often thought. "I don't just give myself to anybody. I deserve more respect."

This woman seemed to be treading dangerously close to a fatally attracted attitude. Lyla would think to herself, "of course not," but it certainly appeared that way. She really cared for Dan and continued to care since the day she left his house.

Dan cared too, but in an entirely different way. He made what he considered to be a mistake in making love to (fucking) his boss, regretting his decision ever since it happened. He wanted to call her and try and patch things up, but didn't have a clue as to where he would start. The guy was not a Romeo with words and he would probably end up making her angrier. Dan wondered why some people couldn't merely have "no strings attached" sex and go in their respective directions. It was obvious to him that men could do that much easier than women could, or would, for that matter. Men have a lack of emotional skills and it shows all too often. Some of the girls he dated *seemed* to be interested in no-strings-attached sex, but again, he could be wrong. A number of women were fighting for the right to be with this guy and sex was a part of the deal for Dan. If he'd lived in New York City or LA, he wouldn't get the time of day from some of these ladies. Living in small town Nebraska limited the females' choices of mates, so Dan ranked at or near the top of their lists.

*

Lyla tried to forget, but couldn't. She saw Dan at court and would continue to see him each day until the trial was over, or until they testified and were finished. Then what? Would he come back to Animal Control?

Would she have to work with him again? Could she? All these questions just kept rattling around in her mind. No matter what she did, be it shopping, housework, or gardening, Dan stayed in her thoughts. She was falling, or had already fallen for him. She was captivated with something that she only now realized was unattainable. Sometimes, that caused Lyla to think irrational thoughts. She considered telling the police he raped her, but changed her mind, mainly due to the fact that Dan in prison meant she could never ever see him again, not to mention that she was no liar. She also thought about telling everybody on her e-mail friend list that Dan had slept with her, and then tossed her out on her bum. That route would also be no good because she, not Dan, would end up being more embarrassed and appear slutty to others. There were not many options remaining. Except, that is, possibly *shooting him in the head.* This was too much like having him put in prison, though, because she wouldn't see him again, and she wasn't certain she wanted that. The other choice that kept creeping in was murder-suicide. Perhaps she could kill him, kill herself, and then they would be together forever in the afterlife. She seriously thought it to be a viable option. The only two things holding her up were the fear of the unknown and a possible trip to hell, which did not interest the self-professed Christian woman. She also wanted to see Garrison put away for what he did and knew that her and Dan's testimonies would be key. Killing him and herself before testifying may free the madman to kill again. More innocent children could die if Lyla were too selfish about the entire situation. She figured there was a better way. Depression was beginning to grip the woman, so a decision had to be made.

*

Dan originally had no idea how thoroughly upset Lyla was. He originally chalked it up as another sexual encounter, only this time it was with an older woman. Dan wanted to try everything at least once in life, so this was another experience. He thought back to that night often and truly did enjoy it, even though it made him recoil. Lyla was skilled, unlike an early twenties woman, and very good at pleasing a man. He wanted to remember it fondly and he was hoping she felt the same way. Unfortunately, she did not. She was depressed and sad about the entire situation. If Dan had been a little older or more emotionally mature, he would have treated the coupling with a completely different attitude. He would have held her the next morning and at the very least given her the respect she felt was deserved. He didn't, and he would have to deal with the consequences of his actions. How? Only Lyla knew the answer to that.

*

The guns Lyla collected throughout the years lay on her kitchen table. She was in the process of cleaning them and giving them a long, hard look. She owned two rifles, mainly for hunting, but also had her service revolver that had been issued to her as an employee of Animal Control. It was a basic .22 caliber handgun, and was very deadly if used properly. She had been taught how to use the handgun in school while training for her position, and learned how to effectively "shoot-to-kill." All fields of law enforcement, including a dispatch position that dealt with animals, were issued handguns for their protection. The public was sometimes apt to get a little upset when the beloved pets they owned were either being picked up for a trip to the pound, or worse yet, a trip to the "go to sleep" clinic. People tend to be as much, if not more, protective of their animals than they were of their own children.

Lyla continued to think about Dan as she cleaned her firearms. She loaded each piece and put them to the side. She studied them, mulled, studied them further, and mulled further. Would she just take herself out of the picture and leave Dan to his own devices? Perhaps she would simply kill the guy and take a hefty prison sentence, or the electric chair. Maybe, deep in her mind, she thought the murder-suicide idea that had been traveling around inside her head for some time now would be the best choice. Obviously, the ideal route would be to forget about him and move on with her own life. After all, there are other men in the world. So she picked a dud, so what? This was not the first time Lyla ever had sex with a man, so she wasn't feeling some first love self-pity. She just didn't know what to do. Lyla struggled and went over it again and again. She finally reached her ultimate decision, but would keep it under her hat. Lyla put her rifles in the gun case. She then placed her .22 in a holster, and laid it to the side for the night.

*

The case was tough on Dan. He had a huge testimonial in court that would possibly make or break Garrison's future. He knew what he had seen in the black bag and he recognized it was an awful situation. The question was: Would Garrison really try and do something that stupid? He had known John for some time and thought him to be much smarter than that. Yes, he was an old grump and yes, he was belittling, but that was just his personality. There are plenty of people like that in this world that do not kill kids. On the other hand, the kid was, in fact, in that bag. There was no denying the obvious. It was a tug-of-war in Dan's mind. He figured the only right thing to do was testify openly and honestly. It wasn't his decision to make, after all, it was for a jury. You just supply facts that you know. If you don't understand a query, you say so. Other than that, simply answer the questions. Dan thought for a few more moments, then went back to the top of his list: Lyla Helms. Dan hadn't heard from her since "the night." He knew why.

*

What to do….what to do? Call her? Maybe. Ignore her? There was a chance. Perhaps he would try to inch his way back in with flowers or a nice card. Whatever it would be, Dan knew that he had to somehow try to make up with his boss. He had to be very careful with his approach due to the fact that he didn't want to lead her on when there was no feelings of love on his side.

Dan was doing much better now, thanks to Lyla, who gave of herself very unselfishly in helping the young man get back on his feet. If not for that woman, he would probably be in a rubber room wearing a straight jacket. Perhaps he would be unable to take care of himself at all. This woman helped improve Dan's quality of life by leaps and bounds. He had already invited two women back to his apartment and was starting to get back to the old stud boy way. He still loved his life; he just didn't want to spend it all with Lyla. As a matter of fact, he wasn't crazy about spending it with any one woman. He liked variety. To him, it was the spice of life. Blonds, brunettes, long hair, shorthair, gothic, conservative. The choices and the differences went on and on. That was what Dan loved the most about his life. All the choices, all the women, and all the fun. Yet he still needed to figure out how to deal with Lyla.

"If I wouldn't have had sex with her, this would not be an issue," Dan reasoned to himself often. "Had I just kept my pants on, it might be okay. *Nooo,* I had to do the wrong thing. I'm weak."

All of this harkened to one word in the English language that is both scary and handwringing. That word is *regret.* Dan regretted his decision and would have to live with it forever, however long that is. Nobody has really known any regret to ever be good. "I regret doing something I shouldn't have done." "I regret not doing something I should have, in fact, done. I'll probably never have another shot."

Those are just two ways that regret harms and maims. It harms the soul for a lifetime. It maims the mind forever. Whenever that one word crosses the threshold of life, hang on tight, because it stays for an eternity. Hopefully, Dan would not further *regret* his decision to have a sexual encounter with Lyla.

*

Feeling better, Dan resumed his normal daily activities. When the trial ended, he planned on going back to work. He had been on disability, and was getting tired of doing nothing and getting paid for it. Despite the fact that he may be irresponsible in some aspects of life, work was not one of them. Dan loved to work, especially at the job he currently held. He missed going out and trapping critters. He missed the camaraderie with the locals. Most of all, he missed meeting the chicks he'd run into on his route. He felt that he needed to get back to seeing people. Dan was social and the last few months had been a kind of hell for him. If he had to endure another episode of "Days of our Lives," or "The Kardashians," he would probably lose his sanity. If he had to continue looking out his window and seeing everyone except him having a good time, he'd scream. There were just way too many things going on around him and he wanted to be involved. He'd already missed the town fair, which was a boon for picking up the lasses. He was missing other social events that were going on from time to time. People had wondered about him, too. They would ask each other questions about his well-being. That would lead to wild rumors flying. "He was dying!" "He'd lost his marbles and was going to a funny farm." "Dan's sitting in his house, turning into an old miser, and getting mean." All these little gossips could not have been further from the truth. Dan would think to himself, "Geez, can't anyone be sick or a little under the weather anymore without enduring the fifth degree from locals?" He was ready to rejoin society and be a productive member again. Dan Wheeler itched to get back into the swing. After the testimony and trial, he would. *He hoped.*

Truth and Consequences

Another day, another trip to court. John woke up in his cell at about 5:00 in the morning, ready for what could be his day of reckoning. He was completely healed from his heart attack of a couple months ago and wanted to get the trial over with, be found innocent and go on with his life. John still struggled with the fact that the case had gone this far with so weak evidence. The prosecutor and governor-elect were after him and he could do nothing but sit back and hope the fine citizens of Lincoln saw the light and let him go home. He knew that was doubtful, especially with the way some of the jurors were eyeballing him in court. John had an uncanny feeling that they would, in fact, find him guilty *AND* send him to his execution. He did not have any misconceptions about a jury giving him a life sentence, due to the fact that it was children who were killed. Even if they had been adults, the odds were still 70-30 in favor of death. Garrison had read the papers and studied the statistics, though he never once had the slightest idea he would face these horrors himself. Don't be fooled though. He was and always would be a smart aleck and an old grump. He was opinionated and found himself in trouble more than a few times because of it. John was also alone. He had no kids, so since his wife had passed, it was only him. The old coot was okay with that. He would have given his love a child or two and the grandkids that would follow, despite not caring much for children, but he knew going into his marriage that his wife was unable to conceive. He loved her so much he didn't care. It was just one of those things in life that you dealt with and made the sacrifice for when you loved someone unconditionally.

Speaking of life, when John thought about it, he would become angry. This world was what he referred to as a septic tank that he lived in until death, after which the wonderful things awaited him. His wife was lucky enough to already be enjoying the fruits of her afterlife, and regardless, death, life in prison, or even the longshot of freedom, he knew his days were numbered. He had already suffered a heart attack and wished the inmate next to him would have kept his mouth shut and let him die on the floor. Nothing would have been more satisfying than dying before they could try him. It would have been John's coup d'état. A huge middle finger directly in the system's face. Oh, how that would have been the cherry on his sundae. It was not to be, though. Unless he died today, which was very unlikely, he would have to face the music he was being forced to listen to. Garrison would never give up on the dream of being free again, because he thought conceding was for cowards with no backbone.

"A man ain't whipped 'till he gives up," John always said.

He would take what he had been given and deal with it. When the powers that be give you lemons, try to make lemonade. John continued his mental preparations for the day in court-a day that could yield his future plans.

*

The visions were getting more forceful. The dreams Amy was having were getting more vivid and much scarier. She felt a presence getting closer and closer every day. Maybe the good Doctor was right. Perhaps Amy should be continuing the treatment. It had only been a few days since her run in with Baxter at the office, and already it was getting worse. She knew that she needed to finish the case first, however, because her independent nature would not allow her to council with anyone until it was over. She left a message for her doctor promising to return to therapy, but needed medicine to see her through until then. Dr. Baxter okayed the prescription and Amy began taking the med right away. Although it had been just a couple of days without it, she had hoped this would subdue the visions and dreams. She had a backup pill or two, but hadn't been able to find them. In a short time, the visions had returned with a vengeance. It did not seem like the med had made so much of a difference that two or three days without it should matter, and it probably didn't. The pressure Amy was under was immense. She had to set herself straight and get to court for the biggest day of the trial. The most important witnesses would take the stand and it was up to Amy, and Amy alone, to protect John.

She heard her name, yet ignored it. Everywhere she looked, the younger version was there, staring back into her eyes. A mirror? Young Amy. A backseat in the car? There she was. Young Amy was now pursuing the adult with more strength. "Don't let Garrison die. Don't let little Jimmy's death go in vain. Pay attention to your past and accept it."

These sentences were repeating over and over in Amy's mind. The entire night before the biggest and most important court testimony should have been spent in a deep sleep. It wasn't to be. The night consisted of tossing and turning, trying to ignore the voices and visions. Young Amy was attacking with a purpose. But why? Amy would ask this question over and over. "Why do you pursue me? Go away and leave me be. You have no business with me. Your past and gone."

No matter, because the visions persisted. To anyone who was watching, Amy would appear to be acting strange. She would be gesturing and talking to blank spaces. Amy was reacting to nothing. She knew this. She knew the voices and visions were illusions brought on by stress, or PTSD, which the Doctor guessed to be the culprit. The deeper the trial, the more intense the eeriness. As frightened as the young attorney had been of these entities, she managed to freak out less and less when confronted with them. Dead dogs being dined upon, burning hair, electrocuted John and dismembered parents had a way of creeping out the toughest and most hardened individual, but after enough of this, Amy was becoming de-sensitized. In the latest visions, the young Amy appeared to be reaching out with the cold blue hands in an attempt to actually clutch the attorney. Each time Amy avoided the contact. The hands were getting nearer and nearer, as if she wanted Amy for her own. What if she actually grabbed Amy? What would happen then? Would the young ghost kill her? Hug her? Drag her someplace she did not wish to go? Those were inquiries that no one could answer, not even good old Dr. Baxter. Amy convinced herself that the medication would take hold again and the ghosts would back off. She expected that to be the result. Just a couple more days remained in the trial and Amy had to forge ahead with determination and fervor. It would be very tough, but if anyone could overcome such obstacles, it would be one Amy Fraser.

*

Ms. Fraser had to get ready to go, despite being absolutely exhausted from her night of very little sleep. She had large black rings under her eyes that mascara and shadow struggled to conceal. Her newly shortened hair brought out her facial features much more than before when she had nice long locks. She hated her haircut. She hated it more that it came about the way it did. “It just isn’t right,” she thought. “Why the hair?

“It was better than perhaps my face or nose. Everything can be worse. Nothing is as bad as it seems, right? The pendulum could always swing even lower, as long as you’re alive. In death, you’ve reached ‘rock bottom.’ How much lower could it be than that? Some would say hell, some would say conscious eternal darkness, while others would say both, but with fire burning you up 24-7. Ouch!” Amy felt better thinking in a more positive manner.

Amy spent part of her overnight hours looking up “Ghostly visions” and “Voices in your head” on her

PC. She found some fairly interesting facts, some a little frightening. As far as "ghostly spirits," she found information about eye disease. "The eyes' weakening causes the brain to overextend itself when trying to decipher what you're seeing." Other strange theories include sleep paralysis, and just plain, old-fashioned ghosts. Hearing voices in your head is explained away by claiming it to be the ghosts of other spirits, spirit guides or flat-out insanity. What bothered Amy the most was the one connection both events had in common; Post Traumatic Stress Disorder. The Doctor had told her more than once that it could very well be the cause of her troubles. "Just a touch of it," Baxter told her.

"Who can tell for sure? Maybe I'm truly seeing and hearing those things. Could it be that they're real?" Amy figured she would have a million nickels if she could accurately answer these questions.

In the meantime, she had to finish getting prepared for a very big day indeed. She gave the ghost thoughts a rest and focused on her paperwork for court over the customary toast and coffee breakfast.

*

The ring of attorney general appealed to Richard. Sonya liked it even better. She was interested in the ring of money jingling around in her purse as she shopped to her heart's content. Richard took a good attitude going into this day. He was almost assured of victory in court. His suit fit better today, his face looked cleaner, and the bruise was lightening. All was well in Richard's world except for one tiny thing: a loss in court today would probably mean swimming with the fishes, courtesy of Jack. He believed a defeat today would spell the end of not only his career, but his existence on the earth. Would Jack really whack him out if he lost? "You'd better believe it!" He nervously convinced himself. Those thoughts sent chills down Richard's spine and he put forth great effort to avoid them. He was further developing a twitch in his right eye. He unconsciously rubbed it away.

He had to come up with a strategy in case Garrison was acquitted. He would have his car parked as close as possible and he'd dash out of the courthouse and flee for wherever Jack wouldn't be. I guess that means "Hello Timbuktu!" All this could be avoided with one word: guilty. If that lone word was uttered by the jury foreperson, all would be smooth and back to normal. Everything would be lifted off Richard's shoulders and he would move on to the attorney general position. When Richard thought about things that way, the relief he felt was incredible. What a wonderful feeling it would be to have a great job, more money, and most of all, a happy governor.

*

Sonya Headly continued spending money that Richard had not yet earned. She was shopping much more and buying expensive gifts *(for herself)* which included rings, necklaces, shoes, clothes, and whatever else she could get her hands on. Sonya had never been this lucky in her whole life! When Richard was starting out as an attorney, they were fortunate to bring home $50,000 a year. It grew to $60-$70-$80, then finally $100,000 per year. It still wasn't enough for Sonya. "Our bills are cramped up? Our bank account is low? No matter. Richard, I need money. Richard, give me CASH!"

He tried to tell her to be patient and wait until he was making it before she spent it, but that was like talking to a steel girder under a bridge. In one side, out the other, yet the girder doesn't move. It doesn't hear, either. "Please, Sonya, relax until I get the job. We can't afford all this stuff right now." A twitch of Richard's eye.

"You'll get the job dear. I have no doubt whatsoever."

"Well la-di-frickin'-da!" was always Richard's thought. He could do absolutely naught about it anyway, unless he tied her down when he wasn't around. "She'd get loose," he figured, "then spend twice as much to make up for it." Perhaps he'd just kill her. The thought hadn't escaped Mr. Headly.

He continued to put his hope on getting the job Jack was offering. If he was to lose and disappear, *by his own accord*, after court, it would be without Sonya. She could sit back and deal with all the bill collectors that would come, "if she wasn't six feet under," he thought. There was no way Richard would take her with him. Perhaps he *could* just kill her and be done with it altogether! Richard surprised himself with such radical thoughts. "Maybe I'm the one going nuts. Everyone's driving me crazy!" The right eye twitched.

Richard tidied up, ate some breakfast and readied for his day. He told Sonya to stay away from court today and bribed her with $200 bucks with which to shop. She was easily amused when it came to cash. He needed her to stay away, though, for obvious reasons. He didn't pack anything to make an escape with. It was only Richard, his car, and a full tank of gas. If necessary, he would simply start anew.

Jack's First Loss

Jack Beauregard. The governor and recently crowned "big man" on campus. No one could describe his newfound character without mentioning the words arrogant, obnoxious, entitled, and pompous. All of these adjectives described Jack to a tee according to the people closest to him. His family and friends thought he was changing. He was becoming a king in his world, but a jerk in others.

Jack had already crawled under Soo's skin more than once and he was doing it again. A conversation about a wedding date turned volatile in a matter of a few errant seconds.

Soo had been shopping for wedding bands and dresses for her nuptials with Jack. The date of the wedding had not been set, but one can always prepare for the happy day. Soo came to Jack's home to tell him all about her latest wedding related excursions. She had been angry with the governor-elect off and on for a while, but it was nothing that could not be worked out between two mature adults.

"I'm so excited, Jack, I can't wait to show you everything I've done to prepare."

"Yep, okay. What have you got to show me?"

"Well, I went to Macy's and I…." Jack suddenly interrupted. "Macys? What the hell, Soo, you think I'm made of money?"

"Jack, I'm just looking, not buying."

"Good! If you buy, you can pay too."

Soo looked at her fiancé with shock and outrage. She could not believe he was being such a cad over a simple shopping trip.

"Well screw you, Jack. If you'd listen for once and think of somebody besides yourself, you may hear the whole story, which might end differently than you think."

"How dare you talk to me that way, Soo. I do everything for you. I was elected *the* top state official and I think you owe me a bit of respect."

"Oh, excuse me, shall I get to my knees and bow to the great Jack? The biggest thing in Nebraska since rows of corn?"

Jack was beginning to get angry. His face turned a reddish purple color and he rose off the couch to continue this little squabble standing up. He saw the bursts of light again. The flashes of anger, he thought.

"Don't be patronizing, Soo. You know I could boot you out the door in a split second and you'd be on your own. Don't think I won't do it."

"Ew, I so scared Jack." Soo's Asian dialect started interfering a bit due to the level of her anger.

"Why you don't do it, big man. Kick me out big shot."

Soo was thoroughly infuriated. She wasn't backing down and fought with an attitude of which few have seen.

"C'mon Jack. You'd stink as governor. You just got lucky to win. 똥구멍!"

Jack stepped closer to his woman and issued a stern warning. "So help me, Soo, if you don't back off I'll…"

"You *what* Jack? Huh, Jack? Are you going to hit me Jack? Are *you* big tough guy *who* slap me silly, Jack? You want to show me *how's* going to be Jack?"

Another step and one final warning. Soo was beyond livid and it didn't look like she would stop. Her face had also shaded to a bright red.

"What *you* want Jack? Want me to get *on* knees and kiss you ass?"

WHAP! Jack struck Soo with a speeding fist, not an open hand, and Soo flew backward with a fury. Her head swung sharply to one side and a trail of blood exited from her gashed lip and broken tooth. The red splatter hit the wall and began oozing down slowly, like thick molasses. Soo landed on the floor between the couch and the coffee table, books and magazines also took flight as she had tried to grab anything she could get her hands on during her tumble. She grabbed her mouth and lay on the floor sobbing. She was injured for sure, and Jack spoke up loudly.

"That's what I'll do, Soo! I'll beat your ass is what I'll do. Now pack your bags and get out of my fucking house, you two-bit whore." The power flashed stunningly before Jack's eyes.

The words flew with an awful cruelty. Jack didn't care. He was done with Soo, and she with him. It was over. Their relationship would end today. Jack felt relief, while Soo felt pain, physical as well as mental. She stood up, spit blood on Jack's carpet and headed upstairs to pack her things. She had a cut lip and was now missing one tooth on the left front side of her mouth. It was at this time that Kyle walked in and saw Jack wiping the blood off the wall.

"What happened, Dad? Jesus, is that blood? Are you okay?"

"Do me a favor and go to your room until Soo gets her stuff out, OK? I need a little space to work here."

Kyle suspected a rough housing session had just occurred and asked more questions. At least he tried to.

"But Dad, I just wanted to….."

"PLEASE, Kyle go to your room. We'll talk later."

Jack's eyes were bulging and his face remained a crimson red. Kyle decided to heed the advice and went upstairs. When he passed his dad's room, he saw Soo inside packing. He inquired.

"Are you okay Soo? Are you hurt?"

Soo kept her back to Kyle so he couldn't see the damage his father had inflicted. Kyle walked up behind her and gently turned her around.

"Oh man," Kyle said with a grimace. "He really did it this time, huh?"

"I'm out Kyle. You can come and visit me anytime, okay?" Soo put a cold cloth on her mouth.

"Okay. I will. I don't know what his problem is, but I'll find out."

Kyle was headed back towards the bedroom door, but Soo stopped him.

"No Kyle. Leave him. He'll hurt you too. I just want to leave in peace now. You go to your room and let it be."

Kyle agreed and did what Soo asked. He was angered, but really, what could he do? He'd give it an hour or so and talk with his dad over dinner. It was the right way to handle it. Just allow the anger to cool and see what the story was afterward.

Soo finished gathering her things up and had but one trip left to the car before leaving. She walked around the corner and Jack met her with his gun drawn and pointed right at her head. She froze in fear for her life. Jack grabbed her on each side of her mouth with a choke grip, then squeezed, furthering the pain from the split lip and missing tooth. "Soo. If you talk, you die. Guaranteed. Don't be a stupid woman."

Soo nodded her head yes, Jack released her, and she was allowed to continue her clean-up. She grabbed the last of her stuff, stopped by Kyle's room to hug him, and then left out the front door for the last time. Soo would not talk. She knew better. Jack had effectively scared the hell out of her and she wasn't sure what he was capable of.

Kyle came down and found his dad at the kitchen table nursing a cup of coffee. "Dad, what happened?"

"We will never mention this again, son. It's over for Soo and I. That's all I want to say about it."

"But Pops…"

Jack looked over at Kyle, just daring him to say one more thing about the situation. Kyle saw the gun lying on the table and wisely read this. He excused himself from the situation. He went out to dinner by himself and left his dad alone. He had seen into his father's eyes and didn't like it. Not one bit.

The Trial of John Garrison

Day 3

Everyone gathered for the final day of testimony. The case would probably go to a jury this very afternoon. Amy filed in, as did Jack, Richard, and Soo, with her black eye and chipped tooth. She had to be there because she was on standby in case further testimony was needed from her. The excuse she gave anyone who asked was "fender bender." It was an important day and no interviews were being given to the media by either of the lawyering parties. The press would have to wait until the courtroom drama played out, and then try again. The biggest inquiries were on how the attorneys would approach this day. How would their respective witnesses handle the questions? Nobody could answer, so why try? Attempting to predict an outcome would be foolish as well as ill-advised. Who wants to deal with the aftermath if they were wrong?

There would be five participants today. They consisted of Dan, Lyla, and Jack for the State, while Robert and possibly John would go up for the defense.

Amy was waiting to see how it would unfold before making the decision about her client testifying or not. She was already on pins and needles from a lack of sleep, and the visions would surely come as the day presented itself, although she hoped they wouldn't. The Judge entered the courtroom, went over any motions or business the attorneys had (which was very little), excused the witnesses to the hallway, and then called the jury in. Day three was under way.

Richard called Dan Wheeler to the stand. Lyla watched him with a menacing look on her face as he left the hallway and entered the courtroom. It was noted on Amy's scratch pad that there seemed to be a bit of animosity between the two. Perhaps she would ask about it.

"Good morning, Mr. Wheeler. Are you ready for some questions, sir?" Richard pleasantly asked.

Dan nodded his head, said what appeared to be a little prayer. He made a cross with his hand; chin to mid-section, then left then right, and on with the questioning.

Direct Exam by Richard Headly, State Prosecutor:

It started with the usual "where do you work" and "what do you do" inquiries. Then the deep, burning questions came.

"When you went to Mr. Garrison's house, what did you do?"

"I picked up a bag with what I assumed to be a dead dog in it."

"What did you find out later?"

"Upon returning to the office and going straight back to the incinerator to burn the carcass, I opened the bag and saw a dead boy inside." Dan was shaken with this testimony and tried to stay calm.

"What did you do after that, Mr. Wheeler?"

"It's a bit fuzzy, but I remember calling Lyla Helms on my radio and asked her to hightail it out to the burner."

Lyla sat in the hallway squinting her eyes as Dan was testifying, but it was hard to tell by the others if she was angry or having trouble seeing.

"Ms. Helms came out and looked in the bag, then called Jack Beauregard and reported the finding to him."

"Mr. Wheeler, could the bags have been changed on your way from John's house to the Animal Control center? Did you stop anywhere?" Richard asked reluctantly.

"Not that I remember. I think I went straight back, but you know it was a strange day and I was tripping out when I found the body. I forgot a lot of details after that."

"Nothing further."

Amy stood up, fought off the latest manifestation of strange voices and went to work.

Cross Exam by Amy Fraser, Defense Attorney:

"So Mr. Wheeler, is it possible you stopped on your way back to the office?"

"I don't think so, ma'am."

"You don't think so, huh? Sounds like "I don't know" to me. There's a chance you stopped then, right Mr. Wheeler?"

"I guess I could have, but geez, it's foggy."

All that could be heard in the courtroom was writers scratching on their notepads, and an audible "OHHH" from the jury box. The jurors were looking at each other after that last answer by Dan. Amy smiled broadly and then dismissed Dan from the questioning, Headly had just one more small inquiry.

Re-Direct Exam by Richard Headly, State Prosecutor:

"So Mr. Wheeler, there was an equal chance you stopped or did not stop. 50-50, right?"

"No sir. I wouldn't say that. It was more like 80-20."

"Nothing more, Judge."

Amy rejected further questioning. Moving things right along, Wiley called for the State to get their next witness.

"Lyla Helms, Your Honor."

Lyla stepped into the court room and made a wide circle around Dan as he exited. She looked very nice today. Her top was a colorful blouse and the skirt she was wearing was a bit high, exposing more leg than usual. It was an apparent attempt to get Dan's attention. Lyla stepped up into the box, took the oath and answered the questions.

Direct Exam by Richard Headly, State Prosecutor:

"Did you see a dead body in the plastic bag that Mr. Wheeler had ripped open?" Richard smartly asked.

"Sure did. He was deader than a doornail."

The gasp from the Joseph family was heard by Headly and he asked her not to be so insensitive in her descriptions. Lyla agreed and Richard continued.

"Mr. Wheeler testified that you called Jack Beauregard as soon as you saw this. Is that right?"

"Whatever Dan says must be true. He has *all* the answers." Lyla rolled her eyes and crossed her arms tightly across her chest.

Richard was not happy with that answer and asked again in a stern voice, adding a bit of commentary himself. "Ma'am, I do not want you to repeat Mr. Wheeler's answers. I want your own responses. Whatever Mr. Wheeler testified to belongs to him. Do you understand me?" Lyla nodded yes, with a smart and sarcastic look on her face. Richard repeated his question.

"Yes, I called Mr. Beauregard and told him about what I'd found."

"When Mr. Beauregard arrived, had anything been touched at all?"

"Nope, I didn't touch anything and Dan was off to the side retching."

"Nothing further, Your Honor."

Amy was right in the middle of one of her little spells. She looked straight ahead and seemed completely frozen. John gave her a nudge that resulted in nothing, then another nudge, with the same result. Donald Wiley's booming voice finally seemed to do the trick.

"Ms. Fraser, YOUR WITNESS!"

Amy shook her head, widened her eyes and looked around. She snapped out of whatever it was, but not before everyone in the court noticed.

"I'm sorry, Your Honor, I was in deep thought."

Judge Wiley politely urged Ms. Fraser that it was her witness, and then shook his head and tightened his lips in a "what the heck's wrong with her" sort of way. Amy stood, composed herself and cross examined Lyla.

Cross Exam by Amy Fraser, Defense Attorney:

"Ms. Helms, did you actually see Mr. Wheeler open the bag?"

"No. I walked out after he called me. It was obvious he had opened it and freaked out."

"So you don't know what happened between the time Mr. Wheeler picked the bag up at Mr. Garrison's house and his opening of the bag at the incinerator."

"I couldn't possibly know, I wasn't there. I trusted that Dan had a problem and I came running. I just reacted."

"Speaking of reactions, are you and Mr. Wheeler an item? Are you two dating?"

"OBJECTION!" Headly shouted.

Judge Wiley quickly piped in, giving Amy one final warning about her questioning techniques. He was none to happy. "Ms. Fraser, if you ask about witness relationships one more time, I will hold you in contempt and have you arrested. Understood loud and clear, Ms. Fraser? I don't care about where your line of questioning came from and I don't even want to know. This is your final warning."

Amy stood with her mouth open, jaw nearly on the floor as she endured this chewing out. She thought the relationships had a lot to do with it. Witnesses dating each other and then breaking up may smear the testimony. It didn't matter now, though, because she would have to avoid that type of inquiry no matter what. She finished up the best she could.

"The bottom line, Ms. Helms, is that you do not know what happened between the time your driver picked up the bag and called you on the radio, correct?"

"It was only an hour or so, but no, I don't know."

"No more questions."

A stunned and crestfallen Amy went back to her table. John shrugged to her. He was as in the dark as she was. Why the Judge acted that way is anybody's guess. John gave his lawyer a kind pat on the back. He knew she was trying, but her hands were being tied in knots. The Judge called for a twenty minute recess, probably to clear his own mind as well as allow everything to calm a bit. Jack was up next and it would be interesting.

Jack be Nimble

The bailiff called out to Jack, "Jack Beauregard, please take the stand, sir."

He assuredly and arrogantly entered the court. He was wearing his very best Italian knit and looked like a million bucks. The governor-elect waltzed to the stand and took his oath- an oath to tell the truth so help him God. Jack would most certainly tell the truth, *or his version of it*. Being the highest-elected official in the state allows one to apparently say and do as they wish. Today would be no different. Jack would answer all the questions *his way*. It was just after 10:00 a.m. when Jack stepped up. Dan and Lyla had already testified and this would represent the State's last witness.

As Jack sat comfortably in the box, Richard came forward to begin the examination. Jack was used to this seat since being a trooper meant testifying often.

Direct Exam by Richard Headly, State Prosecutor:

"Good day, Mr. Beauregard," Richard said very incredulously.

"Mornin', Mr. Headly. I'm ready when you are, sir."

"Boy, Jack was very good at being debonair and polite when he had to be," Richard thought silently.

"Tell us about the night you arrived at Lincoln Animal Control, Mr. Beauregard. What did you encounter?"

"Well, Mr. Headly, it was scary to say the least. Lyla Helms has my cell phone number and she called me when she made the grisly discovery. I was in my office thinking about the murders when she made contact. It was a pretty unique thing, having her contact me while I was pondering."

"What was your next move?"

"I called Lt. Michaels on my radio and told him to get to the office, which he did in less than five minutes and we rode out to the scene together. I called for back-up en route."

"And what did you discover after your arrival at animal control?"

"I quickly went back to the incinerator building and observed Mr. Wheeler vomiting while sitting off to the side. I then approached Ms. Helms, looked in the truck and saw the expired Joseph boy."

Richard paced back and forth in front of Jack while he listened to the answers. Amy was transfixed as she sat at the defense table with John. Garrison was squirming and making a pinched face as he listened. The jurors were taking notes and watching closely.

"What happened after this, Mr. Beauregard?"

"Ms. Helms told me that the bag had been picked up at John Garrison's home in Hickman, so I had the lieutenant put out an A.P.B. and we headed straight over there. I rode with Lt. Michaels and radioed three squad cars for back-up. Two other units stayed back at the scene waiting for the medical examiner to arrive and take the body to the morgue."

"What did you encounter upon reaching the Garrison home, Mr. Beauregard?"

"It was quiet and dark when we arrived. The police lights and hum of activity must have roused Mr. Garrison. He came storming out of the house in a threatening manner while wearing his undergarments. We were forced to shoot him with a Taser."

John wanted to scream at this part of the testimony. This is not how it happened at all. John came out of his house because of helicopters, police lights, *and* a media frenzy. He kept silent this time, scrawling down his notes and sliding them to Amy. Ms. Fraser was staring into the jury box until John broke her "daydream" by poking her arm with the legal pad. Amy seemed to be in and out of awareness of what was going on in court. John was keeping a closer eye on her, making sure she was getting the testimony. She apparently was getting it, because her questioning was effective and to the point, but she appeared distant.

"Did Mr. Garrison resist, sir?"

"No, he went down in a clump and we cuffed him, and then threw him in the paddy wagon. He wasn't armed. I believe we caught him by surprise."

"What happened next, Jack?"

"I had a short presser with the media that had gathered and headed back to the station to interview Mr. Garrison."

"Okay, let's fast forward to the interview with Mr. Garrison. How did that go and what transpired?"

Jack gave a quick and sassy smile as he mulled over this one. He was going to rip the heart right out of any defense that was trying to stand in the way. This was Jack's stage. "He said if I get him coffee and a phone call, he'd spill the truth."

The chatter in the courtroom picked up immediately. Heads were turning and whispers abounded. Wiley smacked his gavel. "Order, order please!" The throng calmed and Jack continued. "I went and fetched coffee and let him make his call, and then he reneged and wouldn't tell me a thing without a lawyer. I found it to be a low class move."

"So he said he'd talk and then backed off? Is that right? What did you do next?"

"Ended the interview and sent him to jail. He was arrested on suspicion of murder, at least one count. I gave him every opportunity to speak up, but he decided to clam up instead."

The jurors did not look happy. They stared at Garrison with dagger-like eyes. If he would have been the bull's-eye, there would be holes all through him. This did not bode well for the old timer and Amy had to bail him out, if she could.

"No more questions," Richard confidently stated.

"Ms. Fraser, your witness."

Cross Exam by Amy Fraser, Defense Attorney:

Amy walked to Jack's left, then back to his right. She had a pen smartly on the edge of her lips as if it were a lollipop. She paced this way for a good thirty seconds or so, then finally spoke. "Mr. Beauregard, you say the press was at Mr. Garrison's house when you arrived. How did they know there would be a pick-up of a suspect?"

"They must have heard on the police scanner, Ms. Fraser."

"You also said he came out of the house in an offensive manner. Why would someone come out with their underpants on if they were being a threat?"

"I don't always know why people do what they do. It baffles me, too."

"Wouldn't the real story be that you yourself called the media so they could see you bust the "murderer," Mr. Beauregard? Would it also be true that Mr. Garrison was fast asleep when you arrived and simply came out to see what was going on?"

Jack smiled coyly.

"Number one, Amy, I never called the press and number two, I perceived Garrison as a threat. I take that very seriously, ma'am."

"Ms. Fraser is how I'd like you to refer to me, *Mr. Beauregard*. Thank you. My next inquisition involves the interview at the police station. Did you in fact grab my client by the collar and threaten physical harm if he did not tell you he was the murderer?"

"Well, Ms. Fraser," Jack said very sarcastically, "the answer to your question is a simple no, ma'am. I never threaten my suspects and I never put my hands on them. I don't know what you heard, but the real truth hurts."

Jack felt that he was routing Amy. She couldn't get the guy to come close to cracking, and besides, she had very little to go on except John's word. She was afraid she was losing the jury. She was also afraid she was losing her edge. Everything up until this point was difficult, what with the voices, visions and the case itself. Now it had been ratcheted up another notch. Amy could feel the noose tightening around her neck. She decided at this point that asking Beauregard anything else would do more harm than good. She was going to rely on her own defense to try and get John exonerated. She looked at the clock and saw that it was about lunch time, so she ended her cross. Amy was dead on, because Wiley dismissed everyone until one thirty. She would spend her hour and a half with John, gearing him up. Richard threw another curveball and decided that after lunch, he would re-cross Jack, thus making Amy's life even more miserable while at the same time punching huge holes in Garrison's credibility. This even before Robert or John were to testify. Amy tried to keep her enthusiasm, but it was tapering rapidly. The young lawyer was feeling weak in the knees and light-headed. She had to keep going for John. She was too persistent and resolute to stop now. Or was she?

Amy be Quick 1

"I'm concerned, John. It's your word against Jack's and I think he's being believed by the jury. We have to pull a rabbit out of a hat."

"Gotdamn it Amy, what's goin' on in there? Your head's in the clouds or somethin'." She ignored John's question.

Amy sat with her elbows on her knees as she tried to figure out a way to turn the tide. The State had a weak case and she knew it, but it's tough to battle against VIP's when they don't tell the whole truth, which Jack had done masterfully. He was poised and serious with just a touch of sympathy for the jurors to eat right up. Who's to be believed? A Colonel Trooper who was to be governor or a seventy-some year old man who was not only a grump, but had a huge disadvantage because a bag had a body in it? There was no way for Amy to call the real killer to the stand when she had no clue who it was. She did know that it *wasn't* John, though. She had every confidence that the State had set up her client to take the fall. Jack was elected governor by the public because of it. She didn't even vote for the slime ball either. Amy attempted to calm John's nerves.

"We're putting up a good defense. The best defense we can. Let's hope that, coupled with my closing, it will help the jury see the light. I will admit it does not look good, but we don't know what the jurors are thinking at this point. I could be mistaken and they may be on our side."

"You can't cheer me up with some pep speech right now, Amy. I want results. I'm not getting' 'em so far. I thought you were one of the best. I may have been wrong about you."

Now John's head hung low. He was starting to get frightened at the prospects, but deep down he thought any lawyer would have a tough time with this case. There was simply too much "could be" and not enough "absolutely is."

*

John was not afraid to die. Dying might even be better than he thinks. It could be rainbows and candy canes. His wife could be waiting for him at the end of the light with open arms. The mere thought brought a smile to John's face. He figured that he'd lived a good long life and dying now wouldn't be that much different than any other old man who expires due to natural causes or cancer or whatever else takes old people. Still, just because John wasn't afraid did not mean he was ready either. He wanted to do it on nature's terms, not by some goofy cop-turned-governor elect.

He knew all the boys down at Harry's Barbershop were probably watching the proceedings and talking up a storm. He so badly wanted to be with them, mulling about some other guy's misfortune. It wasn't to be. Maybe he would slither through this mess and join them tomorrow or the next day, or perhaps next week. John had been jailed for sometime now and wanted his freedom back. After all, he did nothing. He was simply trying to help keep the environment clean and devoid of dead animals. There's no sin in that. He also wanted to strangle Beauregard for using him as a pawn for political gain. John wondered how somebody could be so cold and calloused as to throw a life away for their own personal gain. He thought that Jack could have won the election without throwing anyone under the bus. He had the lead, and seemingly owned the momentum before all this happened, but John was not one to feel sorry for himself and would not start now. He was a tough and grizzled old codger with attitude and fight left in him. His thought was that Amy was failing him because something was bothering her. He wasn't sure what it was, and he tried to find out, but Amy didn't say too much. She was concentrating on his defense the best she could under very trying circumstances. Her questioning was okay, but not amazing. Her mind just seemed to be somewhere else at the most crucial moments. In the three days of trial, Amy was on a downspin, spiraling a little further south each day. It was far too late to do anything about it now, so John had to go forward this afternoon with hope that she would snap out of it and pick up the pace. He wasn't holding his breath.

*

"What's wrong with me?" Amy inquired to herself in the upstairs bathroom of the courthouse. "Why am I losing *it* like this, whatever "*it*" is?"

Amy Fraser sat on the toilet crying her eyes out. She was losing her grip on reality and needed help. She was tough and abrasive through her life and stood up to any challenges flung in her direction, but she was weakening. Amy was running out of strength and running out of answers. As she sat on the commode ruing her client's fate, she was "blessed" with a visit from the young Amy, who made her presence known from the next stall over. The wall dividing the stalls wore thin, and then disappeared, exposing Amy to her alter ego sitting on the toilet next to her. The ghoulish vision also looked worse for wear. Her eyes were a deep bloodshot, while her face appeared bruised and swollen. The young Amy creepily moved her gaze toward Amy. Her body stayed in a forward-facing direction as her neck twisted to the right grotesquely, eyes meeting eyes.

"I want you, Amy. I need you to complete my journey."

Amy responded with a nasty sneer. "NO! I will not go with you or give myself to you. You leave me alone and allow me to finish my life in peace. It's my life!"

"It's *our* life Amy. You weren't the only victim. I am your soul, I am your spirit. You *will* come with me Amy. You *will* join me in hell."

"I WON'T! I WON'T JOIN YOU ANYWHERE!"

Amy lashed out with her right hand to give the spirit a punch, but only managed to smack her fist squarely on the divider between them. The impact was painful and sharp. Amy looked down and saw that she had broken two fingernails. She began to cry again as the pain swelled up her arm and into her shoulder. The frustration was also bubbling over and sent Amy into a state of flux. She put her head between her knees and muffled her weeps in case someone walked in. The wall again disappeared to expose the remainder of the ghostly figures before her. Jimmy, Mom and Dad, and a burnt-to-a-crisp Garrison. Why Garrison was involved in some of the visions was a mystery unto itself. John was alive. He was downstairs waiting on his supposedly accomplished, professional lawyer.

"What do you want from me?" Amy insisted. "Go away! BE GONE!"

Amy was more angry than frightened, but it didn't matter as the figures simply stood in the stall staring her down. The bathroom door then opened with a "*Reeek*" and the spirits were gone. The partition again lay before her, as brown and solid as it had been to start. One spot of wording formed "Beauregard blows me." How apt. Amy snickered.

The young lawyer stood, put herself together and walked out of the stall and into the bathroom lobby. She faced the mirror and tidied up while another woman used the exact stall where the visions were. A minute later, the stall door creaked open. Amy looked through the mirror in a natural curiosity to see who it was and if she knew her. As the door continued to open, young Amy reappeared. She was still bloody as she sat on the commode. Amy gasped for her breathe and darted her eyes away from the grisly scene.

A voice spoke. "Hi Amy. What's up?"

Amy looked into the mirror again and saw the court stenographer looking right at her. She was just finishing up with reconnecting her belt and walked to the sink next to Amy.

"Tough case, huh Amy?"

"Uh, yes, as a matter of fact it is." Amy's voice was shaky and quivered with her words.

Judge Wiley's stenographer turned toward Amy and gave her a bit of unwanted advice.

"You may want to think about a vacation after the trial. You look like you need a break."

Amy scowled as she responded. "Thanks for the kind word. You don't look so hot yourself, sister."

The stenographer's expression went from smile to frown in that very second. "Well excuse me for trying to be helpful."

"There's no excuse for you dear. Now get away from me." The lady left in haste.

Amy finished washing up and headed back downstairs to go over a few more notes with John.

*

John stewed in his chair. He was waiting for his attorney to return and go over any last minute details. It was quiet in the room. He was cuffed to the table and a guard stood outside the door, but hey, it beat sitting in that disgusting jail cell back at the post. Amy finally returned and was allowed in to see John. The conversation picked up where it left off earlier.

"As I was sayin' Amy, you better get your act together before we go back out there. I have no choice but to keep ya' for the duration."

"Well that's good John. I wouldn't fire me now either. We're not losing as much as we have very little to fight with. It's a paltry amount of evidence either way. Yes, I feel like Beauregard definitely used you, but if I mention that, I'm liable to get thrown out on my ear."

"Well ya' better be effective, Ms. Fraser, or I'll be in the fryin' pan sooner than you can say 'roast duck.'"

The last comment caused Amy to smile, although it wasn't really funny. It was just the way John put together his sentences and spun them in a humorous way. He owns that "old man in the Midwest" accent where "gs" are rarely included at the end of "ing." One needs a touch of levity when thinking about going back inside the court and fighting it out for the second half of the day. It would be a skirmish and Amy had a thing or two up her sleeve, but she knew it probably wouldn't be enough. How frustrating to fight an allegation where the evidence is entirely circumstantial and a body is found at your client's front door. Amy also had that tiny problem with the ghouls she was attempting to deal with at the same time. They were devious in their attack. It didn't matter what Amy might be feeling, they pounced on her all the same. Perhaps mental illness *was* the culprit. It was that or they were real, which is so far-fetched it makes one sick to their stomach. Amy was tired of trying to figure it out. As a matter of fact, she was simply tired.

John decided that he wanted to say a few more things to Amy before they went back into the storm.

"Okay, Amy. I know you're doin' you're best, so I have to have some confidence in you. Just keep on tryin' what you're tryin' and let the cards fall where they may. I don't mean a gotdamn Jack of Spades neither."

"I will, John. I will try the best I can, but you have to know that…."

"I know already, you don't need to say nothin' else. Just fight for me, huh?"

Amy again started to weep, but held it back just in the nick of time. Another millisecond and her face would need another clean-up. She had to suck it up for a while longer and dig down as deep as she could. Amy was losing her grip, but believed she had enough to pull through the trial.

Amy Be Quick 2

Jack took his seat in the witness box and was now ready to throw a huge stick of dynamite at the defense table. Neither Amy nor John had any idea as to what Beauregard was about to do. Richard shuffled through his notes then approached Jack.

Direct Exam by Richard Headly, State Prosecutor:

"Mr. Beauregard, did you and your forensic team search Mr. Garrison's house thoroughly on the night he was arrested?"

"We certainly did. We also did some follow up the very next day."

"Did you find anything of interest? If so, what was it?"

Beauregard looked over at Amy and John and smiled like a Cheshire Cat. He had his ducks in a row and was now going to bare a big one.

"We found five decks of playing cards. The interesting part, though, is that each deck was missing the Jack of Spades."

Audible gasps, coughs, and gurgles filled the room. Donald Wiley, the Judge himself, could not help but widen his eyes at this bit of information.

"OBJECTION!" Amy roared, "We did not see this in discovery. This is new to the defense team."

"Your Honor," Headly reasoned, "we will immediately add this to the exhibits list and we will give Ms. Fraser a copy. This was a forgotten piece of evidence sir."

"Objection sustained. Councils approach my bench please."

The second they approached, Amy screamed for a mistrial based on Headly trying to sway the jury with bias. Headly stuck with his story about "forgotten evidence." Wiley said no to Amy, chastised Headly for his "sleazy" gathering of evidence and then sent them both back to their respective areas. After doing this, he spoke.

"Members of the jury, you will disregard the evidence presented just a moment ago. It will not be admitted and it will not be considered when you deliberate, understood?"

All the jurors nodded yes, and Wiley ordered the questioning to continue.

"Nothing more!" Richard exclaimed.

"Nothing, Judge," was Amy's very angry sounding response.

Jack was excused from the stand and what should have resulted in a mistrial was simply patched up by Wiley in his own non-confrontational way. The positive is that it would help in the event that an appeal was necessary. What doesn't help at all is the fact that the jury heard it, stricken or not, and it would be in their minds. It was a dastardly trick pulled off by Headly and Beauregard. This was their law at its sleaziest, a conviction no matter what. Headly was asked about his next witness and stood before Wiley.

"The State rests Your Honor."

Donald Wiley looked at Amy. She was nervous and apprehensive, but as ready to go as she could be under the circumstances. "Call your first witness, Ms. Fraser."

"The defense calls Robert Long."

Long stood up very tall and slowly meandered to the stand. He had been waiting three days and it was finally his turn. He wore the same suit as day one, but surely he took it off and hung it up at the end of each session. There were no wrinkles and it was clean. The neighbor of John Garrison took the stand, was sworn and sat down. His long legs caused his knees to stick up about four inches above the swinging door. He made himself as comfortable as possible and Amy moved in.

Direct Exam by Amy Fraser, Defense Attorney:

"You know my client, John Garrison. He states you're his next door neighbor, is that right?"

"Yep. He's my neighbor, but we live three miles apart."

"Let's get straight to the point, Mr. Long. Did you go to Mr. Garrison's house, by request, and assist him in a bag-up job?"

"Yep. I helped 'em bag up an ol' dead dog."

"Really? When was this?"

"Same day John made it on TV in his underpants."

Robert smiled broadly and almost busted another gut laughing the way he did that night in question, but managed to keep it to a smile this time. His funny bone had been tickled.

"Okay, Mr. Long. The day you saw John on TV in his undergarments was the day you helped him pack the dog up? Is that right, sir?"

"Yepper! We bagged up that dog 'n left it at the end of the driveway. John said he was gonna call the pound to come pick it up."

Now Amy was getting somewhere. The jurors were scratching notes while she felt a touch of positive energy come back to her.

"Thank you, Mr. Long. State's witness."

Up walked Richard with a sly smile and rubbing his hands together. He was ready for this.

Cross Exam by Richard Headly, State Prosecutor:

"Mr. Long, did you stay with Mr. Garrison until the package was picked up?"

"Nope. John was crabbin' at me, so I went home."

"So you don't know what the Animal Control actually picked up at Mr. Garrison's house?"

"All I know is I helped 'em pack a dead dog."

"Is it possible that Mr. Garrison had time to exchange the dog for an actual body?"

"That depends on what time they picked it up. I didn't stay so I don't know."

"Let me help you Mr. Long. The animal control unit was called at noon and the dispatch was at 12:15 p.m., In Mr. Wheeler's logbook, the package was picked up at 3:10 p.m. Now, sir, does that give Mr. Garrison enough time to switch the packages?"

Robert began feeling the perspiration run down from his armpit to his hip. He was getting edgy, but had to answer the question as honestly as possible. He took an oath after all.

"Yes. He had time to switch 'em."

Another swoosh of whispers and gasps engulfed the room. The jurors looked at each other again and said nothing, but their eyes grew into saucers.

"No more questions."

Amy tried her best to deflect this, but couldn't. She asked Robert if it was, in fact, a dog they bagged. Robert answered affirmatively and he was dismissed from the stand. Amy could only hope that John's testimony would help. Doubtful. The air and energy that had temporarily lifted her spirits quickly disappeared. It was time for her to call John up and see what he had to say, and more importantly, see what the State would do to counterattack. At this point, "Deadly Headly" was routing Amy and her client. Amy called John and they were down to their last gasp. Bottom of the ninth, two outs, and no one on base. Down by four. Little to no hope. A chance, though, and that's all one could ask for at this point. John took his seat and Amy began.

Direct Exam by Amy Fraser, Defense Attorney:

"Mr. Garrison, please tell the jury about the day in question. What did you do that day?"

"Well, I found a dead black dog on my property. I think it was a chow mix or something. I called my buddy, Robert Long over to the house to help me bag it up so Animal Control could come and get it."

"Why did you bother Mr. Garrison? Why not just let it decay in the field?"

"I don't wanna smell no nasty dead dog. It'd stink up my whole property."

Amy gave John a little wink reminder to talk with the best grammar he knew. It was important that he tried to do this. The jury needed to hear a smart, well educated man right about now.

"So you bagged it with Mr. Long's help, called Animal Control, and then what, Mr. Garrison?"

"Then I took a nice nap under the eave of my garage. It was hot out and I wanted to relax a little. No sin in that."

"Did you stay under the eave napping?"

"Not the whole time. At one point I was too hot in my overalls, so I went in and changed into cooler duds."

"How long did that take?"

"A few minutes. I changed, used the toilet, then grabbed a cold beer and went back to my seat. I saw the bag still lying there, so I figured I'd give the truck a few more minutes to show up before I called them back."

John struggled with words like "them," but managed to add the "G" at the end of "ing." It was tough, but he was sounding a bit more intelligent than he had just a few minutes earlier. Amy continued, "So they finally showed up and took the package?"

"Yes. I even helped Dan Wheeler toss it in his truck."

"So in summary, you called animal control because you wanted to be good to the environment. You know, keep things cleaned up?"

"Of course. I don't want the stink and it was dead so it needed disposing. It made sense to me."

"Could those bags have been switched by someone when you walked away for those few minutes to change and get a drink?"

"That's the only thing that could've happened, because I didn't kill no boy and try to pack him off to the incinerator. That's ludicrous."

"No further questions, Judge."

Richard stood up and nonchalantly circled the table. He then paced in front of John. Garrison, not surprisingly, asked the first question. "Are you gonna' talk, or walk?"

"I'll be doing the asking, Mr. Garrison. You just answer, thank you."

"Well, yer welcome," John chimed with chuckles from throughout the gallery.

Cross Exam by Richard Headly, State Prosecutor:

"Mr. Garrison, do you expect the jury to believe that concocted pile of lies you just came up with?"

"Not only do I expect it, it's the whole truth. I never killed nobody."

"Right. Somebody just happened to be walking by with a bag containing a murder victim and switched it for a dead dog? That seems a tad far-fetched, wouldn't you agree?"

"I don't know what in hell happened, but somebody switched it somewhere, and it wasn't me, gotdamn it! Stop tryin' to make it look like it was me!"

Wiley told John to watch his language in court. If it didn't pertain to the case, then it wasn't necessary. John nodded and Headly continued shredding his story.

"Sounds strange to me, Mr. Garrison. I'll bet it sounds strange to everyone. You bagged up a dead boy, didn't you, Mr. Garrison? Now's the time to come clean. Get it off your conscious so you can move on. So the families can move on. Your story really is pathetic."

"You call it what the hell you want, lawyer. You, Beauregard and the State are hornswoggling me and the public. Shame on you, ya gotdamn railroaders!"

"Tsk, Tsk, Mr. Garrison, your temper. No more questions."

Amy stood to do damage control. John was losing his cool. She needed to calm him and ask just a couple of more questions.

Re-Direct by Amy Fraser, Defense Attorney:

"Mr. Garrison, please calm down. Just tell me, did you kill anybody?"

"Well hell no! I ain't no gotdamn murderin' menace."

"So you believe someone framed you, right?"

"Yes ma'am. Not only do I think it, I know it. It was that son-bitch right over there."

John pointed at a now chuckling Beauregard. Jack put his fingers on his nose in a "whoo that stinks" motion and laughed again. This is when Garrison jumped out of the box and headed straight for him.

"I'LL KICK YER GOTDAMN ASS BEAUREGARD. YOU'RE A DOUBLE-DEALIN', FRAMIN' BASTARD."

The bailiff pounced on John about five feet before he reached the governor. Garrison went down in a crumpled heap, was cuffed and dragged out of court and into one of the holding cells on the other side of the door. Judge Wiley bashed his gavel on the counter and demanded order. He told Amy that Garrison would only be allowed back into court completely shackled. Any chance of Garrison's acquittal seemed to disappear when the tantrum erupted. Perhaps John knew this would be the last opportunity to slug out the pompous head of the state.

The real killer sat in court giddy with excitement. The plan was coming along perfectly. Amy was stunned and sat at the defense table with an apparent spell looming over her, as she stared straight ahead. Headly was leaning on the state table with his arms crossed and a big smile, the jury was led out of court and into the jury room, locked in until the closing arguments began.

"I'm calling a thirty minute recess," Wiley shouted. "Until this place quiets down."

As You Were Sayin'

Court reconvened after thirty minutes. It seemed that all parties had settled down and were ready to pick up where they left off, less the riotous behavior. John was brought back to sit with Amy. He was completely shackled and cuffed to the table itself to avoid any opportunity for further temper fits. Amy was bleary eyed and looked very tired. She was fixated on the wall for twenty of the thirty minutes they were given for recess. It appeared to be one of her strange trances. Her hair was disheveled and her skin looked wishy-washy. Being as dark-complected as she was, this was a cause for at least some concern. Jack was back in his seat, this time with body guards on each side to protect him, one of them being Lt. Michaels, who incidentally did not have to testify. Anybody who was involved in the testimony was now welcome to leave, or sit in the court room as they moved on to closing statements. Soo-Chin was the first to go. Lyla followed. Dan, Robert and the Joseph parents stayed. Judge Wiley issued a scolding to the participants that was harsh in nature and especially directed to Garrison, who just couldn't seem to keep that fire hot temper in check.

"I know this makes for great TV, but I am thoroughly disappointed with the conduct shown in

my court. I told everyone at the beginning of this trial that I expected full cooperation and was shown very little. Shame on the parties that couldn't seem to keep their cool and shame on the gallery for playing into it. I thought seriously about emptying the court for the remainder of the trial, but was talked out of it by my bailiff. He promises to place in jail the next person that misbehaves in my court. I will levy fines and I will also give jail time to the next perpetrator. I'm not going to ask if I've made myself clear, because I know I have. Do not embarrass this court any further, or their will be hell to pay!"

Wiley, a normally mellow Judge, had it up to his ears with his courtroom being used as a playground. He was not kidding, as he would have the next instigator placed in lock-up. When the diatribe was over, Judge Wiley called for Headly to deliver his closing argument. Headly was more than happy to oblige.

Richard Headly's closing argument:

"Ladies and gentlemen of the jury, you have seen and heard with your own two eyes and ears exactly what Mr. Garrison is like. He is a hothead with a manipulative attitude. He kills when he feels like killing and to hell with everyone else. John Garrison murdered two boys. He was caught the second time around. If not for that stroke of luck, he would still be killing."

The jurors were paying close attention. A cough here, a throat cleared there, with one hundred percent straight faces owning looks of attentiveness. Amy sat listening, but did not feel very well. She was still a pale color, but had gained back a bit of her aura. She was struggling as she took in Richard's closing. The killer also sat, watching with a smile and a sense of great satisfaction. All was well in his world.

"If we let this monster go free, he will terrorize and kill again. Whose boy would it be next? Yours? Perhaps yours? Maybe even your child." Headly pointed at random jurors as he said this, hoping to bring home the stark realization, at least in his mind. "Don't let a killer walk, people. Do not, under any circumstance, let this man go. We have proven that he, in fact, committed these crimes. A bag in his driveway with a dog in it? Somebody made a switch when Garrison wasn't looking? You don't really believe all of that gibberish do you? We have proved our case. The defense has not proven that he didn't do this. First, they try to push the blame onto someone else; second, they concoct a very questionable story. They are simply drawing at straws people. What more is needed? What more is necessary? Nothing more, that's what. Come back with the guilty verdict this man deserves and has earned. If you do not, you put everyone's kids in danger. Thank you."

Amy was teetering on the edge of exhaustion. If she could just make it a little further, it would be over. She arose and walked to the jury box, ready for her last ditch effort to free John.

Amy Fraser's closing argument:

"Hello again. For the last few days you've heard absolutely nothing. No evidence, no proof, and no one able to prove that John did anything. Not one person saw Mr. Garrison conceal a child. Not one person ever saw any kids around him. How can anyone say with any certainty that this man is a killer of young boys? There was no DNA evidence linking my client and the State Pathologist herself said she found nothing…NOTHING implicating Mr. Garrison. Let me ask you this, jurors. Why would Mr. Garrison call Animal Control to dispose of a body when he could have done it himself? He could have set a fire in his large yard and simply burned the evidence. Why on earth would he take a chance on being caught?"

Amy stopped for a moment and steadied herself against the jury box railing in front of her. She looked at her feet, which were a tad fuzzy, and shook her head, attempting to ward off the queasiness. After a few seconds, she managed to continue. "Finding this man guilty is the same as condemning both of those dead children. You would not be doing them any favors by sending this innocent man to the prison. You would not be serving the justice that these boys deserve. You would be making the entirely wrong choice if guilty is your verdict. Don't send John to jail just so everyone can say "we got 'em," or "That's the end of that." It would not properly serve this court or the justice system adequately. Don't be sway…ed by e..mo..tion….or….by…."

Amy stopped again and felt a warmth run from her feet all the way up to the top of her skull. She was again swaying dangerously on the edge of unconsciousness. The room began looking dim and the lights around her began to whirl. She was losing her balance and BAM! Down she went. She crumpled next to the jury box, managing to hang on to the rail for a second, before weakening and letting go. She did not fall hard, but it was more than apparent she was out cold. Some members of the jury, who sat next to the rail, attempted to catch Ms. Fraser, but her initial tumble was too quick.

"Bailiff, call an ambulance please." Wiley ordered, "Ladies and gentlemen keep your seats and please stay quiet. We will get her help."

Even Richard came over and checked on Amy. He bent down and lightly slapped her face to try and roust her. He noticed she was as hot as a fireplace and had to be running a fever. He fanned a notepad over her to try and give her cool air. Amy began to come around. She opened her eyes and saw Headly looking at her with concern.

"Thank you, counselor." Amy said weakly.

"Just stay quiet, Ms. Fraser. Help is on the way."

Amy gave Richard a gentle shove and rose back to her feet. She was coming around and wanted so badly to finish her closing.

"Judge, let me finish, and then I'll go to the hospital."

"Are you certain, Ms. Fraser? You don't have to. We can finish later."

"No, no. I'd like to finish now."

The EMS team had reached the courtroom, but stayed back in the gallery while Amy finished her closing arguments. This was a tough girl, but no one knew how strong she really was.

"Jurors, allow me to apologize for the minor mishap. I just have a couple more things to say and I'll be finished. The State, Dan Wheeler and Mr. Garrison all testified to the fact that the bag lay in the driveway for a substantial amount of time. Long enough for a switch to be made. The real killer could easily have set Mr. Garrison up to take the fall. I say the "real killer" because it's not the man I'm defending. My client didn't and wouldn't kill children. As I said before, don't let him go to jail. Don't condemn an innocent man. Be smart about your decision, not emotional. Don't let John fall victim to what so many have fallen victim to already, which is a snap decision, a knee-jerk reaction to send someone, anyone, to prison, or worse, death. Since the death penalty was established in Nebraska twenty years ago, 14 men have been executed and 20, yes I said 20, men have been exonerated due to DNA evidence which proved they were not the real murderers. How many of the 14 who did die were actually guilty? Ask yourself, please. I implore you. You cannot convict without evidence. You cannot condemn without proof. Thank you for your time."

Amy gingerly walked over to the EMS workers and they lightly led her out of court. John sat at the table alone as Richard still had his rebuttal to attend to.

Richard Headly's rebuttal:

"I know you just saw a very difficult situation, people." Richard attested, "but do not let that bit of unscripted drama leave you feeling sorry for Mr. Garrison. If you'd like to feel a spell of concern for Ms. Fraser, then please, by all means, but don't feel it for that beast sitting right there. A killer switched bodies? Please. We are all more intelligent than to fall for a weak, manipulative argument such as that. Throw that man away. He's a cold-blooded killer of children." Headly pointed straight at John as he said this.

"Screw you Mr. Headly. Screw you, Mr. Beauregard, and fuck you, court system!" John calmly stated.

"Take him to jail bailiff. I warned everyone and especially you Mr. Garrison. Your outburst just cost you."

"Cost me what, Judge? My life? My dignity? My freedom? Screw you too, Your Honor! You're no better than any of these railroadin' pieces of shit."

The bailiff finally was able to free the cuffs from the table and quickly shooed John out, but not before he spewed one last poison dart. "To hell with you jurors, too! You ain't no better!"

The door slammed shut and Garrison was gone, perhaps for good.

"The State rests its entire case, Your Honor." Richard advised, "Nothing more needs to be said."

John Falls on the Candlestick 1

"Ladies and gentlemen of the jury, you have heard from both sides in this case. You will now be sent back to deliberate Mr. Garrison's guilt or innocence in this matter."

Judge Wiley carefully spoke with the jurors before sending them back to negotiate John's fate. He wanted to make sure they understood their duties as citizens and decision makers. He continued his kind lecture to the peers. "If you think, beyond a reasonable doubt, that Mr. Garrison murdered these children, then you must find him guilty. If you do not think, beyond a reasonable doubt, that he committed murder, then you must acquit him. There are also separate counts of kidnapping on the verdict sheet. If you believe Mr. Garrison committed these murders, then he will automatically be found guilty of the other offenses. If you think he's innocent, he will automatically be found innocent of the other charges. It will be "guilty as charged," or "not guilty." That's all you need to worry about. You will now be led back to the jury room to deliberate. You will let the bailiff know when you come to a decision. Please elect a jury foreperson when you go back, and then do your deliberating. Thank you and good luck."

The jurors filed back to the jury room and the clock started. They would now decide Garrison's fate. They had seen a lot of excitement in three and a half days. Everything from a smart-mouthed defendant to a woozy, then collapsing defense attorney. It was quite a spectacle, to say the least. Upon entering and taking their seats, the jurors agreed to vote immediately on a foreperson. Juror number eleven, Oscar, was the unanimous choice. Oscar even voted for himself. He was an older gentleman who seemed to have a flair for being smart. Whether he was or not was beside the point, because he sure looked intelligent.

Oscar called for a vote right away on John's innocence or guilt. The jurors voted and slid their secret ballot to the center of the table. Oscar collected them and began his announcement of each casting.

"Guilty, guilty, guilty, guilty, guilty, guilty, not guilty, guilty, guilty, guilty, not guilty, guilty. That's ten guilty and two not guilty. Will the two not guilties please raise your hands?" Oscar ordered. Juror number seven, James and juror number one, Liz both raised their respective hands. The arguments would begin.

*

Lying in the hospital bed with an IV in her arm and a scowl on her face, Amy was looking better. She was tired and dehydrated, though. She had a severe lack of fluid and a bad headache, which was beginning to straighten itself out. The trial was an emotional train wreck for her and she tried to process all that happened in that room the past few days. It was a very tough go for the young lawyer and she needed a long break. If

Garrison was found innocent, that would be fantastic. Assuming he wouldn't, she had to prepare her appeal to the State. She would take a vacation afterwards. Right now, a nap was in order, so Amy shut her eyes to doze. She'd wish she hadn't.

Amy opened her bleary eyes and found that she was hungry and thirsty. She looked for, found, and rang the call button to summon a nurse ASAP. The door creaked open and in walked six figures, all wearing cloaked robes. Their faces were hidden and one of them carried a tray with juice and bread. It was brought over and placed on Amy's lap. The figures then lined up in a circle around her bed. As a very frightened Amy tried to take a drink, she noticed the juice had been replaced with a thick, smelly concoction of gruel. She threw the glass to the side and looked at her plate. The bread was now covered with maggots and worms. The figures all laughed at her with raspy, throaty sounds. Amy demanded an answer.

"Who are you and what did you do to my food?"

The figures just stood around her, saying nothing. Amy crawled backwards in her bed, almost pushing herself against the wall behind her.

"I said who are you? What do you want?"

One of the cloaked figures pulled its hands out and removed its hood. It was the young Amy. She was looking straight at Amy with glowing, ember-like eyes.

"What we have come for is you, Amy. You have failed in your quest to rescue Mr. Garrison and we want you to pay the price."

"He hasn't been found guilty or innocent. How can you say that when it's not over yet?"

Another of the hooded figures stepped forward and removed its cover. It was the charred John, looking at her with the same glowing stare. "You've let me die, Amy. You must pay."

The third and fourth figures approached, revealing their identities. This time Amy's mother and father grimly looked her over. Their auto accident injuries still prevalent. Mother spoke first. "You have let me down Amy. You are nothing. I told you would never amount to anything and I was right."

Dad spoke next, "Hello Amy. You look so beautiful. I want to touch you Amy. I want to feel you. I want to remember what you were like Amy." He reached out and touched her cheek with a cold hand, sending shivers down her spine.

The fifth stepped forward and removed its hood. It was little Jimmy. He was white and strangled. As dead as he was the day he was found. He spoke. "We've come for you Amy. You belong to us."

The figures all stepped forward and reached out to her. They were inches from her when the sixth, most mysterious figure spoke loudly through the mask it wore.

"Silence! *Do not touch her. She will answer to me first!"*

The cloak slid off and it exposed its face.

*

"Why in God's name would ya have questions?" Cylinda, juror number four asked. "Dis man without a doubt did dis. You guys crazy."

"Wait a minute, Cylinda," Oscar said, "they have a right to speak. Could you please tell the jurors why you feel this way? Liz, you go first."

"I want to make sure I'm doing the right thing here. A man's life hangs in the balance and I want to make a good solid decision. You guys have to convince me."

"Fair enough. How about you, James?"

"I just have a lot of trouble convicting when no evidence exists. It bothers me."

"What chu mean no evidence exist?" Cylinda interrupted. "Da body was in da guy's driveway. Wha's wrong wit chu people?"

Oscar again implored Cylinda to stand down and listen to what the other folks had to say. It was only right to let everyone say and feel as they wished. They were only at the beginning and Cylinda's attitude could do much more harm than good.

"Cylinda, you voted. You said 'guilty.' Now give these other people a chance. You're not the only juror in the room."

The other jurors spoke up and agreed with Oscar, causing Cylinda to sit down and keep her mouth closed, at least for a while. Oscar, with a wave, motioned to the pair that they should carry on their points. The two continued on about being one hundred percent sure and wanting to make a good, sound decision. While the other jurors again nodded in agreement, Cylinda simply sat with her arms crossed and a scowl splashed across her face. No way was she even considering freeing this man, so let them argue, she thought.

Oscar stood up, walked over to the easel that was placed in the room with dry erase markers and wrote down the ten names for, and two names against conviction.

"Are any of the ten willing to change their minds and vote 'not guilty?'

Every one of the ten shook their heads no.

"Okay, it's simple. We will either end up with a guilty verdict or a hung jury. I personally do not want us to hang up, but I want a fair deal."

This is where the jury room began to look a bit like an episode of "Big Brother." Cylinda stood with the other eight guilties, minus Oscar, on one side of the table, while the two not-guilties, Liz and James sat at the other side. Oscar sat at the head of the table.

Liz spoke up, sobbing, "I don't know what to do. I want it to be fair, but I just don't know. There's no evidence here. How can I convict with no evidence?" She began to cry and was handed a tissue by, of all people, Cylinda. She whispered in Liz's ear when she approached.

"Don't make da wrong choice, Liz. Dis man murdered two little kids. It's not you responsibility to look after dat old man. You saw how he act in the court. He a damn fool. Only someone who killed act like such a hothead. You need'a vote wit us, Liz. No worries fer you, dear. You be okay."

Liz lifted her head, looked at Oscar and asked him if she could look at the exhibits.

"You sure can." He laid the black straps, two Jacks of Spades and the trash bags on the table.

"Were these the actual tools that were used for the murders?" Liz asked.

"Those are the actual ones, Hun. These here tools strangled and held the boys. It's pretty shocking, eh?"

"I need a few minutes," Liz stated. She excused herself to the other side of the room, thought about that strap being tightened around a child's neck, and then returned to her chair twenty minutes later. She glanced at James, then at the other jurors voting guilty.

"They must be right," Liz thought to herself, "How could all those people not be right?"

Liz stood, straightened her blouse by pulling it at the waist, and walked to the other side of the table, leaving James by himself. She fell for the peer pressure and went with the crowd. As bad as a decision as that may have been, Oscar smiled and erased his original vote from 10-2 to 11-1.

*

It was a scary, skeleton-like face. No skin, just bone and real eyes. Glowing eyes. It scared Amy into sitting up in her bed at full attention.

"What do you want? I've never seen you before. Who are you and what do you want from me?"

"I am your resistance, Amy. I am the one whom you use to push the others away. I have escaped from your grip, and your opposition is now futile. You cannot get away from your past, and it's here to claim you."

Amy screamed as loud as she could as the young Amy approached her. There was no longer a way out, it seemed. The young Amy reached out and clutched Amy's arm with a force of pressure that was both painful and impossible to slip out of. Amy weakened more, and then shut her eyes, seemingly allowing the ghoul to take her.

*

"Amy, AMY can you hear me? Amy?"

Dr. Baxter was at Amy's side as the attorney was thrashing about in her sleep. She finally calmed down and opened her eyes. She fixated on the Doctor, and then went to a shallow, see right thru you glare. Baxter called for the nurses to get her an eye light and a stethoscope. They did this quickly and the Doctor looked her over. She shined the light in Amy's eyes. No response. She listened to Amy's heart and it was beating strong and without murmurs. Baxter snapped her fingers in front of Amy.

"Amy, are you there? AMY?" No response. Just a deep stare straight into the wall.

"She's had a psychotic break," Baxter said, "we need to stay quiet and see if she shakes out of it."

Amy was not responding to the Doctor, although she could both see and hear her. She felt paralyzed, but also very strange in that she wasn't thinking in a lawyer's sense. It was less mature thinking. It could be compared it the feeling you get when you're frustrated at your parents or when you don't get your way. It wasn't Amy Fraser, Attorney at-Law any longer. It was now sixteen year-old Amy inside the lawyer's grown-up body.

"I want a full CAT scan." Baxter ordered. "I want to see her brain's electrical activity."

Amy was wheeled down to the x-ray room of the hospital for further evaluation.

Dr. Baxter had started her on a drip of Nardil, for anxiety and Fanapt, a drug mainly used for

Schizophrenia, which helps with delusions and strange voices when treating what the Doctor now thought was full blown PTSD. She deduced that Amy was in a catatonic state that may or may not settle. She could stay this way forever, or come back full tilt, normal Amy the next day. There was just no way to tell. In the meantime, the scans showed that Amy's brain was more advanced with stress points that show signs of PTSD than she first thought. The drugs may help, but then again, who really knew. Whatever the case, something shook Amy so hard that her conscious brain went to sleep as a protective measure. What was left was a shell, and Dr. Baxter could only stand by, frustrated, and wait for Amy to let her know what the next step would be.

*

James sat on the other side of the table alone. Cylinda decided she would try her strategy on him as she had on Liz. It worked once, so she figured to go with it.

"Now James, you really do know da old geezer did dis, Right? Ya need ta find im guilty, James. He a menace."

"Get away from me, woman," James demanded. "You let me think about this alone. I do not need your help. You aren't anything except on the warpath anyway. You just want to see him burn, that's all."

Cylinda's mouth dropped to the floor and her ire stood on end.

"How dare ya, ya fuckin' do-gooder. Nobody talk ta Cylinda like that. You a piece a chit!"

Oscar rushed around the table and slid between the two before any more sparks could fly. He, along with the others, did not want to see an assault take place on their watch. Oscar (gently) ordered Cylinda to the other side of the room while he himself spoke with James.

"Are you okay, sir?" Oscar asked, "Is there anything I can do to help?"

Ah, the voice of reason, and soft too. James asked Oscar if he could speak with him in private.

"Oscar, it upsets me because I'm getting a little older myself. It seems a bit like a railroad job, but I think he may have done this. It's obvious to me that something happened here."

"Then maybe you should just take a few minutes to make sure you have this right. We'll leave you be to think about it. Just remember, age means nothing. It's the act that's on trial here. Also remember a couple of other things: Ms. Fraser said that there was time for a body switch in time frame in which the bag sat. A switch? I have to say I'm really resistant to that line of defense. It feels like when your brother or sister break the lamp, and then point at you when Mom and Dad arrive. It's too tough for me to stomach. How in the hell did the 'real killer' possibly know Garrison called Animal Control for a dead dog? It just doesn't add up."

The hung juror asked other jurors how they came to their decision. Nine out of the eleven gave the same story Oscar gave. It seemed too hard to believe that a switch was made. It was even harder to believe that a killer would know about the dog in the first place. The other two jurors thought Mr. Garrison's temper was too fiery and he was more then capable of killing. He did, after all, blow his stack not once, but twice in the courtroom. The whole problem here was that the jury was making its decision not based on fact and proof, or lack thereof, but on the personality of the defendant and a story they didn't personally believe. Cylinda led the charge of ignorance seemingly from the time she was interviewed, and then selected, during Voir Dire. The woman wasn't going to believe anything except what was already in her mind. The same circumstance's applied to the other jurors who voted guilty without so much as a discussion. The fact that they heard a few more things during the deliberations didn't change their minds, because they were set in their ways and weren't going to be talked out of it. This is how innocent men end up jailed, or worse. In trials where an acquittal *seems* to be the only justifiable verdict, it sometimes falls in another direction. This did not bode well for sentence deliberations, which would come up very soon after the verdict. Probably next week.

James sat quietly for about thirty minutes, then stood up and walked to the other side of the table. It was now unanimous: 12-0.

Oscar opened the door and informed the bailiff that they had reached a verdict. The bailiff nodded and told them to hang on for a few minutes while he informed the Judge.

The jurors gathered around the table. They had deliberated for an hour and were now ready to mete out the verdict. This would mean they would also have to decide if John would live in prison for the rest of his life or die in a couple of months. What a pressure filled choice they would have to make. Oscar commended all the jurors on making what he thought to be the right decision, and then sat quietly with the rest of the group.

The bailiff returned and told Oscar that he had informed Judge Wiley of their reaching of a verdict. He would stand by with the jurors until Wiley called them in. Meanwhile in the courtroom, Wiley had instructions for Garrison and the rest of the gallery.

"Mr. Garrison, any outburst by you will be dealt with severely. I understand your lawyer cannot be present. Would you like a stand-in for the verdict?"

"Nope. I don't need nobody holdin' my hand."

"Very well," Wiley told him, "you'd better behave yourself when the jury comes in."

"Or what, Judge?"

"Or what? I will have you placed in solitary for a long time if you're found guilty. If you're found innocent, I'll hold you in contempt and you can stay in our little jail another thirty days. That's what!"

Garrison nodded in agreement with the judge. Wiley also warned the gallery about any outbursts. They all agreed to his rules as well.

"Bring the jury in please."

The twelve filed in orderly and quietly, none meeting Garrison's glance. They all sat in their assigned seats and looked forward, avoiding any eye contact at all. Jack Beauregard and Richard Headly stood side by side behind the prosecutor's table.

"ORDER! Order in the court! All rise." The bailiff announced.

Judge Wiley asked the jury if they reached their verdict.

"Yes, Your Honor, we have."

"Please hand the verdict form to the bailiff, who will in turn hand it to me."

Oscar handed him the form, and it was taken to Judge Wiley. He took a long look at it and made sure it was in its proper order. He then made his next announcement.

"The forms are in order. Would the court clerk please publish the verdict?"

The clerk took the form and walked to the microphone at the stenographer table. The same stenographer that saw Amy acting weird in the restroom sat at the table, wondering what happened to the attorney.

"Would the defendant please rise?" John stood up, shackled and cuffed. The clerk faced him.

"We the jury in the above and titled action find as to count one, murder in the first degree: guilty as charged. This includes guilty as to counts two, kidnapping. As to count three, murder in the first degree: guilty. This includes counts five, kidnapping. So say we all."

"Mr. Garrison, the jury has found you guilty of all charges. You will be remanded to the State Trooper's custody until your sentencing hearing next week. As for the jury, you can go home today, but you will be deciding Mr. Garrison's fate on Monday. Please report to the court at seven sharp Monday morning for the sentencing deliberation. I hereby release you until then."

The jurors quickly filed out. Jack slapped Richard on the shoulder and gave him some good news.

"Way to go, Mr. Attorney General! I told you to quit your worrying."

Richard was still a hair nervous because of a possible appeal, but stayed upbeat. He would not tell Beauregard of his skepticism. He simply shook Jacks hand and smiled, with a twitch of his right eye.

*

Amy sat quietly. She was in a strange place. A place she never thought existed. She could hear and see, but could not talk or move. The medicine was working, but only at keeping her calm, nothing more. The sixteen year-old Amy had seemingly taken over. The attention that she demanded from her older version was now present. Amy Fraser had to deal with her past. The rapes, the abuse, growing up in a tough environment. She had pushed it to the back burner for far too long. As determined as Amy was to force herself through the visions and the voices, it was too difficult a chore to ask of her. The young Amy was in control and there may be no turning back. Therapy and medication were the only hopes left to salvage Amy's life. When Dr. Baxter returned to Amy's room, she found her sitting in the corner with her thumb firmly in her mouth. She had a pen lying next to her from drawing strange and past-related pictures on the wall. The images depicted violent scenes of rape and incest, along with pictures of her stabbing her father. Most alarming, though, were the drawings of a pentagram with a leather-clad figure standing near it. The Jack of Spades was also very noticeable in the images. The young Amy was giving the clues, but no one could possibly recognize them. The good doctor knew it was probably time to send Amy to the infirmary, not only for her own safety, but to also get her the help she really needed. There was nothing else that could be done. Amy was a prisoner in her own body.

*

Jack took Richard and Sonya out to dinner for a celebration of the big court victory. The result was so pleasing to Jack that he could hardly contain himself.

"You worry too much Richard. You're going to give yourself a heart attack if you're not careful."

"Don't fret over my heart, Jack. I've been given a clean bill of health and I don't intend on expiring any time soon. Besides, I have a new job coming up soon."

"You sure do Rich, as long as you can win that election in two years."

Richard was both astonished and outraged over that last comment. "What do you mean *two years* Jack? I thought you were making arrangements. Are you reneging on me? Damn you."

"I can't just remove the newly elected official, now can I Rich? You have to wait until I can pull the proper strings."

Richard rose from his chair and Sonya decided to put her two cents in. "You dirty son-of-a-bitch! You screwed your promise. You're no man of your word." Sonya added, "Jack Beauregard, how dare you! You know how much Richard wants this position and how hard he worked for it. You're a double-dealing pig."

"Sure Sonya," Jack chuckled, "I know how much *you* wanted it. The position does pay well."

As both Richard and Sonya chewed Jack out, they saw that he was laughing very hard. It was an unmistakable loss of control on his part. He laughed and laughed until Richard finally spoke up while almost weeping. "How dare you. How can you hurt people so?"

Jack calmed down and told Richard to do the same. "Boy, you guys are so gullible. I'm just pulling your leg, Rich. You need to learn to have a thicker skin. You should have seen the looks on both your faces. Priceless!"

Richard sat back down and scowled. His right eye twitched. Sonya was beside herself. It wasn't funny in their minds, but they began laughing with Jack. "You almost had us Jack," Richard said with an awkward chuckle, "How can you be such a jerk sometimes?"

Beauregard's smile disappeared, and he bared his teeth. He quickly leaned into the center of the table and said three very important words that struck the couple with a nervous shudder. "Because I can!"

Sudden and uncomfortable silence gripped the couple as Jack's nasty joke turned into a nastier scowl.

Lincoln Times

GUILTY AS CHARGED

Fraser collapses, Garrison faces death

AP- The jury in the John Garrison trial has come back with a verdict of guilty on all charges. After deliberating for approximately two and a half hours, the inevitable became reality. Not one person in or out of court believed it would be any different. Mr. Garrison's defiant attitude and Amy Fraser's shaky defense led to the verdict. Fraser collapsed during her closing argument, thus seeming to seal Garrison's fate. She was taken to a local hospital where she was announced as stable, although nobody can confirm this. It appeared she was awake when the EMS team removed her from court.

What's next for John Garrison? We will find out starting Monday when the jury returns to deliberate his sentence, which will be life in prison with no parole or execution by electricity. The consensus of citizens interviewed seems to be in favor of the death penalty. When Jack Beauregard was questioned upon leaving court, he hoped that death would be the verdict. "While I'm sorry that two kids died by the hands of this perverted killer, I do condone the use of lethal force to make sure this does not happen again." Richard Headly, the State Prosecutor, ignored reporters as he left court for the weekend.

Either way, death or life, one thing is for sure, this man will not ever be allowed to walk the streets of Lincoln again.

-Angela Page

The Trial of John Garrison

The Sentence

John would not have the help of a very ill Amy Fraser, so he had the choice of facing the sentencing phase alone or having a state-mandated attorney step in. It was obvious that John's stubbornness would come into play. Why shouldn't it? Up until then he was as obnoxious and as anti-system as he could be. He waited in the court jail while the jurors, who had started deliberating the sentence, made their decision. The penalty could very well be death. Life in prison was what Amy had hoped for, but she was no longer here to speak up for her client. John was not angry. He came to understand that Amy had done her best under whatever difficult circumstances she had been up against.

Earlier in the day, the jurors had gathered into the courtroom to listen to impact statements by Mr. and Mrs. Joseph, along with whatever John would have to say. The Josephs dried tears from their eyes as they each took a turn speaking. Mrs. Joseph was sure in her words and wanted John to die by strangulation, not the electric chair. She wanted him to feel the same pain and terror her son had felt as the air was sucked out of his tiny body. She begged the jurors to be decisive in their deliberations and have the man slain. Mr. Joseph was also allowed to speak. He stuttered through his words as he tried to make sense out of his son's death. His statement lasted only thirty seconds as he simply broke down and stepped away from the podium. They both gave John cold stares as they walked by him, but the old man would not make eye contact, instead he waved them away in his mind. Judge Wiley listened to the parents intently, and then allowed John five minutes to speak on his own behalf.

"Mr. Garrison, I regret that I must allow you to speak, per Nebraska law, and I regret even more being forced to listen, but the podium is yours. Let me warn you that any cursing or loud mouth antics will not be tolerated. I will expel you if you do not heed my advice."

John stood up at his defense table and began.

"Mr. and Mrs. Joseph, Mr. Headly, and even you Mr. Beauregard; you've all let the system down. You've allowed a killer to continue walkin' the streets while ya put away an old man who'd never kill no one, let alone youngins. I would like to express my deepest regret fer your loss, Mr. and Mrs. Joseph. I never had no kids because my wife couldn't conceive, but I would have loved to have given her a child or two. I can't begin to imagine how much it hurts ya to lose yer boy."

John was speaking quite powerfully and in a softer than usual voice. He went on. "Mr. Beauregard, I believe ya bullied me to enhance your run for governor, which ya won, and which ya would have probably won even without findin' the real killer. It not only disappoints me, but scares the heck out of me to think that others could meet the same fate with you in charge. You are an irresponsible man with an agenda."

Jack sat back in his seat and smiled while rolling his eyes up in his head. He dismissed John's comments with a wave off and an audible "pish."

"Richard Headly. I always respected ya as an attorney and I always backed ya up when I watched ya in action on the TV, but now I know the truth an it ain't pretty. You did Jack Beauregard's biddin' and for that, you should be ashamed."

Headly sat at his table writing on a pad of paper while paying little to no attention to the "rant" of Mr. Garrison. John focused his attention to the jurors.

"As for you, ma peers, I'm greatly disappointed in ya. You've catered to a system of corruption and insanity. Ya sit and think ya made the right decisions, but did so with an obviously closed mind. I'd rather have ya put me to death than sit in that God-forsaken jailhouse for three or four or however many years I got left. Don't make the same mistake twice. Get rid a me. Don't force me ta have to sit around and wait for nothin'."

Cylinda started to stand up in the jury box, hot as a July firecracker, but was swiftly brought back down to her seat by Desmond, who sat next to her. He put a finger to his mouth in a hushing motion and Cylinda behaved.

"Yer Honor, that's all I have, 'cept to say that ya ran a poor trial and ya should probably think about retirin'."

Wiley shook his head and spoke. "I'm glad that's over," he said. "Now get that scumbag out of my court."

The bailiff led John out.

*

Amy was checked into the Lincoln Regional Center for further psychiatric evaluation. She was placed in her own room with a bed and a toilet. She was also given a TV set and could freely walk back and forth down the hallways of the facility if she wished. For now, Amy would just sit in the bed and stare off into space. She kept thinking about the pentagram and the black leathered figure she had drawn earlier at the hospital. Some of the grown-up Amy had slipped through, but it was mostly the younger version that ran the show. The young Amy had drawn the image, but the grown Amy knew about it. It was similar to having two separate personalities, yet it was the same person involved with both. This was a scary thought for Amy, but she was trapped and could not express her emotion outwardly. The young Amy spoke with her inside her mind. It was both tortuous and nerve-wracking.

["You let dad rape us, Amy. You didn't even try to stop it. You wanted him, Amy. You liked it when he hurt us."]

["No. You're wrong. I did not want him. It made me feel dirty and disgusting. It was the worst thing in the whole world. I hated it."]

["If you hated it, why did you lay there and let him do it? Why didn't you resist him? Why did you stay?"]

["You know there was no choice. He would have killed me; us. We would be dead now."]

The young Amy began to anger as she tried to reason with the grown-up. She forced Amy to again watch the rapes. It was hideous. The young one told Amy to watch closely.

["Look at your face, Amy. You're enjoying it. Your eyes are closed when he does it. You let it happen."]

["I pretended. I faked it. I hated it and I hated him. I hate you!"]

The young Amy laughed and allowed this to go on for what seemed like forever. The grown Amy began to think she'd died and gone to hell and that this would go on without end for eternity. When she could not stand another second, the nurse came in and snapped Amy out of her trance.

"Medication, dear. It's time for your meds."

The nurse gave Amy her dose and noticed a scratch pad in her lap. It showed a young teen-ager, perhaps fifteen or sixteen, being sexually assaulted by an adult. This alarmed the nurse enough to try and take the pad, but Amy tightened her grip so hard, she'd need a crow bar to free it. She wrote this down on her progress sheet and left Amy alone. The nurse would turn in her findings to Doctor Baxter.

*

The jury deliberated for only a few minutes before Cylinda spoke up, as she usually does.

"Death to dat old cancer! If he don't die, ain't no justice!"

The rest of the jurors looked at her, especially Oscar, then at each other. They knew what they probably had to do, but that did not make it any easier to swallow. Oscar asked the rest of his peers if they were ready to cast a vote on the issue. He wanted them to simply write down the word "life" or "death," nothing more. Oscar collected the votes and needed only one pile. The jurors had spoken and they informed the bailiff that they were ready to announce their decision.

*

Jack and Richard were sitting in the first row behind the state table when the bailiff came in and informed Richard that the jury had reached a unanimous decision about John Garrison's fate. Rich looked at Jack, who let loose with one of those very annoyingly impish grins. Rich insecurely smiled back, felt his right eye twitch, and then took his normal post at the table. Richard had done a lot of thinking. "Could I be sending an innocent man to his death? Is their the chance he really didn't do it?"

This kind of consideration was very rare for a prosecutor. They tend to be cold, unfeeling and hardened to just about anything. It didn't take long, however, for him to show his true colors. The cowardly Headly decided it was the jury's decision all the way. He simply supplied the facts and let them make the final determination. Richard turned and saw Jack looking at him with what was now an angry eye. Richard winked at Jack, lipped "we got 'em" and turned to face the front of the court. Jack calmed his scowl and turned it back into the grin he so loved to shine at the "little" people.

Judge Wiley reentered the court and announced that the jury had reached a unanimous decision about the sentencing of Mr. Garrison. The jurors filed in and took their seats. This was followed by John entering through the side door and again being chained to his chair. Everyone was accounted for and it was time to begin.

"I understand the jury has reached its verdict?"

"Yes, Judge," announced Oscar.

"Would you please hand the paper to the court clerk so she can publish?"

Oscar did as he was asked and the clerk stood. Wiley asked John to rise and he just shook his head in a left to right direction and stayed seated.

"Bailiff," Wiley ordered, "stand Mr. Garrison up, please."

The bailiff walked over to do just that when John rose on his own. The Judge's handyman stayed next to John in case he changed his mind. Wiley then asked the clerk to publish.

"We the jury in the above and titled actions rule that John Garrison, who we found guilty of all counts, should be put to death by electrocution."

"Very well," Wiley said, "Mr. Garrison, I *happily* sentence you to death by electrocution. The jury has spoken and I back up their findings. Unless you receive a pardon from the governor, who happens to be sitting in court today, you will be executed two months from today at the penitentiary. I find that you are, in fact, a cold-blooded killer with a propensity for children. May God have mercy on your soul. Now get that monster out of my court once and for all!"

From the gallery the killer smiled. He thought to himself, "I'm the only monster in this room." A deep grin crossed his face as white teeth sprang forth in perfect symmetrical order.

John did not react when the sentence was announced. He'd save his final words for the fateful day two months down the road. He wished they'd do it today, but the court system likes to make people sweat it out. It seemed harsher doing it that way. John calmly shuffled out, escorted by the bailiff, and looked forward to his death. John would not file an appeal.

*

Amy was fighting her younger twin and now was coherent enough to ask about the case that had encompassed her for months.

"What happened in court?" A more awake Amy asked Dr. Baxter. "Tell me."

The good Doctor was shocked that Amy spoke. This was a tremendously good sign that she was breaking out of the catatonic stranglehold. She had underestimated Amy's resolve.

"You don't worry about that Amy. It's all taken care of and you can't do anything about it. Just relax and let the chips fall where they may and you move forward."

She really wanted to know what happened. The young Amy had already spoken in her mind, telling her John was going to the chair. How could Amy possibly trust the spirit, or alter-ego, that had so damaged her chances of winning? She couldn't and didn't, even though she was being told the truth.

"Please, Doctor, just tell me. Enlighten me to the truth. The young Amy says I lost and I don't believe her. Just tell me."

Dr. Baxter wanted to ask about the young Amy, but didn't.

"Do you really want to know, Amy? Are you prepared for the truth?"

Amy nodded yes furiously, and Dr. Baxter leveled with her.

"John lost, OK? He was given death. I agree with the verdict and the penalty. I'm sorry Amy, but there were simply too many factors against him for you to overcome. He has also refused to appeal."

Amy was disappointed, but not surprised. She shrugged depressingly and asked Baxter when she could go home.

"You'll be staying here awhile, dear. You have a long battle ahead. Medication, cognitive therapy, group sessions. You were severely abused when you were younger and you need to come to grips with that before I'll release you."

"It's not your choice, Doctor, and you know that. I could leave in five minutes if I so decided. Nobody can just hold me here."

"You're right, Amy. I warn you, however, that the difficulties you've been experiencing will become all the more trying. You could even end up dead. I'm sure you don't want that."

The word "dead" frightened the young woman. She knew what she had to do. She would stay for treatment and try to overcome the spells. Dr. Baxter continued. "The visions will be there and you *will* suffer. At least here we can treat you on the spot, try to make it more tolerable."

The floor nurse was loading up an IV for Amy-a mix of sedative and rehydrating fluids.

"I'm staying, Doctor. I ignored you once and I won't do it again. By the way, thanks."

"You're welcome, dear. Just rest and we will work on this problem." Dr. Baxter gently rubbed Amy's forehead. "I'm glad you're back."

Amy laid her head back on the pillow. The drug was taking effect not one minute after the nurse began the drip. This time Amy felt a bit more relaxed and at ease. No dreams would come this time and Amy would get a good, well deserved rest. She had a long trek ahead of her if she was to beat the affliction that racked her brain.

Lincoln Times

Death

Garrison faces electric chair

AP-John Garrison, the convicted killer of two young boys in the Lincoln area, has been sentenced to death by the same jury that found him guilty of murder last week. Garrison did not have an expression when the sentence was handed out.

Judge Donald Wiley agreed with the penalty, saying that a menace would be taken off the streets. "We have reached a verdict and a penalty that is just in light of the circumstances. I wholeheartedly agree with the jury and I think they did a good job."

Thus ends speculation as to what Garrison would face, life in prison or the electric chair.

The Governor-elect, Jack Beauregard also weighed in on the sentence. "Justice at its finest. The system worked and we now can sleep comfortably knowing our kids are safe in the streets of Lincoln." Beauregard continued, "if you think you can commit murder and get away with it, you would be sadly mistaken. Our approach is to be tough on crime and if it takes an execution to make our point, then so be it."

Anti-death penalty picketers were already on the outside of the prison entrance beginning protests against Garrison's death two months before the scheduled execution. Lynn Bailey of Lincoln was one of the staunchest advocates on hand. "Killing a human for killing humans? That's Neanderthal and Draconian. We need to show an example of punishment that preserves life. An eye for an eye was supposedly phased out centuries ago, but I guess it still exists in the modern age."

Richard Headly, the State's star prosecutor, easily defeated the defense waged by Amy Fraser, who is currently hospitalized in Lincoln with what doctors are calling "severe dehydration and exhaustion." As you may remember, Fraser collapsed during her closing statements, sending shock waves through the courtroom. Headly felt bad for his competitor, but as with Beauregard, preached that murder and other crime will not be tolerated. "While I send my sincerest get well wishes to opposing council, this was another example of a growing intolerance for crime in our state. From sex offenders to arsonists to home invaders, we will try you, convict you, and you will pay a severe price. Perhaps with your life."

The execution is scheduled for two months from now and will be attended by the parents of Jimmy Joseph, one of the murdered children Garrison was convicted of killing. Mrs. Kathy Joseph commented to the Lincoln Times about the conviction and sentence. "He deserves to die for the things he has done. He's a cold-blooded killer of children. Kids died at his hands in a violent, painful way. I hope he feels every watt, amp, or whatever you call it course through his miserable body. I'll be there wide-eyed to watch him die."

John Garrison reportedly has refused to appeal his fate.

-Angela Page

A Killer Laughs

The plan was working better than the killer could possibly expect. With a hand from his master, the chips were falling perfectly in place. Amy Fraser had found her destiny, which was to be trapped in a flux of past and present, hopefully never regaining a foothold on her sanity. The penalties for the rest of them were coming soon. He had watched everything take place from inside the courtroom. The killer was nicely dressed and looked every bit the part of a normal everyday citizen. Not one person was wise to the "other side" of his personality. He laughed at the proceedings that took place. He also laughed at the cowardice, the arrogance, the trysts, and the power some people *thought* they had.

Soo-Chin, Jack's now ex-girlfriend (fiancé), was humiliated and went into hiding. These events were only the start. Each one of the foolish people involved would pay the ultimate price brought on by their actions. The killer would continue to spread his evil around, especially to these sorry individuals. There was no escape for the calloused and power-hungry. The killer would continue praying to his dark leader for the strength and energy to finish the circle.

The lair was dirty and it stunk with the foulness of death. The pentagram that served so well was altered a bit. The pictures now sat in the center of the evil star, around the goat's eyes. A Jack of Spades adorned each point of the design. Five points, five cards. A new prayer to the God of Darkness was ready to begin. The killer lit ten candles, one to represent each player in the evil game that was being played. It was dark and eerie in the den except for the light shone through the waxy wicks. The killer knelt before his Prince and prayed a new incantation of evil.

"DEATH TO THE LAW THAT IS CORRUPT," he chanted, and continued, **"DEATH TO THOSE WHO OPPOSE US."**

The incantations sounded much like a record that is masked backward. The unnatural sound was unsettling, even for the killer. He stopped for a moment, but was urged on with a voice that rang out in his head.

"YOU WILL BRING PRAYER TO ME! YOU WILL NOT WAVER IN YOUR WORSHIP OF ME! DO NOT STOP OR YOU WILL FEEL MY WRATH, WHICH IS WORSE THAN DEATH ITSELF!"

Back down on its knees, the killer continued to chant, more frantically now. **"I'M YOUR SERVANT OH LORD OF DEATH. DON'T FORSAKE ME!"**

This particular chant went on for a full hour. The breezes in the room picked up, then settled. The killer had his master's attention and continued with the prayer until he was interrupted again by the Evil Prince. The Voice of the Dark one was more apparent through the room.

"YOU WILL MAKE THE ULTIMATE SACRIFICE! YOU WILL HEED MY COMMAND AND CARRY IT THROUGH TO COMPLETION, LEST DEATH BE YOURS!"

"Yes, my lord," the killer promised, "I will do your will whatever that may be. I am your servant and doer of the vengeance which belongs to you."

The excitement coursing through the killer's body was dreamy and arousing. A scream of ecstasy was only moments away when the Prince spoke again.

"YOU MUST DO MY BIDDING. I AM YOUR GOD AND I COMMAND YOU TO DO MY BIDDING."

"Yes, my lord." the killer agreed. "What would your will be, oh great one?"

*

Jack Beauregard partied into the night. The alcohol flowed, and the happiness was jutting out of him like a kid in a free candy store. Jack was in his living room soaking up the victory in court, as well as in the election. It would only be a few weeks until he was sworn in and the legacy would continue. Jack continued to party. He was working on his eighth beer, this after a couple shots of his friend Jack Daniels.

"Jack fer Jack!" the Governor-to-be shouted, **"I deserfe you and you deserfe me!"**

The alcohol was beginning to creep up and Jack became as horny as a celibate mountain goat. He decided to make a phone call to get himself laid. The prostitutes knew nothing of Jack. Even if they had, the crack and heroin they snorted, smoked or mainlined would erase any viable memories they may have, at one time, entertained. Jack picked up the phone and made a call.

"I wan' a slan'-eyed li'l Asian ofer to my place in an hour. I'll pay fife grand for the favor," Jack slurred.

On the other end of the line, it was sheer bliss. "Oh yes sir! One oriental doll comin' your way. Did you say five GRAND?"

"Yer goddam right I did, now get 'er ofer here before I bursht in my briches!"

Jack gave his address, then hung up and reached for another beer. It would be a wonder of no *small* proportion if he was even able to "rise to the occasion" when she arrived. No matter, Jack was drunk and getting drunker. He wanted a little oriental girl because it would remind him of Soo. He would never admit it to anybody, but he severely missed his ex-fiancé. As much as she seemed to be a pain in his rear, he loved her and wanted her back. It was the lousiest possible time, but he picked up the phone to call his lost love. Despite it being late, she answered on the third ring.

"Soo, this ish Jack. Come back to me, I mish you."

The silence on the other end was astounding. Jack again spoke, "Pleathe, Soo, pleathe come back."

"You'll never see me again, EVER!" Soo responded.

"Pleathe, Soo, I'm sorry fer hittin' ya. I'm so sorry."

"You're so drunk Jack, and that's all you are. Go fuck yourself and do not call me again. I'm not staying around. You've ruined my life here, but there's a new one somewhere else."

"Oh yeah, bich?" Jack angrily growled, "I got a young slant eyed lady comin' ofer now. I'll screw 'er better than I efer did you. You sorry li'l rat!"

The phone slammed in Jack's ear. It had taken him all of thirty seconds to send Soo on her way again. He didn't care, though. He was the leader of the state and no one could get in his way.

*

One hour later the doorbell rang. Jack staggered to the front and let a beautiful twenty year-old Asian girl in. She was alert and smiling.

"I am Hu-Lin. May I make you feel sooo good?"

Jack threw his drink on the floor and grabbed the young street walker. He ripped her shirt open and tore her bra away, exposing small but perky breasts. She giggled as Jack did this.

"He-he-he. I bring change of clothes for man like you! But money first, yes?"

Jack fished a wad of one hundred dollar bills out of his pants. She took the cash, smiled, and excused herself to the bathroom.

"You sit here and let Hu make self pretty, yes? I come out and give you good, good love, Okay?"

Jack waggled in a drunken stupor. His whole body moved along with the nod of his head. One wrong move and Jack would be looking up from wherever he landed. He made it to the living room, sat on his chair, and waited for the young Asian to return. His flaccid manhood, like a sleeping mouse in his pants, had absolutely no intention of waking up, but he was too drunk to notice. Then the hooker made her announcement.

"Okay. I come out for special surprise now."

The pretty Asian walked into the living room completely naked. It didn't matter, because Jack had passed out on the chair and was loudly snoring.

"Oh, you not think Hu good enough?" She put a shy hand to her mouth and chuckled. "He-he-he." The girl put her clothes back on. "That cost you more mister. Hu look around house." Hu did look around the house alright. She found a watch, a nice I-pod and about five hundred additional dollars. As she was excusing herself from the house, she gave Jack a little peck on the cheek.

"Hu would have given you big love, mister. Too bad you sleep. It okay, Hu make big money. He-he-he." She looked down and saw that Jack had a wet crotch. "OH, you go pee in your pants mister. I no clean you up. That cost too much." Goodbye!"

Hu left and Jack slept; about six grand lighter in cash and merchandise than when the night started.

*

Dan Wheeler was partying too, only he was sexually functional and had been screwing his third girl of the night. The man was a sleaze ball, it seemed, but his hips kept gyrating. The girls didn't seem too concerned, but they had no idea that they were sharing a potentially lethal mixture of bodily fluids with each other. They simply wanted to be "the one." Dan was back in business and the girls couldn't be happier.

Breasts, butts, hips and hoochie; all at Dan's fingertips. Any chick he wanted, he received. When he was finished with one, he excused her, washed up, and before he knew it, the next arrival was knocking. Dan was young and strong. He was also stoned, but his mojo didn't fail. Smoking some grass was one of Dan's hobbies, and the girls liked that too. The wacky tobaccy did not hinder Dan's performance, but rather heightened it to another level.

Lyla Helms, on the other hand, was not as happy as her counterpart. She stewed in her house, on the job and even when she was grocery shopping or doing anything else routine. She was so mad at that young Dan that she would cross her arms over her chest and sit on the couch ruing the future. As she'd done before, Lyla was trying to figure out how to deal with the cad. She had come to a decision on how to handle it, but wanted to make sure it was the right move for her, Dan and all involved.

Occasionally, Lyla would have spells of depression over the young man. She tried to convince herself that it wasn't worth it, but couldn't shake the feelings. Dan made love to (fucked) her and threw her out. This was the most painful experience in Lyla's life. While Dan was playing with his dizzy, bimbo girlfriends, Lyla sat in a state of indecisiveness, hurt, anger and sadness. It wasn't fair that he was having all the fun without her. Lyla wasn't looking as well, either. She had let herself go to some extent. She'd gained about twenty pounds and her hair was disheveled and unkempt. Normally, a "tease here" and a "swish with the brush there" fixed it, but she didn't care as much lately.

Lyla had her final plan for Dan laid out, and after thinking about it for sometime, she decided that yes, she would carry it through. It would not be easy, but it had to be done.

*

"Would you hurry it up, you lazy bum. What's wrong with you?" Kathy Joseph was into her daily browbeating of Kurt and she was being especially nasty. "You're a good for nothing piece of shit, Kurt. Why I ever married you I'll never know. I wish you were dead!"

Kurt kept his mouth shut and his head low. He was smart in that arguing or putting up a stink would simply exaggerate an already fragile situation; not to mention marriage. There was once a time when they were happy, but those days had long since left them. They no longer had any sexual contact and very little in the way of communication. She had so severely subjugated this man that he learned the "head down, keep your mouth shut" routine. There was no telling how much longer he could take it. He had done all of her bidding. He did exactly what was asked of him without quarrel and behaved the best he could to try and keep the offensive and trashy blonde happy. Kurt was reaching his wits end. He had fantasies of murdering her right on the spot. He didn't know what brought him the most joy, playing with himself in the garage while watching porn, or slicing that irritable bitch's throat where she stood.

"It'd b-be such a pl-pleasure to k-kill that n-nasty woman," Kurt thought to himself. "I wa-wish she'd d-d-die so I can have p-peace and q-quiet."

Kathy was not conscious of the extent in which Kurt's hatred developed, and was growing by the day. She had a lover that he didn't know about and spent many a happy day bumping privates with this "real" man. Had Kurt known, she, along with her he-man, would probably be six feet under already. He was unstable enough to do it. Kathy didn't worry because she thought Kurt was too stupid to figure it out. Even if he somehow did, she could talk her way out of it with relative ease. She told her lover how much of a loser she thought Kurt to be. She'd say awful things about her husband behind his back, and not give him the common courtesy to defend himself.

Kurt began going to the garage with more frequency than ever. Kathy didn't care, as it took him out of her hair. He locked the door, though, and that really pissed her off. If she needed something or wanted his undivided attention, she had to wait for him to open up.

"Quit locking that fuckin' door, Kurt. I hate that. What are you doing in there, jackin' off?"

"S-s-sorry, d-dear." Was all Kurt would say, and then he'd lock it again. That space was his only true escape from the woman, unless she was at work or out "shopping."

Banging the hammer on pictures of Kathy or spilling itching powder on items of clothing she wore, Kurt would get a huge sense of relief. Not simply from the hammer hitting or the powder puffing, but from the idea that he was punishing her. The relationship had hit rock bottom. There was no telling where it would go from here.

*

Richard had tensed up since the verdict and sentencing. He no longer feared for his life, but he was still a tad nervous about the attorney general job Jack had promised. He was told it was being worked on, but something deep inside said it wouldn't pan out. Pessimistic thinking was the culprit. Rich was always a negative Nellie, his wife would say.

"Richard, you've won every case since becoming a prosecutor. Why would you lose now?"

Richard never took it for granted and always figured he'd lose. This way it would make winning much sweeter. Yes, he had a guarded confidence. He wanted nothing more than to keep his perfect record, but prepared for defeat.

Now that he had won his biggest case, there was the little issue of A.G. standing over his shoulder. That was the job he coveted, and Beauregard was the only one standing in his way. Another man had won the election for the post in November, but Jack promised a controversy that would force this person to either step down or be ousted. Running people over was more a Jack thing, but Rich was just as guilty because he would stand to the side and watched it happen. That way, he took no responsibility and would ease into the void that was left.

"I can't help what happened, but it won't be the same with me," is how he would reason it to a confused public. "I'm just stepping into a position that the person before me misused."

That had happened a couple times in his career and the excuse was always the same. He was as tough as an unshelled turtle. This man had coward written across his forehead. Anybody above him could easily intimidate the scaredy-cat attorney.

Sonya was thrilled about the appointment, which was supposedly taking place shortly after Jack's entrance into office. Strings would be pulled, palms would be greased, and names would not be taken. As was the case when she found out about the substantial raise her husband would be getting, she kept spending. You know the old saying: "Don't spend it before you have it!" Oh, but spending Sonya did, and very well at that. Purses, shoes, handbags, carpets, furniture, hairdos, and on and on and on. The only thing she seemed to forget was that a bill for all this would come in the mail, and when it did, Richard threw out a head gasket.

"SONYA!" Richard would scream while at the same time twitching his right eye, "You've spent upwards of fifty grand in two months. Two months Sonya! That's almost half of my *gross* income."

"What's gross income, dear? Is this bad?"

"Bad? Yeah, it's bad, and you're making it worse. Number one, stop spending. Number two, take back what you can. Number three; give me those damn credit cards."

Rich herded up the cards and hid them so Sonya couldn't spend another dime.

"What's the big deal, dear? You have a great job lined up. We'll pay it off then."

"Listen to me, woman, Jack has punched me, pointed a gun in my face, and threatened my life if I lost the case. So that's the big goddamn deal. There are no guarantees. Now take all that junk back. **TODAY!"** Another twitch.

Sonya said she would, but didn't. She was of the upmost surety that Rich would get the position and their bills would be history. She had another credit card hidden in a sock drawer that had a ten thousand dollar spending limit. She would max that out in another two-and-a-half weeks. If Richard did not get that job, they would kiss their credit bye-bye. Richard fretted and stressed about this and would continue to do so until he either had a coronary or a stroke, whichever came first. Maybe he'd take care of it in another, more permanent way. His right eye twitched wildly.

*

Tending to John's lawn and house was getting to be a pain for Robert. He sold off the horses John had, and planned on auctioning the interior goodies soon. John had signed over rights to the property to Robert, and the tall lanky neighbor took the responsibility seriously. He cut the grass, saw to the odds and ends around the house and kept things up until the mortgage was in default and the bank would take over. John didn't owe but twenty-five grand, but he just spent fifty g's on his defense, which left but a few thousand in his bank account. The guilty verdict not only would end John's life, if no stay was given, but also cut his pension. The big auto corporation he worked for in

Detroit would only pay surviving members of the immediate family and John was it. They would not pay a convicted killer, however. There wasn't much John could do short of hiring yet another attorney to try and have that continued, but what was the use? The only way he'd enjoy it is if he somehow was granted a stay and a leave of conviction. The chances of that were .0000001%. In other words, forget it.

Robert and the boys at the barbershop missed their grumpy, crass pal, and lamented the court system that convicted him with very minimal evidence. It convinced the boys that the *control machine* was a mess and little hope remained on any kind of turnaround. Robert wrote letters to John in jail, and would read the responses John sent back to all the guys at the shop. They really enjoyed it and looked forward to hearing from the old goat. One letter in particular made them beam with pride, as John wasn't taking any guff from anybody. It read like this:

Dear Fellow Coots,

I'm doin' just fine thank ya very much. These gotdamn guards and their cronies don't scare me much. They try to shake me up, but I'm too tough for 'em. The food in the big joint is much better, though. I get mashed taters, real meat and pie. They even serve coffee here. A good cup of it at that. Well, I miss you old geezers a lot. I can't stand not comin' up there and bustin' yer nuts for ya. I hope Robert's given' you a good dose of B.S., 'cause someone has to. Don't ya old farts worry 'bout me. I'm doin' good and soon it won't matter 'cause they're gonna bar-b-que my ass. It's ok though, so don't ya pout. Soon we'll be together in the old barbershop in the sky! When that happens, there won't be no more bullshit charges levied against any of us. We'll sip coffee, drink beer and play cards 'till our hands fall off. Yep. You SOB's are my best friends. I hope to see ya again (not too) soon!

John

That letter made it onto the wall of fame in the shop, next to some old vanity license plates and a picture of Marilyn Monroe. "Boy what a dish she was!" The old farts agreed. For John's letter to make it on that wall, it must be good. The owner, Sam

Marsh, wouldn't let anyone touch it. They could read it alright, but they'd better keep their greasy paws off of it. It was an honor.

Robert continued to keep up the Garrison home, but he hadn't been feeling so good lately. He'd made an appointment to see his doctor. He was having some chest pain and a bit of a cough. "Nothing more than a touch of dust and pollen," Robert would reason. He was probably right, but seeing a doctor never hurt anybody. He slowed down a bit, but kept his promise to John, just like a good friend would.

*

"HAIL! HAIL!" The killer knelt and chanted, "MASTER!"

It went on for two more hours before the killer finally settled down. The master had told him what he expected to have done. The killer agreed, and knew it was right.

"Your will be done, oh great one. My master's will be done."

The killer laid his face on the pentagram and laughed. He was scared, but wanted to please the prince of Darkness. Upon the death of John Garrison, the plan would go into full motion. The killer wanted everything to be right for the arrival of this date and did not ignore or miss one sign that led to that end.

Satan wanted another sacrifice, this time a child of eight and male. He wanted his minion to do this soon to satisfy the dark one's hunger. The killer nodded in agreement and total dedication, then donned its black leather for a trip to the city.

Less than two hours later, the killer brought a sacrifice to the master. It was an eight year-old boy who was scared out of his wits. The room was dark, only lit by the candles the killer had used in its earlier ritual. The child was bound by his hands and feet, and placed in the center of the pentagram. The killer bowed its head to pray to the demon.

"OH DARK ONE. MAY THE SACRIFICE BE SUITABLE. COME AND CLAIM YOUR PRIZE."

The winds began to howl as the room began to heat up. The prince was present. The killer blindfolded the gagged and bound child, and then knelt on the floor with his face down, so as not to anger the master. Satan then spoke to the killer in his mind.

["YOU HAVE DONE WELL, MINION. NOW LET THE BOY GO TO TELL ALL THAT DEATH IS UPON THEM."]

Baffled, but without question, the killer picked the boy up, put him in the van, and took him back to the spot where he found him. He allowed the boy to be free, but had a message: "Tell everyone what you saw. Tell everyone death will come soon." The boy was released and ran like the wind back to his home. In the coming days, the boy did as he was asked, telling everyone he had seen the killer and that death was coming. First his parents, then his friends. Nobody believed him.

"They caught the killer." Everybody repeated. "Quit making up weird stories."

The boy continued to spread the word, pleading to be believed, but his parents soon worried about his mental health. He was admitted to the same psychiatric facility that Amy called home. He was drugged and monitored. He stopped talking about the "death" issues and would stay in the hospital until his doctor thought him suitable to continue a child's life. Little did everyone know………

After

Water: Autumn, Dusk, Dreams, Emotions

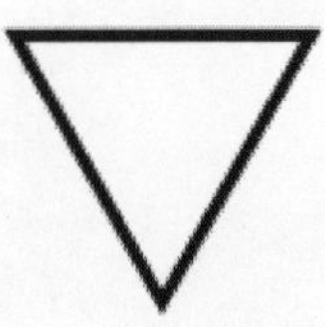

John Falls on the Candlestick 2

Time was not on John's side. The two months had gone by swiftly and he had long since decided that there would be no appeal and no begging the governor for a leave. John knew the chances of winning an appeal were just as close to zero as one could get. The State and Jack Beauregard would have no part of it, so why waste everyone's time? Even if he were to get lucky enough to win an appeal, it would just mean life in prison, and he wanted no part of that either. John simply prayed and took solace in the fact that he would soon see his departed love that died years earlier.

Robert visited John once a week, trying to keep the old man's morale up. Who could be cheered up when you knew you were going to die? The visits were nice and John appreciated it, but he was concerned about his friend. He didn't look so good lately.

"You been to a doctor, dipshit?"

"Naw, I'm gonna' make an appointment, but I'm so damn busy lately, what with yer place and my own."

"I would highly suggest ya' get yer rear-end in, Robert. You look like death warmed over. Why are ya' so gotdamn stubborn?"

"John, why do ya have to break my balls every single time I see ya'? Can't we just have a nice chat and call it good? Yer killin' me."

"I'm killin' ya'? It looks to me like yer killin' yerself, dummy. Get to a doctor."

The conversations always ended with Robert taking off before he was ready, but what would their relationship be like if not for that? It was their way and it would never change. If you could ever count on one thing in life, it'd be these two quarreling up a storm.

Other buddies of John's came to visit. The boys from the barbershop all stopped up a time or two to visit. The local priest also stopped up. John was a devout Catholic and practiced his faith every day. He told the Priest that he was innocent and there would be no judgment from God over this when he arrived at the pearly gates. He did, however, promise the Padre that all involved with his execution were in for it when their times at those same gates came. The Priest never argued with John, nor did he agree. He went about his business as a Priest does and prayed for John. Ninety-nine percent of the parishioners in the church believed John was guilty anyway. The Priest made no judgment.

The meals John was fed were pretty good. When you're on death row, they actually cook you a separate supper than the rest of the prison. In Lincoln, there were only three other men waiting for their fateful day, so it was easy to give them extra comfort. As far as John was concerned, it was the least they could do for someone railroaded into this mess. A couple days a week he was given Burger King or McDonald's, but that was okay with him. He occasionally ate junk food when he was on the outside.

He also wondered about Amy. He missed her and hoped that she was doing okay. He never put any blame on her for what happened. John continued to figure the jury would've convicted no matter who was representing him. He asked the guards about her a couple times, but they just shrugged. "I don't know what happened to her. Who cares?"

John reached a point where he didn't even bother asking anymore. He still wondered. He hoped she would recover from whatever ailed her. In the meantime, John read, ate and relaxed. He slept quite a bit and didn't bother with anybody from the surrounding cells. He just sat and waited. The hour was coming.

*

The day before the scheduled execution, John sat in his cell reading a good John Grisham novel. It had been brought to him by Robert in the hopes of encouraging John in the fact that there were lots of innocent folks in this world who had been convicted of crimes. This book dealt with some guy being wrongly accused in a murder case. Although he did some prison time, he still didn't have to face the death penalty. A social death? Yes. A real live electrocution? No! As much as Robert tried to give sympathy to his friend, John would not allow it. The sentence John faced was severe. There was no denying how awful the system treated him. There was even less denying that tonight (tomorrow) at midnight, the lights would go out for good, at least in this world.

John continued to read until around 2:00 p.m., when a guard arrived at his cell to ask him what he'd like his last meal to be and when he would like to eat. John was grumpy. "Last meal, huh? Why don'cha just stick the last meal where the sun don't shine? Eat it backwards."

"Look, John, I know this stinks," the understanding guard stated, "but I can't do anything about it. So why not just eat what you like before it's time? You know I really do feel kind of bad for you."

"Kinda bad for me? You should feel kinda bad for the gotdamn rat trap called a criminal justice system. You're a part of it, ya know?"

"I'm not like most of them, John. I'm not mean; I'm just trying to feed my family."

"Yep! Guys like me keep business rolling, too. Get me a steak and potatoes. A rare T-Bone with lots of butter for the spuds. Mashed."

"Yes sir. Uh, what time, John?"

"Eight o'clock sharp! I don't wanna have to drop a deuce before the big fireworks party."

"Yes sir, Mr. Garrison, it'll be here."

"Now get the hell outta here, I'm tryin' to read."

John continued reading the book Robert had given him as he waited for dinner at eight.

Seven O'clock came around and so to did Father Gerald, ready to pray with John. They both knelt and worshipped. Father gave John communion and they prayed their Hail Mary's together. The priest asked John if he had any sins to confess before midnight came.

"I have lots a sins, Father; I couldn't fit 'em all in before the hour strikes. Just tell me one thing: Will I see my beautiful wife soon?"

"That's between you and God. I can't answer that for you, but I can tell you that if your sins have been confessed and forgiven, then yes, I believe you'll see her."

"Well that's good. I miss her and I'm glad she was dead before all this shit-*pardoning my French*-came along. It woulda killed 'er."

"John, there isn't another quite like you sir. God busted the mold."

John's dinner arrived at eight, and he requested to eat it alone and in silence. The request was granted and John was taken to the cafeteria, where no prisoners lurked. John was given a table and the guards locked him in. It was exactly what he wanted them to do. He enjoyed every bite.

*

"It's time, Mr. Garrison." The guard had walked up to the cell and made the announcement. The cell door slid open and John stood tall, ready to face *their* music. Along with the guard was Father Gerald, another guard, and of all people, Jack Beauregard.

"What in hell you doin' here Jack-off? I thought you had governor shit to do."

"I'm not governor yet, Garrison. That's not until January. I just want to watch you die close up."

Jack gave that sly chuckle as he said this, trying as hard as he could to rattle the old man. It didn't work. How could you rattle a dead man walkin'?

"Well that's good, ya double-dealin' wretch. I hope I piss on ya when the juice switch is turned."

The Priest wormed between the two, waggled his finger at Jack, and told John to knock it off.

"Gentlemen," the Priest said, "this is no time for childish behavior. Please."

Both men nodded at the Padre and John was led down a long corridor to a side room where preparations were made before the trip to the execution station. It was 11:35 and the guards were to give John a five-minute segment of time to address those in attendance, so they picked up the pace.

"John, drop your pants. We need to stuff you with cotton."

"Why? You afraid the shit's gonna get on ya? Too late ya framin' pigs."

John then did as he was asked and cotton balls were stuffed securely into John's rectum. This was done to avoid any "spraying" that may occur when the voltage hits. This was necessary, as it could get very messy. After this unpleasant task was finished, John was led the rest of the way down the hall, which ended at the death chamber. The door opened and the two guards, Priest, and Jack entered behind Garrison.

The curtain that surrounded the room was drawn so that no one could see in or out. John saw the chair sitting there, ready to claim yet another victim. He was told he would be allowed to stand up and make his final comments, and then he would be led to the chair, strapped down and executed at exactly midnight. John nodded in agreement, took his spot in front of the room and the curtains drew open, exposing John to the onlookers present.

In the front row was Richard Headly sitting next to a police officer. The row behind them featured Mr. and Mrs. Joseph. A policeman sat next to them. In the rear stood three other men, all newspaper reporters, obviously ready to describe what they'd see. John didn't care, he just wanted to make his statement and finish this thing. He lifted up his head, unfolded his paper he had written on, and began to speak.

*

"Ladies and Gentlemen, my name is John Garrison and I'm 'bout to die. I'm gonna be dead because the state troopers, the circuit court and the jury were complete and utter imbeciles. I did not kill anybody at anytime. I'm innocent of all charges."

"Can we stop this idiocy?" Beauregard whispered to the lead guard.

"He has a right to his final words, Jack, just let him spew, then he'll die."

Jack was angry when he first asked the question, but softened a bit knowing the man was going to die. It was only a few minutes away. John continued. "I have been set-up by the man standin' behind me. Jack Beauregard decided that his ticket to the governor's seat'd be through me. Now he has the audacity to want me dead. For him, it's a small price to pay. For me, it means I die."

John dropped his notes on the floor and bent over to pick them up. When he squatted, he pulled the T-Bone from dinner out of his sock. He reared up quickly and yelled, **"I WILL NOT DIE BY THIS STATE'S HANDS!"**

Before anybody could react, John turned the sharp edge of the bone against the carotid artery in his neck and gave a deep slash. The blood violently spewed out of John's vein and against the glass that separated him from the gallery of onlookers. A loud and disgusting moan came from those seated in the spectator's area. John turned from the group in the chamber and ran to the opposite side of the room to bide time for a suitable amount of blood to be wasted onto the walls and floor. When the guards tried to corral him, he fought. The harder he resisted, the more his pulse increased, thus depositing more blood. Jack screamed for them to pin him down, but the old man was strong. Jack did not give a helping hand where needed. He simply blurted out orders. John weakened after forty-five seconds. They were finally able to pin him. It took another thirty seconds to try and contain the cut, but it was long and deep. After three minutes of struggle, bloodshed and finally being wrapped up, John Garrison died on the floor.

*

Jack had the fit of all fits. **"Who fed him his goddamn dinner?"**

The young guard stepped forward. The same guard who was very nice to John earlier.

"It was me, Mr. Beauregard. I fed him his dinner."

"You are hereby fucking FIRED!" Jack yelled so loudly his voice cracked. The guard lowered his head and walked out.

Jack continued his rant about the display of incompetence.

"Are you fucking kidding me with this? Are you the most inept bunch of idiots ever?"

The other guards simply looked at each other and back at Jack, waiting for his next round of screaming.

"Well, you caused the mess, now clean the goddamn thing up."

Jack Beauregard exited the area. The people in the gallery were crying and gasping. It was tough to see what was going on inside because of all the blood on the window. The reporters that were there were jotting notes and seemed almost giddy that it wasn't another boring execution. John Garrison had fought back, and at one minute after midnight, was officially pronounced dead by the doctor who was present for the grisly ceremony.

Beauregard Explodes

What a mess it was. Garrison's blood dripped from the glass partition as he lie in a pool of red death on the floor. The electric chair, along with the straps and buckles, were also blood covered. The man sentenced to die by the State's hands did a good job himself. He hit the artery in the exact spot necessary for maximum spillage. Jack Beauregard blew his top. **"This operation is supposed to be run by professionals, but instead it was an asinine circus of monkeys. Heads will, not might, be rolling come tomorrow. Now get this fucking mess cleaned up!"**

The guards did exactly what they were instructed to do. One guard had left for the locker-room, fired on the spot by the still Colonel of the Nebraska State Police. The gallery stood in stunned silence, trying to make heads or tails out of what they'd just seen. The worst part is that the media had seen it too, so embarrassment would follow. Jack could just see the headlines of the Lincoln Times, splattered with the story of how his unit completely and without fail, blew the entire operation. This angered Jack deeper than he had been when the flaw occurred. The more he thought about it, the hotter he became. He made his way out of the prison and drove straight to the Police headquarters to meet with Lt. Michaels while trying to calm himself. The worst thing Jack could do en route was turn on the radio, but he did. The local news station already had the story in their back pockets and reported from the prison execution site live on the air. Beat reporter Angela Page did the honors.

"What a disaster tonight, folks. The execution of John Garrison has gone horribly wrong. The old man who was convicted of the murder of two young boys managed to take his own life inside the actual execution chamber. A T-bone from his last meal was stuffed in his sock and he managed to yank it out and slash his own throat before the victim's family, the gallery of media, and guards. Even the Governor-elect, Jack Beauregard was present….."

Jack didn't simply shut off the radio; he punched it with a right hand, not only breaking the dial, but scraping his hand up in the process. The radio still played after this rage, so he turned the knob off. He thought indignantly to himself that punching it should have done the trick, so it didn't turn out to be worth it. Jack had escaped the spurting blood at the execution, but now had bled out of his own hand and onto his pressed, and quite expensive, Italian knit slacks, adding insult to injury. Jack shrugged it off with a grimace and continued to make his way towards the substation.

*

Robert Long had known his buddy was going to die tonight and was none too happy about it. The chest pain that had been bothering him was getting worse. He continued to ignore it, as he hoped it was a spot of indigestion or a bad case of heartburn. People have a tendency to do that, hoping and praying that's all it is. It's the prime reason so many die from coronary artery disease. Who wouldn't be scared though? No one *wants* to die. You hope the symptoms ease and you can move on to other things. This evening, the symptoms were not going away, and by Bob's estimation, may have been getting worse. He didn't feel like eating and just wanted to rest. He laid back on his Lazy-boy recliner and took a nap. He flipped on the TV before doing so to keep him company. Bob would wake up later, in time for the 11:00 p.m. news.

*

Jack finally arrived at the station and met Michaels, who was working graveyard shift as a fill-in for the week. He knew when he saw Jack approaching that trouble was brewing. Lt. Michaels had not seen or heard any TV or radio reports about the excitement that took place at the prison. As Jack walked down the hall toward his glassed-in office, Michaels noticed the blood on his pant leg. He thought to himself, "What happened this time?" and blew out a long lungful of air before he met Jack at the door.

"What on God's earth happened to your hand, Jack? You've got blood all over your clothes."

"What happened? *Your* damn guards completely screwed up the execution tonight!"

Lt. Michaels wasn't quite sure how to react, so he stayed with the calm approach. "They're still your men until you take over the mansion, but I'll help you with whatever the trouble is. What happened tonight, Jack?"

"Garrison cut his own throat with a T-bone that he stashed in his sock. He kept it with him after his last meal so he could do the deed at the execution! I fired the man-*your* man, who was supposed to be guarding him during his meal! He obviously wasn't properly briefed by his commander, Lieutenant!"

Lt. Michaels now raised his ire with the Colonel.

"You just wait a damn minute, Jack! Don't try and rub this mistake on my collar! I'm not one of your cronies who'll just take your garbage!"

"You'll take what I give you, Michaels, and you will like it! I want this station, these guards and these troopers properly trained! From now on, you're on probation until I see improvement!"

"Probation? Who in hell do you think you're speaking with? We've been through the ringer together and now, when the going gets tough, you turn your back on me? That's not right and you know it!"

"I don't give a rat's ass what you think is or isn't right, Lt. Michaels! I've been given the greatest responsibility in this great state and I intend to take it seriously! You ARE on probation!"

Jack was toe-to-toe with Michaels and was shoving his finger into his subordinate's chest. Lt. Michaels didn't like it, but had his hands tied, as Jack was still his commander. He expressed his feelings and concerns without pulling punches.

"You're getting a little high and mighty since the election, Jack, and I'm not the only one who's noticed! You better bring it down a notch or two before you get yourself, or someone else in big trouble!"

"One more word Michaels, and I'll fire you! Get these fucking troopers in shape and do not argue with me again! Good night, Lieutenant!"

Jack turned, walked out, and slammed the door behind him. The scowl on his face was mixed with a rich red color and the walk was resolute. Michaels stood in his office shocked, and scratched his head. He was very surprised with the reaction. He flipped on the TV and saw exactly what Jack was talking about. One mistake by a guard had put a wrench into the festivities, but John was still dead, only not the way it was planned. Lt. Michaels knew he had to do as Jack said if he wanted to stay employed, so he spent the rest of his shift organizing a refresher course in police work for every trooper on the payroll. This included dispatchers and office personnel. The same mistake could never happen again, and Michaels was serious about correcting it.

*

Jack drove home, slammed the front door open and shut, and punched the wall with his *left* hand. The drywall buckled in a heap and brought Kyle running down the stairs, practically tripping over himself on the way.

"What was that? What was the noise?" Kyle quizzed excitedly.

"Nothing son. Listen, could you find something to do and leave the old man be? I'm worn out and a hair pissed off."

"What's the matter, Pop? How'd the lynching go? What's wrong with your hand?" Question, question, question.

"Please, Kyle." Jack looked at him with a tinge of poisonous bass coming from his voice.

"Oh. Sorry." Kyle ducked his chin and retreated to his room.

Jack went to his room and removed the soiled thousand dollar suit and rubbed stain-B-gone on it. He found the hydrogen peroxide, washed his injured hand, and landed on the bed, as tired as one could get without doing a sixteen-hour shift of hard labor. He lay there and thought about everything important to Jack: the governorship, the flubbed execution and of course, if Richard Headly was attorney general material. Not once in his selfish and obnoxious thinking was there any room for Soo-Chin, Kyle or humanity for that matter. It was all about Mr. Beauregard. He was the leader of this great state. To hell with whomever questioned it or even thought about a challenge. The self-centered attitude was unmistakable, and all anyone could do was try to exhibit patience.

The clock on Jack's nightstand struck 3:00 a.m., and he tossed and turned, awake and frustrated. He could hear the tick-tock, tick-tock of the clock, while strange noises from raccoons, or whatever critters were milling about, garnered attention from the sleepless Governor-to-be. The thinking continued. He wanted to have a woman in his life, but apparently didn't possess the marriage skills that were necessary. Kyle was not being given the attention he deserved and needed because Jack's fathering skills had also diminished with the drunkenness of power he had gained. The thoughts exited Jack's mind as fast as they entered it. He did not take enough time to think through the important aspects of life. He was a different man now. This was not the same Jack Beauregard that sat in his chair at the police station trying to solve crime. Somewhere he took a wrong turn, but didn't notice. Somehow he forget that which was most important, but did not try to remember. His thinking was that he needed to be tough and thick skinned.

"To hell with this negative thinking. I have a police post that needs straightening. Garrison's execution was flubbed, but he's still dead. Sometimes the end really does justify the means, I suppose."

Jack drifted off, no longer aware of the tick-tock or the critters whimpering. He finally fell into a restful night's sleep. The anger that Jack had felt on this day finally subsided. The ire of Jack was evident, but now he could repose, assured that his power was in place. The respect he thought he had gained on this, the worst day in a long time, made him feel much better about himself. The newspapers ran with the grisly, execution story the next morning.

Lincoln Times

Garrison execution a disaster

Calls to reform death penalty intense

AP- The execution set to take place last evening at midnight turned into a disaster of the highest proportions. John Garrison, convicted child murderer, was led into the death chamber at approximately 11:35 p.m. The curtain for the viewing media and family members was opened and Mr. Garrison was given an opportunity to say last words before being strapped into the electric chair device to be put to death. Approximately five minutes into his speech, or at about 11:52 p.m., Garrison dropped his paper with his written statement. Upon standing back up, Garrison had some kind of a tool, later found out to be a T-bone from his last dinner, and slashed his own throat. Garrison announced a second before stabbing himself that the state would not have the honor of killing him. Garrison died a short time later on the floor of the death chamber. Blood ran down the glass partition as the convicted murderer fought the two guards trying to take control of him. It appeared, according to the doctor on duty, that Garrison lost a vast amount of blood very quickly, thus sabotaging any hope of saving his *life*, so that he could be put to *death*. Garrison was pronounced dead at 12:01 a.m., or about the same time officials believed the electrocution would've taken place. Governor-elect Jack Beauregard was in the chamber for the execution and escaped without injury. He left the facility without comment. Anti-death penalty advocates rallied outside the prison walls in record numbers after the botched execution, calling for elimination of what they feel is a draconian and cruel punishment for offenders. We will supply more details about last night's events as they become available.

-Angela Page

Jack read this as he choked down his morning coffee. He was trying to stay calm and collected, but was finding it difficult to do.

"What happened last night, Dad?" Kyle inquired.

"Read for yourself son. It was a complete and utter screw up by people who are supposed to be professionals. I'm so disappointed."

"What are you going to do? Will you repeal the death penalty while you're in office?"

Jack took a long look at his son as he sat at the breakfast table, also depositing coffee and toast into his gullet.

"Let's talk about something else, Kyle. This really does get my fury up."

"Okay, Dad, but you always say that. You should talk with me more when you're angry. I may be able to help."

The eyes rolled up in Jack's head and a "che" sound escaped his lips. "Not for you to worry about kiddo, I've got it all under control."

Kyle shrugged his slender shoulders and slurped his coffee.

Instability

The night was filled with restlessness. The moon shone through the window and you could almost feel the cold breeze by merely looking outside. The bed was uncomfortable, the pillow hard as a rock, and the room as sterile as an alcohol swab. Amy tried to lay on her left, her right, her back, and her belly. Soon the pillow flew across the room. She kicked the sheets with a squeal. Frustrated, she paced the floor. It was a horrible night for the young lawyer, as Garrison's execution had been completely flubbed and she watched the news with a sick body and mind. She felt that she let him down horribly. Amy beat herself up over the fact that she should have dismissed herself from the case, but was too stubborn and selfish to do so. It seemed like a very winnable trial, what with no evidence against her client, but alas, trying to do something as simple as prove innocence when a garbage sack was found in the driveway turned out to be impossible. The pacing kept up; the tears began to run down Amy's face. The young woman felt the young Amy trying to tighten the firm grip on her mind yet again. Amy stood unyielding.

Amy thought because she had been taking the medication and talking again with her doctor that the sanity was starting to creep back into her realm. This was her time to face her past once and for all. Could she get a grip on the awful acts of abuse that her father put her through? Did Amy have the mental capacity to sort these problems out in her mind before they took her over once and for all? Who knew? Amy certainly didn't. As much as the woman tried to fight off the crosses she bore, it was never quite enough. The past always had a way of catching up and taking over. In Amy's case, it was a matter of PSTD. She had been carrying it around for some time, but something in her mind snapped. Why? Who could possibly answer that question? All she knew is that the evil could return at any time it so chose, causing another calamitous breakdown of epic proportions. This is part of the reason she walked the floor this evening. She had a strange feeling that very soon her world was to be turned completely upside down, this time possibly to the point of no return. She heard the voices far off, and they were coming. She saw quick snapshots of herself being ruined by her father. She felt the goose bumps and the cold chill of regret and denial. It was so much to overcome. She was tired. How could she possibly go through it again? The woman was in her mid-twenties and felt eighty. She was beautiful, but felt ugly. She was a good person, but felt like a nasty ogre.

Amy rubbed her head, ran her fingers through her hair and gripped her hands together in a prayerful cluster at her chin. She paced, rubbed and clenched her teeth. Amy prayed and begged her Lord to rid her of the guilt, which was literally eating her from the inside out. She thought herself responsible for John's death. She thought herself responsible for her father's disgusting abuse. Perhaps the young Amy was right. Maybe she had sprawled on the bed and enjoyed her father's devious and awful intentions. Could it be that she hoped her mom would pass out on the couch from drunkenness so her dad could take advantage of her beauty? So much thought and so much pressure. Amy cried. Amy clenched her hands together and paced. Amy ran across the room and hit the fifth floor window with a loud crash!

*

Robert woke up and was frightened. His chest hurt more than ever and breathing had become extremely labored. He felt the unsteadiness when he tried to stand. A cold sweat ran down his forehead and across his face. The heat started in his toes and shot through him like a cannon, encompassing his body until it reached his face. He wasn't sure, but he thought he may be having a heart attack.

"Never…felt…this…way," he writhed with a hand clutching his chest.

A phone was what he needed, and NOW! He reached the cordless and quickly dialed 911. The operator answered.

"911, what's your emergency?"

Robert could no longer breathe. He was struggling to maintain consciousness.

"911, WHAT'S YOUR EMERGENCY, PLEASE?"

"Uhh...mmphh…I….arrt….ttack! Ple elp."

"Sir, I can't understand you, could you please speak clearly? Sir, sir? Hello? Sir? Are you still with me? Sir? Sir?"

Robert was slumped on the floor still holding the phone. His face was as white as a bleached bed sheet. He was barely hanging on. He could faintly hear the 911 operator when the lights went out. The dispatcher ran a trace and found out where the call was coming from. She called EMS and told them to hightail it. She pointed out that a man may be having a heart attack.

*

EMS arrived and lifted Long up onto a gurney, rushing him to the hospital. Fast work was needed if Robert was to survive. His pulse rate was weak and his blood pressure dropped en route. The IV's and nitro were coursing through his veins in an attempt to clear up whatever could've been blocking his arteries. The arrival at Lincoln Memorial was lightning quick. The paramedics swiftly wheeled Mr. Long into the emergency entrance and doctors took over. Before anyone could blink, Robert was in surgery to insert a stent through a vein in his thigh and towards his sickened heart. The hope was that they reached his ticker in time and could relieve the ailment before too much damage was done. Robert was stirring a bit, since the introduction of medication in his system was beginning to take hold. His breathing calmed and his pressure rose back up to a safer level. Robert tried to speak.

"Wha…what's goin' on? Where am I?"

"You're in the ER, Mr. Long, in good hands. Please try to relax while we work."

Robert acted like any normal person who found themselves suddenly in a place where you're surrounded by many people wearing white coats and facemasks. That's a shocking situation when you begin to come around. Robert wanted to move but was told to lie still. He began to thrash about, so the medics gave him a mild sedative. It worked and Robert calmed, allowing the doctor to do his precision work. The relief he felt upon the procedure's success was instant and incredible. Robert was pleased with the fact that he could once again breath regularly. The pain also evaporated and he sunk into a nice sleep as he was sent to ICU for monitoring.

*

Luckily, the bars on the window didn't give, knocking Amy back onto the floor behind her. She was cut on her arms, but not severely. Amy stood back up and shook her head, disconnecting the cobwebs that formed on impact. Instead of continuing her crying and the pity party she was throwing, she became angry. Amy realized for the first time that not all circumstances are under her immediate control. In some situations she had absolutely no say in the outcome. It's called rolling with the punches and dealing with adversity. It was at this exact moment that Amy decided she was no longer going to be a lawyer. The simple act of telling herself this truth sent a swath of heavily overloaded boulders off her not-so-broad shoulders. The young woman would not take another second of responsibility for her father's indiscretions, her mother's drunkenness, and most of all, the bullying from certain voices and visions. There would be no further feeding of the power that was, up until now, being held over her. It was not her fault that John was tried, convicted, and then executed. She had given her best effort in a very difficult situation. Amy thought she could win, but didn't. It's the State's fault Garrison was dead, not hers. This was a very important step in Amy's healing process. She called Dr. Baxter and asked if they could meet in the morning. Baxter agreed to come up to the facility and see her before she had to be at the office.

Amy went into the bathroom to clean herself up. She bandaged her minor cuts, brushed her short, yet still beautiful black hair, and freshened up. Amy was starting to feel renewed and looked at herself in the mirror. She saw a young, vibrant woman looking back. There was much more to life than defending unfortunate people. As much as she loved to give back to individuals, she knew it wasn't the right calling. Too much pressure, too many hurt feelings bubbling up. It was time for a major change in her life.

As she continued getting cleaned up, she heard the voice. The voice of the young Amy calling out to her. She stood straight and tall, looked in the mirror, and saw the other side of herself standing behind her in the room. Amy turned around, and with a determined look, walked out of the restroom and faced down her adversary nose-to-nose. This time, Amy held to her beliefs, and a showdown was about to occur.

*

Robert was stable. His vitals normalized and he thanked his lucky stars he was alive. Of course there would be a battery of tests and rehab before he was completely out of the woods. Being among the living and laying in a hospital bed were the most one could ask for. He missed John, and he wanted to get out so he could spruce up the farm before it went to auction. It was the least he could do for a man who showed so much courage and poise in his darkest hours. Now mind you, Robert did not think there was anything glorious about suicide, but under the circumstances, he would have done the same thing if he could have. As much as John harassed him, Robert found that he missed that. Thinking about it in retrospect, he knew the old codger was just busting his balls in a friendly way. It was who he was. It was how John expressed himself. If you ever needed anything, he'd be there for you. He might've snapped a few sarcastic quips and perhaps the occasional growl, but he'd help you in a pinch. Had he been here today, Robert had zero doubt that his friend would be sitting next to him in the hospital. It probably would have made things in this antiseptic-smelling joint a little more interesting. John would be hitting on the nurses, fussing about this and that, and making sure his buddy was comfortable. A tear or two streamed down Robert's cheek when the nurse of every fifteen minutes came in.

"Hi Mr. Long. What are you crying about? You okay?"

"I ain't cryin', I just got something' in ma eye."

"Oh, I see, that's your story and you're sticking to it, huh?"

"It ain't no damn story to stick to. It's the real truth. Besides, what do you care?"

"I care, Mr. Long. I care about you as if you were my own."

Robert smiled at that comment. He was in good hands and he knew it. He inquired about his condition.

"Well, Mr. Long, the doctor will be here about eleven, maybe a little later. He'll be here today though. Now you just rest and I'll be checking in."

The thoughts and fond memories continued after the nurse left. This time, there were no tears, in fear of someone seeing him. Robert came from the time when men did not cry around others, if at all. It would be considered a weakness. He sat back in his bed and drifted off to sleep, comforted in the fact that he was to live longer. How many more years, he didn't know, but he'd make them good ones. He missed his friend.

*

"It's time for you and me to finish this little war," Amy told her altar-ego. "I don't have any more time for you in my life." Amy stood her ground.

"I haven't come to fight you, Amy. I've come to say good-bye. You have realized that it's not you who is the perpetrator. You are the victim." Amy was caught off guard.

"Then why did you torment me so? Where are the others who've tried my sanity?"

"There are no others. They were not here because they wanted to torment you, Amy. They were here because you called them here."

Amy was having a difficult time trying to figure out exactly what she was being told. She also wanted to know why the spirits hung around after she shooed them away.

"You didn't have to haunt me, terrorize me, or destroy my chances for success."

"Listen to me closely," the young twin said. "We did nothing of the sort. Your guilt, stubbornness, and sarcastic refusal to give up the past brought us. Now that you have come to the realization of what you must do, we have no further power over you. That is, unless you choose to bring us back."

"I never want to see any of the spirits again."

"We are not spirits, Amy, we are figments and reminders. We are in your mind, no one else's. This was entirely your choice."

As the conversation continued to run its course, the young version of Amy began to fade into static. She was disappearing from Amy's sight, and not a moment too soon.

"Why don't you chastise me for letting Garrison die? Why stop now?"

"You have come to accept that it's not your fault Amy. Nobody chastised you, *except you*."

Young Amy faded and evaporated before her eyes. The voices stopped and the visions were gone. Amy felt a strong surge of energy course through her body as this phenomenon happened. Perhaps the young Amy had disappeared forever. Time would certainly tell.

The nurse on duty entered Amy's room and asked what happened to the glass. Amy told her she threw her tray at the wall and broke the window on accident. After a minor scolding, Amy was told to pack up her stuff so they could find another area with unbroken glass. Amy had known that if she told the nurse that she tried to fling herself out; it would be suicide watch for sure. She was too far along to go there. Amy had faced her demons and apparently defeated them. It was the hugest victory of her life. The nurse, upon admitting Amy to a new room, told her that Garrison's friend Mr. Long was in the cardiac wing of the Lincoln Memorial Hospital, and perhaps Dr. Baxter would take her to visit if she asked. Amy would do just that when she came to see her.

Snuffed Out

What was Lyla to do? She had been going back and forth ever since Dan blew her off and she wasn't getting anywhere. She had contemplated just shooting him after he gave his testimony, but that, she thought, would be too rash. Lyla also considered simple suicide with an overdose, which also turned out to be a bad idea in her mind. If she were to do that, Dan would hear about her death, shrug his shoulders and move on. She wanted to do something that would draw his attention and keep it. The ultimate decision she had originally made was scrapped because she didn't have the courage at the time. That tune was quickly changing and focusing back into view. It held a catch, though. She wanted it to be the most spectacular of attention-garnering ploys she ever used. Lyla not only wanted Dan's attention, but she wanted to leave a lasting impression so that he'd never forget her. She would allow Dan to live his life in pain. The pain of ignoring that that meant nothing to him, but everything to her. Lyla packed a few important items into her knapsack, including her .22 caliber handgun. She gave Dan a call.

"Hello? Dan? This is Lyla. Do you have time to meet me so we can talk?

"I'm kinda' in the middle of something. Can we do it later?"

Dan was in the middle of something alright. Her name was Karen.

"C'mon, Dan. It'll only take a little while, and then you can go back to what you were doing."

"What's this about, Lyla? Are you going to guilt trip me?"

"No. As a matter of fact, I want to show you my forgiving side. The side of me that you haven't seen for some time."

Karen, the girl lying naked in Dan's bed, moaned for his return. He put up his index finger, indicating that she wait a second.

"Alright, Lyla. I'll meet you. Where?"

"Oh, I could just come to your place, Dan." Lyla knew Dan had a woman in his bed and would put the kibosh on that idea.

"Nah. My place is a mess. Any other ideas?"

"Okay, meet me at the Tin Lizard. That bar in town." Lyla thought this a good spot to go over her "thoughts" with Dan. It was a country-western, three-story bar on the west side of Lincoln. Only a twenty-minute drive and not very busy on this, a weeknight.

"Okay Lyla, meet you there at say, ten?"

"Deal, see you there. You won't regret this Dan. I promise."

"Are we going to talk about me getting back to work full-time?"

After a short hesitation, she sighed. "See ya at ten, Dan."

Lyla hung up, smiled, and then took twenty Oxycontins in two handfuls and two swallow of water.

She had to meet him in one hour, and the Oxys shouldn't hit until 9:45.

*

After hanging up, Dan grabbed the edge of the bed sheet and pulled hard, exposing his "flavor of the day" Karen's full nakedness. She giggled with childlike impishness.

"I gotta' go Karen. Get up and get dressed."

"Where you going, big guy? I want some more lovin'."

It was tough for Dan to turn her away. He ogled her up and down. Full, firm breasts and a nicely trimmed lower region was calling loudly. Dan disciplined himself, though, and shooed her away.

"C'mon, c'mon. You can come back tomorrow."

"Maybe I won't be so horny tomorrow. Let's cuddle up sweet-ums."

Dan grew impatient. He took her by the arm and guided her out of bed. Her giggles turned to scowls. He threw her clothes at her and ordered her to get dressed.

"You're a jerk, Dan. What's your deal?"

"Just get dressed and get the fuck out, okay? I have to get moving here. Damn!"

Karen gathered the rest of her stuff and headed for the door. She turned around and gave Dan a nasty one finger salute, to which Dan replied;

"I hate to see you go, but I love watchin' ya' leave!"

She slammed the door behind her. He chuckled.

Dan thought this little meet up with Lyla may help to rebuild some of the burnt bridges. He never meant to hurt her, but he couldn't possibly work a love relationship with her, either.

"She should have known that," Dan would think to himself.

Perhaps he could get back to work full-time doing what he loved. Maybe he and Lyla were finally ready to take the step needed to repair the hard feelings.

Dan brushed his teeth, combed his hair and slapped on a little "Brut for men" aftershave. Hey, when you're a bachelor living alone, you go with the cheap stuff. The young man was nervous, but had no more than moderate tension. It was a very tolerable stress to endure. Dan grabbed his jacket and headed out to fix what had gone wrong earlier.

*

"Screw 'em!" Lyla said loudly in her car. "To hell with that piece of shit. He used me and he took my love without paying for it. He's a jerk and he deserves what he'll get tonight."

Lyla was already headed to the bar. The Oxycontin were just beginning to take affect and the dose she took would undoubtedly be lethal in her tiny frame. She turned on the radio and listened to some Heavy Metal. It was the song "Snuff" by a group called Slipknot. The riff of the music gave her a jolt of energy and the wherewithal to carry out her plan on this cool starlit, evening. She knew she had to get to the bar soon so she could get herself setup for Dan, *her man's,* arrival. Lyla ran two stop signs and three red lights on her journey, darn near sabotaging the entire operation. She kept her wits and continued onward.

Dan drove toward the Tin Lizard with a smile and a song. He was glad to be seeing Lyla and hoped this would bury the animosity once and for all.

"She knows the type of guy I am, so it really shouldn't be a problem."

Dan laughed at his latest newfound wit as he continued forward.

"If you love me let me go, and run away before I know, my heart is just to dark to care, I can't destroy what isn't there."

His radio was belting out "Snuff" by his favorite band, Slipknot, and all was well in his world. He arrived at the Lizard and parked next to Lyla's car, which he found near the back of the lot. Dan had just stuffed his keys in his pockets when he looked up, and saw Lyla standing on the roof of the establishment. It appeared as if she had a rope around her neck and a gun in her hand. This was not good, not good at all…..

*

Chucky Jenson was manning the bar that evening, serving only six or seven customers since his shift started at three. There were two guys left, yakking it up at the other end of the room. Chucky, a very plucky 5'6", could easily destroy someone twice his size. He had been a bricklayer until his back couldn't take it any longer, so bartending seemed the logical thing to do. Little impact, high tips. Chucky was built near to the ground and had to bull rush his share of patrons, but it was still much easier than hauling bricks around.

Not to mention that it didn't happen too often. The drinkers watched Chucky and learned that a blow from him could mean a trip to the ER, which was not a good way to end the evening.

Cleaning the last of the glasses and rehanging them above the bar, Chucky noticed it was just after ten and wanted to close early on this slow weekday. "Last call, you two, drink or split."

The men called for one more round each and told Chucky they'd leave right after they finished. Chucky was okay with that, but decided to lock the door in case someone else came along and decided to drown their sorrows for another two hours.

"I'm locking the door, boys. Let me know when you're ready to go."

A wave by one of the men let Chuck know they heard him. Upon reaching the front of the bar, Chucky saw some guy standing outside looking up to the roof of the building. Curious, he went out to see what was up. Dan noticed him and waved him over, then pointed up where Lyla was rocking back and forth with the rope around her neck.

"What in the hell's goin' on here, dude?" Chucky impatiently asked. "What's that woman doin' up there?"

Dan wasn't quite sure himself, but knew for a fact it was not ideal.

"She told me to meet her here and I find this. Don't ask me why."

"Well, when will the cops be here?"

"Cops? I didn't call them."

Chucky looked at Dan like he was as nutty as a fruitcake.

"What do you mean "you 'didn't call 'em?' You got shit for brains or somethin'?"

The bartender took out his cell to call 911 when Lyla spoke up.

"Do-an bother call-in' any-one," Lyla slowly slurred, "I ain't com-in' down, at leathe not how ya' think."

Lyla wobbled and rocked, slurring her words into a garble. The drugs were hitting hard now and both Dan and Chucky knew it.

"Hey you," Lyla lazily pointed at Chucky, "Go inthide, this do-an pertain ta you."

"I ain't goin' nowhere lady, now get yer ass down 'fore I come up and get cha down myself!"

Dan tried the more reasonable approach. "C'mon, Lyla, don't do anything dumb, okay? Let's work this out."

"Wo-hurk it outh? You a pieth of shit, Dan. You ruinth my life."

Lyla put the gun barrel to the back of her head.

"NO LYLA!" Dan shouted, but it was too late. The gun went off, blowing Lyla's brain matter off the side of the building and down to where the two men stood. Both had Lyla's DNA all over them. She was forced off the building by the impact and the rope caught about five feet off the ground. A loud and disgusting crack echoed through the lot as the rope went taught. She swung slowly back and forth about six feet from Dan and Chuckey's faces.

"Ho-ly fuck-in' shit!" Chucky said slowly. Dan stood in stunned silence. He felt that awful nausea coursing through him. It was the same sick feeling he had when he found the dead child. Dan backed up, sat on the curb, and puked as he did before. He felt his senses weakening while slipping into shock. Chucky called 911 and summoned the police and whoever else could come, ASAP. He then went into the bar and told the two patrons, who heard the gunshot and were standing at the glass entrance door, to stay where they were until the police came. The two nodded with mouths agape. Chuck saw a slip of paper sitting on the ground near where Lyla's bloody and distorted body hung. It was labeled "DAN WHEELER."

"This yours, buddy?" Chuck asked Dan, who was unresponsive to his question. Dan just stared forward, vomit dripping from his lower lip, and made no move whatsoever. Chucky unfolded the note and it had a simple one-sentence statement, 'Now you'll never forget me again, Dan.'

Jack Takes Over

Jack made it to the scene with Lt. Michaels. Both men stood and scratched their heads as they studied Lyla: hung, shot, and swinging ever so slightly in the chilly breeze. Jack looked to Michaels and wanted answers. He had his hands on his hips. Both men saw flashes. Jack and Ed looked around and saw nothing. Ed chalked it up as a fritzy street light, while Jack, of course, took is as another sign of his power.

"What's going on in your town, Lieutenant? Are you in control, or not?"

Michaels looked at Jack with an element of surprise. "What kind of stupid question is that, Jack? Could it be that you're insinuating I should've stopped something *before* it happened?"

"As a matter of fact, yes! You need to take control of the town where you're in charge. So far, I've seen nothing that suggests that. First it was the botched execution, and now this."

Lt. Michaels had to step away from Beauregard. These were fighting words where he came from, and fisticuffs would not be suitable at this moment. Instead, he talked with Chucky, who gave him the note he found next to Lyla, and then gently approached Dan.

"Hey son. What happened here? What did you see?"

Dan sat shivering with his knees up by his chin and his arms wrapped around his legs. No words came out of his mouth. He rocked back and forth. It was obvious that the young man was in a state of shock and would need medical attention. EMS was on the scene, and Michaels waved them over. After looking over Dan, they placed him on a gurney for a trip to the ER. Michaels turned his attention back to Beauregard, who was checking the scene and speaking with Chucky.

"Jack, it's my scene. You can go on home. I'll see to it from here."

That statement riled the Colonel's ire. **"I'm still your Colonel and boss until I start my term in January! You do not give me any orders whatsoever!"**

Lt. Michaels butted up chest to chest with Jack. **"Then you start supporting me, damn it! Just remember that kids were dying on your watch, so don't be throwing stones when you live in a glass house!"** Michaels felt an aura of liberation with this comment, and appeared to have Jack's attention.

"Getting tough now, huh Michaels? Let me just tell you that I solved the cases of the murdered kids! I put that slime ball away for good! Don't ever forget that, sir!"

"Did you, Jack? Did you put away the killer? On the other hand, did you put away someone to help you get that blasted election vote? Is the killer really caught, or is more murder coming?"

Jack cocked back to throw a punch, but was interrupted by a police officer who found something of the upmost importance.

*

The killer watched the whole proceeding from the top of the building across the street. He was wearing the black leather outfit. The power that he felt was astounding. The scene was set right below and Lyla Helms hung dead for the world to see; her head cocked grotesquely to the right. The prayers to Satan were paying off, he thought. The picture of Lyla that the killer had in the center of the pentagram would now be burned, along with the Jack of Spades that adorned her photo. Dan's picture and card would receive the same treatment, as this episode would undoubtedly set the young man back, severely, in his quest for deliverance from the awful things he'd witnessed. The prayers had also caused Amy Fraser to slip in and out of sanity, Robert Long to have a heart attack and the events of this very evening. Worshiping the Satan master did not always result in death for those prayed against; it also brought hardship and pain, all evil to the killer. He delighted in what was thought to be a direct result of the sacrifices and rituals. The only setback so far was the release of the young boy so he could tell of the pending doom. He ended up at the psych ward. Perhaps this event would open people's eyes and ears to the hideous results of their sins against humanity.

A black Jack of Spades was in the killer's hand, but it wasn't an ordinary card. The killer himself had drawn up a special Jack. It showed a person, gender unknown, standing with two bloody spears crossed over its chest and a look of contempt. After rubbing and kissing it, the murderer released it over the side of the building. It cascaded down like a baby rocking in a cradle, going unnoticed and landing about forty feet from Lyla's body. It settled on the sidewalk waiting to be found. The killer saw Jack and Lt. Michaels mixing it up as if they would fight. Perfect. The killer was so satisfied and pleased that it was bringing this disorder upon its victims. After another five minutes, he disappeared into the shadows. He had seen enough and there was much more to come, including the next phases, which would really hit home with these sinful people living in Lincoln.

*

"Lieutenant, I found this on the sidewalk over there." The police officer gave Michaels a hand drawn Jack of Spades card. It sent a tingle down Beauregard's spine.

"Let me see that!" Jack demanded. "Where did this come from?" The officer pointed to the sidewalk.

Michaels mulled, looked toward Jack, glanced up to the opposite building, and then commented sarcastically. "What in the hell is going on in this town, Jack? I thought you had our damn killer."

Jack struggled for an answer. "We do. We did. Garrison's dead, this is just a coincidence. Maybe it's a sick joke."

"A coincidence?" Michaels attempted to make sense of it, but could not, "I have never in my life, up until the child murders, ever seen a Jack of Spades at any crime scene I've ever been a part of. Could it be that you collared the wrong man, Jack?"

Jack had a look of contempt for Michaels even having the gull to suggest such nonsense. "I'm not going to dignify your stupid statement with a comment. That's the dumbest theory I've ever heard and I think you agree."

"Well, Jack, you better hope so. I couldn't begin to imagine the uproar this town would be in if it turned out you had the wrong man executed. It could cost you your job as governor."

This caused Jack to stand tall and firm. It also spawned a nasty feeling of traitorous tones coming from his career-long police buddy.

"How dare you even suggest such irreverence, Michaels. I'll have you know that I, in fact, am still in charge of this department and this investigation. I will relieve you of that playing card in your hand, as *I* will collect and process the evidence, not you. Lt. Michaels, please get that woman's body down and sent to the morgue. The scene is upsetting."

Lt. Michaels was hesitant, but knew his job depended on cooperating with Beauregard, who was, after all, still in charge. He handed over the Jack of Spades and did what he was told, but not before one more teeny-weeny jibe crossed his lips.

"If you're the boss, Jack, then act like it! One second you want me to be responsible, then the next you're taking over again. Make up my mind."

Michaels walked over to Lyla's still hanging body and asked the EMS personnel to help him get her down and delivered to the morgue.

Jack stood scratching at his chin trying to figure out why Lyla did this. It certainly sounded as if she was a spurned lover, but without Dan's statement, and he certainly did not have to give one, it would be chalked up as a suicide, especially after reading the note Lyla had left. Jack placed the playing card in his breast pocket, confident that it had nothing to do with this crime scene. He would destroy it after declaring this an official suicide.

*

The colors in Dan's eyes were gray. He had no idea where he was. He had just witnessed the death of Lyla Helms, but was in the attempted process of blocking it from his mind. The EMS workers kept asking questions, but Dan couldn't, or wouldn't answer. He saw Jack Beauregard and Lt. Michaels approach, but the only thing he heard were blurred mumbles coming from their mouths. He had no idea what it was they said, nor did he care. Dan had Lyla's brain matter on his shirt, but did not notice. The blood from Lyla's wound was speckled on his face in a fine mist. The EMS tech wiped it off after the morgue attendant took a couple of snapshots. Dan was in some sort of a vacancy. No words or emotions would sum it up. He felt as if he could think to some extent, but it was foggy and unclear. Dan was having a shock episode and the ambulance team had loaded him on a stretcher for a trip to the hospital. During the drive, Dan continued to be unresponsive. His vital stats were good. Blood pressure, temperature, and heart rate all checked out. It was inside his mind that was damaged.

Not like brain damage, but emotional chaos. It hadn't been that long since he was privy to the dead child, but this was worse, and Lyla knew it would be. She knew that by doing it this way, it would affect Dan for a very long time, if not for the rest of his life. He simply was not equipped mentally to take on such violence and graphic content. In a movie? Of course, because it was fake. In real life? No chance.

After arriving at the hospital, Dan was taken to the psych ward for a complete examination and monitoring to see if his situation or condition had changed. He would spend a lot of time in this ward, fighting the fear and waves of guilt that Lyla gifted him. Dan Wheeler may never be the same man again. This could end his days as the town gigolo, and the woman who had just recently returned to his bed would again disappear in midair, like a cruel magic trick. The event that unfolded before his eyes was simply too much for the young man to endure. Lyla made her point and it was taken, violently, by Dan's self-conscious.

*

Since Jack took over the investigation, it was his job to visit Lyla's house and find any clues that may exist. Lyla lived in a tiny A-frame just south of town. It was enough for a single woman in her forties. She kept it clean and orderly, just as she had done with her job at animal control. Jack had always admired her for her dedication and professionalism and rarely had a problem with her. He was annoyed that she had slipped into whatever delusion engulfed her and wished she had talked with someone before committing such a violent act.

Jack found an empty pill bottle in the little trash can next to the sink in her restroom. He figured she had taken her fill of the Oxy tablets and probably didn't feel but a smidgen of pain when the bullet forced its way through her skull. He continued his inspection and found a photo album filled with pictures of Dan Wheeler. The photos showed some of the sexual exploits of the young bachelor. He certainly had his share of women and the album was far too hot to be handled. Jack was awed.

"So that's what she looks like naked. I've often wondered." Jack said to himself as he looked at pictures of Dan's conquests, which Lyla had collected by spying and peeping.

He was alone in Lyla's home and soon found himself developing an erection as he looked over the amatory photos. After scanning the room and closing the blinds so no one could see him, the Governor-to-be pulled out his penis and began masturbating as he looked at the exposed girls. Had someone been looking, the scene would be disgusting, as Jack did the deed while he was hunched over like a crippled Sasquatch. It only took two minutes before he reached his climax. He made sure to cover himself with a tissue that could easily collect the fluid he deposited so it could be flushed away in the toilet.

After Jack had finished his business, he collected all the pictures he could find for evidence. *His own personal stash of pornographic evidence*. These erotic photos would go into Jack's safe, tucked away neatly for any future exploits in which he could use them.

Whether it be framing up or manipulating some of the women in town, or for his own use when bored, they would be there and not one person would be wiser to it.

It was obvious that Lyla had been stalking the young man, so Jack really couldn't hold anything against him, and after his find, he really didn't want to. If Dan had, in fact, been having a sexual relationship with his boss and she turned eerie over it that was his problem. He would have to deal with the ramifications that developed from it. In this case, it was the suicide of Lyla right before Dan's timid eyes.

*

Lt. Michaels was sick about Jack taking the reigns out of his hand. It was a cheap shot and proved to him that Beauregard had zero confidence in anyone but himself. A slap in the face. A kick in the rear. Any contrary phrase would work.

Michaels had to try and rebound from this setback and take solace in the knowledge that Jack would be history in two short months. After his departure to the mansion, Michaels would no longer have to answer to him directly. There was a chance that Beauregard would meddle from time to time, but he would not have nearly enough hours in the day to get all the things he wanted to do done, including following up on Michael's investigations. Lt. Michaels also had issues with the new laws and rules Jack wanted to try and pass through State Congress when he started his term. The most annoying was Jack wanting to exile all sex offenders out of cities and towns and put them in their own little community on the southwest side of the state. This would be a mistake of colossal proportions, as Lt. Michaels thought it would increase the influx of crime in that area. Don't be fooled, Michaels couldn't care less about these offenders; he was more concerned with the pressure that would be put on other police forces. Another aspect of Beauregard's agenda that Michaels did not like was trying to turn Nebraska into a right-to-work state. Lt. Michaels had belonged to the FOP in Nebraska all his career and did not want non-union flunkies coming into the fray and causing what he thought would be a ton of dissension between older cops and newer ones. These things, along with statewide privatization, would be costly for everyone involved. Michaels had friends who would find themselves out of jobs and in poverty soon after. It didn't matter to Jack, because he would be saving millions for the state, he reasoned, thus lining his pockets big time.

"I wished I'd never voted for that guy," Michaels thought in retrospect. "He's going to run this state straight into the ground."

Lt. Michaels continued his work and would continue to be second in command until Jack left.

"Fine. I don't need the aggravation anyway. I'll have enough of it to deal with if his stupid laws get passed."

Lincoln Times

Woman hangs self at town watering hole

Lyla Helms, Lincoln Animal Control Officer dies

AP- Lyla Helms, the Lincoln Animal Control Dispatcher, hung herself at the Tin Lizard in downtown Lincoln last night. Although details are sketchy, it appears that Helms shot herself in the head on the roof of the establishment, then fell two stories with a noose around her neck. She was pronounced dead at the scene. Tin Lizard owner Chucky Shuman witnessed the carnage and commented to the Lincoln Times.

“I don’t know why she did it, but it appears she was distraught about a lost love. The police have asked me to keep anything I know quiet. I guess they’ll question me later.

Helms was in her forties and had no family living in the Lincoln area. A funeral has been set for later this week, with details upcoming.
-Angela Page

Dead Headlys

"Damn it, Sonya. Get in here!" Richard was shouting and Sonya knew exactly why. The mail had come and she failed to intercept it before Richard could see the *new* credit card statement that came in.

"Yes, dear?" she warily asked. "Is everything alright, honey?"

When she entered the den, she saw that Richard was sitting at his desk with a gun in his hand. His right eye was twitching wildly. "Why do you have that gun, Richard? Are you really okay?"

"Oh, this gun?" Richard lazily waved it as he spoke. "I have this gun, Sonya, because I see you've charged up another ten grand on the card you had hidden and I'm thinking about killing you."

Sonya took a step back. She felt as though the world was closing in on her. She did not want to die. Richard ordered her to have a seat on the chair across from him.

"Sit down, Sonya. Were going to have a chat."

She did as she was told and Richard started lecturing her.

"For the umpteen numbers of years we've been married, I have been nothing but a pussy about every single crisis we've had together. I go to work every day, I have people thrown in jail every day, and I even have some sent to the chair. I come home from all this and I expect nothing but a touch of sympathy. Just a few minor words of encouragement, Sonya, that's all…"

She tried to speak, cutting off Richard mid-sentence. "But Ric…"

"Shut the fuck up, Sonya. If you interrupt me again, I will shoot you in the kneecap. Do you understand?"

Sonya nodded. She was beginning to hyperventilate.

"Good. I'm doing the talking here for once and you will stay silent. I have listened to you for what seems like a lifetime. Now you listen to me you two-bit, spendaholic, gold-digger of a wife."

Sonya was questioning to herself if Richard had flown straight off the deep end. To her, it appeared that he'd been pushed too far. The only hope was to sit and listen so he may have time to calm a bit and come to his senses. The twitching in his eye worried her.

"My dear Sonya. In the mob, when they lend you money, you pay them back five fold or you get a broken bone; Leg, arm, hand, it doesn't really matter, as long as the tactic is effective." Richard was waggling his index finger as he made his point. "Would you please place your right hand on the table Sonya?"

Her eyes darted left to right, her throat swelled, and her stress level rose even more than she thought it could. Her heart raced furiously as she wondered what he had in mind.

"I'll count to three, Sonya. If your hand is not on that table, I will shoot you. Oh, and do not question or interrupt, or I will shoot you. ONE, TWO…"

Sonya quickly placed her right hand on the table.

"Good Sonya. If you move it off the table, I will shoot you. Now close your eyes."

She did as she was told and could hear Richard rise up out of his leather chair and approach her.

"Do not open your eyes, Sonya, until I say so, or I will shoot you."

Sonya nodded yes. Richard reached under the table she had put her hand on and pulled out a small sledgehammer. He cocked it back behind his head and told her to open her eyes. As the hammer came down in the center of her hand, she had absolutely no time to move it. It hit squarely and sent electric pain up her arm as a scream violently escaped her lips. The bones shattered with the hit. The four knuckles that were affixed to each finger were destroyed. She looked and saw that her hand had bent inward. She pulled the broken stub back and tucked it into her stomach just under her breasts. Sonya tried to rise from the chair, but Richard pushed her back down with his foot.

"Sit, Sonya, you are not excused. By the way, how does that hand feel? You can tell me."

"EEK. I-I owww," was all she could muster.

"I guess that means it hurts, huh Sonya? I'll bet it sure does, whew-doggy. Sonya, please place the left hand on the table."

She shook her head *no* and tried to speak as the tears flowed down her cheeks. She was squeaking a plea not to hurt her again when Richard raised the pistol and shot her in the kneecap. She fell out of the chair in a heap, pain in the hand and knee enormous and unyielding.

"I told you not to interrupt," Richard lazily scolded. "Yet you can't even follow that order."

As she lay on the floor clutching at her knee with her good hand, she saw that her kneecap no longer existed. It was gone. All that was left was blood, cartilage and burn marks. The pain was excruciating as shock began to set in, causing her to tremble. Richard walked over, pinned her left hand down with his foot, and then smashed that hand with the sledgehammer. Sonya went white. The world as she had known it was fading out very quickly. Now the shock was full tilt and passing out was seconds away. Richard did not want that though. He wanted her awake for the grand finale.

"Sonya? Oh Sonya, wakey-wakey."

Richard had busted open an ammonia packet and waved it under her nose. It brought her around quickly. Her two hands lay at her side completely incapacitated and her knee was throbbing in a most dramatically painful way. Blood was splattered about the room and on Richard's face. He whispered in her ear.

"If I've told you once, I've told you a hundred times. I do not have that fucking job yet, so could you please stop spending up money we do not have?"

Sonya nodded with enthusiasm as she thought he may actually spare her life.

"Sorry, dear, I simply don't trust you anymore. He pointed the gun at Sonya's face and pulled the trigger. Lights out.

*

The cell phone rang in Jack's pocket. It was Richard and it was important.

"Jack, could you come on over to my house? We need to talk."

"Look Rich, give me some time on this attorney general thing…."

"It's not about that, Jack. I thought you'd be interested to know that I murdered my wife."

Jack fumbled his cell phone and it landed on the floor with a heavy CLUNK. He quickly retrieved it and asked Richard if he really said what he thought he'd just said.

"Sure did, Jack." Richard explained indifferently, "I pounded the hell out of her, and then shot her *right* between the eyes."

"Why did you do that, Rich? You know that pretty much takes care of your life, right?"

Jack snapped his phone shut and made a b-line straight to the Prosecutor's home. Jack made sure his gun was loaded and the safety off in case he needed it. He started thinking about the happenings in his town. The murdered children, Garrison, Helms, and now Headly's wife. "What's the story?" He wondered in his mind. "Has this town been cursed?" Ever since the botched execution, strange things had been going on. Jack thought about the need for a meeting among his police troops, but for now there was a bigger fish to fry, and it lived about ten minutes away.

*

Jack entered Richard's home very slowly and very carefully with his gun drawn. He was taking no chances with a man that was obviously capable of killing, and in an apparently violent way. Jack could have called for backup, but with his confidence level at a ridiculously high level, he thought himself untouchable.

"Rich, RICHIE!" Jack shouted, "WHERE YOU AT PARTNER?"

"My den Jack, I'm in the den."

Jack continued slowly and when he rounded the corner, he saw the dim light at the end of the corridor. He stepped in with his gun still drawn and found Rich sitting at his desk smoking a big fat cigar.

"Hey Jack, c'mon in. Watch your step though, there's a little mess there."

Richard couldn't have been less accurate. There was a mess all right, only it wasn't little. It was a bloody, gruesome scene. Sonya lay there with a blown out head and kneecap, and her hands were as raw as fresh cuts of uncooked steaks.

"What happened, Richard? What did you do here?"

"She spent a bit more than I was prepared to pay for, Jack. We're now about a hundred grand in debt because of her sheer stupidity. I had to make sure it never happened again." Richard said this with a grin and a twitch of his right eye.

Jack was shaken not only by Sonya's remains, but Rich looked very eerie next to the dim light shining upward on his face at the desk. Jack proceeded with caution.

"You know what, Jack? This is partly your fault. If you hadn't promised me that job, this never would have happened. In a way, you cost my wife her life."

"Don't be an idiot, Headly. You flat out murdered her and it's you that's going to pay, no one else. Don't sit there and try laying this one on me."

"You say whatever you want, Beauregard, but you're going to have to pay the other half of the price here."

Jack saw that Rich had the gun he undoubtedly used sitting on the desk within a whisker of his right hand. The only move for Beauregard to make was to try getting him away from the weapon.

"Get on the floor, Richard. Put your hands out in front of you. You're under arrest."

"Oh, I don't think so Jack. As a matter of fact, I'm declaring a citizens arrest against you. The charge would be murder, Jack. The murder of John Garrison and the murder of my wife. You're taking the heat, big guy."

Jack was perplexed and stunned. Headly was trying to put this murder on him. He could not allow such nonsense. Richard continued.

"You know Garrison didn't kill those kids, Jack. You put the collar on him to get elected. I did the easy stuff in court, but I was only thinking of myself. Now I see the light and you're going down."

With no choices left, Beauregard quickly aimed and pulled the trigger. The gun sitting on Richard's desk flew back against the wall. It was a direct hit and Jack quickly rushed, slid over the desk, and pinned Headly to the floor. Jack punched him once to knock him senseless. A square hit to the jawbone. He dragged Headly over to Sonya's body and laid him next to her.

"I'm the guinea pig, huh? I'm the fucking fall guy? I don't think so, Richie Rich. This looks like a murder-suicide in my book."

Jack walked over and picked up Headly's weapon with a handkerchief. The gun was still warm from the two bullets that claimed Sonya's knee, then her life. He took it back to where the two lie on the floor.

"Wake up, dipshit." Jack slapped Rich across the face. Headly only mumbled a bit, so Jack went to work. He took Richard's hand and placed the gun in it, being careful not to leave any prints, and then placed the barrel in Richard's mouth. Jack wrapped his index finger in the hanky, put Headly's finger on the trigger and helped him pull it. Now it was a murder-suicide. It was actually a murderer murdered, but no one was here to prove that.

Jack calmly opened his cell and called Michaels. "Get your forensics team over to Richard Headly's house. There's a mess here."

Jack knew there was no way they could come close to fingering him. He did what he had to do and came only when called by Headly. This, in Jack's mind, is how he found the two.

Jack holstered his weapon, let out a burst of laughter, and looked right at the half-headless Richard. A quick flash burst before Jack's eyes. It was ecstasy.

"I didn't want a worrier like you on my staff anyways."

The Devil Made 'em Do It

Amy collapsed in court under the weight of voices and visions. Robert Long had a heart attack. Garrison was found guilty of murder and put himself to death. Lyla Helms hung herself outside of the Tin Lizard, while Richard Headly killed his wife and Jack helped Richard kill himself. All very odd for those involved in the trial. Soo-Chin was gone. She packed up and left town, so there's no telling what's happening with her. Jack Beauregard sat on his couch with Kyle trying to make heads or tails of it.

"What's your take, Kyle?"

A shrug of the shoulders was his take as the Kardashians continued shaking their substantial asses on the TV.

"Kyle! Earth to Kyle, come in."

"Oh, sorry Dad. What did you say?"

Jack clicked off the program, breaking his son's spell on the trashy show.

"I said, what's your thinking about everything that's been happening lately with the people surrounding Garrison's trial?"

"I have no idea Pop. Maybe the court Gods are mad." Kyle chuckled at his wit. Jack did not.

"I'm serious son. This is strange and eerie. What if I'm next on this little circle of terror?"

"Did you say, 'circle of terror?' I think you should start watching the Kardashians with me. 'Circle of terror?' Think about that Dad." Kyle was amused.

Jack considered his son, and then tried one last time to chisel through his teen-age mind.

"Yeah! I said circle of terror."

"You really want to know what I think Dad. I'll tell you in two words: shit happens."

A huge blurt of laughter jumped out of Jack's belly. Kyle followed suit. Now they were both laughing so hard they lost their breath. Jack had tears coming from his eyes while Kyle's abs started to hurt. They laughed for another minute or so before Jack was able to come to his senses and speak.

"Kyle, that's the stupidest thing I've ever heard." More giggles. "Are you serious with that?"

"Yea Dad. As serious as Robert Long's heart attack."

This time they laughed so hard Jack dribbled urine into his underpants and ran for the toilet. Kyle followed him and roared until he was out of breath. The two spent the rest of the evening in joyous moods.

*

The recovery was going well. No voices and no visions for some time. Amy felt relief that she thought no longer existed. She decided that this was as good a time as any to visit Mr. Long in cardiac care. She was okayed by Dr. Baxter to roam around the facility as long as she promised not to leave. She looked around with enthusiasm and a whole new perspective. Amy no longer took the blame for Garrison's death, her dad's perversion, or anything else that was out of her control. It was a huge burden off her shoulders, not to mention the other monkeys that were one time firmly attached to her back.

Robert was recovering well. His doctor told him he could soon move on with his life and would probably have a good number of years left. Its difficult being a doctor and telling an older man well past his prime years that he could continue living a full life, being that its only ten or so years longer. Nonetheless, that's what Robert was told, so he took it and ran. He thought he should probably be dead now, if not for God's mercy that was bestowed upon him. The angels sung in heaven, Bob figured, but weren't ready for him to join their chorus.

Amy meandered around the hospital for a while, stopping at the gift shop to buy a balloon and get well card for Mr. Long. She greeted people excitedly and with a new shine in her eyes. Amy appeared to have quite a bounce in her step as life was now treating her kinder. In actuality, she was treating herself kinder and that made all the difference. She made her way to the cardiac unit, card and balloon in tow. She reached Long's room and knocked.

"Yep! C'mon in, whoever it is."

As soon as Robert looked up and saw the young lawyer, he popped up in his bed with a huge smile and a perkiness that had eluded him lately.

"For me?" Robert said when seeing the gifts Amy bore.

"Yessir, it isn't much, but it's what the gift shop had to offer."

She sat next to his bed and the two talked on and on about everything from the weather to their health. Old men and women like to talk about what's ailing them, but the youthful Amy sat with a patient demeanor and let Mr. Long speak. The conversation finally reached the trial, Garrison's death and the funny stuff going on since then.

"So Amy, what have ya' heard through the grapevine 'bout all this nonsense happening since the execution?"

"I don't call it an execution," Amy said with discontent, "I call it torture. They tortured him and John took it upon himself to finish the job. I would expect nothing less from that old codger."

"Yep. Me too! He wasn't lettin' them jailers do it, that's for sure! Too much pride and orneriness inside that old man. I'm willin' to bet he wasn't scared neither."

Robert considered Amy for a moment, and then mentioned how pretty he thought she was. This time, Amy thanked him for the compliment. No threat, no warning, just thanks. It was actually okay for someone to compliment her on her beauty. She was, after all, striking to the eye. This was another new step for the young woman, and boy did it feel good to her.

The conversation then shifted to the death of Lyla Helms.

"I think they were having an affair," Amy said, "and he must have dumped her. She freaked out and did what she thought was needed. It was a bad idea, though. I wish I could have spoken with her."

"How do ya know they was doin' it?" Robert bluntly asked.

"I looked at both of them in court. You could just tell. Call it a woman's intuition."

The two surviving combatants for Garrison spoke a while longer, then Bob tired and Amy headed back through the hospital. During her walk, she saw a newspaper sitting on a lobby table. The front page grabbed her by the throat:

The Lincoln Times

Richard Headly kills wife, self

Colonel Beauregard investigates murder-suicide

AP- Richard Headly, the lead prosecutor for Lincoln, was found dead at his home last night with his wife, Sonya Headly dead at his side. It appears to be a murder-suicide instigated by Mr. Headly. Colonel and Governor-elect Jack Beauregard was called to the scene by Mr. Headly himself and upon arriving, found both husband and wife dead. Mrs. Headly had suffered two broken hands, and had been shot multiple times, while Mr. Headly had a single gunshot wound to the head. Beauregard said he had reason to think it was Mr. Headly who did the dirty work.

"Richard Headly called me on my cell and told me he'd killed his wife. He also stated that he was going to kill himself. He apparently did so as I was en route."

While no one can possibly know what Mr. Headly was thinking at the time, it appears as though financial woes may be at least partly to blame. Beauregard would not comment any further except to say he thinks there was a definite money problem going on. He did say that a marriage under fiscal pressure can dissolve quickly into violence.

"If anyone ever needs help, they need to pick up the phone and contact social services. There is always help out there if it's needed."

This event closely follows Lyla Helm's suicide and brings into question pressure from John Garrison's trial.

Funeral arrangements are pending. We will supply more information as it becomes available.

-Angela Page

Amy mulled over this bad news and wondered if she should be thanking her lucky stars it didn't come to that in her situation. Then a scary thought entered her mind: "What if this is some kind of curse and all of us involved in the trial are going to get our "comeuppance" soon." After brooding over this for a few moments, Amy dismissed it as nonsense. A gentleman walked up to her and asked her if she was finished with the paper.

"Oh, sure, here you go." Amy handed it to him. The man looked at her and then the front page. He asked, "What do you think of this stuff?"

Amy considered this, smiled, and then stated the obvious, "The devil made 'em do it."

*

Jack was sitting at home reading the same article Amy read. The difference was that Jack knew exactly what happened. Jack Beauregard, like it or not, was a murderer. He was a killer the same way the child murderer was. He was a cold-blooded, calculating, evil man. Of course, he refused to believe that. He was the champion of this town and nobody was going to touch him, so he disposed of a problem. No big deal in his mind and better yet, no big loss. He figured himself to be doing a greater service to the public and they didn't need to know all the circumstances anyway. Jack's cell phone started chirping. It was Lt. Michaels.

"Tell me what happened, Jack. I really need to know the truth."

"I have it under control, Michaels. Mind the other stuff that needs minding. I'll see that you get a report for the file."

"Good. I was going to ask you about that."

Jack took a long drag off the cigarette he was smoking and gave Michaels more advice. "That's the difference between us, Ed. I already had this taken care of, while you ride in late. You better get your head out of your rear, son, or this job will eat you up. As a matter of fact, I've been wondering if you're even the right man for the gig. Perhaps when I'm sworn in, I'll make a change or two to the department."

Lt. Michaels was seething on the other end of the line. He kept his cool, but wanted to beat Jack to a pulp.

"Just make sure I get that report, Jack. I need it." Click.

Michaels hung up and Jack thought over whether to fire him that instant. He decided to bide his time for when he took the oath. It was only a month or so away, so he had time to think.

In the police station, Michaels was growing more suspicious of the governor-elect. Two deaths in a few days and Beauregard's fingers right in the middle of them. What if it had been people in which Jack had no interest? Would Jack be this involved? He thought not. Lt. Michaels figured that he and Jack had more to discuss, but where and when was up in the air. Hell, if Beauregard decided to fire him today, there wouldn't be much Ed could do but protest it. He hoped it would not come to that.

Jack wrote up the report for the file, truth not withstanding. He wrote that he received the call, went over to Headly's home, and then found them both dead on the floor. A murder-suicide that could never be touched. Jack had even been alert enough to retrieve the slug that was stuck in the wall after he shot Richard's gun off the desk. It was cut and dried. There was no way on God's green earth that anyone could finger him in this case. It did make Jack feel a bit squeamish, but he recovered from that very quickly. He did what he thought he had to do and it was over…..for now.

A Killer Lashes Out

"It's working. The evil plan is working thanks to my leader. The Prince of Darkness is seeing it through. I'm his helper. I'm the chosen one who assists in Satan's death and debauchery."

The killer was proud to be Satan's crony. Up to now, everything was nearly perfect. Lyla Helms was dead. Dan Wheeler would never be the same, and the Headly's were suffering in hell where they belonged. To the killer, hell was not the same habitation the Devil came from. The Evil Prince being worshiped came from a dwelling beyond comprehension. As a reward for his dedicated service, the killer expected there would be every indecency available. Sex, drugs, alcohol, and anything else that went against the grain of society. The killer's heaven would be the wickedness and destruction of the evil world in which he lived.

He knew that Amy Fraser and Bob Long had been spared death by the master, but they were suffering all the same. Death is not always the end result of Satan's plan. Sometimes the disabling of the human spirit worked as well, if not better. The pictures, along with their jacks of spades, were gathered up and stacked in the center of the pentagram adorning the floor of the killer's rapidly dilapidating shed in the swamp. It wouldn't be much longer before new digs would be needed. The stink was almost too much even for the killer to bear. The swiftly rotting carcass of the dead dog still lay next to the shed wrapped in plastic and Lyme. This kept the smell down and the dog only half-decomposed so it could be used again in the final, most evil degradation yet.

The killer began to chant his incantations as he lit the cards and pictures on fire in the center of the goat's face. The fire represented the burning sulfur of eternal suffering and the ashes would be used as a sacrifice to the great one.

"Oh Great and Noble one, I am your servant and I give you these souls of evil as a sacrifice to you in the form of ash and sulfur. Accept my sacrifice oh evil one, for the good of our cause against the powers of society."

The floor began to rumble and the killer ducked down face first on the floor as a sign of respect to the Master of Darkness. Soon the breezes picked up in the cabin and the roar of a monster made itself heard. The Devil was in the room and the killer only hoped the sacrifice was suitable.

"Oh Satan of the dark, please accept this sac…."

"SILENCE!"

This was the first time the killer was visibly shaken. The master had barked loudly and made itself heard loud and clear. The only thing the murderer could do was stay down and keep quiet.

"MY MINION OF EVIL!" the entity shouted, **"RAISE YOUR FACE AND BEHOLD ME."**

The leather-clad murderer was reluctant.

"RAISE YOUR HEAD NOW! I WILL KILL YOU IF YOU DO NOT OBEY!"

The killer raised his head and saw the beast before him. It wore a black robe with a hood pulled over its head. The hood was too low to see the face, but smoke exited its mouth with each breath it took. The killer looked down and saw not feet, but hooves. Clawed toes were coming off of them. Upon closer inspection, the killer could see rings on the two toes from each hoof. The rings had small pictures depicting Jesus dying on the cross. Only the cross was upside down and the suffering was far more intense than what is described in the Bible. As the killer made his way back up towards the face of the beast, he saw that its two hands were clawed with very sharp looking nails on them. These nails glistened in the light and could easily shred anything to ribbons with the slightest touch. After this bit of study, the killer looked up further and the master removed its hood.

The demon was handsome. It had the face of a man with dark black hair, about mid-neck length, perfectly tanned skin and a deep five o'clock shadow that brought out his dark tone. The only strange things were his fire red eyes. The pupils were completely dilated and red. This gave him a very menacing stare. He glared at his slave with a wide grin. The devil then laughed, exposing razor sharp teeth along two rows, upper and lower. Its teeth were as white as snow, but as sharp as thumbtacks. They started normally at the gum line, but tapered into canines. The killer was no longer scared. He surveyed his master, and then dropped to his knees in worship.

"ARISE, FOOL! YOU ARE NOT WORTHY OF MY GUIDANCE, YET I HAVE THE ULTIMATE JOB FOR YOU DESPITE YOUR INIQUITIES. YOU WILL EXPOSE JACK BEAUREGARD FOR THE FRAUD THAT HE IS. YOU WILL USE A BOY IN THIS DEED." I WANT BEAUREGARD'S SOUL.

The killer was pleased. The evil entity was letting him go on his own to destroy Jack Beauregard. In the blink of an eye, the man was gone. No further direction, simply gone. The killer shouted out; **"I will do it as you have ordered. I am of the understanding that you are my master!"**

It did not matter how loud the killer yelled, because there was no further reaction from anywhere. He looked over the lair and found it to be the same old junkie hut he had used for some time now. The pentagram adorned the dusty floor and the smell of dead dog permeated through the shack. There was nothing more. Had this been a dream? Was everything a figment of the killer's warped fantasy? It appeared so. The anger that seethed through the killer's veins was an ugly, demonic, and vengeful anger. There would be hell to pay, and the killer was going to exact that payment.

*

Click-Clack-Click-Clack. Jack watched the silvery steel balls transfer energy back and forth while he thought long and hard about the murder he had committed. He tried with all his might to excuse his action as "good for the state," but had a very tough time with the reasoning. It certainly wasn't as if he actually committed "murder." He simply did what he thought was best under the circumstances. While Richard had a gun on the desk near his hand, Jack had him covered so there was no chance of Headly getting off a shot before Jack could plug him. After shooting the gun off the desk, Jack could have simply arrested Richard and taken him in. He murdered to excuse himself from having to deal with Richard one more day. Beauregard was cold-blooded, no different from the leather-clad being that killed children. No different from anyone who murdered and didn't feel the remorse. Jack felt only a (tiny) touch of the guilt that should have been associated with the death of Headly. It was not going to change.

There had been no children murdered or missing since Garrison's capture and Jack thought that situation to be resolved. There was the one child who claimed to have seen the killer, but Jack waved that off as nonsense. If he had really seen the killer, he'd already have been dead. Other people may have thought he was trying to up the political ante with the whole situation, but it was turning out that he may have guessed right on Garrison. He had his doubts at times, but no other murders meant just that. Beauregard also considered charging Dan Wheeler with some sort of crime in Lyla Helm's death, but the case would fall apart due to the fact that nothing pointed in Dan's direction. So Dan may have had a relationship with Lyla, so what? It didn't mean she had to kill herself. It didn't mean she had to load up on Oxycontin and force herself off a building after blowing her brains out. It was obvious to the governor-elect that Lyla was jilted and wanted Dan to remember her for the rest of his life. Her point was well taken. Dan sat in the mental infirmary trying to sort out the confusion in his head. Doing that could take the rest of his days on earth to do. Possibly even beyond. That was punishment enough. Dan had no clue that the woman was going to act so irrationally.

*

The governorship transfer was going to take place and Jack needed to get his ducks in a row. Spending bills, the medical marijuana debate, privatization of union jobs, and everything else that would need his attention waited. Jack planned on making life miserable for whoever did not agree with his ideas and principles. Medical marijuana was legal, but not in Jack's eyes. Unions were blasphemous according to Jack. The people voted him in on the issue of solving the child murders. They did not stop to think about how much damage this man could do to their state and livelihoods. Jack didn't care. He was looking after one person: Jack Beauregard. To hell with the people that didn't go with the program. He would ignore them and cater to the do-gooders who were speckled throughout Nebraska. The ultra conservative lunatics would be his best friends. He knew he could use their fears to bring about the changes he planned. It was a dirty trick to play on the people, but hey, they voted and spoke, so that was the bottom line. This man thought himself untouchable and could not be stopped.

A Killer Strikes Again

The terror would start once again. It was time for the killer to strike. He was angry and rancorous. Jack, and others, would pay for their sins, as ordered from the master. The final piece of the murderer's plan was to be set in motion. Another, more ultimate sacrifice was in the offing, and the stalking, black leather-clad killer would go into action. Who would it be? Whom would the killer trap and bring back to the lair for the master plan? It would be a child, that much was known. The killer had the plot in his malevolent mind and nothing would stand in the way. He would kill a child and have a huge surprise in store that would shake Nebraska's foundations. Not only in Lincoln, but the whole state and beyond. The people would be talking about this for a long time. It would be the ultimate degradation and embarrassment for the sinfulness. The killer donned the leather mask; made sure he had a black strap and a black Jack of Spades, and then headed out for the hunt.

*

The killer stalked the prey. The youngster, a boy, was seven or eight years-old and was not staying in his mom and dad's sightline. It was so easy to abduct and murder, and then go undetected. People simply did not keep their eyes open to the danger that lurked around them. It was simple to have the legislatures and senators pass laws to "protect" the kids, but what about the parents themselves? Did they think that since such laws were, in fact, passed that it ridded them of the responsibility of watching their own children? They were sorely mistaken. The killer knew he could snatch these kids up whenever he wanted to and never had to answer for it. The child stepped just a foot too far and SNAP! The killer had him and ran through the dark alley, imperceptible. He knew all the ins and outs of the city of Lincoln. He knew which paths to follow, which yards to cut through, and which tunnels in which to hide. Not one person had ever seen the dark demon. He was simply too fast and too quiet to be detected. Through the city, along the wooded areas, until finally they arrived at the lair.

*

As the child sat bound in the corner, with hands and feet tied, and mouth gagged, the killer looked about the room and could not find the pentagram that had been drawn on the floor. It was gone. It had disappeared into nothing. The floor showed no sign of anything except the dirt and dust of an unswept cabin, along with Jack of Spades playing cards strewn about in no distinctive order. This further angered the killer. The child whimpered and the killer screamed for him to shut up. This only made the boy more upset and weepy. The killer gripped each side of his own head with the gloved hands and tried to make sense out of the change that had been dealt. The killer grabbed the child from the corner, wrapped the strap around his neck and dragged him to the center of the floor. The noose had not been tightened as of yet, and the child cried for his young life. Again the killer strained, trying not to completely lose his mind. He paced back and forth across the dusty wooden floor. The child sat in the center with prayers of survival. It was little hope, yet it still existed. The boy became quiet. The killer stopped lurking and gave attention to the young one. Perhaps he didn't need to die. Maybe the killer could spare his life. Was there was another, even better plan in the works? Could there be a possibility of penalizing without the murder of another kid? The biggest question of all, though, was if the killer may be growing a conscience. The urge to kill was there, but the bigger urge for revenge loomed. How could the killer get his point across without actually slaying this young child? Perhaps he couldn't. It could be that he would, in fact, have to kill the child. The confusion bounced around in the killer's brain.

*

The boy's parents went straight to the State Police Post as soon as they saw that their child was missing from their sight. They were met by Lt. Michaels after they entered the facility. It was a sad scene as the mother cried and the father tried to console. Michaels brought them back to his office for a few questions before allowing them to go on home. The minute they left, he called Jack.

"Jack? Michaels here. You need to come on down to the station. We have another missing boy."

"How long has he been missing," Jack asked.

"About two or three hours."

"You know they have to be missing at least twenty-four before we consider it a missing child case, right?"

"Jack, could you just come down? We'll talk about it here."

Michaels hung up and waited for Beauregard to arrive. He knew in his heart of hearts that a killer of children still remained. The looming question was, is this a copycat or the real deal.

Jack arrived a half hour later, stopped by the lobby for coffee, then made his way to Michaels office. He was acting calm and collected, as if nothing were really wrong. Michaels was not so cool. He started in on Jack almost immediately.

"I don't know about you Jack, but I think a killer is still out there."

Jack mulled over Michael's point and tried very hard to stay focused and not get angry about the possible accusation that it was his own fault that the child came up missing.

"Number one, Lieutenant, is that you have not waited the law-mandated twenty-four hours before declaring this a missing child, and number two, it could be that something else is going on. Maybe it's the parents, or the child just wandered off with a relative. You simply don't know." Michaels approached Jack.

"Let me tell you Jack, I'm getting tired of your excuses about everything that takes place around here! I personally think that Lyla's death, Long's

heart attack, and Amy's mental difficulties are all a part of the Garrison situation that caused you to overreact! I also think you had a hand in Richard's death! I saw the hole in the wall behind his desk, Jack! Forensics matches the hole to your caliber of handgun! Funny, though, they couldn't find the slug! I don't think you're being completely honest with me, or the public!"

Jack stood up, threw his hands in the air, and reacted with intensity. **"What you *personally* feel doesn't matter, does it? What you may *think* means nothing! You are the one overreacting, Lt. Michaels! I will be removing you from your job effective immediately!"**

"No you won't Jack! I have an ongoing investigation into you, sir, and I cannot be removed until such investigation is complete! Those are the rules and you know them as well as I do! You have gone over the top, Jack, and I intend on bringing you back down!"

His mouth wide open, not believing what he was hearing, Jack pulled out his talons and dug in further against any "unfounded" and "damaging" allegations levied against him. He decided to approach the matter with a slightly calmer attitude. The screaming at each other method was not working.

"Did you know, Lieutenant, that it's illegal to threaten an elected official, especially a governor?"

"That's governor-elect, Jack, and it's not illegal if probable cause exists."

"Why don't you just enlighten me, Michaels? What probable cause do you have? A hole in the wall? The fact that these things have been happening since the trial? Its pure coincidence and you know it."

Both men sat down tight in their chairs while staring at each other. It was almost as if it were a "who would blink first" contest. This would go on for a while until Michael's phone rang.

*

The boy was on the floor with a strap around his neck, but was still alive because the killer had not tightened it. The killer knew what he would do. He picked up a cell phone it had and placed a call straight to the State Police Post. In a low growl, it asked for Lt. Michaels.

"Michaels here, can I help you?"

After a brief pause, the killer breathed into the phone with the snarling whisper. "I have the boy. I will kill him soon if you don't take heed of my request."

Lt. Michaels did not know whether to believe it or not, so he went with it just in case. "What do you want? Where are you?"

"Stupid fucking questions," the killer moaned. "I won't be on long enough to allow your trace either. Listen or the boy dies."

"Go on, I'm listening."

"I want that fraud Jack Beauregard to give up his governor bid, or the boy perishes...slowly."

Lt. Michaels had put the phone on speaker, so Jack heard the request and reacted. **"Go screw yourself! I'm not giving up anything! I don't even think you're the killer!"**

The phone clicked off and the killer was gone. Michaels looked at Jack as if he was crazy.

"Are you nuts, Jack? Who in the hell do you think you are? If that were really the killer, you'd put your governorship above a child's life?"

"It isn't the killer, so it's a moot point," Jack lazily waved, "I'd like to go home Michaels, I'm tired."

"You're not going home until this is resolved. Understood?"

"I've relieved you of your duty, sir. You have no jurisdiction over me at all."

Again the two sat and glared at each other, stewing over the statements each made and trying to figure out the best way to figure out the problem. Before they knew it, the situation would resolve itself, for good.

Inevitable

"Shut up, kid! I've heard enough out of you. Don't make me tighten that strap."

The killer was hissing at the child in a very menacing manner. The boy was fortunate to be alive. He could have been strangled by now.

"Are you thirsty, kid?" the killer asked. The boy nodded yes and was given some water. It seemed that there may indeed have been a slight change of heart by the killer, but that remained to be seen. He hadn't been nice to any of the kids he killed so far, so this was a completely different variation. The fact that the pentagram was gone riled the killer, but with the orders of his master, it gave him new perspective. He needed to focus on the problem. That problem being Jack Beauregard. The killer had watched Lyla Helms hang herself downtown, and noticed Jack's presence. He also knew *for a fact* that Jack had killed Richard Headly. The master was right. Something needed to be done about this fraud of a lawman. Jack Beauregard, in the killer's mind, had gotten away with too much and needed to be reeled in. It dawned on the killer that he could make *the* difference in Jack's future. A better, revised plan started forming in his head as he tried to think of a good way to make Jack look like the fraudulent politician he really was. The phone call to the police station had aggravated the killer, what with Jack ignoring his plea to step down, so the child would serve as a shining example that Beauregard was wrong about John Garrison. The killer approached the child, causing the little boy to shudder and scoot back up against the wall. He grabbed the young fellow and set his plan in motion. A scream was heard from the child, then silence.

*

"I am officially naming you as a suspect in the Headly deaths. I see through you Jack."

Jack wanted to leave now. He had heard quite enough of this preposterous dribble coming from Michael's mouth.

"You let me go now, Lieutenant, and I will consider allowing you to continue on as a simple trooper. You have zero evidence against me, and I intend to fight this nonsense tooth and nail."

Michaels knew he had to let Beauregard go. You cannot simply hold someone of Jack's importance because you *think* that he may be the culprit. He needed some kind of solid proof before he could go to the public and spew out allegations against the governor-elect. If this had been some Joe Blow off the street, like Garrison, it would be different. Lt. Michaels could just place a nobody in a cell and lock 'em up. In this case, that was impossible, as the media and public would go crazy over it.

"I guess you can go for now, Jack," Michael's dejectedly informed him. "We all know the rules, though. Don't leave town. I'll have men watching your every move. You are a prime suspect for murder."

Jack waved Lt. Michaels off and headed for his own office down the hall. He needed to get his paperwork and other items in order before he left the station. He decided he would try to stay a step ahead of Michaels by calling a news conference, thus explaining his stance and putting the onus on the Lieutenant himself. Jack was determined not to be the fall guy for Michael's hair-brained scheme. This was his thinking, even though Michaels was right on the ball with the allegations. It would be a challenge for the Lieutenant to arrest, charge and try Jack, but as he saw with the Garrison case, anything was possible. The last thing Beauregard wanted was to die in that damn electric chair. The thought caused cold goose bumps to rise on his skin.

*

The killer gathered two black garbage bags, both full, and loaded them in the white van. He also had a stack of cards, all Jacks of Spades. There was plenty of work to do, and the time was nigh. He was to expose the fraud that was Jack Beauregard, and whatever that took was fine with him. The killer mounted the driver seat and, clad in black leather, made his way into town. He drove like a madman, turning the corners violently and causing the bags to roll to and fro in the back, banging against the sides of the van. The killer calmed himself and continued the journey a bit more cautiously, not wanting to attract attention, or worse, get pulled over. Soon the destination would be reached and the real terror would begin.

*

Lt. Michaels scratched his head and wondered. He was trying to make a logical and unbiased decision about what to do. After all, he had been friends with Jack for many years. They had seen a lot of good and bad happen in the streets of Lincoln. This was a fine town they patrolled and lived in, and Michaels wanted it to go back to the way it used to be. There was not much in the way of gang violence, rape, murder or even mugging in this considerably safe city. Lately it had changed some. If not for a child killer and the awful events that took place, it would have remained quiet in the small Midwestern town.

Jack, meanwhile, sat in his office not far from Michaels and attempted to piece together a legitimate story that would explain everything. This was a monumental task, as Jack never figured Michaels to be so damn insistent on his being involved in a murder investigation. Beauregard had no idea how close he was to being a, *the,* central figure in the entire mess. This would undoubtedly destroy his governorship before it had even begun. That was a major worry for the beleaguered trooper. Jack checked his pistol, just in case a situation arose that would call for its use. You just never knew when someone, *or ones*, would need to be eliminated from the scene. Jack continued to sit and ponder. *Click-clack, Click-clack.*

*

It was only minutes before the killer would arrive at the destination. The adrenaline flowed through his veins with every heartbeat. He also felt a sense of new found calm and compassion. This is something he had never before experienced. The death of John Garrison, the killer felt, was all for naught as the powers of the city continued to abuse their gifts. It served as the perfect excuse to destroy Beauregard.

"The truth is," he thought to himself, "it happens everywhere from coast to coast, city to city, and country to country. This was a civilization of calloused, uncaring souls who abuse the very people who put them in charge, and do anything they can to get an advantage in life. This world has become a society of throwing blame around and pointing fingers. Very rarely was a finger pointer ever visible in public."

The killer wanted that to change. He decided that he would try to do something different. As hard as it was to believe, he had seemingly tossed some of the hate to the side and buddied up with logic. The only reason for this was because orders from his master were to focus on uncovering Beauregard. Had that not happened, the killer's attitude would be very different. The killer arrived at the destination.

Jack's Second Loss

The killer parked the van behind the police station and opened up the side doors, exposing the two full black trash bags that he had brought on the trip. The killer pinned the entire stack of Jack of Spades on his leather outfit and grabbed the two sacks, dragging them behind. He also carried a pistol in case anyone was to get in the way of his objective. The killer had a clear path to the side door of the trooper station, which was locked. He shot a hole in the window and stuck his hand in to unlock it from the inside.

Lt. Michaels, Jack and the ten troopers who were inside the building heard the shot and ran to the front of the station. The security cameras placed outside the building were running and filming, but the overseer of said video had to use the restroom, thus leaving the monitors for just a few moments. It was enough to allow the killer to shoot the door, unlock it, and escape into the poorly lit corridor just fifty feet away from the front desk. The officer's stepped with caution while Jack stayed back in a dark area behind a door. The perspective he held gave him full sight to the front lobby desk as Michaels and other troopers carefully stepped into the area. The lobby had two entrances. The front main entrance and a side door that led to the stairway. Able to see out the front door, the officers focused on the stairwell entrance, figuring that whoever took that shot would undoubtedly enter that way. It could also be a fact that whoever took the shot had already departed the scene. Since the officer in charge of security had not seen anything, no one was able to tell which way the shooter went. Just then, the stairwell door slowly creaked open. It was impossible to see what was on the other side when suddenly, a trooper's hat skidded in along the floor and settled to a stop just short of Michael's feet. This gripped the troopers with a nervous feeling as they squeezed their triggers tighter.

"Don't shoot guys!" Trooper Myers said. "I'm covered by a dude in leather. Don't shoot or I die."

"Come in here then," Michael's ordered. "Come in and show yourself, Myers."

"I'm coming in, but this "thing" has a gun to my ear. He wants you to drop your weapons and scoot them away."

"No can do, Myers, sorry." Michaels then added, "We won't lay down our arms."

"Then I *will* die tonight boss," Myers professed from the stairwell. "Just put down the weapons. This man in leather promises no one gets hurt if you do that."

Lt. Michaels looked over his troopers and waved them to lower the weapons. He then refocused his gaze on the slightly ajar door.

"Deal. We will lose the guns, but no violence or we will rush. Whoever it is can't shoot all of us."

The door squeaked open and the killer in black leather walked in with the kidnapped cop. Trooper Myers dragged the two black garbage bags behind him while the killer had a gun to the back of his ear. The leather-clad man had the Jack of Spades pinned all over the leather he adorned. Sweat poured out of the eyelets and bottom of the killer's mask. He whispered in Myer's ear to open the bag on the left and deposit the contents on the floor. Myers made the announcement to the guys that this was the plan.

"Do it then Myers. We won't shoot. Our guns are down."

Myers opened the bag and a waft of stink filled the room. It was the eye-watering stench of death. Death from long ago. Myers poured out the bag revealing half of a dead black dog. The killer whispered in his ear and Myers spoke again.

"This is the dog from Garrison's driveway; the killer said he switched bodies when Garrison wasn't looking."

Jack, who had snuck in and was watching from around the corner, felt his stomach tighten considerably at the revelation. If true, it would prove half of Michael's case that Jack guessed wrong about Garrison. Despite this, Jack stood firm, not revealing his location. He would have the best shot at the killer if it presented itself.

Myers spoke for the killer again. "He wants to leave before you open the other bag."

"No deal," Michael's said, "You're in this, Mr. Leather whatever."

This was not a good answer, not good at all. The killer repointed its gun from the back of Myer's ear, out toward Michaels exclusively. He again whispered to Myers.

“He’ll shoot if you do not do as it asks. Someone will die no matter what.”

Without warning, Jack Beauregard sprang through the door and barrel rolled across the floor. This surprised everyone including the killer, whose gun refocused on Myers. He pulled the trigger, scattering the trooper’s brains into the air toward the officers. Jack fired. He fired again. The killer was struck and forced backward. He kept his balance though, and rang off another round, hitting a trooper standing to the left of Michaels. It was a hit to the shoulder, thus decking the cop. Jack fired again. Everyone hit the deck at this point, making it a tougher target for the killer. Jack had the masked killer floundering. He finally fell to his knees. Blood was running down from the killer’s chest, just under the heart. It was a lung hit that left the killer without energy. He dropped the weapon on the floor. Jack then approached the killer, who looked up and met him eye to eye.

“So you’re the troublemaker in my state, huh? Are you ready to die?”

Jack did not wait for an answer, he just fired. He had four bullets remaining and they all sunk into the killer’s dying body. He fell backward onto the floor next to the unopened bag and lay completely still. Blood was now running from four new openings. The leather outfit was destroyed, as were many of the playing cards that were attached to it. Cards were strewn about the lobby. Jack reached down slowly and felt for a pulse. It no longer existed. The killer in black was dead at Jack’s feet. This would surely make Jack a hero in Michael’s eyes, not to mention the rest of the troopers who had just witnessed his bravery.

Jack bent down to the killer's face and then looked at his fellow comrades.

"Allow me to unmask this sickened creep. I will take great joy in this."

Jack ripped the mask off the killer's head and revealed the culprit.

*

"What the hell?" Jack exclaimed. "What the hell is this?" His voice cracked.

Jack was frozen solid. He was looking at his dead son Kyle lying on the police station floor. Jack's own bullets had done the trick all right. His bullets ripped through his son's internal organs. Jack had killed his own child. Kyle's blank, still opened eyes looked up at his father. Lt. Michaels approached while Jack swooned overtop of his son. He dragged the other, unopened bag toward him. It slid easily in the pools of blood that had been spread on the floor from the carnage. Michaels untied the bag and looked inside. It was the missing boy. The boy that just hours earlier had been reported abducted in Lincoln. He was breathing. The arms and legs were tied and his mouth gagged, but he was breathing. He quickly removed the boy from the bag and untied him. He was unharmed except for a temporary lack of oxygen from being inside the sack. When Michaels removed the gag, the boy screamed a wonderful, breathy scream and clutched the officer around his neck. Lt. Michaels had a tear drip down his face as he clutched the boy back. In the meantime, Jack wept. "This is not my son. This can't be him. I did not teach him this kind of behavior."

"It's him alright Jack," Michaels managed. "Your boy was a child murderer."

Jack was sick with pity. He stood up and confronted Michaels for the last time. "Me and you, we were friends once. We watched each other's backs and we covered our bases. Those days are gone, huh Lieutenant?"

Lt. Michaels looked at the floor.

"You know my son is no killer! He's a good boy. This is some kind of a set-up."

A note that was found in the bag with the boy described the murders to a "T." Kyle left the location of the shack, which he was planning to abandon. He also wrote that items from the other children could be found there, thus proving he was, in fact, the murderer. He also described a small crawl space behind the headboard of his bed at home, which was also Jack's home. Kyle had planned to find a new hideaway in a different town and stay there to continue his prowling undetected. Kyle did not, however, plan on dying.

*

The crawlspace contained straps, cards and newspaper articles from the killings, among other things. Jack's son had been the one doing the dirty work, all under his father's nose. Kyle had in fact planned on disappearing after exposing his dad, but that was impossible now. It truly was Jack's second loss. He had lost Soo-Chin, who ducked out just in the nick of time, and he had lost his son, *by his own hand.*

The payback was painful in its poisonous sting. This unfortunate series of events took the wind out of Jack's sails. The pompous, arrogant, would-have-been governor now had to answer as to why his son was able to pull this off right under Dad's watchful eye. He would have to answer to the execution, if you would call it that, of John Garrison. The next part in Jack's journey, though, would be answering for Richard and Sonya Headly's deaths. He was under direct investigation by Michaels and his crew and it would intensify in the upcoming days. This was truly a sad day in Jack Beauregard's pathetic life.

*

Lt. Michaels called the coroner's office and told them to come to the station to help clean the mess. He also had Jack placed in a private cell in the back of the jail and watched closely for any possible suicide attempts. The next thing Michaels had to do was call a press conference in front of the station for noon the following day. It would be tough, but he had to explain to the media and people of Nebraska, Lincoln what exactly had happened. Corruption and greed were bringing Jack down. Michaels was left to pick up the pieces. The coroner arrived and began the procedure of clean-up and processing of the scene. It was a somber group as they thumbed through the carnage of Trooper Myers and Kyle Beauregard. There was also a dead dog, a *long since dead* dog, which needed attention. Lt. Michaels asked for two troopers and a shovel. They went in the furthest corner behind the station and buried the canine, something that, Michaels thought, should have been done a long time ago. They put a makeshift cross up to mark the grave.

*

The following morning, with everything cleaned up in the station, Lt. Michaels pulled the lectern out of the trunk for the news conference, which was upcoming at noon. He proceeded to tear off the gubernatorial seal and set the podium up in the station's front yard. He had a microphone attached to it and seats set out for about one hundred. Michaels went into the jail section to have one last chat with Jack Beauregard.

Jack was wearing jail scrubs and was not very happy about the incarceration. He called for his lawyer and Michaels would oblige him, but asked him to take a couple minutes and listen. Jack agreed and Michaels spoke.

"We went to the shack in the swamp last night Jack. The note your son left was accurate. We found everything he said we'd find and he also wrote a few more tidbits."

Jack was listening with his arms crossed, waiting for whatever came next. He had a grimace on his face.

"We found a ton of stuff behind your boy's bed, under the carpet in a crawl space he dug out. There wasn't enough room to fit a person in, but he was able to stash all the personal stuff like newspaper articles, playing cards-Jacks of Spades only, and a couple other interesting things."

Jack raised his eye brow.

"Videotapes and pictures, Jack. Videotapes of you and Soo-Chin having sex, eating, and sleeping. There was also a blurb on a video showing you, Jack, hitting her and threatening her with a weapon. That's assault with a deadly weapon, Jack. That *is* a felony."

Jack continued listening, but his head lowered.

"Guess what else we saw, Jack? Can you guess?"

Jack could, but wouldn't. "Seems your son followed you to Headly's house, Jack. He was closer to you than you thought. He recorded everything that went on from the time you arrived at Rich's home. I must apologize, because I thought you killed Sonya too, but I was wrong. Richard had already completed that grim task before you arrived. You know what I saw Jack, don't you?"

Jack very slowly nodded yes. He now knew that the flashes of light he had seen from time to time were not from power, but his son's camera.

"I'm going to give you a choice Jack. You hereby give up the governorship, plead guilty to the murder and the abuse, and I'll see that you do not fry. That's the only choice you have. It's all on video and I have it in my hot little hands. By the way, how many times did you smack Kyle around in his life? I counted at least a hundred just on the video. That boy of yours was watching closely Jack. You let your guard down with the wrong person."

Jack signed the letter Michaels offered him, thus giving up the mansion and taking responsibility for at least some of his actions. Smart move by the former governor-elect of Nebraska.

*

The press conference went off, shocks and gasps moving around the chilly breeze. Jack Beauregard would be going away for a long time and nothing in the world would stop it.

The Lincoln Times

Jack Beauregard indicted; Kyle Beauregard dead

Governorship dissolved, Critchett to win by default

AP-In a stunning development, Jack Beauregard has been charged with second degree murder and felonious assault, while Kyle Beauregard, Jack's son, was identified as the real Jack of Spades killer in Lincoln. Lt. Ed Michaels announced this at a press conference on the lawn of the State Police post in Lincoln. These developments mean that Jack Beauregard gives up the Governorship, which will be awarded to Mel Critchett, the runner-up in the election. All this comes just a couple weeks before Jack was to be sworn in. As for his son Kyle, he was gunned down by his very own father during a showdown with police in the substation lobby. Lt. Michaels would not elaborate. He did, however, inform the media that Jack Beauregard had signed an official confession indicting him in Richard Headly's death and with felonious assault against his former girlfriend, Soo-Chin Xing. The case will go straight to the sentencing phase in court just two weeks from now. Beauregard faces life in prison, but not death, in the crime spree. More details will follow as soon as they become available.

-Angela Page

Epilogue

Air: Spring, Childhood, Sunrise, Beginnings

Amy and Robert

The doors opened at the front of the hospital and out popped a pair of refocused individuals who were on the upswing in life. A lot of rough things occurred in Lincoln during the tumultuous child killer case. The last year had been a test in endurance and grit. While both Robert and Amy had their fair share of tough luck, they managed to survive. That says a lot about their character and determination. Before leaving each other and going on their separate ways, coffee was in order at the local café. It was here that they discussed their futures and tried very hard to close the book on the past.

"I think being an architect is my real calling," Amy told Robert. "I have a knack for building, or at least planning what to build."

"Yup. I think you'd make a fine architect, Amy. I'd walk into yer buildin' anytime. I'd trust that the floors and ceilin's would hold up."

Amy chuckled at this as Robert continued, this time with fond memories.

"I have to make a trip to the barbershop fer sure. I wonder how all the old dipshits are doin'. I ain't seen 'em in a long time."

"I'm sure they've missed you greatly, Bob. You'll be a hit when you get there."

"I just hope they're still around. Some of 'em could be dead, you know?"

Amy took a huge breath of the early spring air. The sun shone down on the two as they sat at the outdoor café. Her hair had for the most part grown back, and she looked like the beautiful, raven-locked woman that existed before the start of all the challenges.

"Robert, I've finally come to grips with my past. The medication and therapy have helped with that, but you know, I think I'd be fine without it. The weight of clutching on to the past is too much for anyone to bear. I truly hope the future holds all good things. Perhaps a husband, maybe children, a lower stress career. Do you get my drift?"

"Sure I do. I feel the same way, only my future holds the three B's. Baked, broiled or boiled. No more heart attacks for this old timer. The doc says my ticker's in good shape fer a man my age. I suppose the stents and rehab have somethin' to do with it. I have ta be careful though."

Robert had lost a few pounds while he was hospitalized. He looked pretty darn good, though. He was so tall and lanky that the loss drew his cheeks in a bit, but his skin had a good, rosy color and his heart never missed a beat. He felt like a new man, but retirement from any real physical activity, like chopping wood or shoveling snow was in the offing. The old man really wanted to live a while longer, and with a smart approach, he most certainly would. Amy was focused on her future, too. This time the intensity would be drawn down a few notches. It felt wonderful to let the past slide away and remove those pesky monkeys off her back.

"I know I did my best for John under tough conditions. I wish I could have saved him, but it wasn't up to me."

"John's eatin' steak in Heaven, Amy. I'll bet he's the same smart-ass too! He's probably arguin' with God right now. I'll never forget the old coot."

"Nor will I Robert, nor will I."

The two finished off their coffees and gave each other a big hug. Robert went left, Amy right, and all was well in their respective worlds.

*

Amy went back to NU for further studies, this time in architectural design. She did not exhibit quite the same intensity as far as her study habits went. This didn't mean she wasn't nose to the grindstone, it simply meant she was more relaxed and at ease with her new career choice. Amy wasn't trying to prove anything to anyone, nor was she feeling the pressure of having to save people's hides. All there was to worry about was designing safe facilities in which to work and live. The chances for failure in this field still existed, but it didn't equate to life or death. Amy was also fortunate enough to meet a very handsome man named Hank. He was also studying in this field and they hit it off splendidly. After a series of dates and a yearlong commitment to each other, Hank and Amy moved to Seattle where they live together. They're working at a mildly successful architectural firm. They had a few bids accepted and a few rejected, but again, it wasn't a matter of life or limb. It was just nice to be happy and rolling along with someone you loved. They would continue to work, something Amy desires, and most of all, they would have fun together without the worries that had preceded these wonderful times. They seemed to have bright a future ahead. Amy still had the crime background, though, which was very hard to let go of. She never knew when or where it would come in handy again.

*

Robert still lived in that old house down the road from Garrison's place, which had been steamrolled earlier in the year. Despite that, Robert went down there once a week and laid a flower on the field in which the house once stood. He also visited John's grave site once or twice a month to pay homage to a man that was his friend and confidant. Robert was still making the daily trip to the town barbershop, visiting with not only the buddies who still lived, but a few more old fogeys who recently called the place their home away from home. John's picture adorns the wall to this day. His grumpy frown and squinted eyes always made you feel as if this guy still had something to say. Oh, be sure he did. It wouldn't ever be the same without old John looking over the mates at the old barbershop. Robert misses his old friend, but knows that not far down the road, he'll see him again.

Colonel Michaels and Governor Critchett

That's right. Colonel, not Lieutenant. Edward Michaels was promoted to Colonel of the Nebraska State Troopers. This was a huge gift for him and his family. It was one of those rare instances when someone who deserved and belonged in the position was actually in said position. Michaels was firm in upholding the law, but was also very fair and sometimes too lenient. He worked with the kids and did his best to see them move in the right direction through not only jail, but tough love. He had a good relationship with Mel Critchett, who took over as the State's Governor. These two worked together to bring about positive change, not just change for the sake of it.

They decided that medical marijuana would be watched, not raided every other day. If someone were getting a bit out of hand, or selling illegally, they would be asked to "cease and desist." If the problem continued, then they would come down on you.

The sex offender registry had gotten so out of hand that one in three Nebraska residents held a spot on it. This was pared down through legislative change to include exclusively those who were violent offenders, i.e. forcible rape, sodomy, child porn, etc. The people who had wet on a dumpster, been involved in "he said, she said" cases, and those who were eighteen and had sex with their fifteen year-old girlfriends were removed from the registry altogether. After all the paring down and adjusting, one in ten, rather than one in three, remained on the registry. As long as they fulfilled their requirements for five consecutive years, and were not getting in any other trouble, they too were to be removed.

It was a breath of fresh air for the folks in this great Midwest state, and it actually helped crime lessen rather than increase. Other smaller laws were tweaked and changed, and Nebraska would enjoy prosperity not seen or heard of in years.

Ed still thought about Jack and kicked himself a few times for not stepping in sooner and putting a stop to the nonsense. Ultimately, though, you have to be able to forgive yourself, and Ed was able do that.

Dan's Demise

The mental ward had its share of strange characters. Among them was Dan Wheeler. The day he saw the murdered child changed Dan, but he managed to escape most of the aftershock and depression that went with it with the help of Lyla Helms. However, the playbacks in his mind of watching Lyla die were too much for him to handle. No matter what he thought or did, Dan would be haunted by the grisly image of Lyla shooting herself, then falling and hanging from that building in downtown Lincoln. The crack of Lyla's spine upon impact played over and over in Dan's mind, driving him to the brink. The entrance and exit to the roof of that establishment had since been boarded up. The fire escapes are now monitored on a camera that relays its use to the inside where Chucky resides. He'd be damned if that would ever happen again on his watch.

No more women would ever come back into Dan's life. He was too unstable for such things. The girls weren't about to go through another bout of depressed Dan. After his year long stay in the mental facility, Dan returned to his apartment, which was paid for from collecting disability. His new love became heroin. Dan knew the local dealers, and made sure that they visited him at least four times a week. He snorted and shot it. He was a full-blown addict and he was losing teeth and hair, sure signs of his dilapidation. Dan stayed cloistered in his digs, only coming out once per week to get a few groceries and cigarettes. That was all the young man was interested in. He wore dark shades and a baseball hat whenever leaving, and paid no mind to anyone who would attempt conversing with him. Out to the store; get what he needed; then back home quickly to use more heroin. The days, weeks and months passed and Dan became worse. He was seventy-five pounds underweight, lost most of his teeth, and no longer bathed. The dealers would ask about his well-being when they stopped over, but Dan was not interested in discussing it.

"Just give me my drugs and I'll see you in three days," was all Dan mustered.

It was pretty bad when the people selling you the drug asked about your health, then sold the garbage to you anyway. I guess it was an investment check. They really didn't care how he was doing as long as he was alive and bought more dope.

*

It reached the point when Dan no longer went out for food or smokes. He no longer answered the door for his dope, either. Colonel Michaels took a couple of troopers over one day when the store keepers who were leasing to Dan complained about the rent not being paid When they knocked, Dan wouldn't answer. The store owners had thought about busting in but thought better of it and instead called the police. It had been two weeks since Dan had gone downstairs and concern mounted. When Michaels went over, he broke the door down and found Dan dead on the sofa, a needle stuck in his arm, and dried blood running from the vein entrance down to his hand. It was a grisly sight, as Dan had stiffened up and was into the rotting stage of his "afterlife." "He must've died about a week-and-a-half earlier," was the educated guess of the coroner. The apartment stunk of death and unfortunately, Dan went to the great dope factory in the sky. It would take three weeks of constant fumigation to rid the apartment of the foul odors. There was a small funeral for Dan, with about twenty people showing up, including a couple of family members from out of town, and a few of the girls he had once dated. It was a sad day, because the young man had a ton of potential. The choices Dan made cost him his life. He could never get a grip on Lyla's death. Some people guessed that he truly loved her, but also wanted an open, non-committed life so he could continue with his conquests. If he had devoted himself to Lyla, the younger women would have fled. If he was seen with her, he may risk embarrassment because he was dating a female much older than himself. Truth was, there was no need for him to be embarrassed because people would've understood. Besides, no one should ever let another person's thoughts dictate their own lives. Dan allowed too many outside influences get to him.

Dan Wheeler died too soon.

Soo-Chin's Great Escape

"Whew, that was close!" Soo knew that by hanging around Lincoln, she could have easily ended up on Jack's list of people not to trust. She also knew she may be lying six feet under if not for her escape to Eugene, Oregon.

Soo-Chin was now working for the Oregon State Pathology team. She was not a supervisor or head of the unit, as she was in Lincoln. Soo was simply one of the employees who helped perform autopsies and reported findings to the boss. She let them have the spotlight, facing the cameras and whatever came with it. This was a much needed break for the embattled woman. She was still single and wasn't interested in boyfriends after her experiences with Jack. Being smacked around was a real wake-up call for the oriental beauty.

Jack had hit her hard. He broke a couple of teeth that she had surgically repaired. He also busted some capillary arteries in her nose and cheek. One hit was all she needed to know that moving on was the right thing to do. Soo normally would never let anyone bully her, but ever since Jack had been elected Governor, his attitude changed for the worse. He was tough to deal with on a simple police officer level, but he had a good nature that she thought would be of no great consequence in her relationship with him. Being elected Governor erased all that. He turned into a power hungry politician with a propensity for violence if things did not go his way. Soo turned out to be a lot smarter than people thought. Some women take the punishment and come back for more, thinking things will get better, and that they cannot improve their spouse or significant other by working with them. This has much to do with being stripped of any self-worth that they may have had before being beaten within inches of their lives. Soo refused to go down such a path. This woman had no interest in being tossed around and even less interest in dying. She believed staying with Jack would have resulted in her being the subject *(victim)* of a murder case.

She read the newspapers on-line. She was very interested in what was happening in her former hometown. Upon finding out that Kyle was the child murderer, she cried for days. She never suspected it and was shocked to hear of his death. Soo was less surprised that it was by Jack's hand that Kyle was killed. Of course, there was probably no way Jack would have ever suspected his own child either, but had he paid more attention to the needs of his boy, it probably would have come out different. That's sheer speculation. Nothing in this life is a "for sure."

Soo would continue working in Oregon and would also turn down offers to become the State's Lead Pathologist. Doing simple autopsies and keeping her nose out of the limelight was what she preferred. As for men and a family, time would tell. There was no great rush to get to that point. One day at a time was her motto. She was also glad to see that Jack was right where he belonged. She shed no tears for that.

Jack's Final Loss

The knife felt like cold steel as it plunged deeply into Jack's spinal cord. The initial feelings he had were that his arms and legs instantly went numb. He correctly thought that he himself was being murdered. The inmate had snuck right up behind with nary a sound and plunged the homemade weapon as deep as he could. It was a pain Jack had never felt before in his entire life, and this man had felt some pain. The agony left quickly as vertebrae and nerve endings severed under the knife's skill. The blood rushed out on the floor under him as he lay in a suspended sort of animation. He was not here, but he wasn't there either, wherever "there" was. He saw guards and prisoners alike fussing over him. The stabber disappeared into the crowd, unknown and undetected. The weapon was already gone, passed between one hundred hands and deposited into a storm drain in the prison yard. Jack now lay dying, the light of the day slowly disappearing. Everything started becoming blurry as the breath slipped from him in a labored manor. It was time to die. It was time to meet the maker. Jack never thought it would end this way, on the floor in the penitentiary.

*

Jack had pled out in court. He knew a trial was useless, on account of his son videotaping and snapping pictures of his every move. Colonel Michaels and the State prosecution team had him dead to rights. He would be sentenced to a term of twenty-five to fifty years in prison, a soft sentence compared to the no names that would easily have been given life, or *death*. His years as a law enforcement figure, combined with his "clean" record, spared him a life sentence, yet he would be an old useless goat by the time of his release. Jack never thought for one second that the sentence would actually turn out to be death. There was no way the prisoners would let him slide if the chance ever existed to kill the man who sent a high percentage of these men to this very prison.

*

The light continued to drift. The guard tried to speak to him.

"Jack, Jack Beauregard? Are you still with us, Jack?"

Those were the last clear words Jack would hear. He slipped into the darkness, and then into a completely different realm. The tunnel he found himself in held a red, misty glow. Jack was walking down a long corridor with walls made of rock, with blood oozing from the cracks. It was a scary dwelling, to be sure, but Jack was prompted by some inner force to continue his journey. He walked and he walked, hearing voices from behind him fade. It was seemingly miles down this "hallway," when he finally reached the end and was met by a cloaked, robed figure. This figure had hoofs for feet and long, sharp fingernails. He lifted his head and the figure remove the hood. What Jack saw was a man, or so he thought to be a man, with tanned skin and a deep, rich five o'clock shadow. The eyes were red and the teeth were razor sharp. He greeted Jack with a sly smile. "Hello, Jack! I do believe we've been expecting you."

The "man" stepped to the side and Jack saw what seemed like millions of people being whipped, beaten, raped and tortured. The next thing in Jack's mind was pure fear.

"Is this hell? Am I in hell?"

"Good call, Jack. Yes. You are in a world that you made and will never escape from," the man-beast said.

Jack's eyes were like tea saucers, round and prominent. He saw someone approaching. It was another hooded figure with hoofs for feet.

"Jack, I'd like you to meet someone. He did my bidding on earth. I think you'll find him very interesting."

Kyle removed the hood and greeted his earthly father. He also had red eyes and sharp teeth.

"Hello, Jack. Long time, no see."

Both red-eyed beasts shared a laugh as Jack fell to his knees sobbing and begging forgiveness.

"It's way too late for that. You should have taken care of these things while you had the chance. By the way, check this out."

Kyle opened his shirt, exposing the six bullet holes that Jack had gifted to him.

"It didn't hurt much. It was quick."

Jack screamed with a combination of tears and terror as he looked at his son's wounds.

"ENOUGH," the leader said. "Take him, Kyle, and do what you will."

Kyle grabbed Jack by the throat and lifted him. His strength was extraordinary.

"It's just you and me. Forever and ever. I have such fun things in store for you."

Kyle held him above his head and looked deep into his eyes.

"Oh, by the way, you are NOT my father any longer. Now you're my slave. You will want to die every five minutes or so, but won't. The pain will be legendary. You are no longer Jack Beauregard. You are just another of hell's minions. Come, slave, and let's get started."

Jack was clamped with a heavy chain around his neck and stripped naked. Hell started now, with no ending….. EVER!

Lest we Forget….

Kathy Joseph left Kurt as suddenly as leaves blow off a tree on a windy fall day. She had been having an affair with a strong, tough and rich man and wanted to come out in the open with it. She'd had enough of the meek Kurt, who couldn't even achieve a decent, lasting erection any longer. Kathy loved being held and made love to by a handsome, confident man. This new stud sent Kathy into shuddering orgasms and made her feel special every moment. He was also loaded with cash, which was the main underlying reason for her departure from Kurt. She was a different woman without Kurt "bogging her down." He simply didn't have it any longer. He had let himself go and that was not going to cut it in Kathy's world of plastic and silicone. She was all about the outside. What someone looked like physically and in their wallet was much more important to her than what they possessed in their heart. Kurt had gained a little weight and was more deficient and indecisive than he ever had been before.

*

Kathy came home one day and, out of the blue, told Kurt she was finished. This saddened the man who had a child with this woman. He had no idea that she was seeing another person, as Kurt was never really all that perceptive to begin with. She kept it under her hat, telling him she simply needed a change of scenery and a new start. Kathy knew telling him about her lover could cause a spark of anger to flicker, and who could know what he'd do if he was upset by another male stealing his wife. Better to keep that one quiet. It was a dark day for the insecure Mr. Joseph, and it would only get darker.

She packed what she could, and walked out the door with nary a further expression or a comment. Kurt was shell-shocked. He took to the garage, where he hung out for most of the time, and began smashing everything with a hammer. Pictures, computers, TV's, and whatever else was worthy of being destroyed. He stuttered and cried, calling out Kathy's name the entire time. His control was lost. He went in the house and trashed everything he could there too. When he was finally finished, the house looked like a wrecking ball had plowed through it. He would not clean the mess up.

The person he relied on was history. Kathy left him like a bag of old trash at the corner. She didn't want the house, cars, or anything else associated with her former husband. She filed for and received her divorce, simply keeping her momentum moving forward. She later married the "affair", thus sealing her new deal. What Kurt failed to realize, is that he was much better off without the bossy Kathy in his life. He should have been happy that she went with another of her kind: a muscle bound kick-sand-in-your-face style. He had so heavily relied on Kathy that he could not overcome the shock of being without her.

*

Kurt continued living at the house, but had turned into a recluse. Neighbors rarely saw him while family and friends didn't want anything to do with the "weirdo". It started to stink from the hoarding and the lawn, once beautiful, was dying. Kurt no longer cared about the outside appearance. Only when the city would bug him about the disheveled look would he fire up the mower and give it a quick once over. All the while, inside the cluttered house, Kurt stayed busy. He was busy finishing the sewing on the black leather mask and outfit he had been working on for so long. He even went so far as to sew the actual Jack of Spades playing cards into the leather material. He was almost ready to take over where the young Kyle had left off. It was told to him in a vision. He was to be the next Black Jack of Spades killer. Only this time he would prey on those who hurt him in the past. He would stalk and kill those who ridiculed him the most. The carnage would start anew. His first victim would be a tall, blond-haired woman named Kathy.

*

Black. That was the color of choice for the killer…

.....The end

Afterword

Several of the characters in this book suffered from emotional and mental disorders. These disorders were the result of stress or traumatic events and were also exacerbated by tension, pressure, or anxiety. Schizophrenia, Post Traumatic Stress Disorder and Anxiety/Panic Attacks are often treatable with therapy and medication. Their inclusion in this Afterword is intended to illustrate how circumstances may aggravate these conditions; not only in the lives of my characters, but to some degree, in all of us.

Schizophrenia

Paranoid Schizophrenia is one of several types of schizophrenia, a chronic mental illness in which reality is interpreted abnormally (psychosis). The classic features of paranoid schizophrenia are having beliefs that have no basis in reality (delusions) and hearing things that aren't real (auditory hallucinations).

With paranoid schizophrenia, your ability to think and function in daily life may be better than with other types of schizophrenia. You may not have as many problems with memory, concentration or dulled emotions. Still, paranoid schizophrenia is a serious, lifelong condition that can lead to many complications, including suicidal behavior. However, with effective treatment, you can manage the symptoms of paranoid schizophrenia and work toward leading a happier, healthier life. [2]

*

Have you ever been on the edge of sleep and hear your name shouted out? It wakes you right up and gets your attention. How about mid-sleep paralysis that

---

[2] © 1998-2010 Mayo Foundation for Medical Education and Research (MFMER). All rights reserved.

gives you that terrifying sensation of being out of control? These are little mini-touches of Schizophrenia.

Most people have a few of these strange little episodes throughout their lives. It is both scary and interesting. Dreams can seem so real, yet when you wake up, you feel that ultimate sense of relief. We all have a little bit of that peculiarity inside us. We also have a fuse that seemingly burns and burns. You hope it never reaches the dynamite at the end, but what if it did? What if the voices we heard never stopped? What if the paralysis stayed with us when we awoke? Those thoughts can certainly give you the creeps. If you know anyone who suffers from these unfortunate afflictions, remember to be patient and seek professional help. You can't tell a depressed person to "cheer up", and you can't tell a Schizophrenic to "shake it off". These diseases must be dealt with through medication, therapy, and most importantly, support from friends and family.

Post-Traumatic Stress Disorder

Signs and symptoms of post-traumatic stress disorder typically begin within three months of a traumatic event. In a small number of cases, though, PTSD symptoms may not occur until years after the event.

Post-traumatic stress disorder symptoms are commonly grouped into three types: intrusive memories, avoidance and numbing, and increased anxiety or emotional arousal (hyper arousal).

Symptoms of intrusive memories may include:

Flashbacks or reliving the traumatic event for minutes or even days at a time.
Upsetting dreams about the traumatic event.

Symptoms of avoidance and emotional numbing may include:

Trying to avoid thinking or talking about the traumatic event.
Feeling emotionally numb.
Avoiding activities you once enjoyed.
Hopelessness about the future.

Memory problems.
Trouble concentrating.
Difficulty maintaining close relationships.

Symptoms of anxiety and increased emotional arousal may include:

Irritability or anger.
Overwhelming guilt or shame.
Self-destructive behavior, such as drinking too much.
Trouble sleeping.
Being easily startled or frightened.
Hearing or seeing things that aren't there.

Post-traumatic stress disorder symptoms can come and go. You may have more post-traumatic stress disorder symptoms during times of higher stress or when you experience reminders of what you went through. You may hear a car backfire and relive combat experiences, for instance. On the other hand, you may see a report on the news about a rape, and feel again the horror and fear of your own assault.[3]

Anxiety and Panic Attacks

A panic attack is a sudden episode of intense fear that develops for no apparent reason and triggers severe physical reactions. Panic attacks can be very frightening. When panic attacks occur, you might think you're losing control, having a heart attack or even dying. You may have only one or two attacks in your lifetime. However, if you have had several attacks and have spent long periods in constant fear of another, you may have a chronic condition called panic disorder. Panic attacks were once dismissed as nerves or stress, but they're now recognized as a real medical condition. Although attacks can significantly affect your quality of life, treatment is very effective.

Panic attack symptoms can make your heart pound and cause you to feel short of breath, dizzy, nauseated and flushed. Because attacks can resemble life-threatening conditions, it's important to seek an accurate diagnosis and treatment. Attacks typically include a few or many of these following symptoms.

A sense of impending doom or death.

Rapid heart rate.

Sweating.

Trembling.

Shortness of breath.

Hyperventilation.

Chills.

Hot flashes.

Nausea.

Abdominal cramping.

Chest pain.

Headache.

Dizziness.

Faintness.

Tightness in your throat.

Trouble swallowing.

Panic attacks typically begin suddenly, without warning. They can strike at almost any time; when you're driving the school car pool, at the mall,

sound asleep or in the middle of a business meeting. Attacks have many variations, but symptoms usually peak within 10 minutes and last about half an hour. You may feel fatigued and worn out after the attack subsides.

One of the worst things about panic attacks is the intense fear that you'll have another attack. If you have had four or more attacks and have spent a month or more in constant fear of another attack, you may have a condition called panic disorder, a type of chronic anxiety disorder.

With panic disorder, you may fear having a panic attack so much that you avoid situations where they may occur. You may even be unable to leave your home (agoraphobia), because no place feels safe.

When to see a doctor

If you have any panic attack symptoms, seek medical help as soon as possible. Attacks are hard to manage on your own, and they may get worse without treatment. In addition, because the symptoms can also resemble other serious health problems, such as a heart attack, it's important to get evaluated by your health care provider if you aren't sure what's causing the symptoms.[4]

---

[4] © 1998-2010 Mayo Foundation for Medical Education and Research (MFMER). All rights reserved.

My Comments

One day I was cleaning up around my property when I saw a dark, furry looking object lying next to the field that sat next to my yard. I was very skeptical about approaching it. If it was a raccoon or something else equally vicious, I was not interested in causing it a feeling of having to defend itself. After seeing that it wasn't moving, I summoned up the courage to take a closer look and saw that it was a dog that had expired. I felt terrible, as I'd recently lost my own beloved family pet. I went to my shed and retrieved a black garbage bag, carefully placed the body of the animal in the sack and carried it to the driveway. I was in the difficult process of trying to bag it up with not one, but two sacks, when my neighbor ventured out, obviously interested in what I was doing. He pulled out a roll of duct tape from his back pocket (my neighbor is very handy), and started sealing up the critter. My neighbor is also a hunter, so in comparison to cleaning out a deer, this was easy for him. He quickly and neatly finished up the job. I placed the bagged carcass in my driveway and called animal control. I was told to leave it in the driveway and they'd be along to pick it up. A few hours later I looked out my front window, and the critter was gone.

*

This was how the work was born. I started thinking of what ifs. *What if*…the police came back and said I had a dead body in the bag? How would I be able to prove there wasn't? Only my neighbor's word would help me. *What if*…I was arrested and taken to jail for murder? People have certainly been taken away for much less. *What if*…the nightmares about being framed came true? How would you fight a rap like that? *What if*…I'd been set-up by a real killer? Only I could get that lucky. I decided that it could make an interesting story, so I pulled out some paper and a pen, went in the yard near where I'd found the dog, and started writing. The writing turned out to be Black Jacks.

*

The title Black Jacks was born out of a combination of the dog being black, the direction the story was headed, and surfing the internet. I stumbled upon some artwork I found to be incredibly different. It was a set of Jack of Spades drawings done by a young woman from Canada calling herself Trish the Stalker. She had done so many variations I couldn't believe it. Looking through them, I found one that had a man on it that looked like he was somewhat, but not completely evil. This reminded me of the leather-clad killer of whom the story was centered. One thing led to another and voila, an idea for a title and book cover was hatched. It took me about a month to track down the artist, but once I did, I was given permission for the use of the image.

Soon I was looking at a rough draft. At times while I was writing, something came over me and I just wrote for hours on end. It was much like meditation. The story strayed left, screeched back to the right, and then turned left again. I would look back and almost scream with excitement. My wife would throw ideas at me, I'd start writing them down, but it wouldn't turn out quite the way she meant. I kept moving toward a darker, almost gothic angle. Ultimately, it came out the way I wanted it and onward I crept. Ten months of writing, followed by five months of editing, which, by the way, is numbingly difficult.

At any rate, I hope you enjoyed it. It was extremely gratifying for me and I can't wait to get started on my next work, which, by the way, has been born. Until then, stay safe and keep reading.

Other work recommended by Shaun Webb:

Blaze by Richard Bachman

The Frankenstein series by Dean Koontz

An Innocent Man by John Grisham

The Dark Tower series by Stephen King

The Catcher in the Rye by John Salinger

The Talisman by Stephen King w/ Peter Straub

Creepers by David Morrell

Predator by Jack Olsen

The Plantation by Chris Kuzneski

Sword of God by Chris Kuzneski

About the Author

Shaun Webb lives in Waterford, Michigan with his wife, Nancy. They have three children, Bill, Mary and Alycia, and a Grandchild, Ruth Ann. When Shaun's not writing, he enjoys music, sports and working outdoors.

"Black Jacks" represents Shaun's second novel. His first, called "A Motion for Innocence" deals with false allegations and injustice. A Motion for Innocence, Second Edition has been released in paperback and is also available. All works can be found at Amazon.com, along with other various booksellers.

You can also see what Shaun's up to at his site, www.amotionforinnocence.blogspot.com

7795021R0

Made in the USA
Charleston, SC
10 April 2011